FIC   Lelchuk, Alan.
         Brooklyn boy

$19.95

DATE		

Brooklyn Boy

Brooklyn Boy

A Novel by
ALAN LELCHUK

McGRAW-HILL PUBLISHING COMPANY
New York   St. Louis   San Francisco   Bogotá
Hamburg   Madrid   Milan   Mexico   Paris
São Paulo   Tokyo   Montreal   Toronto

1 2 3 4 5 6 7 8 9 DOC DOC 8 9 2 1 0 9

ISBN 0-07-037163-6

LIBRARY OF CONGRESS CATALOGING-IN-PUBLICATION DATA

Lelchuk, Alan.
    Brooklyn boy / Alan Lelchuk.
        p.   cm.
    ISBN 0-07-037163-6
    I. Title.
PS3562.E464B7   1989
813'.54—dc19   89-2689
                                                    CIP

Book design by Eve L. Kirch

In memory of Harry Lelchuk
and also Ralph Halpern

Beginnings: Breucklyn Boy

Early evenings, the short woman with the bunned hair and smell of linens would lift him into her arms, and sing in a lulling voice,

Oyfen pripetshok brent a fayerl,
Un in shtub iz heys.
Un der rebe lernt kleyned kinderlech
Dem alef-beys.
Dem alef-boys.

And by the middle of the Yiddish song he'd be set back down in his crib, adrift with sleep.

A few years later, the boy sat on his father's lap, and listened to the deep, strong voices coming from the phonograph. The father sang along with the army of male voices, in Russian, while the boy, trying to follow the pronunciation, imagined the men hauling the barges along the Volga River,

Ei ukhnem! Ei ukhnem!
Eshcho razik, eshche raz!

Razovyom my beryozu
Razovyom my kudriavu
Ai-da da, ai-da
Razvyom my kudriavu.

At the end of the second side, he was allowed to raise up the needle carefully and lift with both hands the heavy plastic record, and help Papa slip it back into its light brown jacket, with the small golden angel lounging on a disc in the corner. Once a week they listened to the Red Army Chorus, occasionally to Al Jolson, while his teenage sister regularly compared crooners like Dick Haynes and Mel Torme with bow-tied Frankie. Before sleep he pronounced the word "crooners," and practiced the deep "razovyom." His mother disliked the Russian that his father spoke to him, so the boy tried to keep it only between them, secretly.

In the large *Times*, his father had always shown him the maps of the war, with the Allies attacking with black arrows and black lines, and the Nazis getting pushed back into a narrower and narrower dotted-line chunk of Germany. (Why did Mr. Heatter call it a "theater" of war? It wasn't like the Sutter or the Pitkin theaters, not a bit.) Staying in his head were battles like Guadalcanal, Stalingrad, Battle of the Bulge, and generals with funny names: Omar, Georgi, Monty, Timo-something.

And one day, after the father had rubbed and made a horseradish (*chreyn*) so strong you couldn't walk into the kitchen without tears rising, he sat with the boy and displayed a gift presented to him for his Air Raid Warden service by Abe Stark, the borough president. It was a small, boxed set of five booklets, printed by the *Brooklyn Eagle*, about Brooklyn, plus a rolled-up map of the old borough.

At the mahogany secretary, on the hinged fold-down desk, they sat together and Father pointed out the six original villages, Bushwick, Brooklyn, Flatbush in the upper part, New Utrecht and Gravesend at the bottom, and Flatlands on the right side (or east). Though Brownsville didn't show on the map, New Lots, which included Brownsville and East New York, was set in the upper end of Flatbush. His father surprised him by explaining that five of the towns were originally Dutch. Only Gravesend, which had

Coney Island and Sheepshead Bay, was settled by the English.
"You mean we're Dutch also," the boy asked, alarmed and confused, "not only American and Russian?"

Water surrounded the borough, and he felt proud that he had
already been to the East River, the Narrows—you could see the
reason for the name now—and the Atlantic Ocean. But he had
not yet been to Jamaica Bay. It was an oddly shaped place all
around, hardly any straight easy borders, just chunks, "wedges,"
and curls protruding. His father showed him where the Brooklyn
Navy Yard was (on the western side), Coney Island (the south),
City Hall (the center), Eastern Parkway, the Brooklyn Bridge. The
boy waited patiently, and then asked, "But where's Ebbets Field?"
Of course Papa didn't know *that*. When the boy tried to copy
the map he made a mess of it, while his father, in one sweeping
unbroken line, outlined it accurately. A few practices later, the
boy did better. His father placed the tracings in one of the desk
pigeonholes, and the boxed set itself on the bookshelf above, alongside the blue set of *Wonderland of Knowledge*. Father closed the
window door, turning the key to keep the door shut. To himself
the boy made a pact to study the map, and get the place in his
memory, especially where the Dodgers played, naturally. After all,
he figured, if it was home ground, it should be in his head as well
as on paper.

At eleven, he discovered he was a sinner, and an atheist. He
was standing in the synagogue, standing between Papa and Walter,
his prayer book in his hands and the crowded congregation already
swaying and chanting. It was the eve of Yom Kippur, the holiest
day of the year, and the rabbi was beginning the service with the
singing of Kol Nidre. Using the black *Standard Machsor*, he followed
along in his passable Hebrew:

*Kol nidrei. Ve'esarei. V'konamei. V'chinuyei. V'kinusei.
U'sh'vu'ot, dindarna. U'di'eshtvana. U'diacharemna V'di 'asarna
al narshatana. M'yom kippurim zeh ad Yom kippurim
haba aleinu l'tovah. Kalhon i'charatna v'hon.*

3

He glanced at the other side of the page, to check out the English. "All vows and self-prohibitions, oaths, vows of abstinence and promise, vows with self-imposed penalties and obligations, which we may vow, swear, promise, and bind ourselves from this day of Atonement, unto the next day of Atonement . . . we repent them all." Privately he shook his head, repenting nothing, almost from spite. He fingered his heavy trousers, thinking, what a holiday! Twenty-four hours of atoning and fasting. With no escape, from here anyway, not for a few hours at least. Never again, he vowed, would he be forced into this ordeal. At least not when he was grown up. The congregation poured it on, in their religious mumbo jumbo, and finally they were allowed to sit.

He turned the pages, fingering his blue and white silk tallis. And concentrated. The Dodgers were in a real dogfight with Saint Looie. The new pitcher, Newcombe, was having a swell year and going to pitch this weekend. And Jackie was simply the best there was. Who would have dreamed he'd be leading the league in hitting? Well, the weekend ahead with the Cards would tell a lot, *if* we could take two out of three. . . . But beating Howie Pollet and Harry the Cat was not going to be easy.

His father leaned over to catch him up, and soon they were standing again. God he wished he was a girl for these occasions, so he could sit upstairs in the "women's court," and not be squeezed and pickled down here.

The droning continued, on and on, about those vows and oaths, self-prohibitions and abstinence, and he felt himself sweating and daydreaming. . . .

The next day, he wickedly focused his energies on baseball, not atonement and punishments—especially as he grabbed a sandwich—just to see what would happen on the weekend.

And when the Bums indeed took two out of three from the Cards at home, he knew that they and he were home free, winners! A pennant for them in the National League, and a victory for him in the big Religion League. Better to be a Dodger sinner, he knew now for sure, than a pious believer. Oh, he'd still take pleasure in Passover seders and Sholem Aleichem stories and ancient heroes like Joseph and David, but anything religious was out of bounds, foul for good.

Years later, after playing an American Legion baseball game at the Parade Grounds, the sixteen-year-old youngster walked over to the Brooklyn Public Library to finish a project for his senior journalism class. He ambled through the Grand Army Plaza with its elaborate Soldiers and Sailors Memorial Arch at the Plaza entrance to Prospect Park, dedicated to the memory of the Union defenders, 1861–65. Foolish and stunning, this noble monument, with its bronze equestrian bas-reliefs of Lincoln and Grant—he researched it—never failed to move him. Inside the library, he felt funny, carrying his spikes and glove in his warm-up bag, and still wearing his dirt-smeared uniform. But that was okay. The huge rotunda, with the high dome above, made him feel slightly holy. In the open stacks, he found the B subject area, a nearby table and seat, and selected his somewhat familiar stack of books. He opened first the old one by the British photographer Moses King because it showed the arch on the cover. *King's Views of Brooklyn 1904* was a series of black and white photos, which looked like engravings, of the old town. He took a curious pleasure in the shady, detailed pictures of the turn-of-the-century office buildings, the amusement parks and quiet streets and squares, the great bridges and Navy Yard; all his, in a way, Aaron felt. Odd, wasn't it, that this Englishman should be the appreciator of *his* town. But that just seemed to give the town more credit, more worldly approval.

And presently, leafing through the other texts he had already studied on previous Saturdays, he had out his narrow five-by-eight loose-leaf book and fountain pen, and was writing his report, in his straight-up-and-down scrawl, an awkward, stiff penmanship, on single-spaced lines. Tomorrow maybe he could revise it, and perhaps make it a bit clearer, and give it a proper title, not merely "A Brief History of King's County." If it was good enough, Mr. Drackler wanted him to publish it in *The Liberty Bell.*

"In the beginning came the Walloons, farmers from the south

of Belgium, and settled, maybe in 1625, the first hamlet, naming it Wallabout (or Walloon's) Bay, near the present Navy Yard. [Of course he'd have to get in here that earlier, about 1609, the Dutchman Henry Hudson sailed the *Half Moon* into "the great bay between Sandy Hook, Staten Island, and Amboy" (Strong), and touched soil in Gravesend, the first white man perhaps to land in New York State. Though the village itself wasn't settled until 1643.] Other settlements came farther along the East River, by Gowanus Bay, and, on the eastern side of the peninsula, in the Flatlands (Amersfoort) by Walloons and other Hollanders, in 1636–37. The colony was part of the Dutch East India Company. The first recorded land deed was given by Governor Kieft to one Abraham Rycken in 1638, and the earliest grant to Thomas Besker in 1639. Kieft was an arrogant sort, and maybe *the* cause of the Indian wars, 1643–44. [Could he say it just like that?] So the borough began. And nine years later, in honor of the old Dutch city whence many of the colonists had emigrated, the settlement received the name of 'Breucklyn.' The first Church, in this 'City of Churches,' was erected at Midwout (Flatbush) in 1654, after nearly thirty years of parishioners having to cross over to Nieuw Amsterdam to attend service. Later, after the first Dutch immigrants, came the English, and the settlement was incorporated under the name 'Brooklyn' as a village in 1816. Already, in the 1700s, it had absorbed the districts of New Utrecht, New Lots, Flatbush.

"In 1834 the township, consolidating the outlying regions of Williamsburgh and Bushwick, was chartered as a city. Suddenly, Brooklyn became the third largest city in the U.S. By 1898, when it became a borough of Greater New York, its population was about one million. Only Manhattan, Chicago, and Philadelphia exceeded it in inhabitants, and only Chicago, New Orleans, and Philadelphia were larger in square mileage (seventy-one square miles—eight miles in its greatest width, a little over eleven at its greatest length)."

He sat back, craning his neck, knowing it was too dry, but he felt he had to get all the pertinent facts in first. Then maybe he could loosen up, maybe write about a specific figure. . . .

"The Dutch especially made it into a city of parks, homes, churches, neighborhoods. Seeing the commercial value of the ocean and bay waterfront, they also had the habit of greenery, and everywhere, it seems, set parks, trees, flowers and shrubs, green neighborhoods surrounded by blue seas, like old Netherlands. They were citizen-farmers of taste, and shaped the borough beautiful. The superb park system, for example, contained over a thousand acres by the turn of the century. Of course the biggest was Prospect Park, over five hundred acres, and included a large intricate lake, and in an adjacent park, a Botanic Garden, Zoological Gardens, Museum, and a vast central library. And on the other far end a series of baseball fields were added, the Parade Grounds he regularly played on. [The only problem with inserting this here was that the park was designed by Olmstead and Vaux, who had designed Central Park in Manhattan, and not by any early Dutchman.] Huge elms were planted in plenty, and tulips bloomed everywhere. Churches bloomed, too, all sorts. The first was the Reformed Protestant Dutch Church of Flatbush, built in 1654 (the present building dating from 1796), and in another century the Episcopal churches of the English [in the Holy Trinity, a Gothic landmark on Clinton and Montague built in 1846, he had heard his first musical service] the Catholic of the Italians, the synagogues of the Jews. [Did this need much more detailing?] The Dutch Reformed Church on Kane and Court in downtown became, in 1846, the first synagogue, ironically enough. Rectitude and religious tolerance came early, accompanied by orderliness, a sense of beauty, prosperity. [And what about sports, rowdiness, hanging out?]

"Superior farmers and landscapers, the Dutch (and English) were also veterans of commerce, finance, and trading [not to mention wars and killing, huh?]. By 1900 the borough had become a first-class financial center, with impressive surpluses of capital in its savings banks and trust companies. And early on, the settlers made shrewd use of the thirty-three miles of ocean and river waterfront in their Breucklyn, developing manufacturing facilities, shipbuilding establishments, a number of grain elevators, private and customs warehouses, and the piers of a great navy of merchant ships. The shores from Long Island City to Bay Ridge gradually became dotted with foundries, oil and sugar refineries, mills for the production of machinery, foodstuffs, chemicals, clothing, etc.

Little wonder that the U. S. Navy Yard in Williamsburg became the foremost naval station in the country.

"Interestingly, perhaps starting with later colonial days and extending to the early nation's days, New Englanders began to move down to this thriving borough at the western end of Long Island. As early as 1643, Lady Deborah Moody arrived, with a band of New England followers, to settle southerly Gravesend. [The story of this gutsy Great Lady needs lots more development.] They brought with them some Bay State ways and manners, giving the place a touch of a New England town within its large borders, though, fortunately, not ever taming or suffocating it with the same ways and manners. [Again, show here Lady Moody leaving Rhode Island because of Roger Williams's religious intolerance.] Was this because of the Dutch and European mix, the free space of primitive forests and empty wildlands, the adventuring seas and rough hustling spirit?

"In the wars, too, the borough played its role. During the American Revolution, the first strategic conflict was fought here, the Battle of Long Island (August 27–30, 1776). General Washington sent a part of his small army over to Brooklyn Heights to defend New York City and the lower Hudson Valley, but the British forces, massed in great numbers in Staten Island under Sir William Howe, recalling the lesson of Bunker Hill, decided to lay siege instead of attacking and forced an evacuation, back to Manhattan (which led to the northern retreat). Within the confines of Prospect Park [he had an urge here to jump up and shout his news to his fellow readers and loungers!] there is a commemoration, Battle Pass, which attests to this hard episode. And during the Civil War, no other city contributed a larger quota to the Union Army, or raised and forwarded as many supplies. Not to mention the other bloody battles, and battlefield cemeteries. The young soldierly dead had defended Brooklyn as fiercely as their immigrant parents and grandparents had first shaped it, landscaped it, invigorated it, giving Brooklyn its distinct, native character."

When he stopped and looked up, a girl about his age was staring at him, from across the table.

"Do you always concentrate that way?"

Embarrassed, and still rapt in his material, he shrugged.

"I go to Erasmus. And you?"

"Jefferson," he said, torn between this sudden brown-haired attraction and the pull of his scrawled words and the past.

"Ssshh," cut in another girl at the table, and he saw Erasmus shoot her a furious glance.

But he was set free to re-concentrate, for the time being anyway, on his report. So he skimmed his pages, checking his warm-up bag with his foot.

Oh, it was still too dry, a kind of listing of things. Certain phrases, words, he admired—"rectitude," just learned, for example, or "soldierly," he liked the heroic tinge of "soldierly dead," or the last sentence—but mostly, he'd have to go through the whole thing again, once or twice. Where was the surging feel of Brooklyn, Miss Fitzgerald's "Whitmanesque spirit"? . . . And what about the Canarsie and Far Rockaway Indians, who had been in the borough long before the white man had come along? Their relation to the land had been much deeper than the Dutch or white man would ever understand, for example. Which was why the Dutch had to buy the same land several times, not once. . . . Lady Moody: well, she needed a whole paper (or narrative) unto herself, that daring widow departing first from England because of outrageous laws about residing in your manor house or losing it, and then leaving old Massachusetts and Rhode Island because she would not be bound by narrow puritanical ways and laws. Only in Gravesend did she finally feel free, constitutionally and personally. . . . And what did it feel like to be a Jewish boy then, in the early Dutch days? Or for that matter, to be a Dutch kid, a real one who didn't much like stuffy rules or father's orders. Would he seek out a Canarsie squaw and drive his and her parents crazy? Well, he'd have to imagine all that in a short story, not any old report.

"Hey, Jefferson, let's take a break and leave old grundge sourpuss alone here."

Yeah, it was a good time for a break. "Sure," he said, getting up and automatically bringing his precious bag along.

As they wandered out, the pretty girl, wearing a kind of

pageboy hairstyle and a long cardigan sweater with three Greek letters on the front, said, "You know, when you first came in here, wearing this uniform, I thought, uh-oh, is he gonna be a pain or what?" She flashed a radiant smile. "To show you how much *I* know."

Outside the sun baked warmly, and they sat on the top of the high steps, off to one corner.

"Is Jeff fun?" she wondered.

"Well, yeah, it's pretty good."

She tossed her hair a bit, looking up sideways. "Which college you going to go to?"

Should he tell her the truth, that he preferred the sea and Norwegian freighters? "Uh, I'll probably stay out for a year first."

Holding her knees, she looked at him as if he had said the wisest thing in the world. "God, that's a great idea! I wish my parents would let me do that. It's easier for a boy though. I *want* Cornell or Wellesley, but I *may* have to settle for something less. Rothman's English and junior-year trig sunk my average. How 'bout you?"

He wasn't sure what to say. "Do you realize that this is one of the highest pieces of land in Brooklyn?"

"Huh? No, I didn't."

"And that just over a hundred years ago they were fighting the Civil War here? Dying right here?"

She shook her head slowly, impressed.

After a proper silence, she offered, "Well, I still can't wait to get out, no matter what the history. God, when I see this"—and she indicated the whole Plaza area, with kids running up and down the steps, and the cars whizzing by—"and that *fake* Arc de Triomphe, I can't wait to get away." She paused once more, "This summer it looks like Paris for me."

"Oh."

She glanced at him, strangely.

"Wouldn't you like to be somewhere else right now? Anywhere?"

"Sure," he said, leaning toward this Rheingold queen. "Over a few blocks, at Ebbets Field. They're playing the Braves today, and Spahn is pitching."

Her small-featured face scrunched in puzzlement. Then she laughed wonderfully and pointed to the bag. "What's the treasure?"

He unzipped it, showing her the spikes and glove.

Gradually she nodded, figuring. "You really are a little different . . . from the guys I date. I mean your goals and all."

But he had already started drifting back to his paper, as much as he liked her and her teasing "Arista" differences. "Hey, I better go back in, and get to work again." Standing up, he looked beyond her, shading his eyes and surveying the busy highway spokes of the Plaza architecture, with the green park and stately rows of brick apartment buildings along Eastern Parkway, and the "fake arch" that gave him goose pimples when he'd stand underneath it and recall its somber meaning. Well, this was his Paris all right, he knew, but he kept that to himself as they walked back in.

Sitting again in his seat, and staring at the swirls in the oak table, he tried to re-enter his regal realm of Brooklyn. He looked over what he had written and further notes, and he realized the Canarsie and Rockaway Indians had not gotten their fair due, at all. How to get in the rich stuff that interested him? Like their peculiar, fierce game of baggataway, a rough mix of lacrosse and football, where they used a sewn bladder of a pig for a ball, and kicked, ran, and tackled for hours on end, all day long. Did Dutch boys join young Canarsies on the sly for baggataway and soccer, for example, despite their parents being on the warpath? . . . And where to put in his favorite list, the price paid by the Dutch for the old Flatbush, including New Lots and East New York, when they purchased it from the Rockaways around 1667 (after having purchased it some thirty years earlier from the Canarsies)? Oh, that list was priceless as he reread it now, having unearthed it in his father's old *Brooklyn Eagle* pamphlets. The Dutch couldn't have done any better at Klein's Bargain Basement, he figured.

PRICE FOR OLD FLATBUSH (Indian Sale No. 2)
10 Fathoms of black seewant or (wampum).
10 Fathoms of white seewant or (wampum).
5 Match coats of Duffells.
4 Blankets.

2 Gunners sight guns.

2 Pistols.

5 Double handfuls of Powder (gispen bunches of powder).

5 Bars of Lead.

10 Knives.

2 Secret aprons of Duffells (Cuppas of Duffell).

1 Half fat or half barrel of Strong Beer.

3 Cans of Brandy.

6 Shirts.

Nowadays, when he rumbled above the midsection of Brooklyn on the New Lots Ave El, he had a better appreciation of the bargain.

Leaving facts for his imagination, he also realized that maybe the richest parts of his town were going to be left out of his paper, censored by school manners. Like what? he asked himself. Like this, he answered, in writing.

"But Brooklyn, my Brooklyn, is really best known for its collection of odd and mangy characters (and happenings?) through the years, characters with cockeyed accents and cocky ways. As much for gangsters like Bugsy and Louie in Brownsville as for great Hassidic rebbes who immigrated to Williamsburg; as much for tommy guns and barbershop murders as for payess curls and an eighteenth-century Polish village relocated. As much for the dropped syllables and rat-tat-tat rhythm of speech, throwing a nasty curve into the language, as for its museums or libraries. For a baseball team that was infamous for its major calamities, such as dropping third strikes in World Series games or sending two men home at once to score, only to get two outs at once. As much—"

A notecard slid toward him; would he like her phone number? Signed, Bobby.

His attention shifted. He smiled at her, this Roberta-Bobby, and nodded. And as she wrote it down, left-handed, he wondered if Breucklyn boys had longed for Amsterdam and Dutch girls or were quite satisfied hunting in the Flatbush wilds?

Now, where was he? feeling a little like Coleridge and his man from Porlock, interrupted by this young woman from Erasmus . . .

Oh, yes, Brooklyn uncensored.

Little Mr. Don Juan

The first time she had punished him, he was furious. He had done something minor, hiding Jackie Greenfield's jacket in the wide wall closet just before recess, and Mrs. MonteLeon informed him that he was to sit it out for the entire hour.

"But there's a punchball game today!" he protested.

"Sorry, but not one for you."

And suddenly he hated her, everything about her. The gravelly sensual voice, the gold-trimmed eyeglasses that hung upon the chest, the loose black-knit sweater and the pulling swell of her full breasts (sometimes jiggling loosely, startling the kids). He sat in the schoolyard, bitterly disappointed in the sunshine, while his pals discovered he had been grounded, and scrambled around for a replacement for left field. *His* left field. She had betrayed him, and he wouldn't forgive her!

He watched as Boodie slapped the ball down the left-field line, foolishly left open by Jackie. Easy double. Good, serves them right. Funny thing was, she was his friend, he had thought. She had protected him early on when that battle-ax Baxter had come around and tried to pin some stolen eraser on him. MonteLeon had told her to disappear and mind her own business. Bitch Baxter took it like a shot in the face, coloring. Oh, Monte was knightly then. Just as she had been when he first came into her class, with a record of trouble and mischief from the fifth grade, and MonteLeon told him his slate was clean with her. The past was the past. So why the hell did she pull this on him?

"Well, you still brooding?" She was standing by him suddenly, sporting her dark glasses, long and mysterious like Marlene Dietrich. "Still angry with me?"

He glanced away, and then looked straight ahead, at the concrete field.

"Look"—she leaned down on her haunches, close enough so that he could smell her perfume—"self-pity is self-defeating. And staying angry with me won't change matters. Wait for something more troublesome to happen, a real humdinger—then you can really tie one on against me. You did something small and foolish, and you're getting a small punishment for it. That's all there is to it. Now, look at me." She tugged at his shoulder, and he rotated slowly. "Is it over?" She put her hand out.

Against his will, he took it. "Yeah."

"Was it dumb what you did? A *kid's* joke?"

He mumbled, "I guess so."

"Good. It's over. Simple, see? Now why don't you check out the garden for me, and see if there's any more room to plant our tulips or daffodils?"

When she stood up and moved off to attend to Rosemarie, injured again, he got up and walked across the schoolyard to the fenced-off garden area. His pals were shouting and a pink ball was bounding by him between outfielders. Her attention to him had turned the trick all right, and he knew it. He was in her hands once more. Powerless to stay angry. And now doing her bidding! But wasn't that what he had wanted anyway, he figured, opening the door in the hurricane fence, and walking amidst the hardening furrowed rows. The midafternoon sun was slanting down, making prison bars on the earth. Feeling of some sort was returning to his heart. Some ambiguous sort. In a far corner, near the handball courts, he saw a patch of empty ground. Room there to plant her Dutch tulips straight from Holland. She had fought hard for this garden, each and every year. The fantastic spring blooming was due to her, and her alone; and to her students, like him, whom she had recruited to the gardening team. Against the wishes of the principal and her colleagues. Excited, he half-ran to tell her of the available patch.

She had been the first teacher who had so entered, and so complicated—at times tormented—his feelings. Sure, he had liked others, like young Miss Fitzgerald in the first grade, and looney spinster Gidden in the third, but those were different. Even Helen, his girlfriend, had kidded him about this. With a small smile, she had said to him, "I think sometimes you prefer Mrs. MonteLeon over me."

"Why do you say that?"

"Oh, just the way you talk about her sometimes. And maybe the way she handles you. Oh, she scolds you severely at times, but well it's kind of clear that she likes you too. Lots maybe." She paused, and tried her best at irony, "She knows you have to be watched."

He tossed his pink Spaldeen in the air, not high, and caught it in one hand. "Well, you're not really in competition with her, you know," he offered.

"Sometimes," Helen said, looking wonderful in her pea jacket and new short haircut, "I think *she's* in competition with all the girls. The way she dresses. I mean, you can practically *see right through* some of those sweaters she wears!"

He moved closer, whispered, "Know what? I like you better than her, even though I never get to see through any of your sweaters." He kissed her lips right there on the stoop of her two-family house. Softly he added, "I always have to wait until they're off."

"You rat!" and she tried to slap him, only half-playful.

He liked her best just then, when her small, well-featured face was agitated, and the pale white color flushed slightly from her anger, as much as she could muster anyway. Boy, she was pretty, with that pert nose and white pearly smile, and he had liked her since the second grade, and gone with her since about the third. (Though not "steady-ish" till the fourth.) The bad boy and the pretty, good girl. Well, not all that bad, and not all that good.

Now he slipped his arm around her trim waist, and said, "Are we still good for the birthday party on Saturday?"

"Not if you act like a wise guy and make fun of me."

He turned her face to him. "You can always make fun of me." Knowing that he hadn't really made fun of her at all. "Honest."

"Well, it's not the same. You . . . you can take it better. And *don't* kiss me here, please."

"No more kisses on Montgomery Street, I promise. Scout's honor." She laughed. "You don't even belong to the Scouts."

"I know, but I have my own version." And he did feel like a Scout, sort of.

Which was unlike the way he felt with some of the other girls. Carol Kahn and Frances Kushner. Carol was noisy, skinny, unsmart, four-eyed, and fatherless. But she was well-developed in the chest, and for certain kids like Aaron, she was naughty. She "put out." In darkened rooms at parties, or afterwards outside by the bushes, she'd French-kiss you and let you raise her sweater and play with her large breasts. Laughing mockingly if you were too nervous or awkward to unfasten her brassiere in back, she'd undo it for you, and then thrust out her prizes. While he lifted and kneaded them —round, warm, firm—he felt the thrill of danger as much as pleasure slide across his brain. And in her low, masculine voice, she'd ask, with superiority, "You like this, huh? Go ahead, squeeze harder, that's it . . . *that's* it." But if you tried to stray beyond, meaning below, she'd pinch you hard, or even knee you in your groin, as a warning. So you laid off. And if she were in a special fooling-around mood, she'd put her hand on you, and, driving you mad, smile narrowly, like a cat licking her mouth after a meal of a mouse. During those fifteen or twenty minutes, the eleven-and-a-half-year-old felt the enormous transforming power of a young girl; the power to turn herself suddenly from a homely duckling into a queen, and the power of her naughty attraction for him.

Frances was very different. Brown-haired and sweet-voiced, a violin player and an able student, she taught Aaron another lesson: the secret life of physical intimacy. When they were alone, during "Post Office," that quiet student changed into a wanting, aggressive girl, asking him only "to promise totally" never to tell "anyone, anyone!" (Especially since her mom was "nuts," and her "enemy.") In a daze, he promised, lost in her big brown eyes, and feeling the passion of her young, lithe body, as she wound herself around him like some naked vine. He fondled her fine breasts and, through her underpants, touched her vagina gently; her hand seemed to lead him to her places of sensation, until she almost bit his shoulder, and he had to muffle her moan. And in another session, she handled and stroked his penis, and kissed it too, making him nearly cry out with pleasure; and when he emitted some sort of colorless liquid, he quaked with as much fear and bewilderment as excitement. In class they adhered to Franny's wishes, exchanging looks but hardly speaking, as though they were secret criminals, on the verge of being disclosed and caught at any moment. Her private life was revealed to him irregularly, every four to six weeks—she wouldn't have it any other way—and he kept his promise, honored the intimacy.

Reading *The Deerslayer* and *The Last of the Mohicans* in his *Classic Comics*, he wondered whether Leatherstocking really had had any wilder adventures in his youth. And he figured there was adventure out there in the wilds and there was adventure back here in the basements.

Playing ball.

Punchball was a primary pleasure in life too. He played during spring and fall months, around softball, and hardball, or baseball. He played on the Ralph Avenue vacant lot, stony and hilly as it was, and in the PS 189 schoolyard, on the concrete. In left field he was king, nothing flying or slipping by him or eluding his grasp once he got his hands on it. Always catching the pink Spaldeen with two hands if he could help it. The art was in judging it: a line drive, a high fly, a sudden slice? He had an instant to make up his mind, and then race for it. The best catches sometimes looked the easiest, the ones where the ball was punched on a line into the alley between center and left, and he raced immediately to the spot and then turned, and found the pink ball coming down out of the sky right to where he was waiting, as though he were on both ends of the same rubber band. Whereupon he immediately threw the ball to the infield, to hold the base runners. "Atta way to go!" and "Nice catch, Schlossie!" filled the air and scooped his heart.

She didn't watch much, unless his class was playing another class in an important game, and then she'd say, in her gravelly voice, "Now don't get cocky because you've made a good catch. Let's see what you do when you're up at bat this inning."

Not surprisingly, when he found the hole in right center for a double, she nodded from the sidelines, coolly. And that was that. As always she *trusted* him to meet her high expectations.

Odd, who and what she was, he'd think, watching and listening to her teach. A long-legged imposing woman, maybe forty (like his mother), long dirty-blond hair occasionally shoulder-length loose but mostly tied up and bunched high, with a full, curving figure made stronger by her forceful personality. You didn't sass her back in class, no sir. Her husky-voiced sarcasm would destroy you. "She's a tough bitch," claimed Howie Mindich, a straightforward clunker. But Aaron knew better. His homeroom teacher, she taught sixth-grade reading, writing (and penmanship), arithmetic, social studies, grammar, history, preparing them for junior high, and, for the brightest six or so, the possibility of 7SP, the Special Progress class that would skip the eighth grade, and go straight into ninth. But the most important instruction came in the grayer areas, no place for it on the report card, like what was right and wrong, what were good manners, what was gentlemanly conduct. Odd to think, hard to believe, that she had a pair of twins right here in the school—tall, nice kids too—and a husband somewhere; she seemed so absolutely on her own, independent, rough and ready. The ordinary facts surrounding her, like kids or husband, seemed to have little to do with her *essential* nature, according to the boy's perception (and to some extent, every-one at PS 189). Part-woman, part-teacher, part-mystery, she lived in a territory of her own, beyond the boundaries of ordinary grown-ups.

He was a smart boy, cleverer than most, but also restless, mischievous, forever getting into small scrapes. He loved kidding around, provoking kids, especially since he picked up the class lessons immediately, and then had to sit at his small student desk waiting an eternity for the rest of his classmates to get the point.

Sitting in the fourth seat of the third row, having been displaced from the SP row for talking too often, he felt a little like a black bishop commanding two long diagonals of the chess board. There, he'd pass the time by reading, writing out the Dodger and opponent lineups, making up stories associated with Ali Baba or the French Foreign Legion, or passing outrageous and comical notes to *his* Helen (Levine), to quiet Judy Monblatt, or to Franny (a mistake, he saw immediately, when she reddened and almost cried from his one and only, flattering note to her). Best of all, of course, was when he'd cause one of the "good boys" to get into trouble, someone like Joel Ruskin or Jeffrey Frye, who wanted to be A in conduct as well as studies. Well, tough on them!

For his mischief, his small troublemaker ways, she'd punish him by stern and swift talks, by bans from the recess-hour sport, by having him stay an extra hour after school. Well, he minded and he didn't. Sometimes, when she'd call him up to her large oak desk in front of the classroom, and chastise him strongly (but quietly) while the class wrote out an assignment, he was able to focus on his favorite features: the high cheekbones—Indian?—of her mobile face, the delicious impression of the full breasts against the loose sweater, the sharp well-featured legs crossed at the knees and revealed by the somewhat short skirt, and that gravelly voice that traveled to his boyish heart like some sultry movie actress speaking to him directly. Of course she was right, too, in admonishing him for his "constant disregard of the class's calm and orderliness," and for "diverting his classmates' attention from classwork." But her moral critiques, rather than dissuading him from further shenanigans, served rather to elevate her in his passionate regard, like truth accompanying beauty. Curious, he found it, that her high, moral preaching should translate itself into such a different channel in his blood.

Winter passed into spring, indoor gym basketball shifted back to schoolyard activities—wise-guy ways were kept at a manageable level—and his class grades stayed at A, practically insuring him a place in the SP. His bond with Mrs. MonteLeon had grown firmer too, a bond of mutual trust and feeling. To a certain degree, she accepted his excessive gabbing, the occasional passing of notes, the hiding of pens or jackets. In exchange he gave her his deeper loyalty and his obedience, listening to her on the important matters without his past habit of rebellious defiance. (Naturally, he kept his fantasy life about her to himself, and sometimes from himself, letting it out, or not voluntarily censoring it, at night in his bed, in the hazy twilight zone between sleep and wakefulness, when consciousness was loosened, and imagination and memory roamed at will, running wild like a pair of colts out on the erotic range.)

With Helen too he stayed firmly attached, though she had learned to kid him now about forgetting her once they entered Winthrop (Junior High), and he was in his fast-lane class. "What'll you want with a slowpoke like me?" She put up one finger and followed the bumpy slope of his prominent nose, and he responded, "Do you think I go with you for your *brains*?" causing her to belt him. He stared at her fine serene face, and the devoted eyes, and said, "Don't worry, brains are useless without beauty, so I suppose I'll never be able to give you up, no matter what." She made a face, and he held her and kissed her, off-limits in the long clothes closet, after everyone had raced down to recess. (Well, almost everyone, he realized, as someone—a girlish figure?—slipped out the door. Who had been spying? he wondered, getting his jacket, and not saying anything to prim Helen.)

A few weeks later, on a sunny April Friday, a special treat: a softball game in the schoolyard, against 6B-3, their chief rival. Both classes were rooting on the sidelines. Two umpires, and the teachers who were trying their best to look and be impartial, were watching as fans. Again he played left, and had already snared two sure doubles, one down the line by positioning himself just right, and one in the alley on an instinctive crack-of-the-bat run. And he had gotten a big hit too, a clean single, driving in two runs in the fourth. Well, they were leading by one in the sixth inning, with one inning left, and he was crouching out in left, wearing his Dodger cap and just hoping another shot would come his way, when, for some reason or other, time was called, play was held up, and he waited while the teachers held a brief conference with a messenger who had just appeared. And now, suddenly, he was being hailed, waved on in, by MonteLeon.

What the hell was up? he thought, running in.

"The monitor here has a note from the principal's office. Mr. Geller wants to see you, immediately." She looked at him, and he shook his head back, dumbly.

"Now?" he asked.

She nodded, and showed him the note, with the word "immediately" underlined.

His heart fell, as he realized it probably meant an accident at home. Shifting gear, and taking his beloved mitt with him, he followed the monitor off the field, and through the hurricane fence door, hearing the moans and confusions of the onlookers, and wondering whether it was Mom or Dad, or maybe even his sister? "Damn!" he muttered, hurrying along, sweating and trying to forget the game and focus on the new development.

He had been in the principal's office once before, when Baxter had tried to pin something on him, and Geller, true to his reputation, had been fierce at first, but then fair. It had worked out okay, and swiftly too. But the office remained scary, like some inner sanctum. Mr. Geller looked up from the telephone, and motioned him to a chair.

He sat, his feet dangling off the ground, the mitt in his lap. Catching his breath, he felt the perspiration pimpling his brow, and he used his sleeve to wipe it. While the principal talked, the boy observed the large photos of a smiling FDR and businesslike Harry Truman hanging on the wall, with Old Glory unfurled on a long flagpole and set up in the corner. Half-listening in, Aaron didn't think Mr. Geller was speaking to any hospital, or even about his case. Hmmm. He scratched his nose, wiped his forehead again, wished he had a glass of water, and waited. Christ, his pals better not blow that one-run lead!

Geller, laughing, hung up the phone. Then, turning his attention to Aaron, his face and manner changed abruptly, and he said, "Well, young man, that promise you made to me about a year ago, so you've gone and broken it." With some pleasure he walked around the vast oak desk and sat on it, towering above the young, shocked boy. "And gotten yourself in real hot water this time, eh?" He folded his arms, and nodded, eyeing the young criminal.

"But . . ." he stumbled, shifting his legs, "what have I done?"

"Oh, are you going to play the innocent now? And make it harder on yourself?"

He shook his head, bewildered, blinking his eyes rapidly.

"Frances. Young Frances Kushner. I got a call from Mrs. Kushner yesterday, and this letter today." He held up the evidence. "Shall I read it to you, son?"

He breathed deeply, and made a pocket in his glove. He shook his head, not knowing what to say, what to think.

" 'Dear Mr. Geller,' " he read slowly, solemnly, " 'I have the painful duty of having to report to you that my daughter Frances has been subjected to repeated sexual molesting by an obviously dangerous or sick young man, Aaron Schlossberg. The incidents in question have gone on, it seems, throughout this year at different times. The details are simply too sordid for me to go into here. I suggest you speak to the boy in question himself, obtain the details from him, and then decide for yourself the proper form of punishment. At this point I don't know whether to call the police in or not, hire a lawyer, or what. I have wanted to keep Frances out from classes so long as the boy is still there, but she has insisted on going. This has been a terrible ordeal, for all of us, and I know that if I were to tell my husband, Sidney, all hell would break loose. And he has enough headaches already. Therefore I leave it to your best judgment as to what to do, and shall not pursue any action subject to your wise decision. Signed, Etta Kushner.' " Mr. Geller looked up, and sighed. "Well, son, what do you think? And where would you like to begin?" His look was a mix of scowl and smile, a perverse smile.

Stunned, and bewildered, Aaron said, "Sir, may I have a drink of water?"

Mr. Geller eyed him, for a long minute, as though he were a biologist studying a microbe. Finally he said, "You stay right there, don't move, and I'll see that you get it."

While the principal went to the door to call his assistant, the boy frantically tried to figure out a plan of defense, but was hounded by the how and why of it all, especially why? If his mother were to be called in on this, or father . . . The thought that only ten minutes ago he was standing in sunny left field, high with the pleasure of the game, struck him as a discrepancy to remember. Another thought hit him as he weakly pounded his mitt: Was this how you got paid back for your good times?

Presently he was being handed a tall glass of water, and allowed to drink it, while prosecutor Geller stood before him, arms crossed, following his every gulp. God, it was awful, and his chest pounded with fury and fear together.

"Well, my little Mister Don Juan, what's been going on?"

Was *he* a criminal too? He searched for his voice, and began, "Well, sir, I don't really know myself, to tell you the truth. I mean, uh, I've seen the girl a little yeah, and we've sort of fooled around a bit, but I've never uh 'abused' her sir, I mean I never did anything that *she* didn't participate in . . . or agree to. Not that I'm blaming her, sir, I don't mean that at all!" But even as he said these things, muttered his fragments of logic and pieces of the puzzle, he knew he was deep in the soup, and his words alone were not going to get him out of it. He needed help in all this, especially from Franny—if she would talk freely. Little chance of that, though. And he certainly didn't want to implicate her needlessly, even though he already had. Damn, damn, damn!

"Look, my boy, you better come clean here with me or you'll have a bigger problem with the girl's mother, I assure you." The principal moved away from the desk and pulled an armchair up to the boy to emphasize what was at stake here. "And who knows, maybe with the law too."

He restrained his tears, and felt alone, terribly alone.

"Squirming won't help you. Just tell me what happened, lay out the facts, and we'll see where you and everyone concerned stands in all this." He shook his head, affecting a stance of forgiveness lurking somewhere. "Look, it may be we can save you from . . . from most difficult circumstances, *if* I'm sure you're being completely honest and open with me. Now, what have you been doing with this girl?"

And as he proceeded, for the next hour or so, to give a version of what had occurred, a version that tried in its way to protect the absent Franny as much as assume a certain responsibility for the present Aaron, in other words to concoct a cocoon of innocence in which they both had existed, he fixed his gaze mostly on the slants of afternoon sun filtering through the windows, and on the smooth-shaven face of FDR, his eyeglasses radiating light and wisdom. He had become a leader despite his polio liability, so couldn't Aaron rise above his present sickness one day too? Every now and then he had to face Geller, and his stern angular face with the unforgiving eyes, and he did so with hesitation.

At the end, Geller said, "Well, we'll have to check out your story of course, because if you've uttered one word of untruth to me"—and he wagged his long finger at Aaron—"you're in severe trouble." He shook his head. "I just don't know where you . . . developed such premature habits and ungodly tendencies, son. But get rid of them, fast. We'll do what we can to see if we can keep your parents out of this, and somehow pacify Mrs. Kushner—and I'm not promising that I can, you realize."

He nodded, silent, allowing Geller to do the talking now, and realizing that convenience and practicality were the principal's main concerns, no matter what words he preached.

Finally he heard the words of release, and stood to go, feeling fatigued and exhausted. But still in one piece.

He thanked Mr. Geller and was at the door when he heard the parting shot, "Of course this may have a negative impact on your SP chances, I'm afraid. Conduct and citizenship are very much part of the total consideration for Special Progress students."

As he closed the door feebly, he felt slowly shattered, the whole of him crumbling, coming apart. Unfair! screamed his soul. Unfair!

He sat in his cushioned seat in the darkened theater and watched the giant screen up front as Barbara Stanwyck, the greedy wife, and Fred McMurray, the hooked insurance agent, plotted their double-indemnity way through the murder of her husband for the insurance money, working against Edward G. Robinson, the company boss, who suspected a rat. Usually, such a cat and mouse story of murder and intrigue would hold the boy spellbound at a Saturday matinee. Today, however, the spell slipped, the movie rode right on by him, his heart elsewhere. Huddled in his seat, he sat still, heavy with the problem he wanted to escape from, and didn't even mind the kid kicking his seat from behind. Indeed the stuff up there on the screen, regularly so scary, now seemed harmless. His own life seemed, well, not so much scary as weighted down, dreary. And yet, what had he done wrong?

A beam of flashlight pinned him, and the masculine voice of "Greenstreet," the huge female usher, scratched at him: "Don't *you* start anything today, or I'll herd you right out of here! I have a packed house on my hands, and any trouble from you—"

He didn't even bother to mimic her back, or devise a plan of torment, but sat there and wondered if Geller would drop him from the SP track? His father would forever hold it against him. . . . And if either of his parents was forced to come up to school, that would be rough too. Cheesus, what a fix he was in.

He recalled trying to see Franny on Friday, to get her to speak for him in some way, or even to find out why she had done this to him, but she looked at him as though he were a leper, and raced off.

Now, the movie finished, Werter, Kamph, Dennis, Tavel, Mel, and Davis were surprised that he wouldn't join them over at Al's for ice-cream custard and hanging around. "Nah, I'll see you guys later," he said, and walked off by himself down Ralph Avenue, along the trolley tracks. He walked and walked, beneath the El on East 98th Street, hearing the subway trains periodically thundering overhead, smelling the carbon monoxide fumes particularly, and not feeling much like any Leatherstocking, or even Don Juan.

On Monday he sat in class, mute, sensing that the guillotine was going to fall soon, and feeling helpless and alone in defending himself. Everyone knew about him and the charges, he felt, and was trying to avoid staring at him. The worst of it maybe was not having anyone to tell the real story to, his side or the shadings of his side, and having to live bottled up. God, just in the three days it was getting to the point that he himself hardly knew anymore if he was guilty or innocent. Up front, MonteLeon was talking about the gentleman from Virginia, George Washington, as opposed to the General or the President, and how important it was to understand that he was a man, not a god. When she asked about the chopping-down-the-cherry-tree-and-not-lying-about-it story, he thought for sure she was somehow referring to him. But when she asked what the class thought of that legend, he sat quietly, not venturing any word, not even caring.

Afterwards, in the schoolyard, she came to him and said, "Do you want to talk to me?"

He shrugged his shoulders, not really knowing.

"Look at me."

He looked at her, the wind blowing strands of her hair loose, and at her smart outfit of brown leather jacket and white scarf. "You're getting to look like a pilot."

She laughed, put her arm around his shoulder, and said, "Come on, let's take a little walk. Tell me what happened between you and Frances. I've heard one version from the principal."

How did she manage that? he wondered. And, as she shepherded them toward the distant, remote part of the schoolyard, away from the ball-playing classes, he couldn't resist her, and began spilling forth the story.

Through the glass-clear day he spun his tale of puzzlement and intimacy, relating shyly at first the outlines of the times alone with Franny. But MonteLeon pushed him for details, and more details, and by the time they reached the high concrete handball wall, where a game was in progress in one court, she had pretty much understood the whole story.

She shook her head at him—in dismay?—and motioned toward the garden, adjacent to the courts. There, she sat them down on the ground, backs leaning on the hurricane fence, and rumps on their jackets.

"What the hell do you think you're doing?" she began. "If you get into this sort of mess now, what you are going to do in teenage?"

He shook his head, not knowing.

"So you never forced yourself upon her? *Not once?*"

"No. Not once."

"Will Franny confirm this?"

He shrugged. "I don't know. But then I never figured out why she . . . turned me in, in the first place. To her mother, I mean.

Especially after she told me that her parents were sort of nuts, and she didn't get along well with them, especially the mother."

The pink ball from the handball court bounced their way, and she fielded it and tossed it back to the player, all in one motion.

He admired the athletic ease, and wanted to ask, "Was it so bad what I did?" but for some reason held off.

Instead he put, "Mr. Geller says my SP chances are threatened now, by this. You think he would do that?"

"From what I hear, Mrs. Kushner is pretty angry," she said, adding, almost to herself, "probably as much at her daughter as at you. It was a pretty stupid thing to do, all around." She shook her head, exasperated. "You have plenty of time to fool around with sex. You don't need this kind of pressure, or this incredible tangle, at your age. Do you understand me?"

He nodded, and observed a low killer shot hit by one of the kids.

"You have your whole damn life to get mixed up with girls, and *you will*, believe me. Right now, for god sakes, stick to your schoolwork, and friends, and sports—isn't that enough?"

"Yeah, it is."

She took out a cigarette and lit it, cupping her hands. "If you start climbing into these things too early, prematurely, you'll make a mess of trouble for yourself, and spoil all the fun that's possible later on. You get me?"

He nodded.

She took several puffs, exhaling slowly. "Look, sex can be pleasurable, and splendid—and also awful—but it's not simply a matter of bodies. It's also a matter of minds, of feelings and emotions, just as much as bodies. The point is, it gets complicated. *Darn* complicated. And you're what, *eleven years old*?" As though she had just discovered that fact. "Are you crazy?"

He mumbled, "Soon twelve." But he understood what she was saying, and whose side she was on.

"Look at me."

He did, and she lowered her dark glasses, for the first time, facing him with her shrewd and appealing gray-green eyes.

"It's just too complicated for you to be involved in such matters now, do you see? No matter how much the teenage wise guys or older jerks may taunt or provoke you, or try to boast about it themselves. Ninety percent of what they say is strictly bull. You understand?"

He wanted to tell her right there and then what *she* meant to him, but could only nod very slowly.

Up in the wide blue sky a silvery airplane streaked, a twin-engine DC-3 shimmering in the sunlight. Surer and simpler than things below, he thought.

"Whadja mean before by 'awful'?" he wondered aloud.

She shot him a glance, and said, "You don't miss much, do you? Ever." She inhaled. "I mean that it's a complicated business, that sometimes it can be the most awkward and difficult moment in your life, and that you're not ready for it and shouldn't be yet." She took her last few puffs, exhaling leisurely, and ground the butt onto the asphalt. "Come on, let's get back."

She stood up, and slipped her leather jacket over her shoulders —as he had seen it worn by European movie directors—and readjusted a few pins in her hair.

He stood too, and watched her, barely hearing one of the kids calling for the wayward handball.

She looped his arm in hers, adult-style, filling him with pride, and excited confusion.

As they wandered back, she declared, "What a mess. And now I have to try to straighten it out." Looking at him, she observed, "I hope you prove to be worth it, my friend. You hear me?"

Oh, he heard her, saying "I'll try," but the sounds and the frequencies were more various and rich than he could acknowledge aloud, perhaps even to himself. One thing he knew, though, and knew: *It* wouldn't be "awful" with her, not ever, no matter what.

On Tuesday evening he accompanied his father to his club, the old storefront that used to house the Brownsville Air Raid Wardens Club. Presently, all the talk centered on Truman's sudden firing of General MacArthur for seeking to enlarge the Korean conflict to include Red China. Aaron sat at a chess board, playing Mr.

Mindich, and half-listened to the heated discussion in the cigar-smoky room. At the next table his father was playing pinochle with three friends and arguing against their pro-MacArthur sentiments.

"This is the finest thing Truman has ever done," his father was saying. "MacArthur may be a smart general but he's a dangerous man. A war monger, plain and simple. Fight the Red Chinese on their soil? Eh, he's a *meshugenah*."

"Harry, if they don't fight 'em now, they'll have to fight 'em later on," sparred Louie Ratner, "so what's wrong with now?"

"Especially now," Levine emphasized, "when we have the Bomb."

"He's right, Herschel," put in red-haired Skolnick, "MacArthur knows what he's doing, no? He's the military genius. If the Reds are supplying the reserve soldiers, then they have to face the music."

"And what are *we* supplying?" my father returned. "The catering service? Here, how's this piece of trump, Mr. Ratner? Not too bad, eh?"

Aaron played his chess game, poorly though, still focused on his own problem. Distracted and sluggish, it took him years to defeat Mindich, when it should have taken him twenty minutes.

Before they left, Louie asked, "So, Harry, how's the boy doing at school?"

"Are you kidding, *him*?" answered Mr. Mindich instead. "My Howie should be so lucky. Tell me, Aaron, have you ever gotten under an A in any subject?"

"Yeah," he stated proudly, "I got a C in Conduct last year."

"Ha. *Conduct*. What about real subjects?"

He shrugged.

"And the Special Progress list—it's been announced yet?" inquired Louie.

Aaron shook his head.

"Why? You need a list to make sure this *momser* is on it? Do you have to check to make sure Rome has a Pope?"

The adults chuckled.

Shortly, walking outside along Topscott, his father bemoaned, "Oy, what brains inside there, eh? MacArthur wants to be a little dictator, and they're all for it. Sheep." Papa shook his head. "*Nu*, what's new in school, boyala? Anything of interest?"

What could he say? "Nah, just the usual stuff."

The next morning he got to school early in order to find out whatever inside scoop he could from Mrs. Hennessy, the stern but friendly assistant principal. As she wasn't in yet, he sat on the long bench outside the offices, waiting. He opened his hardback Composition notebook, checking out homework, and stopped to glance through the Bill of Rights on the inside cover. He sure could have used an Amendment to cover his situation.

Just then he heard some voices grow louder, into an argument, coming from the principal's office. Mr. Geller was in a kind of shouting match with someone. Moving over, he was able in a moment to identify the opponent, by her unmistakable, husky voice. They were fighting all right, and there was no doubt about what the subject was. His heart pounding, he was dying to go inside and slug it out with him too! Instead, he spotted Mrs. Hennessy, and decided to depart.

On his slanted desk that afternoon he found a note, the penmanship large and clear, so unlike his own.

Aaron,
It's all my fault. I got angry at you when I saw you smooching Helen right in class, one thing led to another, and I wound up telling my sister about some of the things we did. And she went and told my mother, who twisted the whole thing in her usual way. What can I do to help you out now, please tell me? I feel AWFUL. And yet I'd feel HUMILIATED having to tell the whole truth to an outsider, a stranger. What can I do?   •
Franny

He was grateful for the note, but had little idea what to do with it, or with her offer. Bring her to Mr. Geller? Out of the question. To MonteLeon? No, not even to her. Good for Franny for being honest with him, period. He looked over at her, two rows away, clad in white blouse and bent over her work, determinedly not looking his way. A new lesson dawned on him; the classroom closet was really not the place for acting impulsively, or for playing Little Mister Don Juan, was it? (Having discovered who *he* was.)

When the bell rang at three o'clock, MonteLeon asked him to stay a few minutes. Sombre and elegant in black sweater and strand of pearls, she said, "Well, I don't know where you stand. I argued your case with the principal, but I'm afraid he's under a lot more pressure now. It seems Sam Kushner found out about the matter, and has made his own threats. So—" She reached over and lifted his shirt collar outside his sweater. "Be prepared for the worst, all right?"

He nodded, blood pumping.

"You don't need the SP to know you're as bright as anyone, do you?"

He shook his head, biting down on his teeth to restrain his emotion as his house of aspiration began tumbling down.

"And you don't need me to tell you what I think of you as a young man, do you?"

He shook his head, lying again.

She grasped him by his shoulders. "Sometimes there are consequences that are simply unjust, like a foul ball called fair. And there's nothing to be done about the call, but play on. You understand?"

He nodded, close enough to smell her perfume, and feel her full presence.

She nodded, and fixed on his eyes.

He faced her too, pounded by ambiguous feeling, fighting down any wetness in his eyes.

She shifted tone. "Let's see what happens. I must run, my boys are waiting for me." Then, squeezing his arm, she commanded, "You'll be all right, yes? Promise?"

"Yes," he squeezed out.

She nodded and sent him off, out of the room.

Once in the corridor he ran, reeling with baffled passion and stinging hurt.

Two weeks later. A bright, sunny May afternoon, and they were on an outing (MonteLeon's idea), up at the Botanic Garden. Three sixth-grade classes all at once, escorted by three teachers, and taken around by an official guide. They moved in and out of the spectacular blooming gardens, which were ablaze with hills of bright color and alive with planter boxes of delicate flowers. From Magnolia Plaza they strolled down through the Japanese Garden and then, amidst the flowering crab apples and large peonies, a field of red, yellow, and pink. The air was filled with a thousand fragrances, shifting at every turn.

At his side, Helen said, "It was just terrible yesterday, when Geller announced the kids for the SP and left you off of the list. Everyone knew it was unfair, and knew why, too."

Rejecting her hand, he shrugged. "Yeah," he said, walking.

She stayed right with him, though.

"I've been unfair toward you too. Out of jealousy. Once the word got around what had happened, between you and *her*."

"Nah, you've been fine," he said, squeezing her hand. He didn't try to tell her that she had the wrong *her* in mind, in any case.

"Do you remember the field of poppies in *The Wizard of Oz*?" she asked.

He shook his head.

"It's really a poison field, where the Cowardly Lion and Dorothy are put to sleep, almost for good, until the Tin Woodsman and Scarecrow get them out of there. I always kind of doubted that hundreds of field mice could lift the Lion up, and off that way."

Before he could get the drift of her meaning, the Botanic guide called out, in her Englishy accent, "Lilacs and wisterias next, everyone!"

The whole flock turned and headed in that direction.

He must have strayed, for the next thing he knew he was alone at the Overlook, surveying the scene, and maybe looking beyond, somewhere.

"Scouting the site?" MonteLeon asked.

"Yeah," he said, and for some reason said, "In case the British should attack again."

She gave her raspy laugh. "Well, you'd handle them just fine, I imagine. At least *I* wouldn't worry too much if you were defending."

"Oh, yeah?"

"*Oh, yeah*," she mocked him, and, locking his arm in hers securely, as though forever, led him back toward the class and the lilacs.

Fathers and Sons

Are the fathers and sons of the suburban life to be compared to the immigrant father and his son, reared in the post-Depression city? Can they even be considered to be the same species? Consider the question. A spacious lawn for pigskin tosses, an Olds or Chevy for cool evening drives or holiday trips, a Saturday of weekend teamwork for raking and removing the autumn leaves, maybe a good run or race around the local reservoir, all the casual rituals of native fathers and suburban sons. Life in the secure zone.

Along with secure, the zone of ease. America the Beautiful and the Good stands for the Easy Life, and the suburban life had come, more and more, to signify this life. Thy Purple Mountains of Majesty had become this cape or colonial or ranch, on a large lot. More space, more leisure, more fun. One's own home, one's own room, one's own car, taken for granted. If you needed to escape from father, you could. If he wanted to flee from you, he could. Space all around to roam in, to feel free in. Private dens and backyard gardens of domestic illusion came with the package.

Life with the immigrant father, in the city, was another matter. Especially if the immigrant missed his old home, didn't quite understand this present New World, felt in permanent exile. The mentality of exile, the foreignness with all things native, the every-day press of eking out a living, added up to pressure. Compounded by a son growing up American, with a love of dungarees, Dodgers, Saturday matinees, fudgsicles and forward passes, the sports pages, and *The Shadow* or *Inner Sanctum* on the radio—you know, all the crucial paraphernalia of daily life. How could immigrant Papa compete against all that?

This father never owned a car or house, never afforded the boy a room of his own, never managed a holiday with the boy, never took him fishing or camping, accompanied him to a game, or had a catch with him. Intellectualish, priggish, European-formal—what can you say on his behalf?

Well, he managed his rituals, sure: chess at the Air Raid Wardens Club on Sunday mornings, Russian movies uptown afterwards, and regular trips to the boxing arenas, to see the fights. But a few times a week at least, there was the cultural buzz ringing, and interrupting—America calling, sir. (Can your father really wear that blue serge monkey suit everywhere? Doesn't he even know the rules of baseball or football? Soccer—are you kidding?) And the father would lose the son to the native culture. Which would only serve to intensify the pressure of feeling on the outside, looking in. Not merely immigrant, but Jewish, and left-wing (thereby setting him apart even from the neighborhood). Really on the outside then.

If you added this pressure to a short fuse on the temper, an authoritarian personality, a dogmatic fatherliness, a lost rich past, well, you can see the trouble the poor fellow was in.

And yet, he needed love more than most. And increasingly, love and respect from the native son.

Years later, the boy, about twenty-two, a grad student at Stanford, stopped over in Manhattan on his way to London for a dissertation year there. The boy was shocked to see, after some six years of absence, a short potato sack of a man, with a sudden belly and a bulbous nose. What had happened to the sturdy powerful father of his childhood and adolescence, the man with the strongest handgrip on the block?

And over dinner, on Second Avenue, the father's physical decay was mirrored by his mental state when the boy dared to criticize JFK's nuclear confrontation policy. "Sshh," the father cautioned quietly, glancing around in fear, and amazement.

"What do you mean, sshh?"

The father leaned closer over the table, his plain brown tie just missing his brisket of beef, and said, sheepishly, "Who knows who's sitting in this restaurant? Be careful what you say." And the boy, amazed himself (and growing angry) at the father's tawdry fear, said the same thing even louder, as much to punish the father as to challenge the agents or informers. The father blinked rapidly, his face blanched, he turned uneasily in his seat, and he stared bewildered at the strange young man across from him.

And the young man, filled to the brim with the arrogance of youth, health, and Stanford-ease, smiled derisively at the defeated father.

It was only many years later, another twenty say, when the young man, himself in his forties, would awake in the middle of wintry New Hampshire nights and be filled with the father—his strong scent, his vest undershirts, his bristly face and his hairy body, which as a boy he loved to lie against, and all the other details of his energetic life—until suddenly he'd remember the last meeting on the Lower East Side. And then, curiously enough, his own derisive smile and arrogant devilishness seemed a proper due, a fitting payment for his years of filial neglect. The only thing was, now, in winter, with his wife lying peacefully asleep, the son was clinging to a ghost, not wanting to let him go, as gradually in the shadows the ghost had had enough, as it were, had reappeared just long enough to be remembered and relived, and then slipped away swiftly, back into nothingness, leaving the son alone, a forlorn man.

And the forlorn man understood, accepted, and even summoned the ghost of retribution to reappear, as much for the sake of the retribution as for the pleasure of the old company.

The Manly Art

The fights were on Monday or Thursday evenings, so as not to conflict with the Friday night fights at Madison Square Garden, and we generally went about once a month. Of course we never missed a bout where Green was fighting, 'cause Harold lived right there on our block, and was Dad's friend. Well, a kind of friend. A middleweight with a strong left hook but a boxer's brain couldn't quite be a real pal of Papa's, you know. But he was proud of Harold, proud of the friendship, and, as I said, we never missed a chance to watch him fight. Like that Thursday night in April.

After an early dinner, Papa would shave, for the second time that day, using his soft bristle brush to lather on the fluffy cream, and his barber's razor. (I never knew why, as I practiced with his lathering mug and brush, he didn't use a Gillette razor, which sponsored Don Dumphy and the Friday night radio matches, my weekly fare. Papa said it was a lousy razor, that's why.) Then he'd dress, putting on his dark blue suit and tie, while I had to get into my own monkey outfit, either my tweed knicker suit or my sports jacket and clean shirt. Comb my hair too. It was awful, of course, but I had to follow the rules or I wouldn't get to go. And who was going to miss a fight over some duds?

We said goodbye to Mom, promising to come home right after the fight, since I had school the next morning, and we were on our way. We marched the usual twenty minutes up Ralph to East New York, and over to Howard Avenue, then north to Eastern Parkway. I had heard about that Boulevard in Paris, but could it be finer, or more elaborate than our Parkway, which ran practically the length of the borough, from Highland Park in East New York through Brownsville and East Flatbush and straight up past Ebbets Field and Grand Army Plaza. I mean, it was long, it was grand. With its huge elms, wide-walking promenade, wooden benches, and citizens strolling at all times of day or night, Eastern Parkway made you love Brooklyn. And there were even chess games along the way, where you could stop and kibitz, or play, or argue politics, as we occasionally did, though not on fight nights, of course. And could the Champs Elysées lead you directly to a boxing arena?

Naturally Dad always ran into two or three chums he knew on the way, but on such an occasion, he only said hello or waved, explaining we were on our way to the fights. At those times Floyd Patterson or Harold Green were more important than McCarthyism, the fate of the proletariat, or the Hiss case. Always a rigid, formal man, he seemed to relax out here, amidst the swaying trees and darkening sky of a spring evening, as though he was headed for some holy place, not the local club for fights. I could feel that even in the way he held my hand, not the usual grip of ownership as much as, well, comradeship.

Eastern Parkway Arena was a roller-skate hall that turned into a fight club on those evenings, cramming in about two thousand fans. And just as soon as we had entered, and were hit by the tobacco smoke and the echoing din, the place cast its full spell upon my father. The ushers by now knew him, and, with the sort of smiles saved for tippers, one of them escorted us down the aisles toward our expensive two-dollar-fifty seats. (We never told Mom the cost of those seats, of course.) The early prelims were already in progress, and the filling crowd was half-cheering, half-audience-gazing.

As we entered our row, just beyond ringside, Father was greeted enthusiastically by two or three souls who called out his name and waved to him.

"Did you see Abe yet?" one asked, referring to the borough president Abe Stark.

"Of course, what then?" he replied, exaggerating his connection, I knew.

Smiling comfortably, unusual for him, he took his seat, removing his coat but keeping his fedora on. I sat alongside him, starting to feel heady from the excitement of the place. We were about eight rows from the ring itself, and you could hear the thuds from the gloves and grunts from the fighters. And even though these boxers were mostly beginners or over-the-hill veterans, they still grabbed your attention when they landed a hard blow or received one, and still managed to stand up. You see, being inside the arena was like being on a different planet, with a whole new atmosphere, with new aromas and sights, and it kind of made you see things differently, maybe yourself too.

Yet Papa, strangely enough, was at home there. He joked with familiar acquaintances and occasionally cheered on the boxers, while smoking his Lucky Strikes easily, and even allowing me to have an ice cream and soda pop without fuss. His pallid face took on color as he'd call out, "Jab, jab, use the jab!"

Thus Father, who knew nothing about baseball or football, basketball or hockey, and mocked them as a frivolous waste of time, reveled in this rough sport.

Papa, who knew so little about America, and felt so outside his adopted country of over thirty years, was at home here, at the fights.

The audience, a rich mix, maybe helped him. Sitting right around us, for example, was a fancily dressed couple from uptown in Manhattan, the slim woman wearing a fur stole and tossing her blond hair back every so often, and the gentleman hardly ever uttering a word aloud, but looking so natty in his Scotch plaid suit and, whenever a fighter was really beating up on another, leaning forward, and nodding, ever so slightly. Then there were the three middle-aged Irish fellows, good-naturedly laughing and drinking, wearing mackinaws in winter and old high school jackets in spring, always offering to buy Dad a beer, and treating him like a buddy. (And me, too.) And just in front of us sat the elderly Negro gentleman, who seemed to know all the trainers and many boxers, who wore a red vest with watch fob, carried a walking stick with the head of a lion, and sported his own mane of white hair. He was the shrewdest judge, my father felt, saying things like, "When that boy learns how to use combinations, he'll be a kettle of boiling water." On view also were the remaining regulars, the leather-jacketed Italian tough guys (tame and well-behaved here), the ordinary "mothballs" (my term for the weird characters in scarves and earlaps), the sprinkling of greenhorns from East Europe, with their funny accents and center-parted hairstyles. A motley crew, you might say, but a vivid one, an American one. And one which father fitted into easily, almost naturally.

Something he didn't do in life outside the arena. He was a strange bird, no doubt about it, like that one ornery pigeon in Davey Walter's coop, who was forever leaving the flock and straying off on his own. For Papa, the flock was still in Russia of course, his whole family of brothers, sisters, and mother, and he always wanted to migrate back. I remembered those meticulously written letters, written in Russian, that floated back and forth across the ocean during World War II like carrier pigeons, between the family and the youngest son. They were still waiting for him to return, sipping their borscht and shav over there in Minsk and Kiev, and he was still hoping to return. Like living out of a suitcase for forty years or so, feeling strange, temporary, in permanent exile, and still living by the old habits and ways. You know, Chaplin instead of Clark Gable, Red Army Chorus not Benny Goodman or Duke Ellington, chess openings by Novomyesky in place of curve balls by Sain. Was there another father in the neighborhood who had never owned a pair of dungarees or worn a pair of real sneakers?

But to watch him here, increasingly easing up and letting himself go, joining in with the crowd, was another matter.

Like now, as he actually accepted a foamy beer from Frank, and toasted his thanks. Papa, beer? Oh, he'd drink his schnapps or vodka, but beer?

"How will your boy do tonight, Harry?" Frank asked.

Father winked, and pronounced, "Fifth or sixth round knockout, or he's a bum."

The curly-haired Billy shook his head. "Tough veteran he's up against tonight, Harry. Reif won't go down easy."

Papa sipped his beer, and laughed easily. "He will tonight."

By the time we got past the last prelim, he had loosened his tie and even taken off his jacket, leaving him exposed in his white shirt alone. Thanks to the fan behind us, his soft-brimmed hat had come off too, revealing his balding head. And he had begun cheering more openly as the bouts had worn on, urging on this or that boxer with cupped hand shouts. Oh, how I wanted my mother to see him now, drinking beer, shouting out, leaning forward in his shirt-sleeves, a sports fan. Not as she regularly saw him, standing off to the side, an unyielding, mocking Bolshevik, criticizing everyone, and everything, hereabouts.

Just then the crowd began standing and clapping, and we all turned to see the main eventers coming down the aisle.

First came Reif, walking rather smartly, wearing a fine red and gold robe, smiling to well-wishers. Handsome fellow.

Our Harold, approaching now, was a different matter. In his cheap wool robe and side-to-side bob, he swaggered toward us like some punch-drunk bum. Father squeezed past two people to get to the aisle, where he greeted Harold, whose face looked like a kind of giant soft mushroom smiling. Slowing down to find me, Harold raised a gloved fist in greeting. My heart surged.

"Fifth round, you hear?" My father held up a forefinger, warning Harold, who was already past.

Papa's face was reddening, half from excitement, half pride, as he returned to my side.

For some reason I felt embarrassed, seeing him react that way. It wasn't like him at all.

He leaned down toward me now, and asked, in a whisper of concern so unlike him, if I could see well enough? Sure, I told him.

"So, a knockout, sonny boy?"

"A knockout, Papa."

Floating through this simple exchange, however, was a complicated connection, intimacy, and I felt suddenly near to him—his hairy flesh, his unfulfilled dreams. I was happy for the fights, and promised myself I'd never hold the rest of him—his bullying, his Communism, his temper—against him.

Now came the time of getting ready for the highlight of the night, the main event. The crowd settled into their seats, the boxers danced, skipped, and shadowboxed, the corner men occasionally stopped them to dab another touch of Vaseline over the eyes. The announcer introduced the fighters, giving the records, weights (there was a 160-pound limit), hometowns, color of trunks, as though they were crucial words to remember. And then the eyeball-to-eyeball confrontation, where the referee instructed them on the rules of the fight, the same Queensbury rules that that Marquees had made over in England for boxing in the last century, I knew. (A fact I had researched in our World Book Encyclopedia, which pleased Father, since a door-to-door salesman had sold him the volumes one evening in our apartment.)

The lights lowered, save for the cone of light pouring down over the ring, like a transforming halo. The bell rang, the fight began, a new intense world appeared. And I realized I was as nearly interested in watching my father as I was the fight itself. Not that I wanted to, I mean, but that's just the way it happened. The two boxers circled, jabbed, felt each other out, and Papa sat up on the edge of his seat. Something he never did for his Yiddish theater, for his Russian films. The opponent, Reif, danced away and boxed cagily, while Harold pursued him doggedly around the ring. Nothing much happened for the rest of the round, really, except at one point Reif caught Harold with a decent uppercut, and Harold retaliated with a swinging left hook, but missed. But the force of the swing made the crowd almost gasp with fear, or anticipation.

In between rounds we watched Green, in our corner, wiped down and advised by his familiar trainers, Ray Arcel and Freddie Brown, and Gold, his manager. If Harold won this bout, they were taking him to the Garden for a middleweight showdown against the Frenchman, Marcel Cerdan. I could see his neck's thick width, the full biceps of his arms, his thick curly hair. In contrast, his black sneakers looked old and worn, and the Everlast trunks rode down absurdly on his short frame. As Harold stood and tapped his gloves, waiting for the bell to ring, Father winked at me and smiled, his face widening with excitement.

For four rounds, they fought that way, Reif, taller, slenderer, swifter, jabbing and occasionally stopping and hitting, making Green look foolish, slow-footed. Around the eighteen-foot ring, Green pursued, taking the punches and hardly blinking, but starting to slam hard at Reif's midsection as he tried to clinch, causing the older fighter to wince aloud twice, and take a few deep breaths through his mouth in the fourth.

But the fifth passed harmlessly, with Reif even landing a few good shots to Harold's head, including one which reddened his cauliflower ear. After the round, the trainers slapped Harold's arms, and his manager began to lecture him angrily.

And Dad looked concerned too, shaking his head.

Frank turned back to us, saying, "Reif looks too clever, Harry. I think he's going to take him the distance." He took out a bill and said, "A sawbuck says he will."

Father smiled, his sheepish helpless smile, and could hardly speak, challenged this way, and already the one losing. "Sure," he blurted out.

But he hadn't even gotten any odds, I realized, with only five rounds to go.

Now, when Green stood, Papa stood too and called out, "Catch him, Heshy! Catch him and klop him good!"

The burst of enthusiasm and Yiddish words made some people smile, I saw.

"Atta boy, Harry," Billy said, either complimenting him or, maybe, condescending, "wake him up or he'll blow his big chance."

Into the sixth they proceeded, the same pattern following, and Papa said to me, his face growing colorless, "He's a bum, isn't he? A real *ferd*. Feh, I'll never trust him again!"

"Don't worry, Papa, he'll get him," I said, hardly believing it, "it's only the sixth, remember. Come on, Harold, come on!"

For the next two rounds, while Harold began to cut down the ring space of Reif, my father was caught up as never before, intent, devoted. At one point he nodded, and whispered, "*Nu*, will he

45

catch the fox? He's learning his tricks, you see?" Without realizing it, he held my arm tightly, with rising pleasure.

The crowd too sensed the hunt closing down, and watched quietly in the eighth as the two boxers circled.

The round was two minutes gone, Frank had already turned to say something to Father, when suddenly Reif, coming in and attacking, peppering Harold with two jabs and starting to throw his right, was lifted up off the canvas by Harold's left hook, which shot out short inside the right and landed squarely on Reif's chin, a short swift blow of no more than eight or ten inches. So short, so fast, that I'm not even sure I saw it. The taller boxer was lifted up maybe six inches from the canvas, a moan escaped from somewhere, and when he fell, he fell straight forward, thudding against the canvas. For some reason I thought immediately of a hanging, watching a man's life taken suddenly as he was cut down, and maybe it was that shadow of the otherworld that shocked the crowd for ten long seconds. A stunning silence.

The crowd awoke, stood, and cheered, Papa along with them. His face was red and glowing now, and he was even cocking his fist, running it through the air. I felt the oddest sensation watching him. Was this him, really? Or a stranger? Was this what it took to make him feel at home, easy? Was this the inside of the man who had read all those Russian books on history and politics in our Winthrop secretary, and could argue down anyone at the club?

He grabbed me in his strong arms and kissed me on the cheek, saying, "We showed them, eh, *boitchek*! We showed them!"

But excited as I myself was by the knockout, and as wonderful as it was to feel his hands hold me warmly and his smoothly shaved cheek against mine, I felt other things as well. Other emotions I mean. Mixed ones, new ones, that I couldn't easily identify, or name, like one of those strange hybrid flowers at the Botanic.

I wasn't even sure that they all concerned Papa even. . . .

Anyway, in the next minute, normalcy returned in the arena, and slowly in me. Frank paid off the bet to Dad, and he, Kevin, and Billy were congratulating Father, as though he had won the bout himself. "Well, Harry, you knew your goods. I'll bet he stands a real chance against the Frenchie in June."

The crowd in the ring had now parted, and Reif was in his corner, sitting on his stool, receiving smelling salts. Harold went over, shook the dazed fighter's hand, and returned to his own corner, and meager robe. Presently, the ring announcer gave the time of the knockout, two-forty of the eighth, and then raised Green's glove. He looked almost embarrassed now, in victory.

He departed the ring, and came up the aisle, and Papa was there, beaming his congratulations. Harold smiled back.

Soon enough, we were outside, in the soft night, walking again. On our promenade, beneath the wide dark sky filled with bright stars, we paraded. A group of three acquaintances spotted us and moved along with us for a while, praising Harold and asking father what he thought of his chances against the classy French fighter. Papa laughed lightly, and said it was too early to tell. But he seemed glad to have been asked, an authority again. At Howard Avenue they veered off and left us.

"So, boyala, quite a night, eh?"

"Yeah, Harold came through all right."

He shook his head, marveling, I saw. "He's strong as a horse. Imagine a Jewish boy who can hit like a goy! Of course he acts like one too—he'll throw his purse away on the ponies. Aah!"

We walked, holding hands, and though I was only twelve, I felt older, in some ways older than Papa. Was it that I sensed something about him now that maybe he didn't know? Almost against my will, I felt sort of protective—about him, about that secret. Or something like that. Certainly I could never tell Mom about it, she would use it against him, and that wasn't fair. A slight wind fluttered up, strangely warm and sultry.

"Some rain, Dad?"

"Why not? Come, we'll walk faster."

The trees swayed and rustled too, and we got a move on it. By East New York Avenue we passed the local synagogue, and I thought how I had never seen Papa reveal as much emotion there, or such pleasure, as he had at the arena tonight.

Rain fell swiftly and hard, and to my surprise, Papa laughed, and called over, "Come, silly boy, come!" And he was actually running. He ran funny, swaying his hips from side to side like a girl, and sort of using his elbows not arms, but his strength gave him his speed.

I ran too, excited, just barely keeping up with him, to my amazement. You see, I don't think I had ever seen him run before.

We must have run two blocks or so before the shower let up, and so did we, pretty exhausted. Rather exhilarated.

Soaking wet, breathing hard, we turned down Ralph, and walked down the darkened sidewalk, which was glistening from the rain. He had taken my hand again, and I was glad for it. The new leaves from the trees were shining, the occasional puddles glimmered with reflections, and the deserted streets sprouted red and green rainbows gleaming in the lamppost light. The whole street was fresh and breathing with the fragrance of the sudden shower.

"I've never seen you run that way," I said.

Coughing slightly, catching his breath still, he offered, "It's easier with a horse under you."

By the vacant lot where I played punchball, I asked, "Did you really use to ride out in the rain, over there?"

He looked at me, wiping his forehead. "Of course. Why not? It could be very nice sometimes to get caught in a shower riding in the woods." He paused to tie his shoelace, using a car bumper. "Eh, I miss that."

The word struck me, and I wondered how much else he missed—the large house and private stables, the school called "gymnasium" and the peasant village, the brothers and sisters, mother and father, dining on freshly caught rabbit and speaking Russian?

Just then we arrived at our apartment building, where Sam Tavel was standing on the front step, protected by an overhang. "What are you guys, going crazy?" the tallish, mustached man said, smoking his cigar. "It's been pissin' like crazy out there, you'll catch pneumonia!"

"Oy, Shloime, are you a baby," countered my father. "A little fresh rain never hurt anyone." He lit a cigarette, and inhaled deeply.

"Where have you been, on a night like this?"

My father smiled and shook his head. "What would you do on a really bad night? Outside your apartment, and bourgeois comforts, I mean."

"We've been to the fights, Mr. Tavel," I quickly announced. "Green knocked him out in the eighth with one punch!"

The stoop-backed accountant shot me a look. "Boxing again? I don't know what you see in it, Harry. It's a terrible sport. They should ban the whole thing."

But I knew what he saw in it, didn't I? I was about to defend the sport, but Papa was already shaking his head and half-smiling with that look of hopeless disdain. It was the same look that he'd break into as when he was arguing the workers' revolution to Mr. Tavel or one of the other "bourgeois" neighbors.

And although it was a look that I usually hated, I didn't mind it so much now, for it signaled to me that all was back to normal again, Papa lecturing arrogantly, and foolishly, hardly hearing his own words, hardly revealing himself.

"To the Garden, *Harold*?" asked Mr. Tavel now, raising his voice in disbelief. "Does he really have a chance?"

And while father responded, offering up his valuable opinion to the amateur fan, I noted his suit and shirt still glistening with droplets, and recalled his funny girlish running, and the pleasures of his evening.

"And you, Aaron, you mean you like going to the fights too? Somehow, I can't imagine you enjoying all that blood and gore!"

"That's not the most interesting part, Mr. Tavel," I answered honestly. "Not at all."

Sundays

However well I liked Sundays as a boy, a small terror always found its way into my heart as they approached. It was the day I would spend with my father, going to his club or occasionally traveling uptown on the subway to a Russian movie at the Stanley. The movies were mostly war movies that took place in Russia, and I remember soldiers, large woolen coats with fur collars and furry hats, running and falling in the snow-filled fields. The pictures were exciting, but sometimes I was frightened by the thunder of the artillery guns and by the bundled soldiers, who were always looking to warm their hands or feet in the freezing cold. I would roll up my paper program into a long spiral like a telescope, and, tucking it inside my jacket, slide low into my seat and shroud my head with my jacket. If my father noticed me then, he would lean over and say, "Aaron, that's not nice, sit up straight, be a big boy," and I would sit up.

On Sundays it was understood that I was to wear the gray tweed suit and cap that my father had picked out for me. Instead of long trousers there were knickers—woolen and itchy. And the socks. So long, dark blue, and also woolen. I had to wear garters to keep them up, but luckily no one ever saw them. In the naked night my legs, below the ridges of the garter marks, were red-striped from the day's scratching.

And whenever I climbed the two flights of marble steps to call for Steven Stern in the early afternoon, before my father captured my Sundays, that knicker suit with its garters made my heart shake. Sitting straight and squeezed in the Stern's small kitchen, I answered politely Mrs. Stern's questions about my family and watched Steven gulping down two white-bread sandwiches.

"You should look so nice on a Sunday for a change," Mrs. Stern said to Steven, whose head kept diving in and down and back and up, eating. Pinched and uncomfortable, I fingered my shirt collar. "Aaaah, but you'll always be a slob, look at you"—her hands on her weighted hips, her breasts sagging. "You want more milk, Stevie?"

He nodded, his jaws moving. Mrs. Stern poured him another glassful.

"Are you going to play ball today, Aaron?" Mr. Stern's blue eyes twinkled. He always shadowboxed with the kids, and I liked him.

"I can't, not today," I mumbled.

"Just my nut of a son and his wild friends knock themselves out on Sundays," said Mr. Stern, with a flare of pride in his voice. He cuffed Steven playfully on his arm—"Heh, nut?"—and my friend swallowed his milk throatily and rose to the game. He hit his father with a left hand in the side and with a mock seriousness they began to box in the vestibule.

"Look at them, Aaron, heh? Honestly, they're nuts!" Mrs. Stern was becoming annoyed. "All right, Louie, enough, enough." In spite of myself I smiled and felt warm.

When I headed for the door, however, with Steven behind me in the hallway, instinctively I would turn my head under the pretense of saying something to Steven and glance back at Mr. and Mrs. Stern, who were exchanging grins. It wasn't necessary to hear my family name, though I did once, to know that they were talking about my father, the way he dressed me and did things. In that instant, tears welled up in my eyes and I would grimly catch the doorknob. I hated my father then because he made me wear the horrible wooly knickers and didn't let me play on Sundays, but mainly because the Sterns were laughing at him. But as soon as I had opened the door and was out on the landing, my face tightened and I knew I hated the Sterns more because they were laughing at my father. And I swore to myself that I wouldn't scratch all day, no matter what.

On Sunday morning my father and I got up early. He made me wash my face and ears with soap before I could come into the kitchen. Outside the bathroom he put his fingers to his lips. "Sshhh, your mother's sleeping for a change," and I smiled intimately with him.

He stood by the stove with a spoon in his hand stirring cereal in a pot. Slippers, a worn pair of trousers, hair escaping the top of his undershirt, dishcloth flung over his shoulder. The hot Ralston was always the way I liked it, never lumpy or uneven, but smoothed down into a sandy plain.

"Boy, I could eat this all day this way."

"A little different than the way your mother cooks it, huh, sonny boy? Here, put a little more salt on it, it needs it."

"But it's good the way it is, not so much," I protested weakly.

"Don't be a *nar*, listen to me."

Usually the salt ruined the taste for me, and I bitterly ate in silence. And I wasn't a fool, I thought.

But after we finished our soft-boiled eggs, eating one at a time, never cracking and mixing them the way my mother did it for me, I exulted in the ceremony of coffee. Real coffee! And once we dipped the challah into the magical brown liquid, making sure to dunk the crust fully, the day was transformed into Sunday.

Then he began telling me about his father's estate in Russia before the Revolution: the fifty acres of farmland, the double-gabled white frame house, the horse that he owned when he was twelve. Sometimes he drew a picture of it all, the house, the land, the small stables; and they even had an orchard with peach trees that my father would draw on a separate sheet of paper, using two pencils, one for shading. But just as my craving was fed, he would stop and tell me it was getting late, or else then I would hear my mother rising. And when she appeared at the kitchen door, her once-firm figure loosened by a thousand Sundays, my father would say, "Well, well, look who's up," in a mocking, surprised tone that I couldn't resist.

I ran to my mother and hugged her tightly. She asked me whether I had eaten already, but my father answered, "*Nu*, what then, I'd let him wait for you?" And while I smiled I was sorry that I hadn't waited for my mother.

My mother cleared the dishes while my father read the Yiddish daily, *Der Tag*. Periodically he pointed at a difficult sentence, and I stumbled out a translation. After a time he said, "Come, Aaron, let's go into the living room," and we stood up.

Before leaving the room, however, he stopped by my mother, who was washing the dishes. Her torso was fleshy in the nightgown, but her neck was slender and delicate. I knew what he was going to do and I wanted to run around, or tell him not to, but I did neither. He patted her buttock and then squeezed it, winking at me.

I wasn't sure whether I fully saw his look or heard my mother say, you bastard, you dirty bastard. I was looking at the clumps of hair on the backs of my father's fingers. I was ashamed at myself for accepting his wink without protest, his wink that made me an accessory.

"Very nice words, very nice," my father said, nodding. "You should be proud of yourself, the words you use in front of your son."

"Don't you worry about the words I use with him—just keep those filthy hands off me."

"I just touch you, and you talk that way to me, *du goy* what you are."

"*Du goy, du goy*, that's all he knows, like an idiot he repeats it." She was on her knees, looking in the low closet. She got up holding an empty jar, and let out a groan of pain, her free hand going to her back. Seeing a hole in her nightgown beneath her breast, I wanted to run to her and cover the sudden flash of white. I didn't move.

"Very nice words, Rose, I'll leave the boy to you so that he can grow up to be a truck driver." He stood with his hands folded, and my mother had to walk around him.

"Go to hell," she said, close to his face. She poured herself a cup of coffee and sat at the table.

"Ah, are you intelligent, such intelligence—"

"You dirty dog! Get out of here! Let me enjoy my food in peace, you rotten *hoont!*"

He started out, then turned and said, "Wait, you'll be sorry one day for carrying on like this." I moved from his reach, and he walked out.

I sat by the window, staring at the chipped bars of the fire escape. I rubbed my eyes and turned toward my mother. Cream cheese was oozing out from the roll she was biting. She brushed back some strands of brown hair and wiped her forehead with her arm. I stayed in the kitchen with her while she ate, feeling grateful when she said, "Aaron, *ketzelah*, be a good boy and get me a napkin from the closet." I strained and was able to reach it without standing on a chair.

"Thanks, *mein schein kind*," and she grabbed me to her as if she'd just looked up and suddenly remembered who I was, and planted a wet kiss on my cheek. "Ooh, I love it." I tried to squirm loose from her grip when I heard the bathroom faucet running and I knew my father was getting ready to shave. I stopped struggling. "My little pussycat—"

Outside, the September day was hot and gray. My father nodded to the people sitting in front of our apartment house, some on chrome-backed kitchen chairs, others sharing orange crates. Mrs. Lubin, a big woman with a pocked, red face, reached out for me with her long arms, but I skipped away. My father didn't even greet her. To me he called her a "cow" as we walked on, and I laughed and held on to his hand. Marching along Sutter Avenue, I wanted to stop and look at the fielder's mitt in the window of Irving's Sporting Goods shop, but I decided another time would be better.

My father waved to Phil Hoffman, who was slicing a corned beef in his delicatessen store. Just then I saw Mr. Goichberg approaching.

"Hello, Herschel! Hello! And how have you been, we haven't seen you for so long."

My father shook his hand. "Yes, Goichberg, I've been meaning to come around and see you, but—" And he smiled and moved his shoulder. "Aaron keeps me informed, though, how things go." My father's hand felt cold on my neck.

Mr. Goichberg's dark face looked down at me, and I beamed at him. "Aaah, Herschel," my teacher enthused, "what a boy this is, what a boy—trouble I get plenty from you, heh, Aaron?" He gripped my shoulder good-naturedly. Even in the cheder when I would whisper the wrong answer to Arnie Applebaum or hide Alan Katz's *Geschichte* and Mr. Goichberg would grab me roughly and shake me—even then I knew he never wanted to hurt me. "But a head he's got, Herschel, and when he's ready for it, if he wants, you should let him go to the Mittelshul in the city. He would do well."

"Well, boyala, you heard what *Lehrer* Goichberg says," my father said proudly. Looking down, I saw how high my socks were, and my face reddened.

Mr. Goichberg spoke quickly. "And how is Rose, Harry, how has she been?" I had always thought that he was old-fashioned, and I joked with the kids about the way the *Lehrer* wore his ties with the underneath part longer, or the full shoes he had that were like rubber galoshes, but one day Ronnie Rosenberg told me that he saw small blue numbers on Mr. Goichberg's forearm and that meant he had been in a concentration camp. After that I looked at Mr. Goichberg's face, red-brown with a network of lines in the forehead, and clear blue eyes, and shook his hand just to feel it, calloused and hard, and decided that I was wrong. I felt very stupid, ashamed, and for him, some deeper emotion.

"Rose, Rose is Rose, how should Rose be? Sleeps, *noshes* some cake, talks a little, and *schlafs*."

"Herschel, Herschel, don't talk that way, even in fun. Your Rose is a gem. Come."

I had a whiff of the hot pastrami as someone held the delicatessen door open. A small boy began crying, and I turned to see a man spanking his behind and pointing at the street. For some reason I hoped that Mr. Goichberg wouldn't talk any longer with my father.

"And tell me, Goichberg, where are you headed for on a Sunday? Church, maybe, *du ganif?*" My father tapped Goichberg's arm playfully.

"No, Harry, I have to do some work at the library in the city."

"Work? On a Sunday, Goichberg?"

"And what for a holiday is Sunday?"

"You work too hard, Goichberg. And leaving Sammy alone to protect Esther all day by himself? Ah, Goichberg." My father looked at him with sham disapproval.

"Sammy? Sammy has enough to do, the violin lesson, then naturally a little chess with his friend Aaron." He smiled. "But about Esther, Herschel." I looked away so that Mr. Goichberg wouldn't lower his voice too much. "Between you and me, she has me a little worried lately."

"What's wrong, Goichberg?"

Mr. Goichberg shook his head, and opened his hands outward in bewilderment. "*Ich veis nit, Herschel, ich veis nit.* It seems it's better if I leave her by herself lately. She seems to like it better that way. Eh, I don't know, Harry, I don't know."

"Have you taken her to see a doctor?"

"*Vas far* a doctor? It's not that . . . but wait till she sees Aaron today, she'll feel better!" and his hand lifted my face.

"I won't forget, Mr. Goichberg," I said, as if I owed it to him. Most Sundays at about four-thirty I called for Sammy Goichberg, but never earlier because his music lesson lasted until four o'clock and he was never home for another half hour. The Goichbergs lived two houses away from my father's club, and Mrs. Goichberg—I was never able to call her "Esther" although she asked me to—always gave Sammy and me milk and sponge cake before we went to play chess. She liked me, I could tell, but she was a strange woman. Once she caught me to her and put her hand down inside my pants and asked me what I had there. But I never told anyone about it. I was very young when it happened, but I remembered it.

"Well, Herschel, don't make a stranger of yourself, come to the next school meeting. You'll enjoy yourself."

"I will, I will."

"You will, you will—and what's so wrong with the Goichbergs' home that you can't pay a visit there with Rose sometimes? Take

Rose out and don't be such a *mysterishe* and so busy, busy all the time—*du herst Herschel?*"

My father was laughing, and Mr. Goichberg had already taken my hand and said goodbye to us. We moved along a few steps. Then I turned and tried to follow Mr. Goichberg's tall, straight back and gray-white hair flying about, but I lost him behind a woman with a red-feathered hat. It seemed as if there was something that I had forgotten to tell Mr. Goichberg and now it was too late.

"*Nu*, Aaron, come!" And I was taken from my reverie.

As we entered the club, some man yelled, "Herschel! Herschel!" and, "Come over here, Harry, sit by us here!" We went and said hello to several people and then joined one of the groups.

The club was one square room, with a tiny bathroom, that used to be a fish store; but when Mr. Cohen's son went to war, Mr. Cohen gave the store to the Brownsville Air Raid Wardens. It was very strange one day when I went for a quarter pound of belly lox and saw a man wearing a funny gray mask with an elephant's trunk coming out of it. I asked my father if I could wear his, but he never let me. The store was at the end of a quiet, tree-lined block of attached two-and four-family brick houses. The Air Raid Wardens had painted the inside of the store windows black so that you couldn't see in. My father was president, and behind his desk was a large picture of President Roosevelt, an American flag, and a paper in a frame that he told me was an "Oath of Loyalty." The walls were a dull blue and there were several tables, wooden and folding, with chairs around them and a few benches against the walls.

"How is school, Aaron?" Howard Frey's father asked me.

"Fine."

"Howard tells me you're one of the best students in the class."

I didn't know what to answer. Mr. Frey had a black mustache and small dark eyes. Once I told Howie a new dirty word, and a few days later he told me that his father didn't want him to play with me anymore. But Mr. Frey never said a word about it to me. He was always very courteous and polite. Howie once said that he hated his father, and I felt sorry for him after that and always picked him for my side when we played punchball in the schoolyard. Chubby and awkward, he was always dropping pegs to second or running too slowly on the bases. In class he giggled a lot, and I never could forgive him for not being a little more quiet because he made all those punchball errors.

"*Hast du a maydl*, Aaron?" Mr. Schneider sat across the round table, talking out of a squinted face with a cigar in one corner of his mouth.

A girlfriend? My fingers tightened around the band of my cap.

"The boy's shy, Harry, look at him," said fat-cheeked Mr. Peck. "Not a chip off the old block, heh, Herschel?"

I hadn't understood what he meant, but my father shook his head at him. "No, Harold, that's not nice," and smiled. Then he bent over and told me to sit up straight, that it didn't look nice the way I was slouching.

In a little while more men had entered the room, and my father went to his desk and called the meeting to order. Mr. Feibleman read the minutes and then my father read a letter from the State Department commending the "outstanding civilian work your organization has accomplished to help America's cause during the war." Here my father paused, and he looked as if he were going to put away the paper when someone called out for him to finish reading it. "Your own achievement," he went on, "Mr. Schlossberg, in providing the kind of patriotic leadership which you have shown, is a great one. You are a great example to your family and community. The United States of America is deeply grateful for your service and loyalty. . . ." At this point the room resounded with applause and cheering. Somebody slapped me gently on the back and told me how proud I should be, and I squirmed.

The meeting came to a close soon after, but the buzz of light talk and laughter remained, with the smell of cigars. My thighs itched terribly, and I sneaked off to the bathroom and scratched them with long, relieving strokes. I hoped the day would soon come to an end.

I was sure there were many pairs of eyes upon me when I emerged from the bathroom. I sat by my father, who had Mr. Madansky on his side in a game of pinochle against Mr. Peck and Mr. Schneider. Some kibitzers were idly sitting or standing by the table. The room was now cluttered with card games, but I didn't see anyone for me to play chess with. My father had entered me in my first chess tournament, and I could tell he was excited about it.

The first hand of the pinochle game was an even one, but my father took the last trick with a low piece of trump, and that made the difference. He began shuffling the cards.

"Aah, Harry, you're all right for an old man," said Mr. Schneider. "Your father's all right, heh, Aaron?"

"What are you talking, Schneider? Count your cards."

Mr. Schneider stopped long enough to say, "I have twelve—it's probably your card, Madansky," and he shoved the card toward him and started arranging his own hand. "Peck, *nu*? Let's do something today."

Mr. Peck still hesitated. "Never once can I get a hand from this man—my God, my bubba's *tam* he gives me."

"I'll bet Herschel's hand has a different *tam*, all right," said Mr. Schneider, grinning. Taste, I thought. He looked up at Howie's father, winked, and floated a curl of cigar smoke out of his mouth, which I turned away from.

Three more hands passed, my father's side winning them.

"You can't beat this man," said Mr. Peck. I wanted to pile up my father's nickels and dimes that he had in front of him, but I knew he didn't like it when I interfered in a game. I felt odd about his winning all the time, and I knew Mr. Schneider was getting upset. But I couldn't understand some of the things Mr. Schneider was saying.

"In playing cards, getting votes, ladies, you can't beat this man—you're right, Peck."

"Schneider, play cards, yuh?" my father said.

"Harry, play with *roita Perela a bissel*, yuh?" Mr. Schneider had an awful grin on his face. I understood the words, but they didn't make sense to me: play with red-headed Pearl a little, yes? I looked hard at Mr. Schneider in bewilderment.

"Schneider," said Mr. Madansky, "have a little sense, the boy understands Yiddish!" He stared at his cards, then at Mr. Schneider.

My father put his arm around me. "Ah, Aaron, here's

Newman—play him a game of chess until Sammy gets home. Newman, hey there, Newman! *Du* lazy good-for-nothing, why don't you set up the board and give Aaron a decent game of chess?" My father poked Mr. Newman in the arm.

"Of course, Herschel, of course," and he was off.

"Just this hand I'll watch," I said. Perhaps I would hear something further, I thought. *Roita Perela.*

"Aaahh, Aaron, we just kid, you know that, don't you?"

"Yes, Mr. Schneider."

"Me and your father are just having some fun."

"Yes, I understand," and I smiled, surprised at myself.

"The boy's no fool, Harry," said Mr. Madansky, "and you should think of him more when you talk in front of him." He had two cards left in his hand, and played an ace of hearts.

"Aha!" Mr. Peck yelled. "Finally caught you two!" And he played a nine of spades, trump, and took that trick and showed a ten of clubs in his palm and took the remaining cards from everyone.

"And *bist du a nar, Mister* Maddenskee!" My father condescended, head rolling from side to side.

"There was no way for me to know, Herschel, that—"

"You don't know the game, Madansky, and you never will. *Come* with the ace, what are you fiddling around for all game? You see I had no more trump—what's the good, you never learn, Madansky."

I got up from the chair and was about to join Mr. Newman when Mr. Schneider waved me over.

"Here, Aaron, here's a pack of chewing gum for later." He put it into my hand and closed my fist over it. "Go, go show Newman how to lose his queen," and he pinched my cheek lightly.

Mr. Newman had already set the pieces up on the board. Holding my cap with my legs, I opened my fist and put the gum into the lining. Sticking out from one edge of the Juicy Fruit packet was a coin. I slowly pulled the shiny silver out—a dime!

"Eh, Aaron, frightened already?" Mr. Newman's light eyes danced in their tired sockets. He had pushed the king's pawn two boxes and was waiting for me.

After moving my own pawn, I saw Mr. Schneider offering Mr. Madansky a cigar and grinning to Mr. Frey. My coin glittered. I put the gum and the dime in my pocket and tried to pay attention to the chess game. I had let Mr. Newman advance his horse.

When the game was nearly over, I decided to go to my father again, but I saw that he was not at the table. Mr. Goldstein was at his place, holding cards in one hand and with the other caressing the Boston bulldog cupped in his lap.

In the midst of arranging the pieces for a third game, after winning the first two, I saw that it was only three-thirty by Mr. Newman's watch. I felt restless and turned to see Mr. Goldstein still sitting there.

"Are you going to be playing with Sammy Goichberg later, Aaron?" asked Mr. Newman.

"Yes, I expect so."

"Take a break, maybe you should then, rest awhile, enjoy yourself. Too much is no good neither." Yawning, he stood up and put his hand on my shoulder. "Aaron, you're a good boy and sense also you have." His gray-blue eyes were looking down at me, and I thought he was going to say something further, but he simply stood wearily for a few seconds and then walked away. I was glad the words didn't come because I was embarrassed.

Almost an hour before Sammy would get home. In my pocket I felt the pack of gum. Juicy Fruit. Too sweet. I picked up the white queen that Mr. Newman had lost in both games and held it in my palm, staring at the empty black and white squares of the board.

I went to the front door, and Mr. Newman walked past me and outside, saying, "Aaron, get some fresh air, it'll do you some good—but do it now, before it rains."

"Yes, sir, I think I will."

"If you'd like to go for a walk with an old man, Aaron, I'd be glad to have you." A car screeched to a stop and Mr. Newman jerked about momentarily, then turned back and shook his head.

"Thank you, Mr. Newman, but I'll probably wait here for my father."

He waved his hand in the air and walked off. The deep wrinkles on the back of his neck reminded me of Mr. Goichberg. I leaned against the entrance. Although Sammy probably wasn't home yet, I remembered that Mrs. Goichberg wasn't feeling well and that I had promised to see her. I began walking toward her house, feeling a rush of hot air.

Mr. Newman was right about the rain—it was getting sticky out. The large elm trees looked very still.

I jumped the eight concrete steps two at a time. She might be resting. I opened the outside door quietly and made my way along the dark hall toward the Goichberg's front apartment. The door was unlocked on Sundays when I called for Sammy so I turned the knob and slipped in.

I walked through the dark foyer and sat at the kitchen table. The place was empty and quiet. I played desultorily with my cap on the tablecloth, and then remembered with a spurt of joy Mr. Goichberg's chess books in the living room. For a second I wondered if it was fair to Sammy, reading up before a game.

On the bottom shelf of the tall walnut bookcase I found Nimzovich, *My System*, and Lasker, *Chess Strategy*. Still on my knees, I carefully opened the Lasker and began browsing. There was a section emphasizing the importance of the middle four squares of the board, then one on the art of deception. For example, deceive your opponent by setting up a decoy attack on one flank, attract his attention there, and strike elsewhere. Or get him used to a certain routine of one piece, only to alter suddenly his habits in a crucial test. I had never thought of that.

I heard a sound. Laughter. I listened . . . quiet. I put the books back and half-stood, balancing on the balls of my feet, when I heard the creaking of what sounded like springs. I stood fastened there, sweating. In that crouched position I stole past the couch until my knees sank noiselessly to the rug by the bedroom door, which was ajar about six inches. A navy-blue square of the colored glass doors reflected my face. A creaking, then a whisper . . . stopped.

I slowly moved my head to the space between the doors. On a dressing table were Lucky Strikes, gold cuff links, bobby pins, a glass ashtray with a cigarette dangling, and a wedding photograph of Mr. and Mrs. Goichberg. A trail of gray smoke traveled through the crack, and I closed my eyes and swallowed hard to keep from coughing. My eyes burned. A slender hand reached up for the cigarette; then a sharp cough was followed by Mrs. Goichberg's shrill little laugh. A drop of perspiration rolled down my nose. The cigarette came back and the smoke seared my eyes, but I kept them open. Another hand reached out past the ashtray, for the Goichberg photograph. I bit my tongue sharply, my eyes hot and welling up as I saw the clumps of familiar hair.

In the blue glass my face showed ghost white. Another light laugh. I began creeping back, getting to my feet near the kitchen and squeezing my knees.

Outside in the hallway I was unsure about what to do. Sammy would be coming home soon, I thought. I had to get to him before he went in his door. I couldn't wait outside in front of the house so I hid behind the stairs at the back of the hallway.

I huddled in the dark corner with my head tilted to fit the oblique back of the stairway, craning my neck so I could see the front door. My shirt collar was wet in the back from perspiration. The time passed slowly. The front door opened, a path of light imprisoned me, and a young couple carrying packages came in. I stepped back, into the darkness. The shouting of two children, then footsteps above me.

Suddenly a little girl with dark hair was standing very straight, staring at me. I was still. She put her hand to her hair in a grown-up fashion: "Ilene, where are you? Come up here this minute!" And the little girl ran.

After a while the rancid odor of garbage became stronger. I saw two brown bags with orange peels peeking over the top against the wall. I thought of the weather outside, whether it had rained yet. I thought of the softball field, and practiced in my mind running for long drives. I don't know how long I stood before Sammy's black violin case pushed the front door open. I had to take the chance—I ran up to him, grabbed him by the arm, and started pulling him toward the door he had just come through.

"Hi, Aaron, where are you—"

"Sshhh! Come along, come—I'll explain it outside," and I still held his arm as we walked down the steps. The day had grown darker.

"What's going on, Aaron? What's all the mystery?" His light eyes, like his father's, were excited with curiosity.

"I didn't want to wake your mother up, that's all. You knew she wasn't feeling too well, didn't you?"

"She said she had kind of a headache this morning, but—"

"Don't worry, don't worry." I put my arm around him as we walked into the club. "It was just that she was sleeping when I went inside, and I figured that between me *and* you there together, she'd probably wake up. Now we can start right in on the chess." The second after I had patted him affectionately on the shoulder, I was sorry for some reason that I had done it.

We sat at our places before the board. I put my cap on top of his violin case on the floor. When Sammy pushed his king's pawn, glowing with his usual excitement and embarrassment, a feeling of tenderness and hurt, betrayal and confusion, flooded me.

There was soon the small ring of men around us that always watched our games. Although I usually won, I had to play well to beat Sammy. When my knight fork had worked and I was reaching to take off his rook, I was aware of my father standing over Sammy and smiling. I hadn't seen him come in.

"That's all right, Samala, you still have good position," said my father. He laid his hand on Sammy's shoulder. The shoots of hair recalled the rancid odor, and I felt sick in the pit of my stomach.

Sammy looked up and forced a smile. "Oh, Mr. Schlossberg, I didn't see you, sir. Nah, I lost the game just now."

Several of the men nodded their agreement, and one of them said to my father, "Harry, the boy is getting good, very good. I wouldn't be surprised to see him get to the finals in the competition."

"Aaah, who knows? Who knows?" my father said casually.

"You'll see, he'll win like his father does," remarked another, and my father laughed with them.

I played the rest of the game carefully until I saw my chance. I put my queen in a position where it looked as if it were attacking Sammy's bishop and protecting my pawn. Then, after he moved the bishop, I pushed the pawn to further the appearance of an attack. I knew Sammy wouldn't miss it—almost shamefacedly he placed the bishop in the same diagonal where I had my queen. And my queen was being pinned by my king! My queen was lost.

I couldn't resist a glance at the surprise on my father's face.

65

The kibitzers were astonished. The disturbed pose I assumed probably looked good because, really, it was real. The deceit I had played had nothing to do with the sickening feeling inside of me.

Outside it had begun drizzling. I walked by my father's side, my knees weak.

"Aaah, what a *nar du bist*. You'll never learn, a plumber you'll be."

I didn't say anything, but walked straight and stiff, never falling behind. At the corner he took my hand in his, and I clenched my teeth until he released me on the other side. Turning up Sutter Avenue, I could see immediately the yellow light shining from our kitchen window. I scratched my knee where the coarse wool had become wet and itchy.

Upstairs I walked before my father into the kitchen, where my mother was sitting at the table. She had on a white blouse and her hair hung down loose. I ran to her and kissed her on the cheek. I fought to keep the tears back.

"Hello, my *zhabala*," she said, making a part in my hair.

My father stood outside the kitchen, his hands on his hips. "A lot of *sechl* your son showed today in the chess game. You should be very proud of him—he lost to Goichberg's boy."

"So? So what's so terrible?" I stood nearer to her.

"By you nothing's terrible," he responded, "Maybe you'd like him to play a little more baseball or run around some more—ah." He shook his head. "He won't be able to beat the first *goy* he plays in the tournament." He turned away to hang up his coat.

I decided, while I stood with my mother, that I wouldn't scream back at him then that I wasn't going to play in any chess tournament, that I would tell him quietly when I was alone with him.

I sat across from my mother and saw that it was raining harder. I looked at her hazel eyes—mine were the same color—and reached over and ran my fingers over her smooth arm. She asked me how Sammy Goichberg was and I told her that he was the best friend that I ever had. She said that she was surprised to hear that we were that close.

New Man in the House

When I was almost fourteen, in late winter 1952, my mother took her lover into our small Brooklyn apartment, and began living with him only a short time after she had locked the door on my father. Since Sam, the lover, was still, like my mother, married, the situation had to be kept somewhat secretive, though the neighbors in our four-story brick apartment building got the gist soon enough. Sam was a nice fellow too, with soft silvery hair combed in neat rows of small waves, shiny gold-rim eyeglasses (cleaned every day with dishwashing detergent), and a sunny disposition. He had a good job that paid well, working as a photoengraver for the *Long Island Express* newspaper—quite a contrast to my father and his erratic employment as a milliner. And Sam was kindly toward me, talking about sports, asking about school, bringing home special cuts of steak or lamb chops, my favorites. Having only a daughter himself, he tried his best to be a pal to me, I think, and often succeeded.

What surprised me therefore was how certain small things he did used to upset me disproportionately. For example, he was especially fond of hygiene, and it wasn't long before my mother, sitting on a hassock, was manicuring his nails regularly while he read the newspaper or they talked. It struck me as deeply servile, and when I asked her why she did it, she reported matter-of-factly that he liked it, and it was easy for her to do, so why should he spend money on it? That answer quietly infuriated me, but I didn't say anything more. And I told, or warned myself, it was her business, and if he was good to her, as he clearly was, let her do what she wanted. That made sense to me—until the next time she pulled out her emery board, cuticle remover, and polish, and I felt my chest constrict, and I knew I had better leave the room.

Maybe part of the reason why Sam and I used to have periodic fights, despite the fact that he was a decent fellow and treated my mother well—much better than my departed father did—was the compactness, or closeness, of our apartment. I had nowhere to escape. There was only one bedroom, which they occupied, while I slept in the living room on a Hollywood bed, made up as a couch by day. When I had to do my homework I either used the empty kitchen and the old wooden table covered by oilcloth or the one bedroom. When Sam and my mother were watching television in the living room, as they did most evenings, I would take my things into the bedroom and set up my small study-shop. First, of course, I'd close the living-room door, and then open up the foyer closet door to create a double barrier against the TV noise, and for more privacy. Once inside the bedroom, I would unfold a green-webbed aluminum lawn chair and squeeze it in between the mahogany double bed and bureau, a tight fit. For my desk I used the small square bedside table, moving away the vast lamp and adjusting my legal-sized yellow writing pad (for serious work) or loose-leaf book (for homework) at an angle to the table. Finally I was ready. Sitting squeezed in my study-cockpit—I still liked to use the World War II imagery from recent childhood—I was alone at last, able to do schoolwork or, more often, free to fly off into the wild blue yonder and daydream, plan and jot down ideas for stories. Only on occasion did I glance at the double bed and consider its present occupants, and wince. Mostly, I stayed in my own private zone, making lists of places I'd like to adventure to, like Tierra del Fuego or the South Pacific Islands, the Belgian Congo or the Galapagos, the territories of the wild. But in the midst of my imagined journey, I'd be interrupted by my mother, who would ask if I'd mind moving now to the kitchen, since Sam wanted to take his nap before going to work at midnight. Confused, I said nothing, but collected my items and shifted from one end of the burrow to the other, feeling disturbed and displaced.

And he wouldn't return until the next evening (save for weekends), going from work to sleep at his own private home in the fastidious Flatbush section—we lived in grimier Brownsville—sleeping in a separate bedroom from his estranged wife. He lived this double life, he explained to my mother, in order to continue to be near his daughter, a dark-haired beauty of eighteen whom I had met several times when Sam was a friend of the family and not yet a live-in lover. His odd working hours, and his odder living situation, seemed to make me more conscious of his presence in our life. By day I had my familiar routine, journeying by IRT to high school in the morning, then up to my Manhattan bookstore job by afternoon, and returning for dinner by six or so. Frequently, by the time I got home, Sam would be there already, his aftershave lotion wafting toward me just as I had entered our long dark foyer, and I'd feel slightly cheated that I had no free time with my mom. And though I said little about it during our chatty dinners, I'd feel a curious resentment of those fancy rib steaks and "double lamb chops," which were so far superior to my own father's horrible oversalted boiled meats and overcooked vegetables. My father's tastes, I knew painfully, were a result of his Russian past and present poverty. In a way I didn't fully understand, I felt like a secret traitor wolfing down a whopping steak, instead of Papa's beloved boiled meat ("plate flanken"), and listening to Sam's genial banter.

"What do you think of them Knicks, huh?" I'd nod, agreeing, and even add something about Braun or Boryla, knowing my own father knew nothing and cared nothing about the game. Or, "How do you like that cut of tenderloin—you can't get any better. Look at the way he polishes that off, will you, Rose."

And guiltily I'd look down and see he was right, I had gobbled down the whole darned steak, hardly noticing.

Anyway, at the same time that we had a new man in the house, I continued seeing my father once a week, on the surface to get

my allowance. I'd meet him by Jack's corner candy store at the
Sutter Avenue El station or, across the street, by Dave's Blue Room,
a bar and grill he hung around evenings. I had no idea where he
was living then and didn't bother to ask. In fact, I hardly asked
him anything, except for my three dollars, making it clear what I
was there for.

He, on the other hand, had changed character remarkably
in the few weeks since we had thrown him out, his fierce authority suddenly replaced by a strange, fragile appeal. Even his
navy wool overcoat looked newly threadbare to me, frayed at the
collar.

"Do you think it's right, the way your mother has treated me?"

I was taken aback by his absurd query and humble tone. "Yes,
I do."

"I was such a bad husband?"

"Oh, come on," I cut into him, "don't!"

"So you're still on her side, eh?"

My rising anger and fury pleased me, and even steadied me.
"Of course."

"And I was such a bad father, boitchek?" he appealed.

My head was pounding by now. "Look, can I have my
money?"

A sheepish smile came to his pallid face—surprisingly unshaven
—surprising stubble on the cheeks, and the customary brutal temper was nowhere to be seen. "You think it's so easy, eh? Didn't I
put food on the table, and clothe you? Were you, or your sister or
mother, ever short?"

His crazy appeal turned my plan of calm upside down, and I
grew wild. "Are you mad? Do you know how she'd have to fight
to get money for a pair of *new dungarees* for me? Five dollars, and
it would turn into a battle."

He laughed nervously. "Didn't I just buy you a pair a month
ago? Did you go without, sonny boy?" and he reached out his hand
to touch my face.

I pushed it aside, furious and confused. "Look, I have to go.
Do you have my allowance or not?"

He brought out three single dollar bills, I took them, nodded once, like collecting an overdue debt, and said, "I'll see you."

"Maybe you'll say something to your mother, about me?"

I didn't bother to respond, but walked off, just as a train lumbered in overhead, heading away, away from all this. And as I walked off, hot, disturbed, drained, I wondered why I even met with him, lying to myself that it was the money, of course, the allowance, but sensing, somewhere, something deeper.

Maybe the sensing was no more than remembering. For whenever I was in danger of feeling sympathy rising for my father, I would replay certain intimate scenes. And the most forceful one was that most immediate scene which, when my mother heard about it, provoked her into decisive action. She had gone away for the weekend, leaving my father and myself alone for two or three days, an inflammable situation for us over the past two or three years. We had had our usual argument, this time over whether I could stay out late on Friday night with my East 92nd Street friends, an appointment that had been cleared by my mother. My mistake was in announcing this, her approval, to him. He stared at me, and shook his head, in effect saying he was in charge now. Chest surging, I answered that it was already arranged, and I was going to go ahead. Now in most past moments like these, my mother would intrude here and maneuver me away or else my father would stare me into obedience or even slap me hard two or three times. But just then, alone, in the small hot kitchen, emotion and stubbornness took hold of me, and I couldn't back off, repeating I was going out anyway. Our testing of wills had begun.

Subtly, hardly knowing how it happened, I found myself wedged into the space between kitchen table and window, and Father was approaching me with a long carving knife. In a whirring blur, it seemed to me later on, the sort of blur that collects like scar tissue after such scenes, he put the instrument into my hand, lifted my hand toward him, and, grinning eerily, said, "Now you can use it on me, like you want to. Go ahead." When I dropped the knife, shaking, he kept me pinned, bent down, and picked it up and carefully returned it to my hands, closing my grip on it with force. Feebly I let it go, trembling wildly. This time, when he retrieved it, he held on to it, and, setting the sharp blade point-blank against my chest, he uttered calmly, "Would you prefer if I used it on you?" The room in twilight turned, my head spun, oxygen slipped away. I must have lolled my head in some fashion, and time seemed suspended. Finally he shook his head, as though bored with the situation, lowered the weapon, and walked back to the cupboard and put the knife away. Quietly he left the kitchen. My body suddenly released itself, seemed to separate from me and slump against the windowsill, and I stayed put, watching darkness approach and spread its gray-black amorphous shape everywhere.

For the rest of that long weekend I stayed away from him, licking my wounds, soothing my despair, shuddering at intervals. And he, the mad father? He said nothing about the incident, not a word, but went about his business routinely, preparing for us Ralston and soft-boiled eggs for breakfast, and inviting me to dip the challah into his coffee, as usual.

But on Monday, when my mother returned and heard the story, which I tried to hold back but blurted out, quaking un-controllably again in the reconstructing, she decided to act. She called up the locksmith and had the intricate lock on the front door changed; packed up a suitcase of Father's clothes and had me take it to a mutual friend; telephoned Father at his sweatshop in lower Manhattan and told him of the new turn of events. She warned him that if he tried to break in, she would call the police. (Surprisingly, he didn't try, didn't even return, perhaps out of projected humiliation at having to stand out on the landing, knock-ing on the door, with the four other neighbors coming and going.) Thus occurred his removal from our home, after some twenty-eight years of married life, and the uneasy start of my own new life, a young man for real, so unlike the formal declaration I had made when I was thirteen.

I didn't realize then, of course, that in a few short months I would have to make yet another family adjustment.

If my father was a hot-tempered man, a violent father and bully husband, Sam, the lover, was a model of regularity and genial sanity. He hardly ever showed a temper, was easy to talk with, had a variety of interests. Native-born, he was also much more of an ordinary native than my father, an immigrant from a White Russian village who had come here in 1917 after his own father had had his head lopped off by a marauding cossack officer seeking money and goods during the turbulence of the Revolution. And yet, strangely, my father never forgot Mother Russia, or forgave America—for his predicament perhaps, or for *its* modern, democratic ways. Sam owned a car, a home, had a good job, and took native ways and customs naturally, and with affection. All this was fresh and attractive to me, forced to grow up beneath my father's yoke of Russia-yearning all my years. To be able to talk about a pennant race or basketball game, instead of a chess match or political question, was a new and refreshing experience. And to see Sam pick up the Sunday comics and actually read *Dick Tracy* or chuckle over *L'il Abner*, why that was unheard of, that was democracy, that was freedom!

Trying to cope with my disquieting and perplexing mood in those days—maybe trying to like the lover more and hate the father less?—I sought the counsel of a high school teacher, a fortyish man in the athletic department who had taught us a class in Sex Hygiene and who had gotten our respect with his easy seriousness. We began to meet semiregularly, during my study periods, in his office. Over cups of English tea, which seemed daintily out of place in tough Thomas Jefferson High, soft-spoken Mr. Rattner drew me out, and gained my trust by confiding that he was a divorced parent, with a teenage son, and it wasn't easy. The boy was acutely interested in any new female friend of his father's, for example, and acted hostilely whenever he met one. This open recounting of his situation calmed and soothed me. And I began to see that my losses, my hurting, my jealousy, were "understandable, natural," as he put it, handing me another Earl Grey fill-up in my porcelain cup. One thing that he did say, almost in passing, lodged itself in my head: he had waited—or had had to wait—almost a year before a new woman friend could sleep over, so much did it disturb his son. Well, then, what about *this* son, and *his* situation?

* * *

If I took the situation as best as I could, balancing necessities silently like some juvenile juggler, my sister, older, was openly critical. She disapproved strongly of my mother "living in sin" this way. This surprised me for several reasons. First, I hadn't realized that she who had played hookey much of her senior year in high school and who had then married a non-Jew, was now, at twenty-two, so devoted to convention. And next, I found it hard to believe that her sympathies were already shifting toward our father, the same man who had administered to her at least two punishing beatings in our living room, for skipping school and for daring to marry "a goy," beatings stopped only by my mother's physical interference and police threats. The same father who refused to meet her fiancé because he was an Italian Catholic and who told my sister that she was no longer welcome in the home.

So that when my sister insinuated to me how "unnatural" our mother's situation was, of these two married people living together, I felt half-betrayed, and wholly helpless. "But, Hannah, what do you want *me* to do about it?" I asked, and she shrugged and said, "She listens to you. Why don't you tell them to get married?" I explained that I didn't really care if they were married or not, and also that it was nearly impossible, since both Sam's wife and our father refused divorces. "Still," my sister prodded and complained, from the convenience of Long Island distance, "it's not right. Especially with you there."

I felt besieged, confused, sinking. What could I do?

I found myself making mischief in school, and trouble at home.

In school it was a matter of upping the ante on my regular mischief. In poor Mr. Kaufman's algebra class, I began taking undue advantage of the white-haired, incompetent old soul whom I actually cared for and during the term often protected from other troublemakers. Lifting open the large window in back, and gathering snow, I lined up a series of snowballs and arced them at kids around the room, occasionally missing and hitting the blackboard where the old man was working. Large newspapers like the *Times* I turned into huge B-24's, darting and dive-bombing into grave student grinds. And I insulted the kindly teacher by cheating brazenly on an exam, staring directly at the gentle man while handing my paper over to a pal for copying. And then, when he called me up and shook his head sadly, and said he "just had to turn me over to the dean," rocking his head and saying he no longer knew how he could handle me, I put my arm around him, said I understood his anguish, and kissed his scalp. The class roared.

The dean, named Muldorf, was another matter. A sturdy, bald man in his fifties, who wore smart suits and ambushed dumb wise guys, he read me the riot act, saying "You're turning into quite a case, Schlossberg. I thought you were a good kid, in trouble sometimes but nothing serious to worry about, but I've just changed my judgment. I'm having your mother come up, and if you cause any more shenanigans, I'm shipping you out to Boys High. Let them deal with you. Picking on an old guy like that, Christ almighty, you're becoming a *bum*. You're suspended from classes until your mother shows up with you. Get outta here."

Boys High, up in Bedford Stuyvesant, was no joke. Known on the outside for its athletic teams, it was known by us as a mix of Death Row and boot camp, a place where the students, or inmates, were as bad as the wardens and sergeants.

And my mother had never been asked to come to school before. At home, she didn't take the news well either. "What the hell's going on there with you? What's the trouble?"

"Ahh, it was—a mistake, Mom. I just got, sorta carried away."

Just then, Sam surprised me, us, by popping his face out from the bathroom, where he was shaving. "Oh yeah? It started out that way with my daughter too, getting called up to school, and I let Shirley tell me it was nothing, nothing at all."

Furious, I let go. "What the hell's it your business anyway! Who asked you to butt in, huh?"

"Sshh, take it easy." She put her hand on my shoulder. "Sam, he's right, we'll handle this."

Her words and hand consoled and vindicated me.

With the dean too she was composed, and kind of impressive, a firm auburnhaired woman dressed in a wool suit, listening to him without acting cowed or defensive. At the end of his report, in which my series of accumulated offenses had been laid out, she asked me if the list was true. I acknowledged it and she said matter-of-factly, "Well, you'll have to do what you think best, Mr. Muldorf. If he doesn't change"—and she looked over at me—"it'll be his own responsibility."

The dean, his face relaxing from the words of this reasonable woman, changed tone, and asked, "Has anything perhaps changed at home recently? You know, something which may be affecting Aaron's behavior?"

She half-shrugged, and said, "Could be. I'll talk to him about it."

After some polite words, we stood up, and Dean Muldorf put his hand on my arm in a way he had never done before. "You have a mother to be proud of, son. Don't do something foolish you don't need to." I nodded, surprised at seeing that side of him.

On the subway going home, she cautioned me, "If you keep it up, he'll get rid of you, kick you out for good, and you'll have it coming. Doing those things to that old teacher, you should be ashamed." Then, staring at me, she asked, "Does Sam bother you? I thought you liked him."

"Oh, I do, most of the time. Except for—"

"He's a good man, Aaron. He treats me like your father never did. And I think he treats you well too. Oh, sometimes he's foolish, like the other day. He had no business opening his mouth, but mostly, he's kindly to you, isn't he? Tell me the truth."

"Yeah, I guess so," I said without enthusiasm, because the truth seemed more complicated than that question allowed for.

"Look, I know it must be difficult at times, but please, be *kind*, for my sake. Let there be peace. If he does something stupid or foolish with you, you tell me. I'll handle it, yeah?" And she took my hand and waited for my answer, knowing that once she had me close that way, her flesh to my flesh, her hazel eyes upon my eyes, it was impossible for me to disagree or separate and assert myself. Defeated, frustrated, yet happy to be alone with her again, I nodded assent.

But fights with Sam began to erupt more regularly, despite my pledge and despite myself.

At a dinner the next week, he flashed me a big confident smile and asked how that beef brisket was.

Looking up at him, and chewing deliberately, I retorted, "Why are you so concerned with food, huh? That's all you seem to think about."

"Ohh, I see. Well, *thank you.*" And he turned to my mother, fixing a salad. "Hear that, Rose?"

And another evening I made sure that I happened to be watching a television show at just the hour he wanted to see something, and didn't give it up easily or with good spirit.

On Thursday night I dug myself in when I saw my mother getting ready for the biweekly manicure. "Why do you have her do that for you? Why don't you get a manicure at the barber shop?"

"Are you kidding?"

"Do I sound like I am?"

"I didn't know it was your business," he said. "Any time your mother wishes, she doesn't have to do this. But I'll tell you one thing, son, you're getting to be pretty bossy around here. I didn't know *you* were bringing in the support for this house."

My chest filled. "Who needs your goddamned support?"

"Aaron, that's enough, please," my mother implored.

"That's it, folks." Sam had stood up and proceeded to put his shirt on over his undershirt. "Thank you very much. I get the message." He went to search for his shoes.

My mother came over to me as I was getting my jacket on in the foyer and said, "If you can't speak nicely to Sam, don't speak at all. You owe him an apology. *I* want to give him a manicure and I'll do what I want. No man has ever been as good to me as he has, so why shouldn't I want to be nice to him? And I enjoy it. He doesn't force me to do it, I assure you, Aaron."

I got out of there as fast as I could and wandered the wintry streets up to East New York, and along busy Pitkin Avenue, where the Loew's Pitkin was showing *Body and Soul* and the rows of shops and restaurants buzzed and blinked with life. I walked and walked, hardly noticing the pretty girls I used to hunt for there, or the light snow that had begun to fall. The real trouble pricked me: he was right, we did need his money since my father gave my mother nothing. And worse, my mother did really enjoy doing things for him. Shitty life! I kicked a cardboard box of refuse in front of a store, sending it flying, and was chased by the owner. It was only when I had walked beyond the lights and the hot knish-and-chestnut vendors did I realize that I was entering dangerous territory, near Rockaway Avenue, where gangs hung out and strolling innocently was not very smart.

My next appointment with father was on Sunday evening when I was invited to join him for dinner at Dave's Blue Room. He wore the same double-breasted blue serge suit, shirt and tie, black shoes, as always, but once again it took a few minutes for me to get used to his new manners. Kindly, thoughtful, respectful. I met him at the horseshoe bar, where the bartender gave me a big hello and told father that we had better adjourn to a booth, because of my age. Dad took his drink.

In a darkened booth he helped me off with my coat and said he had ordered a Dave's Special for us, and smiled, a smile to please. He started asking about me when a thin blond woman wearing a tight dress and excessive makeup named Molly approached, gave me a hug and hello, said a few words to father, and laughed, leaning on his shoulder. An old friend of my mother's, she seemed to know Papa well too, and it surprised me when he slapped her behind lightly as she departed, just the way he used to slap my mother's in their better days.

"I didn't know she . . . hung around here," I stumbled.

My father shrugged. "Molly," he said, using that tone of casual dismissal that I knew so well. "So, sonny boy, how are you?"

"Okay," I said, feeling two ways about his phrase, which, when I was a little boy, he caressed me with.

"And school?"

"Oh, nothing new there," I lied, not wanting to involve him in my life.

"And your mother?"

"What do you mean?"

He half-laughed in that embarrassed way. "Is she well?"

"Very well," I said.

The waiter brought our dinners, hot roast beef smothered in onions and gravy, with thick french fries, and a Coke. The dinner I loved but had hardly ever had when we were a whole family.

In that lurid, indirect light, I ate with distraction, hearing the dim talking, the tinkle of glasses and dishes, the shuffling sounds of the poolroom overhead. I felt on the verge of adulthood, but wasn't at all sure I wanted to cross over.

"So, I hear she's seeing Sam." He smiled feebly. "Not very nice."

"Why not?" I shot back. Who had told him, lovely sister?

"You think it's nice, silly boy?"

He sipped his liquor, and for a moment I peered at him through the amber ice, and his misshapen face agitated my heart.

I forced out, "She should do what she wants."

"And you, what do you want?" Smiling, with a new look in his usually wild eyes. Fear, was it?

What *did* I want? I wanted him to be drawing his detailed penciled pictures for me of his house and stables in White Russia, while I, age four, sat in his lap. I wanted to be marching with him, in my boy's soldier's suit complete with brimmed cap, in the V-Day parade up Pitkin Avenue. And I wanted to be winning chess games at his Brownsville Air Raid Wardens Club on Sunday mornings, with Papa approving. And then the two of us alone going uptown to the Stanley Theater to see Russian movies, or Charlie Chaplin.

"You had your chance," I mumbled.

He nodded, but instead of fury there appeared, again, that sense of bafflement, of uncomprehended defeat. "I was so bad, tell me?"

And, again, I couldn't believe he was being serious. My breathing quickened, I could hardly talk. "If you keep this up, I'll leave, I promise."

A large thud overhead and, just on cue, it seemed, Molly reappeared now. Draping one arm around me, and the other around father, she cooed, "Why don't we all go to the movies afterwards? Sunday evenings . . . ugh, gloomy!"

Her exotic perfume and her womanly hip brushing my cheek aroused me, and I felt more confused than ever.

Every other week or so Sam and my mother would go away for the weekend, frequently driving to Connecticut, where they invariably stayed with Sam's family. (His family seemed to accept the situation and my mother. They liked her and realized his marital unhappiness, according to Mom.) So I would have the apartment all to myself, a routine I preferred. For ever since I was six, and my sister refused to baby-sit any longer, I had been on my own most evenings, making a cocoon of my solitariness and private friends—radio shows, sports magazines, erector sets, and my heated imagination. Especially now, these weekends served as relaxing retreats, like country vacations maybe, away from unresolvable emotions and tangled relations. It was a relief not to have a well-meaning adult around, a fine but too intimate mother, a father of unplayful paradox. Just three rooms, Ranger hockey and Knickerbocker basketball, Friday night shows such as *The Sheriff* and Madison Square Garden boxing, and my own company. Alone meant richness, resources, physical space, reality-rearranging. And when fear and terror came, by means of *The Shadow*'s scary voice or *Escape*'s grotesque tales of invading red ants, why that too was part of the weekend retreat. Usually.

On this weekend however I was still smarting from a Friday fight with Sam; again, over very little. Sam had made some cutting remark about throwing out all the Commies from the government, as McCarthy was proclaiming, and I said that he was just a bully, and no one had *proved* anything. I surprised myself as much as him, I think, by this stand, since if it were my father arguing I probably would have taken the other side, against my father and his Red sympathies. And yet here I was, suddenly defending those Commies or liberals or whatever.

Sam taunted me, "Hey, look, he's becoming a little pinko. What do you know."

"Yeah, maybe I am," I retorted, "if it means fighting against know-nothings like you."

"They should take the whole bunch of 'em and send them back to Russia," he concluded, lifting the two bags, "if you ask me."

"No one is asking you, Sam, and no one is likely to." Send my father back too? I thought.

My mother now reached the foyer, saw what was happening, and said, "Are you two at it again? Come on, Sam, will you? Take the bags and go, please." And she shooed him out the door. Then, turning to me, she said, "Must you? If he says something foolish, let it pass for once. Come, give me a kiss. Now remember, there's chicken all ready for tonight, just warm it up in the pot, and for tomorrow night there's the T-bone that Sam brought—"

"He can keep his steaks, I don't want them anymore."

"Sshh. Take it easy. If you don't feel like cooking, don't. Go out and get some deli, okay? And don't hold things against him, all right?" She repeated an earlier scene. "He's a good guy and means well, you know that. Come here, *zhabala*," and she used her childhood endearment for me, gathered me in her arms, and gave me a strong hug and kiss.

Against my ambivalent will, I hugged her back.

She flashed me a last look, asking if I was all right, and departed.

But the niggardly fight and Sam's stupid remarks stayed with me, funneling down through the voice of Don Dumphy announcing the slugging Gus Lesnevich 10 P.M. fight, through my turning sleepy thoughts, and through beloved softball on Saturday morning. A usually sure-handed outfielder, I even muffed an easy line drive because my concentration had drifted. The worst of it was that I knew that Sam was decent enough, at the same time that I knew I couldn't get on with him, and we'd always be at odds. I felt alone, terribly alone, isolated by my unresolvable dilemma.

In the early evening I went out and ate Specials and Beans at Phil's Deli, savoring the pungent aromas and flattered by Phil, who reminded me that the time was coming near when I'd be "mature enough" to assist him in the restaurant. Really? Afterwards, I moseyed up Sutter Avenue, past darkened Woolworth's, to hang out with the kids by the movie marquee. After horsing around for a while, we decided to play some ring-a-levio, before heading up to Manhattan later on, maybe to catch *Hit Parade* in the NBC studio and then grab a bite at Horn 'n Hardart. One of our standard Saturday night routines.

Without much enthusiasm, I fell into the game, and raced away while Alan Davis, our designated tag man ("You're it!") cradled his head against a telephone pole and counted to ten. I had little idea where to go, my concentration adrift, and just ran down Ralph, toward the darkened area under the El, where East 98th Street and Ralph joined and formed a wedge. Just there, on that cement promontory, sat the Mobil station, closed and darkened, the Flying Red Winged Horse not running for the weekend. Desolate now, the scary station beckoned, and I looked around for a place to hide out. Of course the best place was below, underground, in the open lubrication pits, where I had never before dared venture. But now I felt strangely impelled, and very carefully edged around the dangerous iron lip bordering the long pit. Then, fighting fear, mocking myself, I descended downward, balancing on the five narrow, greasy iron rungs. My head throbbed loudly.

Down in the sunken pit, I waited, my eyes and ears super-alert for animal noises. Alley cats lived there, stray rabid dogs, rats too, it was rumored. What was I doing there, I asked myself. Hiding out for the game, I answered, half believing it. I pulled my jacket tighter and huddled in a far corner from where I could survey the dim situation. The smells of gasoline and oil mingled with the rancid scent of garbage, and I tried to avoid the thick grease smeared everywhere. I waited.

Overhead, the El trains thundered back and forth like B-17's.

After a while, I don't really know how long, I heard some running, and soon what sounded like Davis calling out, "Ring-a-levio, ring-a-levio, one-two-three, one-two-three!" and then the voices trailed off, away.

I could turn him out, couldn't I? I mean, change the locks on Sam the way my mother changed the locks on my father. Yeah, why not? . . . Some noise in the pit, a quick movement . . . or I could just take off, take the IRT uptown to the George Washington Bridge and begin hitching, it wasn't that difficult. Call Mom after a few days, so she'd know I was okay. . . . The noise came from a small animal or rodent, that was for sure, and I seemed to feel as determined as I was frightened. I held on to the iron railing at the side of the wall, not caring about the grease now, and got ready to defend myself, or, even, to attack. . . .

Voices approached, and presently I heard Kassover booming out my name, "Hey, Aaron, let's go! C'mon, it's getting late, game's over, we wanna make the show. Do you hear me? Sch-loss-y? Hey!"

Well, I did the strangest thing, I did nothing. I mean I wanted to come up and get out of there, naturally, come up for real air and go with them uptown, but I didn't budge. Maybe I couldn't, I don't know. But I stayed on in the dank hole, and said nothing.

"Are you coming? Or we'll leave without you, stupid!"

I felt chained to the grim spot, the greasy coffin-shaped opening. Stupid, all right, I knew that. And why? Why?

Soon the grating voice of Kassover was gone, along with the steps and voices of my pals, along with the uplifting prospects of the familiar evening, and I felt alone, afraid, turbulent. But also right, somehow. My position seemed necessary, my will mechanical, as I felt the creature approaching. Something like a scratch, a low hiss, an emission of some sort. And, steeling myself, I knew very clearly that if I conquered this little situation, this small ordeal making my heart jump, I could somehow overcome the other, bigger one in my life.

And fixing on that precious self-deception, I waited, tears welling in my eyes from my tense staring and acute expectancy.

The Shrine

The square-block, three-tiered coliseum curved to a bow front, with a blue and white striped awning marking the front entrance. In Paris it might have been the entrance to a fashionable brasserie or café; here on home ground it was the entrance to a baseball field. Sacred ball field. Above, from the roof, flew the two important flags: the Stars and Stripes and the Dodger banner. The oval building, lined with rows of old-fashioned arching windows set into the reinforced concrete, always seemed to take on a pinkish-golden tint when the sun splashed it. As though nature, as well as the natives saw fit to honor the site. For this building, with its emerald diamond within, was the place of true worship, the shrine visited weekly by a hundred thousand or more religious devotees, devout followers since childhood, the long faithful. Built in 1935 in honor of Charlie Hercules Ebbets (the manager of the Brooklyn Bridegrooms, in 1898), Ebbets Field demanded more devotion, afforded more pleasure, struck more pain, than any church or synagogue in the borough. The Italians had their Popes, the English and French their Kings and Queens, the Russians their Czars and Empresses, and we, our Dodgers. Glories versus glories. For example, was Pope John XXII as divine as our legendary Dazzy (Vance), Henry VIII as wild as Rex (Barney), or Louis IV as popular as the People's Cherce (Dixie Walker)? Catherine the Great really as supreme as the Rube (Marquard) or the Duke (Snider)?

Faith, hope, charity, and patience were all on trial here, for, you see, the famous Bums, our Dodger teams, had never ever won a World Series, had never been champs—while across town, in the Bronx, the Yankees of New York were perennial champs, and had hardly ever lost a Series. Nonetheless, we, the faithful tribe of Brooklyn, trekked to the Shrine, and preserved our faith. Despite all the comically weak clubs in its long sad history, despite all the consistent persecution against the team (for its antics and odd ways, plus the losing), we persevered. We understood in our bones what it was to feel lowly and humiliated, a failure and a laughingstock —take Mickey Owen's dropping of Casey's third strike in the ninth inning of Game Four of the 1941 World Series, with two out in the top of the ninth against the Yanks, turning a sure victory into an impossible defeat—but we continued to believe. Being the underdog, being the victim of biased Broadway lyrics or vulgar newspaper mocking, only spurred us on. The Dodgers remained our religion; and the very fact that we believed so fervently, without ever having victory bless or reward us, only proved the strength and uniqueness of our faith.

We, the strongest believers, entered the Shrine in two different ways. One was to proceed with a ticket through the turnstile; the other was more unconventional. This meant retrieving a ball hit over the right-field fence in batting practice and trading it in for a grandstand ticket for that day's game (if you didn't wish to keep the baseball and try for a post-game autograph right on it). This procedure was usually done in pairs. The gutsier one would climb up the right-field fence, maybe a third of the way, and, hanging on up there, signal down to the partner below with the baseball glove when a lefty slugger like the Duke or Shotgun Shuba was up. Then Aaron would pound his mitt, and wait, along with the half dozen other kids. Suddenly the cap signal that a batting practice home run was heading their way. Now, a mad scramble to catch the baseball, usually a fierce competition with the banshee-screaming bunch risking their lives and limbs by racing out onto busy Bedford Avenue to try to nab it on the fly. Cars coming? So what!

Often the ball would land first on the asphalt, and bounce high, sometimes shooting across the street over to the Texaco station. Aaron would race with all his might to join a rugby skirmish for the prize. Was there a nobler moment, short of catching a foul ball inside the ballpark, than coming up with the major league ball and, after displaying it, presenting it at the grandstand entrance?

And if he didn't manage to catch one, well, he paid his two quarters and a dime and sat out in the cozy bleachers in center, caught some sun, rooted, and occasionally chatted with an outfielder. Sixty cents was not a bad price for sun, chat, and an unobstructed view from that short centerfield (395 feet in dead center). With the green diamond laid out splendidly in front of him, Aaron, also an outfielder, could study the nearby Duke position himself for each batter, and, from afar could even see the curve from Erskine break a full foot down. With Gladys's organ serenading every so often, why it was a little bit of heaven purchased cheaply. Having sat out yonder often enough, the boy learned to gauge the nature of the hit from the crack of the bat, fly ball, or line drive, a piece of lore equal to any algebra law.

Everyone came to the games. I mean it was a popular, democratic service conducted out there. Baseball was the American sport in those days, the real religion for a free and easygoing people who had their own ideas about independence and good and evil, and their own notions about pomp and ceremony, play and devotion. (Could anyone ever understand an American if he didn't understand what baseball meant to a young boy or girl?) And with the prices so right, a buck and a quarter for grandstand, two-fifty for lower grandstand, three-fifty for boxes, and maybe four-fifty for the best boxes, plus the sixty cents for the bleacher seats, well, everyone could afford to show up. The steamfitters and shipbuilders from the Brooklyn Navy Yard wearing their high school jackets; the bigwigs like the borough president from downtown or business execs who worked uptown in Manhattan, loosening up their ties and rolling up their sleeves; the "hard-guy" toughs with DA's and pegged pants from Bushwick or Greenpoint, whom you wouldn't want to meet out on their turf; the families of Negroes from East New York or Bedford-Stuyvesant, dressing up in neat sports shirts for the memorable occasion of watching the new Negro stars, like Campy or Newk or Jackie; the old-timers, who remembered the game from the turn of the century, and kept mental note of the singular moments and players (from Zack Wheat and Dazzy Vance to "Pistol Pete" and "Da People's Cherce"); and on weekends and night games, the pairs of fathers and sons from Bensonhurst, Bay Ridge, East Flatbush, Sheepshead Bay, Williamsburg, Canarsie (or grandfathers and grandsons too, come in from Westchester or over from Long Island, at the far eastern end of Brooklyn) to watch the game, the only game, and join the faithful. (Maybe only one father-son pair missing.) All citizens of good and noble faith, of all ordinary religion and race, made the pilgrimage to the shrine maybe once or twice a month, like an instinct or gene pulling you there. Yeah, the Ebbets Field gene was alive and working.

And for good reasons: beauty, relaxation, tribal warmth, folk art. Forget the sweatshops, forget the class wars, forget the family troubles, forget the racial antagonisms, forget the daily grind, forget the Depression and the war, forget the anger and quiet despair, forget the ordinary. All the subtle art of baseball was put on display by the Dodgers of those days. And art it was, the popular art of agile physical skills coupled with the built-in nuance and drama of baseball. Was there anything more sudden, more dramatic, than the eighth or ninth inning of a one-run game, say, with two or three men on base and one out, the lonely batter getting set for the pitch, all burden of responsibility for the day's result upon his shoulders, thirty-three thousand folks looking on, maybe quietly praying, while the late afternoon sky changes colors imperceptibly; and the pitcher, his personal antagonist, momentarily responsible and alone too in this battle, like the cowboy or king, finally nods at his squatting catcher's signal for the pitch, looks around and begins his windup, while his eight colleagues get set on the balls of their feet, trying to swiftly figure out for themselves, those that haven't seen the signal, what pitch will be thrown in this situation, curve or fastball or maybe change, and where this left-handed slugger is capable of hitting this pitch—can he pull Branca's fastball with two strikes on him, say?—and shade ever so slightly toward that patch of ground or grass that seems most probable? For these few seconds, and maybe the few minutes of the present situation, the tension climbs, the drama grows fine, and the crowd is gripped as surely as any ancient Greek audience held by an old tragedy; and often enough, by means of this strikeout or that line drive base-clearing double, the knowledgeable, trained fan is rewarded, satisfied (or disappointed) deeply, even, in certain situations, feels that peculiar feeling of everything resolved, the perfectly named catharsis. Truth be told, truth be obvious, many a great Dodger-Cardinal or Giant-Dodger game, many a Yankee-Dodger Series gem, has been as memorable to our native citizenry, has been stamped upon our collective consciousness, as any *Oedipus Rex* or *Medea* or *Electra* was stamped upon those ancient Greeks.

Only in America, perhaps, could they have ripped away that shrine of devotion—the owner moved the team away from Brooklyn in 1957 because the borough wouldn't build him a grander stadium —and later replace it with a housing project—with such impunity, such easy callousness, such casual disregard of the public will, and the city's soul.

And Brooklyn's never been the same since, without Ebbets Field. After all, would Paris be the same without the Cathedral of Notre Dame, Leningrad without its Hermitage, Rome without the Vatican?

The Voice

L ike three million others of the Faithful, Aaron first followed the Dodgers by listening to the radio, and the broadcaster's depiction of the game. In the 1940s the broadcaster attended only the home games at Ebbets Field, but announced all the away games via the Western Union. Some reporters may have tried to hide this—not the 'Ol Redhead. At eight years old, Aaron was already listening regularly to WOR and WHN for the Dodger broadcasts, sometimes scoring with pencil and pad in hand, as the ticker tape, placed close to the mike intentionally, wired a play, and Red then called it out. Or, interpreted it, gave it some feel, some flair, without ever trying to mask the fact that it was coming over the ticker. Red, their man in the booth, was too honest, too accurate, ever to lie to his followers. For in those days, Red Barber was as important to both kids and grown-ups as, say, General Eisenhower or President Roosevelt.

He was the Voice of the Bums, and the voice—maybe conscience—of the borough. It was a measure of Brooklyn's hospitality and worldliness that Aaron and friends had adopted this Mississippi-born, Southern-accented gentleman to speak for them, sing to them. When Red was on the air, telling us about Pistol Pete crashing into the wall yet again or about Fireman Casey coming in from the bull pen to put out another fire, you could hear his special phrases everywhere you went, on the beaches or front stoops, in drugstores or candy stores, in parlors or barbershops, at lunch wagons or pool halls, from car radios, portables, or consoles. He was soft-spoken, scrupulous, knowledgeable, rhythmic, humorous, down-home, eloquent. Always eloquent. His voice filled the streets, shops, seasides of the borough, surrounded and suffused us with its sweetness and moral light; a very different voice from that older Brooklyn singer, Walt Whitman.

He charmed and sang to us, nonetheless. His language was a mix of the homespun, countryish, biblical, uniquely put-together English, delivered with rhythmic cadence and disciplined restraint. And those evocative idioms, which became part of everyday Brooklynese: "We got a rhubarb growin' in the infield," and "Sittin' up here in the catbird seat," and "Tearin' up the pea patches," and "Walkin' in tall cotton," and "The bases are FOB." Full Of Brooklyns, indeed. A code for fans, a bond for citizens. Aaron loved that soft gravelly voice, even when he thought "Old Goldie" for home runs was pretty corny, and not nearly as good as Mel Allen's "Going, going, gone!"

In Aaron's childhood, Red was his gravelly interpreter of baseball, and his worldly traveler to faraway places west of the great Mississippi, like St. Louis, when the Dodgers went out there to play the Cardinals. He'd tell him about Missouri, under what condition and when it joined the Union; about the World's Fair and Sportsman's Park; about the great Card teams like the Gashouse Gang and the '42 Championship club. And when he'd describe Marty "Slats" Marion as, "He's out there at shortstop, movin' easy as a bank of fog," the boy would think about that image for a long time after the game. He didn't just go to the ball games with Mr. Barber to learn about line drives, curveballs, and outfield play; he learned just as much about farm life and history and geography. Without Aaron's quite knowing it, Red was his earliest teacher.

If his voice soothed our ears, his decency invaded our souls. He was a moral man who became a kind of spiritual force. A believer in Mr. Rickey's ways, he immediately and wholeheartedly took to Robinson, even though, as a Deep Southerner, it meant going up against his own background and peers, even among the Dodger players. No matter to Red. He described Jackie's human conduct on the field with as much fervor as he did his antics on the base paths. For in the end Red was as much gentleman as he was fan, and character was a part of the game, a crucial part.

Yet he did not act like a preacherman with fans, but more like an Ariel spirit. In the chain of being, in other words, Red was at the upper end of the scale.

The boy still hears that gravelly voice, still hears the wireless ticker, still hears his 'preciation and "Attaboy!"; still reflects on the pea patches and that bank of fog, whenever he sees Ebbets Field in his mind. The Shrine wouldn't have been the same without him. No sir.

The Stranger

Black as black can be. Ebony, or dark mahogany. The darkness highlighted by white flannel, and by the sea of white players. Every other player on the team white, and every player on every other team white too. The bases white, the baseball white, the umpires white, the boundaries chalk-white, the big leagues white. His blackness was emphatic enough to be blasphemous, lawless, disturbing, menacing; Anti-Christ come to the Christian game. Number 42 on his back, he was an object to be ridiculed, vilified, attacked, crucified. Slash him with your spikes when you hurtled into his second base. Throw the baseball ninety-five mph at his skull and maybe smash the blackness to bits. Tag him with all your might in the face or kidneys, the tag less important than the elbow or fist. However you can, humiliate him: toss black cats on the field and yell out "Black Sambo"; when he's up at bat whisper in his ear, "Nigger, nigger!"; remind him of his slave and gorilla heritage; ask him about the smell of his wife's pussy. However possible, make him lose his cool, and urge him into a fistfight, and humiliate "the boy."

Pigeon-toed and bow-legged and unsmiling-unfriendly, he looked like a Caliban of Ebbets Field, didn't he, a subhuman creature something halfway between human and brute, and deserving to be chased by a pack of dogs. How could he ever be touched by human sorrow, or understand the (white) magician Prospero? The fans in the late forties and fifties flocked to see this strange dark phenomenon perform on the home stage, as interested to observe his human conduct as his baseball ways. Only here, with Prospero played by Mr. Rickey, and Miranda (maybe) by Pee Wee Reese, he had two solid protectors against the teams of enemies on the beautiful but treacherous green diamond isle.

The fabled dark creature kept his cool, however, and took his revenge within the lines and rules of the game. He performed his greatest feats on the bases, turning ordinary plays into baseball myths. No one ever ran the base paths of the game, ninety feet of soft brown dirt between each base, with more daring, more skill, more purposefulness. And no one, in modern times, ever humiliated the opposition more with his baserunning and base stealing. The player fulfilled the metaphor, he was a thief par excellence, not merely stealing a base but insulting the pitcher and catcher in the process. On the base paths he was a one-man vigilante gang, breaking conventions and surpassing ordinary wisdom; mocking the pitcher with his extra-long leads, his arms dangling at his side, daring him to throw over to try to restrain or catch him, going out a step farther than any player dared or coach desired. He became baseball's greatest threat, the black outlaw on the loose and stealing games for his team by his brains and legs.

His specialty was the steal of home, the most difficult and most infuriating play in the game. First he'd take his lead, outrageous lead, off third, staring at the pitcher maybe sixty feet away, arms out and halfback hips jiggling, and when the pitcher wound up to throw to the plate, he'd come halfway home, in a test run. Seeing how the pitcher, and catcher, reacted. Frequently, the pitcher, his attention distracted, tossed a wild pitch or walked the batter. (What he could never seem to do was pick Jackie off third.) Meanwhile, Jackie had done his homework, studying the pitcher's windup in slow motion, and picking up the exact moment when he had started going home with his pitch. Just then, number 42 made his run, not pulling up and stopping this time, but coming, coming. Being a beautiful slider, he'd make up his mind, depending on the location of the pitch, where and how to slide; to hook the inside of the plate with his spikes, or maybe dive with a hand to catch a piece of home plate. Again and again he'd do it, steal the sacred home against the best pitchers and catchers of the time, batteries like Munger and Rice (Cardinals), Borowy and Scheffing (Cubs), Jansen and Westrum (Giants), Bickford and Crandall (Braves). Called safe, he'd get up, wearily, dirt-covered, glory-haloed, and, like Odysseus returning home, make his awkward way to the dugout, without hat-tipping or glamor-smiling, this pigeon-toed journeyer. Leaving the pitcher shaken, the catcher furious, the whole team unsettled.

In his rookie year, he proved to be the most exciting player in the National League; by the second year the phantom figure led the league in fielding; in his third year (1949) he was the best in hitting and stealing bases; and by his fourth year, was probably the all-around most dangerous player. Still, you couldn't nudge him into a fistfight, as they tried, or injure him, as they tried, or contain him, as they tried. The outlaw prevailed.

Nor did he become, during his baseball years, a friendly soul, a converted diplomat, an advertisement for sneakers or bats. He stayed wholly himself: determined, combative, furious, stoical.

I met him once, when I was eight or nine, on the subway, but was afraid to approach him there for his autograph; he stared at me for four or five seconds, his brown eyes fixing mine in some mysterious silent inquiry, as though I were Pip suddenly caught by the escaped convict in the marshes in the opening of Dickens's novel and recruited into a clandestine bond. The train rumbled and I stood transfixed, at the dim end of the car. As he stared before getting off, I wondered, what did he want, or demand? Allegiance? Fairness? Reparation? In any case, he remained in my consciousness as a Robinson-Magwitch, at once stranger, outlaw, and, curiously enough, long-term spiritual benefactor, a baseball hero and defiant conscience. For Dodger fans, and for that boy, he was an odd member of the family, at the same time that he was the stranger in the native game.

The Arm

He had a long Roman nose, hardly ever smiled, and always used two hands to catch the ball. An Italian gardener, say, whose domain was right field, with the high fence looming behind him. Actually, there were three parts to that fence: the black scoreboard high up in right center, the 150-foot-high hurricane fence above and to the right, and the low ten- to twelve-foot base of the wall lined with advertisements that ran the length of right field all the way to the stands. No one ever doubted, for a moment, that Furillo would catch any fly ball or line drive that came his way—in ten years of watching him, the boy never saw him muff one—and that he would manage those tricky bounces and odd ricochets off the walls with consistent skill. In his fielding Carl was always there, always consistent.

The element of elegance entered after he had caught a ball, by means of his golden arm. You see, when it came to throwing a baseball from the outfield with strength and accuracy, Furillo was no longer a gardener, but a prince. Style was added to competence. In fact, when the kids sat out there in the lower right-field grandstand, they rooted for the moment in the game—especially if it were a late inning in a tight game—when an opposing player would hit a shot off the fence and try for a double; or when a player

99

already on the bases tried to make third or home on that shot. When the dare was there, Carl was ready, along with Aaron and pals. Turning and firing on baseball instinct, Furillo threw overhand on a line directly over his shoulder, flinging the small white hardball nearly three hundred feet in the air to a precise point: an infielder's or catcher's glove. Robin Hood was not more accurate with his bow and arrow. And that throw, or peg—a "clothesline," according to Red Barber—was a flight of beauty, a line of poetry amidst the prose of ordinary hits and outs.

It affected its audience, the knowledgeable crowd, like a sudden poetic revelation. For example, take a game against the feared Cards, when the great Musial was up, with two men on base. Now Musial owned the right-field fence; he was probably the best Ebbets Field hitter who ever played there. Two on, two out, in the sixth inning, and the Bums leading by 4–2. The middle-age couple in front of the boy had been arguing the whole damn game, with the straw-hatted pock-faced man repeating how sorry he was to have taken her to the game. "Shit, never again, what a damn waste!" Aaron was tempted to lean over and tell him to knock it off, except it wasn't his eleven-year-old business, and besides, he'd probably get his block knocked off. Anyway, old Stan the Man did his usual thing, lashing out from his corkscrew batting stance and walloping the ball on an upward arc out to the scoreboard, Repulski and Schoendienst on the move, and Carl on the move too. Running to an exact point to play the ricochet, Carl grabs the ball on the fly off the scoreboard, turns, and, in one motion decides where and how to throw. He lets loose his clothesline, a high peg beyond the cutoff man and on a fly to Campy at home. For three long seconds the boys are filled with silent hope and wonder while watching the little white ball traveling on its low arc in the race to beat the Card runner home. Campy has to move maybe a half-step up the third-base line (the right direction) to catch the exacting peg, and confront the runner Schoendienst barreling down at him. An explosion of bodies and a whirl of dust. For a fraction of a second there is quiet, while the ump checks the ball in Campy's grip, and the fans replay the peg, the brazen decision to try to cut down the fleet Red. When he's called out, the crowd lets loose its apprecation, cheering like crazy, while Carl trots in, deadpanned, oblivious, dutiful.

"Would you believe that, Alice? Cutting down Schoendienst!" The ogre in the next row chants, "Would you believe that?" and he grabs his slender wife around and hugs her! And would you believe that from then on the ogre turns into a pussycat for the rest of the game, doing a complete turnabout and treating his wife like a dear soul, never once cussing again?

The prince's arm, and magical peg, could do those sorts of things: turn the nasty into the chivalric, the petty into the poetic. "Attaway, Carl, attaway to go!" Aaron screamed as he half-ran off the field, but Carl treated it as just another play, just another workday.

But just imagine if we could take that peg and put it right up there on a real stage for all the world to see? You know, like a kid's version of a Shakespeare monologue or something. Only I guess it belonged right where it was, on Ebbets Field turf.

The Glove

Toward the hot corner, third base, the balls were slammed the hardest and swiftest, it seemed, and our man out there was the smoothest fielder. His name was Billy Cox, and, playing with the old five-fingered mitt, he made it all look easy. It didn't matter if the ball was a fine bunt, a hard grounder, a line drive, a foul pop down the line. It was all butter-smooth easy. Fielding was his *way*, his habitation, and, like DiMaggio in center, he didn't have to throw his body on the ground and dirty up his uniform to make the plays. He knew the batters, knew what they could and what they couldn't do, and what the inning and the score meant. He was positioned always perfectly, that's all.

The hands were fast, so fast, faster than the fan's eye. Like some gunslinger out West who could outdraw anyone, Cox could get his hands down on the ground or suddenly out into the air swifter than any mortal infielder. If the ball was sometimes slammed up the line in a perfect blur, his glove would somehow be there, scooping the ball easily, the crowd gasping at his skill. If the ball hit a pebble and took a sudden crazy bounce, no problem, Billy's glove was right there, fielding it. A couple of times I saw him catch the ball with his bare hand, out of dire necessity, and his right hand handled it just fine. Frequently he got to the ball so fast that he'd wait a second or two, sometimes even inspecting the ball, before throwing over to first to get the batter by a step. Curious, how often he made the hot corner a position of some leisure, enjoying the cat and mouse game.

Bunts, the cruel bane of so many third basemen, he treated with ease, and a touch of disdain. As though you could try to trick him or cheat the pitcher by trying to get on first base, with a meager fifteen- or twenty-foot tap. No chance. He'd pounce down on the ball, pick it up in that sure right hand, and already, in that same one motion, be tossing the ball sidearm to first. Thus the strategic bunting game was nearly taken away completely from other teams, just as, for right-handed hitters, a whole normal region of safe hitting ground was suddenly an easy out. And you might judge the full unfairness of Billy when certain hitters, robbed of sure hits by those special hands (and his positioning), couldn't help cursing the "sonofabitch" as they crossed the field back to the visitor's dugout. He had no interest in answering them, however, since he was already hunting for stray pebbles amidst the soft dirt that might intrude on the next play. Working all the time, he patroled his turf efficiently, keeping it clean and tidy.

Not a very good hitter, not fleet afoot or possessing a great arm, he had the eye and the fast hands, and the butter glove, to make him the god of third base. In his great years, such as '52 or '53, he made fewer than ten errors during a whole season—neatly immaculate reception for a third baseman—and stole how many hits away? Those hands probably could have made a polished pool-shooter, a feared gunfighter, even a superb surgeon. As it was, he was all smoothness at the toughest infield position. He made fielding into an art, an art for the keen fan, and was cheered for it as richly as any slugger. Brooklyn fans knew the subtleties of the game.

Four Goodly Creatures

How many goodly creatures are there here!
How beauteous mankind is!
　　　　　—Miranda, *The Tempest*

L ook at them out there, in their white flannels and blue numbers—Pee Wee (#1), Campy (#39), the Duke (#4), Gil (#14)—and conclude with Miranda: "How beauteous mankind is!" They were the beloved, the adored, the worshiped.

Up the middle, the crucial middle—in baseball, as in chess—the Dodgers were potent and plentiful. Reese at short, Snider in center, Campanella behind the plate were the daily corps, the everyday clutch players. (With Jackie the spectacular one.) The team glue, say. Each performed his task with a high level of accomplishment, each flashed his own elegance. Together they created an exacting level of expectation. Rarely, in ten years, was there a dropped peg or missed cutoff or signal, so fine were their fundamentals, so tuned their team instincts.

Pee Wee, the Little (Louisville) Colonel, was there first, forming part of the old Dodger infield of 1941 (with Camilli, Lavagetto, Herman). Of his baby-faced shortstop partner, Robinson said, "No one realizes just what he has meant to the Brooklyn club. No one, that is, but his teammates." And to Robinson especially of course. For it was Pee Wee more than any other player who created the moral spirit of the club, by first welcoming Jackie and always being there for him. The quiet Southern white boy took under his wing the fiery and fired-upon black boy, and braced him as a player and a man. The boy, Aaron, was there one day, for example, when, during Robinson's first season, after he had embarrassed the defense with his base running, a Brave reliever threw three straight pitches at Jackie, finally hitting him in the leg. He sunk to the ground, crumpled in pain.

Everyone, umpires included, turned away from the battered player. Not Reese. Number 1 raced out from the dugout and leaned down to his partner, waited, helped him up, and walked with him, a trainer consoling his injured racehorse, who limped about in half-circles, dazed and unsure. Pee Wee cooled him down, and accompanied him to first, holding his waist and arm—a gesture of symbolic meaning in 1947 baseball.

Pee Wee was an early pal, a friend when friendship took courage and signified acceptance. The first open Dodger friend when other players like Dixie and Casey were open enemies. When friendship gave an extra edge to a baseball team, and enabled a great one to come into being.

Reese and Robinson soon formed one of the best shortstop-second base combos in the league, leading it several times in double plays—against the likes of Marion-Schoendienst, Dark-Stanky—and excelling in clutch plays. Pee Wee was also a pretty fair hitter, always getting a piece of the ball and laying down superior bunts. He batted in the .270's generally, with a singularly high number of RBI's for a shortstop, mostly in the mid-70's. And he was a surprising basestealer, finishing second or third in the league several times. The important thing was, he could do everything, and do it steadily and understatedly. So much so that you hardly noticed how he sacrificed a runner to second, turned a nasty grounder in the hole into a forceout at second, cooled down a Branca or Roe in tense circumstances, kept the Dodger spirit alive and well. But Jackie knew it, the players knew it, the fans knew it. Pee Wee was high up in the chain of being, a kind of mortal perfection; history and circumstances allowed his character to reveal the moral side of that force.

*   *   *

The Duke, Snider, in center was an effortless star, a grand power hitter built especially for cozy Ebbets Field (with its short-right and right-center dimensions), and a sure, agile fielder. If he suffered somewhat by comparison with the other two center fielders in Gothamtown in those days, Mickey and Willie, it is enough to say he was fit to be compared with them. (As the boy Aaron did, often, keeping, like any good scientist, his own Dodger statistics in a cherished Composition notebook, its graph pages filled with all the glorious figures of laboratory facts.) For five seasons, 1953 to 1957, Duke was at the top of the game, walloping 42, 40, 42, 43, 40 home runs, knocking in 126, 130, 136, 101, 92 runs, hitting for averages of .303 ('52) .336, .341, .309, .292, and slugging around .600 in percentage. That was hitting, the boy figured, even up against Mantle and Mays. The Duke could also go get 'em with the best. With deceptive speed and improved positioning, he glided to all balls in time to two-hand the catch and make the accurate throw back to the cutoff man. Like his colleagues, and famed competitors, he made few mistakes.

His swing, too, appeared effortless, and a thing of beauty. Even when he swung and missed, a frequent happening, it was a line of baseball pleasure. A left-handed batter, he'd keep the bat high and back, wrapped around his ears and head, wait, and then step into the pitch with his right leg raising slightly off the ground, weight back; and then the big cut, whipping the bat through by rotating his hips and swinging his whole, well-proportioned body through the swing. With that big swing he whiffed a lot, but that didn't defer the true fan from admiring the form. For it was a classic swing—learned in boyhood in Los Angeles and finely honed in Brooklyn, since he spent hardly any time in the minor leagues—and when the boy of nine watched him from behind first base, he kept his eye on the body, the hands, the form, the follow-through, reveling in its swift hard beauty again and again.

Although also nicknamed "the Silver Fox"—for his Rommel-like looks—he was known mostly as "the Duke." By Divine Right he seemed to inherit his center-field throne, you might say, the graceful boy displacing the stern Furillo quite naturally in 1949—thanks to kindly Burt Shotton, the manager—for the good and rightful placing of everyone. Or, to put the matter another way, he was really closest to the original golden boy with the fantastic skills, Pistol Pete Reiser, whose career of great promise was aborted by his endless rendezvous with the outfield walls. The Duke fulfilled the promise of that first Gold Dust Twin (Reese the other) and quickly became a necessary player, a natural star, a bleacher favorite. Behind the big flashing smile and the tip-of-the-hat manners, Snider knew the ins and outs of the game. The Duke was *our* answer to *their* center fielders, a player of proportions, a gentleman with a swing.

Campanella the catcher. Campy, the roly-poly player (5 foot, 9 inches tall, 190 pounds) with the sunny temperament and deceptive will and superb skills. He and Yogi were the best all-round catchers in the two leagues, and again a subject of argument for Dodger vs. Yankee fans. Campy handled the wide assortment of Dodger pitchers—the needy Newcombe, the slow-slower Preacher, the mercurial Loes, the wild Black (and wilder Barney), the curve-baller-change-up artist Carl, the sinker Clem—with adroitness, care, intelligence. Catchers are responsible for pitchers like parents for children—the great pitching staffs always seem to have a knowing catcher, Hegan with the Indians of Lemon, Wynn, and Garcia; Crandall with Milwaukee of Spahn and Sain and Burdette; and Campy was a shrewd father. Under him two great pitchers were developed, Newcombe and Erskine, and a splendid reliever for a few years, Joe Black. Roy knew when to be sympathetic to a disturbed Billy Loes; when to provoke or scold the temperamental Newk, when to signal Burt or Chuck or Walter that Branca had lost his fastball (despite the infamous Bobby Thomson pitch) or Labine his sinker. The catcher is the brain on the field, in many respects, and frequently the caretaker, bearing the largest responsibilities. Roy was the good father, the good brain, the good caretaker.

And there was more. He had a fine arm, with great wrists for throwing, and for hitting. You didn't steal on him because of his quickly snapped accurate throws. And his agility behind the plate belied his appearance: four times he led the league in fielding for catchers. Most memorable was his hitting from that wide-open batting stance: bat back and high, left leg far out to the left of the batter's box, so that it always looked as though he were swinging from the weight of one leg alone. How for godsakes did he hit the ball so well, and pull it to left with such power? With those wrists. Seduced or fooled by a pitch, he nevertheless could turn the tables on the surprised pitcher with a last-second flick of the wrists, twirling the thirty-six ounce bat like a toothpick, and, his right knee practically scraping the ground, rocketing the ball to all parts of the ballpark. It was a stance not to learn from. Yet in 1951 he was fourth in batting average (.325) behind Musial, fourth in RBI's (108), and third in slugging behind Kiner and Musial. And two years later he hit forty-one homers, slugged at 611, and led the league in RBI's, with 142. When he was done, stopped by ice and a telephone pole in January 1958, he had hit more home runs than any catcher in the league. Voted the Most Valuable Player three times. On and on, the stats and honors.

But not for statistics was number 39 to be remembered, or valued. For mastery of the game, for maturity of judgment, for reliableness and even rectitude—these were his qualities. And for a certain *joie de vivre* in the midst of his responsibilities. As he said after the 1953 season, "You have to be a man to be a big leaguer, but you have to have a lot of little boy in you, too."

Hail Campy, the man and the boy!

With Gil it was his vulnerability that raised him to the level of beloved for the Brooklyn fans. He had been a weak-hitting catcher, and the Dodgers, bringing in Campy, tried him out at first base. All he did was become the best in the game, in a year or so. Smooth as vanilla were his short-hop-scoops of pegs in the brown dirt. Sure as daybreak, his handling of over-the-shoulder pop flies, twisting bad-hop grounders, errant high throws. Solidly on target, his throws to second on the bunt, and his 3-4-3 or 3-6-3 double-play coverage. Around the bag he was like a great hawk gliding, his footwork graceful, his big first baseman's mitt an extended hand. As awkward and uncertain as he was as a catcher, he was sure and creative as a first baseman, a natural, the smoothest in the league for a decade.

Hitting was his Achilles' heel, the curveball from the right-handed pitcher his personal bane. With his open right-handed stance, he'd bail out on the curve, meaning he would lean back and away from the plate for a split second, only to see the pitch suddenly break and hit the corner and be called a strike. Sometimes he'd catch a piece of the ball, and feebly pop it up or ground it out. Mostly he swung and missed, or took it for a third strike. Yet there were enough fastballs or change-ups, and enough left-handed pitchers, that he'd get his share of hits, and even home runs, though his average stayed low.

Fans put up with his weakness there, since he had become a splendid first baseman. But when the situation grew terrible, deeply embarrassing, downright humiliating, something peculiar, something Brooklyn, happened: the fans rose to the occasion, rose to his defense, rose to benefaction. During his weeks of shame and impotency in 1952–53, Gil became the loved one. You see, he went into this hitless streak, this incredible streak of utter futility in which he managed one hit or so in fifty to sixty at bats, striking out half of the time. This fallow period started on September 23, 1952, the last week of the season, and extended through the World Series, where he came up to bat twenty-one times and failed to get a single hit. That end-of-season shame was intensified when the next season came, and once again, poor, cursed Gil couldn't hit.

Only a player, and a true fan, will know what it's like to go up there in the warm sunshine, gripping your bat, with twenty or thirty thousand fans in the stands, and men on base frequently, and know that it's hopeless, foredoomed, that your at bat will only heap further dishonor upon you, that you'll get the curve and you'll hesitate and accept the disgrace of a called third strike, or else swing and miss the ball by three, four, five inches, again and again. Then, sunken, and nakedly exposed, Gilbert Ray Hodges from Princeton, Indiana, must make the long walk back to the dugout, a walk every bit as shame-ridden as Achilles' refusal to fight. What had he done to deserve, in baseball youth, that cruel a fate?

The fans of Brooklyn decided to act upon that fate, to try to alter it. As the streak went on after the first few days, the crowd began clapping for hitless Gil when he strode to the plate. Not booing him, as expected from ordinary fans, but clapping, as though he had done something fine and splendid. And as the streak wore on, the citizens of Brooklyn began cheering, along with the priests and nuns, who began praying, for Gil. The fans, you see, were going to restore potency to the player, to collect and gather and transfer to him *their* potency. Somehow or other, they were going to replenish him by means of the power of their ardor—for after all he was a Dodger, a regular to boot; he must be saved, restored. Broken Gil must be made whole Gil again. A hitter again. Fans clapped in cadence at the ballpark, fans gathered by the radio at home, they crossed fingers at the beaches and parks, they prayed in the churches and synagogues. The more he suffered, the steadier was the faith, the deeper the prayer, all through the borough. And like Walter Alston, the loyal manager, the fans wouldn't give up, through fall months and Series loss, through winter and spring. The devoted would hang on no matter how long the curse on the House of Hodges lasted, weeks, months, the whole season if need be. Robbed of his manhood by the gods of baseball, the fans of Brooklyn would restore it to him.

Gil got a hit finally, on the curve, in late April 1953, and, after another month of futility, slowly started to come around. Gradually he began to hit the curve, and even hit it occasionally with power. The curse had been fought, and lifted. The shamans of Brooklyn had won. Religious order was restored. And hitless Gil had a fine 1953 season.

Was it any surprise that, when Hodges became the crosstown manager of the Mets years later, it was as a real Dodger icon returning, a beloved Saint Gil?

So, put them in a painting by Piero della Francesca or a triptych perhaps by van der Weyden, four "goodly creatures" wearing their mitts or swinging their bats: Pee Wee, Duke, Campy, Gil.

Four shining examples of Brooklyn's "beauteous mankind."

Mr. Rickey's Isle

T he boy first observed him in the *Post*'s photo, and then in the grainy Saturday matinee newsreel. He wore a bow tie and spectacles, and smiled genially as he shook hands with Jack Roosevelt Robinson, his new player called up from the Montreal farm team. To Aaron, the boss looked a lot like another hero of his, FDR. Aaron always thought of him as Mr. Rickey—the way he knew his schoolteachers—at the same time that he was struck by the odd first name, Branch. Even though he was the owner of the team, Mr. Rickey was very much part of the team, in the same way, say, that Red Barber was (not to mention the managers, Leo, Burt, Chuck, Walter). They were all Dodgers in the boy's estimation.

Under his reign the magical things occurred, and the country, not merely the borough, was interested. What happened on that cozy emerald isle during those years was a kind of national theater, the boy interpreted later on, with fans and citizens from California to Louisiana to the Dakotas becoming an audience. (The boy met people from those far-off places at the games, and that convinced Aaron that something was really happening out there.) Would the great experiment work, or would baseball itself collapse? Well, the baseball was high class, and the social relations almost made for a second Civil War. Through it all Mr. Rickey stayed calm and cool and unyielding, despite the death threats and family advice and National League rejections, realizing there was more than sports at stake, and counseling his great second baseman to remain the same. He was the Lincoln of baseball, wise and resolute, genial and frugal, loved by the real fans and hated by the mobs.

In high school Aaron did research for a sports piece he was writing about the Dodgers and the borough, and found out that Mr. Rickey had been a lawyer, a teacher, a baseball coach, a general manager. And from Red Barber, in a phone call after he had written the announcer a letter, he discovered a "conversion" that Mr. Rickey had experienced, on the road in a hotel room in South Bend, Indiana, in the late 1930s when he was a young baseball coach at Ohio Wesleyan. The team had arrived there to play Notre Dame, but the clerk at the Oliver Hotel wouldn't register their young catcher, declaring aloud their policy of admitting "No Negroes." Rickey announced then that he'd put him up in his own room, and the clerk gave in. When the coach went into the room to see his catcher, he found the boy pulling at the skin on his hands and crying out, "It's my skin . . . Mr. Rickey . . . if only I could tear it off . . . I'd be like everyone else." From then on, according to Mr. Barber, Branch Rickey was determined that, sometime in his life, he was going to satisfy the lament of that young catcher.

In order to carve his newfound history and break ground on his new mythology—the Dodgers as a national monument, if not a team—he needed his community (Brooklyn), his enemies (the world nearly), his protégé (Jackie), his voice (Red), his principles, his magic. And his private isle of course. For in green Ebbets Field, the fans, sitting practically on top of the field, were intimate with the players, calling them on a first-name basis naturally. For background music and comedy, there was Hilda, exercising with her cowbell, the Dodgers Sym-phony Band, five tattered bums meandering, Gladys and her organ. For nearly a decade this was regular community theater, tribal theater, directed by a Prospero called Branch Rickey.

Curious, how personally connected the boy in Brownsville felt to the cigar-smoking Lincoln sitting in his office uptown at Bedford

Avenue, but he did. It didn't hurt to receive a personal note of appreciation from the great man after he had read Aaron's piece in *The Liberty Bell*. (The boy cherished the two-line note and put it in his scrapbook.) After all, Brooklyn was a village then, a village on the world map, like Paris or Dublin, say.

Age of Heroes

During the spring of 1947, when I was nine and a half, Burt began taking me to the ball games. The real thing, the Dodger games. Burt was twenty-one or two, lived on the third floor of our Brooklyn apartment building, and had been like my big brother ever since I could remember. (Just as Sally, his bun-haired mother, had been the grandmother I never had, rocking me to sleep with lullabies in Polish and Yiddish, in her haberdashery store downstairs on Sutter Avenue.) And when Burt had left college to join the Air Force in 1942 to become a pilot—settling for navigator—he became a real-life hero to me, a live Frank Merriwell or Tom Mix, my radio gods. Moreover, the fact that his B-17 had been shot down over Germany and he had been pronounced "missing in action" for six months before being confirmed as a "prisoner of war"—ah, those heroic tags—only added to his romantic aura. When he returned home in 1945, limping, thin, with a Purple Heart and first lieutenant bars, it was as much a homecoming for me as for him. As he grabbed me in his arms and swung me high and wide, embracing me in a crackling leather aviator jacket and white silk scarf, I felt like I was rotating in a ferris wheel, spinning with indescribable delight.

As I said, he started taking me to the ballpark during that spring of '47, picking me up early from my public school on Rockaway Parkway—I got permission to leave at 2:15 twice a week from crazy Miss Gidden—and either driving up to Ebbets Field in his ratty Nash coupe, or else hailing a taxi to the Utica Avenue subway stop and taking the IRT uptown three stops to Franklin Avenue and then walking ten minutes. The reason for his freedom was his wound. While trying to escape from the Nazis, he had been shot with experimental glass bullets, and the results were thousands of glass shards deposited throughout his body. Hence, he had needed a series of operations to remove the largest, most troublesome pieces, and time in between was given over to recovery, and college. He had returned to NYU downtown, which he attended three or four mornings a week, for his degree in engineering.

In those lingering postwar days of comradely spirit, a veteran who wore his service uniform entered free at the park, and, if he wore his purple star, the ushers saw to it he got a first-rate seat. Since we mostly went on weekdays, it frequently happened that we were allowed to move down from the lower grandstand and sit in the boxes, on the first-base side, which, in cozy Ebbets Field, meant you were right up close to the field, alongside the Dodger dugout. And since a special Brooklyn rookie played first base that year, our seats had an added attraction. For he was no ordinary rookie, as everyone knew. Not his hitting, fielding, or running was the center of attention, but rather his shining ebony skin surrounded by the white flannel of the Brooklyn uniform. Oh, he stuck out all right, an intricate black orchid amidst a field of white daisies.

That Robinson was no ordinary player, in any sense, was apparent the very first time we saw him that spring. The Cardinals were in town for a three-game series, the same feared Cards who had won the pennant the year before, and the team that was considered the most "Southern" club—Southern in temperament as well as in player origin. (When I looked at St. Louis on the map, all I saw was that it was west of the Mississippi, the only team that far west. So far, in fact, that Red Barber had to report the games via the ticker tape, turning a printout triple into a line of lyrical poetry, while I huddled by my radio late into the night.) We arrived in the fourth inning, and had barely taken our seats when the first unusual situation occurred. Enos "Country" Slaughter, the Cards' hustling outfielder, hit a slow grounder to second, where Stanky fielded it and threw a routine peg to first to get the runner. He did, but at the same time Slaughter got Robinson, slashing his planted foot with his spikes as he crossed the bag. It was an obvious cheap shot, and Jackie sank to the ground, twisting in pain. Slaughter meanwhile ran off the infield just by Robinson, flashing him a little smile and nod. With the crowd and myself stunned, the only player who came over to the hurt player was Reese, from shortstop, who helped him up and walked with Robinson as he hobbled around, trying to assess his injury. Just then, too, a pitch-black cat was tossed out onto the field, along with a series of remarks from the Cardinal dugout ("There's your brother, Robinson, go cry to him!"). If that wasn't enough to make my blood pump, we then heard a "Yeah, beat it, black boy!" hurled from the Dodger dugout, aimed at their own player!

Burt, sensing my confused rage, put a hand on my arm.

More of the peculiar stuff happened in the bottom of the inning, when Red Munger, a fastballer who showed fine control in getting out the first two batters, decked Jackie with two straight high hard ones when he came to bat. Not a single line of protest came from the Dodger dugout, however, and hardly a ripple from the crowd either. Everyone seemed to be waiting, watching, before committing their sentiments, or votes. The next pitch was the predictable curve, way wide, which Jackie left alone. Then Munger tried another outside pitch, maybe a strike, and Robinson suddenly laid out his bat daintily and pushed a bunt up the right side of the field, just wide enough for the pitcher to have to cover it. And there was Jackie, almost jogging, timing the pitcher's run from the mound perfectly and then picking up his pace, colliding into Munger and sending him flying. Robinson didn't look back as he made first. For the first time, the crowd now clapped.

"Nigger," called one of the players picking up Munger, "you're finished!"

"Yeah, black Sambo," added another Card, "they're gonna carry you back to Africa!"

From the Brooklyn bench, a single voice said, "Attaway, Jackie."

Burt tapped my arm. "He's got the guts, hasn't he?"

I nodded, entranced.

"Does he have the talent too?"

The game settled down into a pitcher's duel, with Munger out-dueling Vic Lombardi by 2–1, and with no more incidents around first due to Robinson's quick eye and foot. In the home half of the seventh, with Gladys Gooding serenading us on the organ, Robinson came up again, and, with his bat cocked high over his head, he waited, along with us. No knockdown pitches this time, however, and Jackie, after fouling off several tough strikes, took a walk. Down to first in that odd pigeon-toed trot of his, an unlikely looking runner.

One out, and, with the next batter up, Robinson extended his lead off first. Reese was the batter.

"Will he go?" I asked.

"Could be."

Baseball's changing time now slowed to almost a standstill while Pee Wee waited at the plate, Munger went into his stretch and looked around, and Robinson started to do his dance about ten or twelve feet off the bag. Hands stretched out loosely at his sides, crouching like the halfback he had been (at UCLA, as Mr. Rickey had announced), Jackie jiggled this way and that, forcing Munger to throw over to first three times, then step out of the box, then to throw again, almost wildly. Robinson was back to first each time, comfortably.

The count went full, Munger threw over a few more times, then pitched, and Robinson ran. Pee Wee, not getting around fast enough, hit a setup two-bouncer to second, where Schoendienst fielded it easily but, having no chance to double up Jackie, pegged to first. Reese was out by six steps.

Robinson was still running. He had gone into second as though to stop, naturally, and then, just as Schoendienst began his throw, Robinson shifted into high gear and propelled toward third. By the time Musial, at first, realized what was happening, Robinson was three-quarters there, and Musial's throw was a half-second late.

Musial stood with his hands on his hips, staring unbelievingly. Schoendienst picked up a few pebbles and tossed them away. Robinson had already dusted himself off, and was standing upright, on third, hands on hips.

Burt looked over at me, and winked. "Ever seen that before?" I shook my head. "Not in this league."

"And not against the St. Louis Cardinals," he fine-tuned.

Two out now, and Jackie on third—still not much hope. The batter was Bruce Edwards, a right-handed hitter who had done nothing against Munger thus far.

Once again, Robinson began to lead, and Munger, after a consultation with Marion and Kurowski, decided to work from the stretch.

That didn't daunt Robinson in the least. Some sixty feet away from the pitcher, he edged out for his same long lead and jiggle, and, as soon as Munger threw to the plate, he raced halfway home himself, terrifying everyone.

"He's shameless too."

I didn't fully know what that meant, but I was too excited to inquire. All I knew was that I had my fingers crossed, under my legs, hoping against hope . . .

On the fourth pitch to the batter, Jackie again darted for home, the ball sailed low and away from the catcher, and Robinson only had to trot home. We were all now standing, cheering him. At the dugout, however, only two players greeted Robinson for his daring.

"They gotta get used to him, huh?" I wondered.

"They better hurry," Burt advised.

The Dodgers won in the ninth, 3–2, to move into first place.

Periodically then, a few times a week during May and June when the Dodgers were at home, we went up to Ebbets Field to watch them play. For Robinson, the same pattern continued, clubs taunting him ferociously, trying to punish him physically, and he taking them on, spectacularly. He seemed to learn quickly the other teams' vulnerable points—sloppy infielders, big-windup pitchers, reckless catchers—and push toward their break point. It was as if, looking back, he played with wit and irony while the other players were performing straight. For me, at nine already a fan, it was a raw and exciting time, and I too felt like a rookie. The only really bad moments came when, at times, I'd hear a kind of moan at my side and, glancing over, observe Burt's face go ashen, and he'd be gasping. Stitches would be pulling, or bits of glass somewhere would be cutting, and suddenly all the splendid sights and sounds of a ballpark in spring would be eclipsed. And Burt, seeing me in fear and loss, would then ask if I'd get him some water. And by the time I arrived back, he was calm again, and the interlude of darkness was over.

My father, a short stocky man who had never gotten on with America, also felt uneasy about Burt. Both of them were pretty arrogant, but especially with each other, and so they more or less avoided meeting. Burt thought my father was a "greenhorn Commie," which he was, and he resented that. My father believed that the Breams (also immigrants) had spoiled Burt, and he was a smart aleck who was made more abrasive by college. Nor did my father approve of our long friendship, and my total devotion to Burt. Even when I was four, and Burt was helping me to construct a miniature railroad depot—the delight of my childhood—from odd pieces of hardwood, obtained from his cabinetmaker assistant's job, my father would sneer at the two of us sprawled out on the floor, working meticulously. Although I didn't fully understand his animosity toward Burt—jealousy of him? of his family's closeness to me and my mother?—I knew enough to want to keep them apart, and our friendship more and more private.

I was therefore not happy to discover one evening, at dinner, that my father had heard about our Ebbets Field journeys.

While eating the boiled meat and potatoes that he salted heavily and adored (and I despised), he began questioning me, almost slyly, about the trips.

"So you've been going all spring, eh?"

"Well, not exactly."

"And tell me, did you skip school, too, to do this?"

"Of course not," and I explained how carefully I had gotten permission.

"I see," he commented, slicing and salting a piece of rye. Then, the prosecutor prying almost innocently, "Did your mother help you in all this? She agreed, right?"

I squirmed in my chair, and tried to appease him by applying the dreaded salt too.

"She helped you get the teacher's permission, yes?"

The widening eyes and tightening forehead belied his benevolent tone. "No," I managed, only a half-lie.

The small brown eyes flared, and the round face now grew alert with wild anger. "From now on you'll attend to school, and forget that *narishkeit*." Foolishness, I knew. "And you can tell your friend that too." He chewed his rye with gusto.

"But Dad, please, they're fighting for first, and Robinson—"

He took my wrist, and held it firmly, staring at me. Quietly he ordered, "You'll stay in school until three o'clock, and only then leave. And if—"

Just then my mother re-entered the room, unaware of the discussion he had begun when she had left.

"*Bist du klug*," my father began, "*very* smart." He shook his head in disdain as she sat down at the wooden table.

"What are you talking about?"

"Baseball instead of school, that's what. Very nice. What do you care if he grows up to be a truck driver?"

"Aah, stop it, will you? When he stops getting A's, then I'll worry." Her forehead creased with lines of familiar fatigue.

"Well, no more playing hookey with Mister Burt."

"Are you crazy?" she retorted. "What are you saying? No one played 'hookey.' "

"I suppose you skipped Hebrew school too, now and then? Well, no more. No more baseball until school is finished."

"Oh yeah?" I couldn't help challenging him.

He looked at me excitedly, fury mounting and driving him with strange power.

"Aaron, sshh," my mother urged, "you let me handle it, okay?"

I held my tongue, and scraped at the oilcloth on the table.

My father, slightly disappointed, returned to his food. "To soccer games he won't come, but to baseball. Eh."

Yes, it had been stupid of me not to accompany him the last time a European all-star team had come to Ebbets Field to play an exhibition match. But soccer? . . . Well, I already began my strategy for going to the Dodger games on the sly, unbeknownst even to my mother, so she wouldn't—couldn't—be held accountable. I could take his slapping me around, but not her.

Mrs. Gidden sat in her chair, propped up with a pillow because of her diminutive height, little feet encased in black bunion shoes, and nibbled at her chicken leg. At the blackboard was Jay Greenburg, who was trying to figure out how to get through the long division problem she had put to him. I, meanwhile, looked at my watch; just fifteen minutes to go, and I could grab my jacket from the wardrobe and be on my way downstairs. I carefully wrote out the Dodger and Brave lineups for the day, including the starting pitchers. There was just no way I was going to miss this Series, or any other for that matter. No matter what *he'd* do to me. *If* he ever found out. Ryan, Torgeson, Holmes, Elliott . . .

"Aaron, didn't you hear me? Can you help out our friend here?"

I looked up and saw that Mrs. Gidden was speaking to me. Immediately I stood up and hustled to the blackboard, as though I had been studying the equation all along. Sure, she wanted to make sure that the rest of the kids saw clearly that I wasn't getting spoiled, leaving early this way. I looked at the problem, it wasn't much of one actually, and in a second I was scribbling away on the board, already sighting Jackie getting his lead at first. Boy, that would be tough, off of Johnny Sain.

"Thank you, Aaron." She nodded, her rimless eyeglasses reflecting light.

Outside, in the warm sunshine, Burt was already there, and I got into the car.

"Now you're sure you want to go ahead and do this?" He looked at me. "If your father finds out, he'll be pretty upset."

"I know. But he won't find out—unless *you* tell him," I kidded.

"Oh, I just may not," he said, tapping my shoulder.

And as we took off I thought of our journey as some sort of Air Force mission, maybe like one of Burt's B-17 flights over Germany. Something secret, something dangerous.

And the game didn't disappoint, though we didn't win. Sain beat the Bums, 2–1, with his variety of curveballs, and even almost picked off Robinson at first (a great hand slide saved him). "He'll get to know him second time around, huh?" I asked. "Well," Burt responded, "some pitchers you learn are too tough, and Sain may be one of them."

Excitement ballooned, however, when Burt allowed me to wait for the players afterwards, and I hit the jackpot—Robinson's autograph on a Dodger scorecard. Though to be truthful, up close he was scary-serious, the voice soft-gravelly, his face the color of our mahogany bureau. He asked my name, and my heart leaped as he wrote "To Aaron" and signed his name, on a slant, small but legible. Yet when he lifted his high stubborn forehead and stared at me for a second, I felt accused and afraid, as though he . . .

Confused but high by the time I ran to Burt, I was still flying by that evening when I came downstairs after dinner to play punchball with the kids. We played on the vacant lot on Ralph Avenue, where you had to run up a rocky incline to reach the bases. Naturally I kept quiet about my prize, waiting for the right moment to spring it. I played third base, and made a few easy errors, the pink Spaldeen ball eluding my usually firm grip because my mind was elsewhere.

The game ended just before dark, and we naturally gathered together by the street corner of Ralph and Sutter, our social center. The Sutter Theater, a hundred feet away, was showing *The Lost Weekend*, which we would go to the next afternoon, our Saturday matinee ritual. Across the way the New Lots IRT pulled in and out of the station. In the warm June evening, we kids boxed, kidded the girls passing, argued about the pennant race.

"Forget the Dodgers, come September and they'll blow it!" said Alan Kamph, die-hard Yankee fan.

"Yeah, the Cards look strong again," worried Ronald Tavel.

"And don't forget 'Spahn and Sain and two days of rain,' " scholarly Jerry said, referring to the Braves and their pitchers.

"Aah, Brooklyn will murder those guys," asserted Morty Kassover, street bully and Dodger fanatic.

"Well, they didn't murder them today," I put in modestly. "In fact, they looked pretty feeble against Sain."

"Don't tell me you went again, Schlossy?" cried Mel Goldstein.

And so I got to explain how I watched Sain toy with them today, describing his cunning kick and pickoff move, and how Reiser almost cracked his head again going for a Holmes double, and then prepared myself for the usual questions—where'd we sit, did we catch any foul balls, get any autographs?

"Just one," I spoke evenly.

"Oh yeah, who?"

"Arkie Vaughan?" offered Steven Werter sarcastically.

"Robinson."

"Who you joshin'?"

"I don't believe it," chipped in Mel.

"C'mon, let's see it," said pink-cheeked Kamph.

An excited jury of ten circled around me, waiting to see the actual evidence. I produced it, carefully unrolling the program.

"Wow!"

"No shit!"

"Let's see that." And Kassover ripped the program from my hand and studied it up close. "If you're bluffing us—" And he brandished his thick fist. "We can check this out, you know."

"It's for real, I swear," I blurted out, already afraid of his secret network.

Gradually, as the truth sank in, they began to treat me as a kind of hero, someone who had braved bayonets and trenches to secure this booty.

"How'd ya do it?"

"Who'd ya know?"

Well, I got so caught up in the heat of my sudden-found glory that I began to embellish foolishly my feat, saying how I had run after Reese's car and almost got hit by it, and how Jackie had given me a big smile, and—

"Aaron!"

The voice torpedoed my glory, stopped my story.

"Can I see you for a minute?"

"Hello, Mr. Schlossberg," Kamph greeted my father.

"Good evening, Alan," my father returned, cordially as ever.

"Did you see whose autograph he got at the game today?" Morty Kassover jumped in, especially friendly with my father.

What could I say, do? The El train lumbered into the Sutter Avenue station, and the little bulbs on the movie marquee were sizzling suddenly.

Now the kids spread apart like a wagon train to welcome my father, respectfully opening the circle for me to go to him. But my knees were rubbery, and I wished that they would continue to surround me.

The bluish-black rush of the evening descended on me as he took my arm ceremoniously and led me across the street and into 701 Ralph Avenue. Through the yellowing lobby and up the cement steps he led me, while I held on to the cold metal bannister with all my strength.

"Hi, Mr. Schlossberg," spoke Joey Zorn, from the mailboxes below.

My father, taken aback by the shadowy figure, stopped to peer. "Is that you, Joey?" Stunned by society, he retreated into formality. "Why, how are you?"

"Fine, thanks. How's the left fielder doing?" he said, rustling my hair, and beginning to follow us up the stairs.

"Okay," I mumbled, desperately wanting Joey to stay with me.

"Someday you'll have to watch Aaron play the outfield," he enjoined my father. "He can really go get 'em." Coming from Joey, a real player, it was a high compliment.

"Is he?" father said politely, and began to move off with me on our first-floor landing.

From the recessed darkness I called out weakly, "Joey."

He turned at the stairwell. "What's up?"

Father put the subtlest force to his grip, and I could only shake my head. He unlocked the steel door, and we went inside, my heart and stomach astir, the grave mask of Jackie reappearing now, paradoxically comforting and terrifying me as he signed my program.

Father sat me down at the kitchen table, squeezing me between the window and the wall, and began with, "So you disobeyed me."

On Sunday morning, three days later, my father and I left the Brownsville Air Raid Wardens Club on Topscott Street and headed for home. The air was cool and refreshing after a morning of chess (me) and pinochle (him) in the smoke-filled room. Before going uptown to the Stanley Theater to watch a double feature of Russian and Chaplin films, we were going to stop at the house and have a quick bite. Also, Father agreed, finally, that it was too hot for the knicker suit, and I could change to my gabardines. The storm of the other evening had receded, and, if we had not forgiven each other—no, I never would anymore—we at least had arrived at a calmer point. One where turbulent force had returned to the wings, and the actors went through their rehearsed parts quite routinely.

When we arrived at our apartment building, clusters of parents and kids had taken up their customary posts—talking, kibitzing, playing checkers and box ball, sitting on folding chairs or wooden crates. The traffic was lighter on Sundays, including the busses, and I missed the trolleys that used to clang their way past, but which had been recently discontinued. My father was greeted politely, with the usual curiosity, by the neighbors, who looked upon him as a kind of zoo creature, formidable and comic. Not just because everyone knew he was a leftie or Red, but because he was always such an odd fish, forever formal in his double-breasted suit and tie (like today), forever European in preferences and tastes (chess, soccer, Chaplin), aloof and slightly superior. Despite myself, I felt a flow of sympathy for him at those moments, when he amused the citizens.

"So, Herschel, how goes it?" asked Mr. Tavel, his one crony.

My father nodded, and said, "Fine, why not? And you, you lazy-good-for-nothing?"

Mr. Tavel, a hardworking bookkeeper with slumping shoulders, made a so-so gesture with his hands, and replied, "Could be better."

"Hello, Harry," said curly-haired Mr. Werter, looking up from infighting with his son, and laughing at the blows, "the boy here thinks I can still take his hardest shots."

My father smiled. "Try him in those golden gloves, Louie."

"Are you kidding? They'll knock his block off."

"Oh yeah?" cried out Steven pounding away at his dad.

I was secretly glad at all this tumult, distracting everyone's attention from my formal suit and Sunday duties.

We were about to turn into the entrance of our building when the heavy iron door opened, and Burt, in soldier's suit, emerged. With his soft cap that looked like a folded envelope and new trim mustache, he looked deceptively fit and youthfully splendid.

Naturally he put his arm around me, and gave my father a correct hello.

My father nodded. "So, are you off to Palestine, or have you given up that *narishe* idea?" Foolish, I knew.

"No, not at all. Just have to take care of some unfinished business first."

"This baseball business you mean?"

Burt eyed him directly. "College and hospitals."

"A Jewish state will never get off the ground. And an Air Force yet?" He raised his eyebrows in mirth.

"You mean Uncle Joe might not approve?" A reference to Stalin, I sensed, *father's* hero.

"Harry, a little poker later today?" asked Mr. Ainbinder.

"Thanks, Morris, not today."

Burt gave my head a little furtive squeeze of affection.

"By the way," my father said, taking my hand, "no more of this baseball foolishness for Aaron. He'll stay in school, if you don't mind."

Burt tilted his head slightly, and seemed about to relent. Then he said, "You know your trouble, Harry? You live in America, not Russia. Why don't you let Aaron grow up an American boy?"

My chest pounded, and I felt my breathing quicken.

My father's face narrowed, and he paused just a few seconds, in which he weighed the words and the attention they might be attracting.

"I'll bring my son up my way, if you don't mind again."

"Sure, Harry, sure." He backed off, shaking his head.

Interrupting them, Mr. Werter said, "C'mon, gents, instead of talking, how about a little arm wrestling—my boy is dying to see me getting licked."

"Yeah, take him on, Mr. Schlossberg, go ahead teach him a lesson!" And Stevie, shaking his own defeated hand vigorously, then sucker-punched his father, who laughed good-naturedly.

My father, smiling with embarrassment, removed his suit jacket and allowed himself to be seated on a folding chair, opposite Mr. Werter; and, setting their elbows upon a small table, they locked grips.

Knowing his arm strength, and his crazy pride, I was not surprised that he took up the challenge. I was also delighted that he and Burt were separated.

It did not take long. By the time I could count to twenty, he had taken down Mr. Werter's arm, to the squeals of his son, and to my disappointment.

The small crowd that had gathered congratulated Father, who beamed and shook hands with Mr. Werter.

Father was replacing his jacket, already standing when Burt reappeared and said, "Stay, Harry, I'll take you on."

Father's eyes widened in surprise, then he smiled broadly, with something beyond satisfaction.

Removing his tight khaki jacket, Burt took Mr. Werter's seat, and put his elbow down, hand up. I looked twice at the cracks in the sidewalk cement, counted to eight three times, and scratched behind my kneecaps. I put all my superstitious powers to work for Burt. The small crowd had increased by now, and encouragement was shouted to both sides.

At first I thought Burt could do it, and maybe so did he. He had gotten my father's hand down halfway, with steady pressing, and it seemed that it was just a matter of moments before he'd pin him. I saw my father's face then, and it was filling with . . . determination, I thought. But as Burt now pressed for the win, I saw something else—the bare hint of a smile on my father's face. And I knew he had been playing a game of deception with Burt. Slowly now he moved their hands into reverse motion, and carefully forced Burt's hand down onto the table. I saw Burt's face go that same ashen color, and wanted to go to him, maybe bring him water. But at least it was over.

"Come, another?" Harry offered, with cunning magnanimity.

Burt, his mouth twitching slightly, forced himself to comply.

Don't, Burt, don't! I wanted to shout. But my tongue was frozen, cowardly frozen.

Once again they put their arms and hands into lock position, and once again Harry let Burt get the upper hand, before moving him the other way, slowly, slowly, staring at the younger man's face. By the time Burt had been submitted to defeat again, he was near crying from his other pain. Did my father know this?

"Why didn't you tell us you were a *shtarker*, Herschel?" asked one of the men.

I sneaked to Burt's side and asked, "Do you want some water?"

Smiling weakly, badly shaken, he said, "Didn't do so well for us, did I?"

At that point, not caring what my father saw or felt, I buried my head in his side, and felt my wetness dissolve the scene.

Darkness enveloped me, except for the flickering screen up ahead. Russian soldiers, in furry coats and hats, were moving forward against a retreating Nazi army. Snow was falling, and it covered the trees, the tanks, the soldiers' uniforms. The music was that patriotic chanting of the Red Army Chorus, which I knew from my father's records. I sat low in my seat, despite my father's protestations. . . . Gradually, in place of the somber Russian chorus, I began to hear the cheerier sounds of Gladys's organ, and instead of the snowy war front, to see a green baseball diamond splashed by sunlight. And, sure enough, there was Jackie, in his white flannels with "Dodgers" written in blue across the chest, leading off third. And as the pitcher took his stretch, Jackie increased his lead. Edging farther, farther from security, Jackie dared him to throw, either to third or to home, and finally the pitcher threw home—and there was Jackie, racing the ball. And sliding, away from the plate, he managed to reach out and touch home with his hand!

"What's wrong with you, silly boy?" whispered my father, placing his hand upon me with surprising tenderness as I jumped. "Are you all right?"

And my heart, which was whole with hostility, was suddenly torn asunder, a condition which, I sensed then in the shrouding, guilty darkness, would afflict me forever.

That summer, about the middle of July, my mother took me upstate to the mountains for our regular six-week vacation. We went up to White Sulphur Springs in the Catskills and stayed in a small hotel owned and run by a tough, piano-legged Hungarian widow. Because we had gone there the summer before, I had already made friends and could lose myself immediately in country pleasures. With the farmers' sons, I played hardball and helped with chores on the various dairy farms. With the other vacationing city kids, who stayed at nearby hotels or summer bungalows, I played softball and evening basketball, sneaked into the nightly shows at the casinos, watched the waiters and busboys flirting with the girls. Sometimes one of the parents would take us on a small expedition to the town of Liberty, a half-hour drive, to the movies. Of course these were very different from the sort of somber films I saw regularly with father at the Stanley Theater in Manhattan. These were mostly light comedies or musicals.

Everything was green and lucid up there, in the tree-filled hills where the air cooled off so aromatically at night, and the smells of pine and freshly cut hay scented my dreams. And where I didn't have to face my father on a daily basis.

The Dodgers were doing real well, still heading the pack. I followed them on the radio, listening closely to Red Barber's funny descriptions and indelible country idioms. Only he could call a flyball to the outfield a "dying chicken falling out there in the pea patches" and make it sound like part of the game.

Robinson was doing all right as well. There remained little question of his stamina, daring, or skill. In fact, he had become a hero to the fans of Brooklyn, despite the fact that some of his own players still resented him and opposing players were still out to get him. That's just too bad, we all thought . . . well, not all of us, as it turned out; I learned that quite a few of those farmers' kids were pretty prejudiced, and I got into two fistfights over my devotion to Jackie.

Burt, too, seemed to be doing fine. There were no more operations scheduled for the near future, so he was free to go to Palestine to fly planes for the Jews. He was also seeing a woman pretty steadily, a Czech lady who had been in the European "camps" during the war. (Did that mean POW camps? I wondered. Or was it the other kind I had begun to learn about, in which the Nazi Germans had murdered the Jews?) And when I kidded him on the phone about "not getting married or anything dumb like that," he replied, "You never know. But if I do, you'll be the first to hear about it, pal. I'll need a best man, you know." After getting Burt back from the war and the Nazis, the thought of losing him that way pretty much knocked me over.

I didn't think about Papa much, and he made it easy by rarely coming up, always pleading work duties. I really felt much freer and lighter without him; life in the country held its own special routines for me, and there didn't seem to be any need for my father. So, when he'd ask me, over long distance, whether I missed him or not, I was glad for the fuzziness of the connection and uttered something vague and meaningless. I suppose I didn't really take his question or his sincerity seriously.

That's probably why I wasn't looking forward to the weekend in August when he was coming up for a visit.

And "sure as shootin'," an expression I used quite a bit that summer, my fears were fulfilled when he arrived. Father wore his usual striped suit and tie as though he were still going to work or the club in the city. What a joke he was. I could see the hotel guests snicker behind his back on Saturday morning when, sitting outside in the wooden lawn chairs reading their newspapers, they spotted him. Oh, he was as polite as ever, polite and stiff, and I was embarrassed, almost ashamed to be seen with him. Although he was friendly, even warm, to me, I hardly gave him the opportunity to get close. I clearly saw the countryside as *my* territory, and he was out of place there. One thing though: his awkwardness gave me a feeling of revenge, even victory, you might say. It felt good.

That secret sense continued throughout the day and into the evening, when we went to see a show at the nearby Leona Hotel casino. We were entertained by a juggler, a comedian, and a singing act, and everyone in our group, including my mother and me, were having a fine time. Not Father. He watched politely enough, but didn't clap. Afterwards, when someone asked how he liked it, he raised his eyebrows.

"This *chazerai* you like? This crap!" he said to us privately. "Sometime, sonny boy, I'll take you to see a real juggler, and you'll see how fantastic it can be."

My mother's face tightened. "Sure, anything that we have *here* is not good enough for you. Do me a favor. Don't join us next time, yeah? Please."

And she went off to dance with a family friend, joining the crowd of people moving to the rumba music of the band. I watched her—auburn hair flying, hips moving, hands gesturing—at the center of the floor and was glad she was not going to let my father spoil her evening. Without his strict ways and European standards, my mother was freer too.

The next morning my father disappeared after breakfast, and I prepared to go to a morning softball game. Gathering my glove and hat, I waited outside on the long wraparound porch for my friends to join me. The sun was bright and warm, and I hoped that by the time the game was over, it would almost be time for Papa to catch his bus home. Then we'd be free again.

However, just as my pals showed up, we heard a commotion on the large lawn adjoining the hotel and decided to see what was going on.

There was my father, sitting on a huge, chestnut-colored horse. Wearing leather riding boots and looking at home, he glanced around comfortably. Clusters of city vacationers, surprised and curious, had gathered to look at the beautiful animal that was grazing on the lawn. Papa was smiling, a different sort of smile than I had seen before, and I noticed drips of perspiration on his face as well as on the horse. Obviously, they had been riding hard.

Seeing me, he dismounted easily, and the crowd jumped back as the horse jerked his head and backed up a step. Papa merely stroked the horse's neck and said, "Sshhh. *Ess*, Red, *ess*." Eat, Red, eat. "The clover is good, eh." Amazingly, the horse listened and began to graze once more. Red was a lovely reddish-brown and had a white stripe down his long head. His eyes were like big brown plums and seemed almost human.

Father wore his white shirt, but it was open at the neck, and he had rolled up his sleeves. He looked so different—not a stiff greenhorn, but a free and easy country fellow. Taking me around, he said, "So, sonny boy, how about a little ride?" He patted Red's broad but lean side. "He's a good *ferd*, this one."

The guests showed a new respect for Father, putting hesitant, interested questions to him. Papa answered them in an easy, friendly manner. He was not aloof now, but relaxed.

My friend Joe Luftus asked, "Are you gonna ride him?"

I shrugged, trying to hide my excitement and fear.

Benjy Lewis added, "I didn't know your father was a real horseback rider. Why didn't you tell us?"

I smiled, not knowing what to say.

"Come," my father said to me, "I'll lift you up and then climb on myself."

Having no idea what was happening, I found myself hoisted up onto the saddle. Red turned lazily and gazed back at me—with doubt, I thought. Father whispered something to him and then, in one easy motion, lifted himself up behind me.

The crowd moved back, oohing and aahing, and my friends cried out encouragement to me. But I was so excited at just sitting there that I hardly understood their words. Everything looked so different from up there. The grown-ups were smaller, the kids were shrimps, and the grassy ground dropped far below. The sky seemed closer too.

My father showed me how and where to hold on to the saddle. Reins in hand, he touched Red with his heels, and the horse began to walk about. Around the lawn, he, we, paraded, while everyone watched.

Just then my mother appeared, wearing an anxious expression. "You all right?" she asked me.

I nodded.

"Don't you go too fast with him," she warned my father.

I felt my father's strong arms around me as he guided Red with gentle but firm hands and pressing knees. The horse seemed to understand perfectly his every command. After a few minutes, we proceeded outside the hotel's premises and onto the dirt shoulder of the road.

Leaning forward, Papa said, "Hold on now—we'll go a little faster." He made a little clicking sound, nudged the horse's sides, and I began to bounce up and down. It was a different experience—speedier, bouncier, and a little scary. Up and down, up and down, the world bobbed by and my blood jumped too.

At the end of a stretch of road, Papa pulled back on the reins, and we returned to a walk. He guided us across the empty blacktop to the grassy field opposite the hotel.

"How about a little gallop?" he asked, his face close. "All right, sonny?"

"Is it . . . much faster?"

"Sure."

"I'm afraid," I admitted, hating my fear. "Maybe we better not."

"Don't be silly. I have you, and he's a good horse."

"No," I said weakly—for I did want to try faster.

"First we'll just trot toward that farmhouse to make sure of the field," and he put Red onto his path.

I turned for a moment and saw the small crowd gathered by the hotel, observing, growing smaller and smaller, as we distanced ourselves from them. I thought of my friends watching, too, and tried to forget, or surmount, my fear.

When we were within about a hundred feet of the farmhouse,

we turned. "Hold on!" Papa said, and he gave the horse a solid kick with his boots.

With immediate thrust we took off, the ground beneath us disappearing suddenly. Red galloped as though he were flying, his hooves hardly touching the ground. Papa spoke words, but I was too scared to register their meaning and only felt his leaning body. I held on for dear life, tears in my eyes, my heart leaping. At some point I must have slipped to one side, because I felt my father's powerful hand grab and right me with ease. It was like being on a train, traveling so fast that it was impossible to distinguish clearly the passing objects. Grassy fields, rows of trees, and an occasional white house were vanishing, while hotel, crowd, and road were approaching, no line separating the two. Exhilaration mingled with terror in my rushing blood.

We pulled up just short of the blacktop. Father gave Red a loud pat on the neck, and then we walked back across the road. Papa's sweat fell on me, and it felt right.

Releasing my grip, I realized how tightly I had been clutching the saddle. My hands were hurting, my heart was racing. Slowly, the ordinary world was returning to its right size.

My mother was furious, the hotel guests and my pals were cheering and clapping, and I felt my breathing return to normal.

Papa whispered to me, "Not too bad, eh, sonny boy?"

I had a surge of emotion, wanted even to hug and kiss him, but for some reason, I held myself back. Instead, I nodded, at a loss for words.

My father got down off the horse and asked someone the whereabouts of water. Red had already resumed his search for clover. Telling me he'd be right back, Papa asked whether I wanted to wait up there. Well, what could I say? Red grazed, I sat, and the grown-ups and kids surrounded me.

"How was it?"

"How'd ya stay on?"

"Do you know how fast you were traveling?"

"Was your dad in the cavalry or something?"

My mother anxiously asked, "Are you all right, kindelah?"

I nodded, said, "Fine," and, uncharacteristically, leaned away from her reaching hands.

My father returned with a bucket of water, and Red quickly turned his attention there. His nose submerged, he drank contentedly.

To Father, my mother said, *"Bist du mishugah.* You scared the daylights out of me. How could you endanger the boy that way?"

But I knew differently; I knew something else.

Father made a weak gesture with his hands and gave Red a pat.

And I thought, wouldn't it be great if Papa could take Red back home, to Brooklyn, where we could go out for rides with him all the time? He was a different man out there—with the horse, on roads and fields—and different with me too. Why, he wouldn't always need to dream about his old house and old country; he could be happy right here. Then maybe he'd make America his home ground. Why, I could even take him out to see Jackie run and steal the bases!

Papa took me down from the horse, said he'd see me later, and got back on himself. "Time to go home, Red," he said, half-smiling, wholly happy, and he walked the horse out of the lawn pasture.

Once on the road's shoulder, he kicked him lightly and prompted the horse back into that bumpy trot.

Everyone watched in rapt attention.

Benjy turned to me. "Boy, you're a lucky guy to have a pop who can ride like that. Where you been hiding him?"

The sun slanted down, camouflaging horse and rider in black shadow and greenish light. *"Where you been hiding him?"* The question repeated itself in my mind. Watching them both move down the road so easily and naturally, with athletic grace, I wondered the same thing.

Patriotism

The Modern Age of Betrayal: America in the early 1950s. The McCarran-Walter Immigration Act. House Un-American Committee. The Rosenberg case. The era of the double cross of our Constitution and fair-play principles, by the likes of self-styled superpatriots like J. Edgar Hoover, General MacArthur, Senator McCarthy. The use of one of the slyest totalitarian tricks: set friend against friend, and the children against the fathers and mothers. A child's path to hell, with no exit, since enlightened adulthood, if it came, entailed guilt and shame. A political crime as bad as sexual abuse, perhaps.

A Commie under every bed, a potential Red in every heart. The Salem Witch Hunt re-enacted on a national scale. Like the giant U-2 spy plane that blocked out all sunlight, McCarthyism, aided and abetted by J. Edgar and his FBI shock troops, shrouded all our bright Bill of Rights principles and protections. And were the visible culprits really worse than their accomplices—our cowardly congressmen and senators, our timid legal officials and complacent university presidents, our Hollywood moguls and endless minor citizens, who allowed it to happen?

The road from Capitol Hill in Washington to the boy's apartment in Brooklyn was not too long a way for the official hook of intimidation to extend.

The father, a bad businessman and foolish fellow traveler, became a haunted man, a terrified immigrant. And the mother, a good but simple soul, bought the official news and blamed it all on the Russians too. Took McCarthy's side, without quite knowing it. And helped to infect the young son. So the boy participated unwittingly in the trials and judgments on the father. Nice Bolshevik strategy that, now employed by we Americans. The national (cultural) disease led to the family intrigue, which contributed to the family illness, which took years to diagnose, understand, let alone untangle or cure. But is there ever any cure for the childhood years of bad feeling, ruined faith?

What saved the boy perhaps was the deeper loyalty, baseball and the Dodgers. For on the field it didn't matter much whether you were an imagined leftie or actual fellow traveler; if you could hit the curve, scoop the short hop, throw the high hard one, run the bases, that's what really counted. Too bad DiMaggio or Williams or Musial didn't have a little pink in them; having Jolting Joe or the Thumper or Stan the Man go up against one of the HUAC bullies would have made a nice at-bat for democracy, don't you think?

So, in yet another one of the superpatriotic ages of our history, the Cold War was filtering down into small family niches. Yet, who is there to pay for the misjudgments, the calumny, the personal injury, and the family pain—except perhaps the Republic's memory, and the surviving wounded?

If history is a partial record of that memory, then literature is a little drama of the wounded.

An Infantile
Disorder

He lay in his Hollywood bed, reading his *Sport* magazine and
fighting drowsiness, overhearing the heated conversation
going on in the next room, the kitchen. In the shadowy
darkness, his blankets pulled way up, he was supposed to be sleeping, but he used his pen flashlight to read on. Would Pistol Pete
Reiser ever be the same again, after crashing into the center-field
wall so many times? The small printed words took on added mystery, like a Captain Midnight coded message, he thought, lit up
bright yellow by his narrow beam of light. Cars whispered by on
Sutter Avenue, louder than usual because of the light rain falling.
He tried to concentrate on the clatter of rain, and the Dodger write-
up, but the argument developing, mostly in Russian, kept dividing
his attention. Even though he couldn't really understand the language, he had a strong sense about the meaning. It was "Commie
talk," as his mother called it.

Mom wasn't home, and he was glad of that anyway. She was
out playing cards over at Ida's, this being Wednesday night, and
so she might not ever find out that Papa was having his cronies
over again. He hoped she wouldn't anyway. That would just upset
her all over, and probably cause another fight. His revery was
interrupted by that *name* spoken again, or that set of names. Always

"Trotsky," then always "Stalin," set off against each other. That was the fight all right. With Papa on the side of Uncle Joe, the boy knew. And Cousin Morris—not really a cousin, he knew that too—on the side of Trotsky. Well, the boy certainly didn't know who was better, but he liked so much the soothing deep voice of Morris. Besides, Morris always came in to see him, either to give him a small toy, like the wooden car tonight, or to say something amusing. Therefore, he decided to side with Morris, and stay on Trotsky's side. Fayvel was short and chin-bearded and a hothead, though he pretended otherwise, and the boy was always glad when he was bested. Lev, the fourth, seemed to the boy like some wounded sparrow, ready to agree with whichever side was winning, and since Papa was usually winning, by bullying everyone, Lev would side with him. Like tonight, when he seemed to start out neutral, but was already nodding (the boy imagined) and agreeing with his father.

The boy tried to block out the rude garblings of the Russian and return to his ice creamy baseball words. A new center fielder was coming up, someone named Snider—with the wonderful first name of Duke—and he was already being compared defensively to Terry Moore of the Cards. O Spring, where are you? For sure, Snider or Reiser vs. Moore was a thousand times better than Stalin vs. Trotsky. Or Lenin, who was mentioned just as often. Funny thing about the language too. The boy of three or four had loved it when his father used to speak to him tenderly in Russian, but after his mother had told Papa to cut it out, since they lived in America, the language had lost its appeal. So in the apartment he heard English and Yiddish, for the most part, except for when this small group met, once a month maybe.

He crawled down deeper into his cocoon, and felt the satiny edge of the wool blanket. It wasn't that great to be eight years old. You had all these things you wanted to do, but you were always told you couldn't do this, you couldn't do that. And on top of it all, you had a father and mother who disagreed and fought over everything. And he always seemed to get dragged along into the fights. Sometimes he wished he could get up and leave, just walk out or run away. He scratched the back of his head, right down through the thick straight hair to the scalp, pleased by the scratchy sound as well as the digging of the long fingernails. In a way it was better to have it itch like this, and be able to scratch it deliciously, than to have Mom wash it clean.

The voices were rising in the kitchen like the aroma of tobacco (probably his father's Lucky Strikes), and he sensed Papa getting angry. Here and there the boy listened intently, when English or Yiddish was spoken.

"Without Stalin," Papa was saying, "the Nazis would have taken Leningrad and Moscow, Mister Comrade."

"You're dreaming, Herschel," Morris answered. "The Red Army and the people won that war. Because of your Stalin, they almost lost it. And because of your 'Uncle Joe,' the revolution has been betrayed."

The stirring of the tea loudly, father's trademark. "You're a bourgeois *kupp* and always will be. Bolshevik faith and beliefs you never had. Cell meetings are wasted on you."

Usual stuff. "Betrayed" the boy would have to look up. With his "comrades," Papa's anger would come out in argument and sarcasm, but never in force. That he saved for his family. Father and his arrogance, his family temper. The boy rubbed his favored divider ridge on the painted wall.

Did they read sports magazines over in Russia? He knew they played soccer, not real football or any baseball, so they probably didn't even have any *Sport*. Actually, if it weren't for his sister's abscessed ear, back when he was one year old, he might have grown up a Russian boy. That would have been something, something awful. They were all set to take the ship overseas back to see Papa's family, outside Minsk somewhere, when Hannah got her usual bad earache and the doctor insisted that they put her in a hospital for a week or ten days. The doctor and Mom had won out over Papa's strong objection, and that week Germany invaded Poland. Transatlantic journeys were suddenly held up, put off, and he grew up here, on Brooklyn soil. Lucky boy, lucky earache. They had missed the boat, all right, thank god.

Now, in Yiddish, which he three-quarters understood, he heard his father cutting down Fayvel and Morris, dismissing them as *nars* and *ferds* who had never understood the Revolution. Fools and horses, the boy knew. Revolution reminded him of "Shazzam," a magical word. Papa was in the middle of one of his lectures, which grated on the boy's ears, when he heard the front door being unlocked. Mom! His heart jumped with glee, while his head raced with anxiety. He flicked off the flashlight and lay there, growing alert, waiting.

He heard his mother being greeted familiarly by the men: "Come and say hello, Rose!"

He could feel her nod of hello. "Aaron asleep all right?"

"What then? At ten-twenty you want he should be up?"

The sounds of his mother hanging up her coat in the long foyer, and the approach of his favorite moment, when she'd check his covers, and make sure he wasn't cold or sweating. He waited, preparing for his delicate ambush.

The familiar aroma of perfume and body odor swept him wonderfully as she leaned down. "What's going on here?" she asked, discovering the magazine and flashlight.

He giggled, opened his eyes, and drew her face down. "I was waiting for you, that's all!"

"You *goniff!*" she whispered. "What are you doing up this late? Reading all this time?" She shook her head.

"Aw, it's not *that* late, Mom."

"After ten, on a school night? Come on, enough now, close your eyes and get to sleep. Don't be silly."

"Did you win?" he wondered, prolonging her presence.

"Oh, a few dollars, nothing to write home about. Now, *schluff.*"

"A good-night kiss?"

She kissed him on the forehead, and he squeezed her tight, tight, before letting her go. She returned the ten steps to the kitchen, on the other side of the wall.

He heard, "We're just calling it a night, Rose. Unless you stay and have a cup of coffee."

"I'll take a rain check, thanks, Lev. Too late tonight."

She gave her good nights to the others and left again, passing through the living room, where the boy slept, and on into the bathroom, which separated the single bedroom from the living room.

He felt sleep creeping up on him, but fought hard to stay awake, just in case.

The men were breaking it up, and getting their coats from the foyer. "*Nu*, Herschel, everything we didn't solve, but useful? Yes."

Father said, "Go home, Moishe, and do some homework. Re-read your Lenin, you *pastkunok*, *Left-Wing Communism, an Infantile Disorder*. You'll argue better next time." A softer tone now.

When they had departed, Father returned to the kitchen, and the boy could hear him turn to his newspaper, probably *PM*.

Meanwhile, Mom was busy brushing her teeth in the bathroom. Drowsily he repeated the Lenin title, wondering about that *Infantile Disorder*, and beginning to slip off. . . . He was climbing the right-field fence of Ebbets Field . . . playing left field in front of the hurricane fence of PS 189 schoolyard. . . .

Voices in the kitchen stirred him awake, even though he didn't want to be.

"I asked you not to have those meetings here in the house any-more."

"Don't be foolish."

"I don't want the boy to be kept awake because of it. I begged you to take the Applebaum apartment across the hall six months ago so he could have his own room, but you wouldn't hear of it. Five dollars a month more, forty-one stinking dollars a month and you wouldn't do it."

"Five dollars here, five there—to you it grows on trees."

"And I don't want that . . . that 'stuff' talked about here."

"What 'stuff'?"

"You think you're the only smart one in the world, and that all the rest of us are so stupid. And that I'm such a dummy. You know what 'stuff.' You and your damned Communism. One day they'll run you out of the country, and I'll watch it with pleasure, be-lieve me."

The boy, lying in his bed, almost shivered from the father's anticipated reaction.

"You probably would, wouldn't you? Ah, are you smart."

"Why not? And why, if you hate it so much here, why the hell don't you go back there? See for yourself what it's like. Because you'd come running back in a minute, with your tail wagging, *if* they ever let you out. You're so smart, but you know what? You're the stupid one. This is the free country, and all you do is to knock it. 'Overthrow the capitalists.' You and your slogans. Well, no more of that crap here. If they catch you meeting with your 'cells,' let it be elsewhere and not where we live."

" 'Catch you,' that's all she knows. 'Catch you.' Why, am I a criminal? Because I have a different view of society? You're a peasant, Rose, and—"

"I may be a peasant, but I have more common sense in my pinky than you have in your whole big brain. And I appreciate this country. Not like you and your mockie friends. Anyway, I don't want Aaron subjected to your Commie talk."

"Aaron? What are you talking about? First of all, he's been asleep for hours."

"You mean he's been up for hours. Probably getting his head filled with your *meshuggah* ideas."

"Of course *you'd* rather have his head filled with baseball ideas. Or playground ideas. Or other *narishkeit* of great interest."

"Don't you worry about what he learns or picks up. Anything is better than your Bolshevik bullshit."

The boy heard the pause, and tried to pause with them. His heart had begun to race, and he was glad that maybe now it was over.

The teaspoon was once again clanging the glass loudly, however, stirring the tea.

Say nothing to him, Mom, just turn and walk out. Come on. He pulled tight his pajama drawstring, hoping.

But just as she was turning and leaving, Father said, "I won't have twenty dollars for you this week. You'll have to make do with fifteen."

"What?"

"You heard me. It's a difficult week."

"Oh no I won't. You'll bring us the twenty. I promised Aaron a new pair of dungarees over a month ago, and still haven't bought them for him."

"What's wrong with the old pair?"

"You are something. I've been mending seams and holes in them for nearly two years. Look, you attend to your business, and I'll attend to mine, which is this house. I never should have let you talk me down to twenty lousy bucks a week, that was my mistake."

"What do you want me to do, steal for the extra five?"

"I don't care what you do. If you have to steal, steal."

"Sure. You wouldn't care. Well, a thief I won't be, for you or anyone."

"You know what? You are ridiculous. Plain ridiculous. Make sure, Harry, the twenty bucks are here on Friday."

"And tell me, where shall I get it if it's not there?"

"Don't tell me that. You go to work every day, what are you getting for it?"

"You think it's so easy, eh? You go out and try to earn a living."

Was he right, the boy wondered? Was he being pressed unfairly?

"Everyone else does it, why not you? And everyone else is doing it well these days, except you. Why? Because you're a fool in business too. You're just as arrogant and foolish there as you are in politics. You don't know people and never will. You're always trusting the wrong ones. Anyone who flatters you gets your money—when you have money."

"All right, that's enough. You and your big mouth. That's enough now."

"That you don't want to hear, do you? Well, if you can give that shyster Margolis fifteen hundred dollars for three 'bargain' embroidery machines, two of which break down the next month and you're stuck, you can buy your son a pair of new dungarees every two years!"

Then, abruptly, the boy's stomach gasped as he heard the smack, and then a second.

And he was up and out of bed and on his way to the battleground by the time his mother was crying out, "You bastard, you dirty bastard! You'll be paid back for this one day, I promise you!"

"Don't you hit her!" he yelled at the kitchen entrance, and rushed inside.

He was intercepted by his mother, however, who grasped him tightly to her. She said, "No, you stay out of it. I'll handle him, *kind*."

"You keep your hands off of her, if you know what's good for you!" he threatened the father, struggling to get free to face him squarely.

The father shook his head in dismay. "Ahh, you've poisoned his mind against me completely, haven't you?"

"I don't need to poison his mind. He has his own eyes and ears, that's all he needs."

Papa loomed by the stove, his brown eyes hesitating between fury and disappointment. Or was it fear of some sort?

"Come back to bed, sweetheart. Come."

He took one more thorough look at the sturdy, hairy monster, dressed like a gentleman in white shirt, tie, and wide-bottomed trousers. Just try to touch her again, he said to himself, clenching his fist, just try.

The father now reached out to Aaron, saying, "Where can I get the money if it's not there, sonny boy?"

The boy's plan for revenge was interfered with by the sudden plea.

"Come on, back to bed. He's crazy."

So the boy, crazy now too, was led back to the living room, and his bed, by the comforting presence, his heart still shuddering.

Tucked inside his blankets, he inquired, "Are the Commies so bad, Mom? Are they really like criminals? And what's 'infantile'—"

"Go to sleep, honey. It's very late. We'll talk about it some other time." And she kissed him good night again.

But he knew that they wouldn't. He'd have to make his own judgment about that. . . . Would they really chase Papa out of the country because of that stuff? Well, he deserved it, right! . . . Right? . . . Did that mean actually taking him to the boat and putting him on it? With handcuffs even? . . . But hadn't Roosevelt sent father a letter thanking him for his Air Raid Warden work during the war? How then had he been doing anything wrong? He remembered fondly sitting on Papa's lap near the end of the war, listening to Gabriel Heatter or the President on the radio describe the way the Allies were driving toward Berlin. And the Allies meant the Russians as well as the British and Americans. Confusing. For clarity, his mind returned to those two slaps, and he tried to focus on the small scene in the kitchen, losing ground fast to sleep.

The next morning, Papa was in the kitchen early, making breakfast. Soft-boiled eggs, fresh bagels, and lox, his favorites.

"Where's Mom?"

"*Schluffin*, what then?" He smiled at their private joke.

Aaron took his seat at the wooden table, downed his orange juice, and glanced briefly at the early morning workers hurrying past Woolworth's, heading for the El. His bagel had already been prepared for him, with butter, cream cheese, and lox.

Father moved from the stove to the sink to the table, bringing the eggs in a pair of glass egg cups. He wore his vest undershirt, with a dish towel over his shoulder. He set down the eggs, and sat down himself, opposite Aaron.

The boy sliced away the top of the egg with his knife, just as his father had taught him, and salted the egg before dipping his teaspoon in for a bite. The consistency was perfect, though he wouldn't say so aloud.

"So, *boitchek*, what's in school today?"

"Same stuff. Nothing unusual. An exam in long division."

"With that *schmendrik*, what's her name?"

"Miss Fitzpatrick. She's not a *schmendrik*." He chomped on the bagel, made with just the kind of small bites of lox that he liked.

The father salted his eggs heartily, and drank his coffee. At his son he looked cheerfully, his brown eyes open and warm.

"I hear you need dungarees. Why didn't you tell me, sonny boy?"

He looked up at his father, though he didn't want to. "I told Mom, she told you. Ah, it doesn't make any difference."

"Of course you'll have a new pair. Some weeks are bad for me, that's all. But if you need them this week, I'll get the money."

He had been waiting for so long, another few weeks wouldn't matter, he knew. "I don't need them right away, I suppose."

Father sought to take his hand, but the boy slid it away.

"You know, it's not all one-sided. I do my best, *boyala*. You don't always have to believe your mother's version of things."

The boy ate in stubborn silence. Now and then he looked upward, and saw the tufts of chest hair edging up out of the undershirt.

"Could they really send you back?"

"Deport me?" His father looked up, astonished, as though he considered it for the first time. Then he smiled, palely though, and said, "Of course not. Your mother was just talking."

He chewed his bagel. A siren whirled in the streets.

"Why do you always have to hit her?"

The father laughed, embarrassed. He made a weak gesture with his hands, expressing helplessness. "A slap? I didn't hurt her, foolish boy. I wouldn't do that."

"Yes you would. And do." Saying this hurt the boy too, made his head and chest pound, and he had to keep from crying.

The father stared at him, a half-smile frozen on his lips, and slowly shook his head.

Finally he murmured, "Finish your bagel and I'll make you another, yes?"

Yes, he wanted another, but he was moving on another track. "I want you to know," he said, "that if you try to do that again, I'll get you, I really will. And something else." And raising himself up as though to put his eight-year-old body behind his grown-up warning, he plunged forward into another, odder territory of the unknown, declaring, "I think Stalin was wrong, he did betray the Revolution, and from now on I'm going to be on Trotsky's side, no matter what you say!"

For a moment he faced his father straight-on, having little idea of the strength of his news, only of the whereabouts of the target. Yet, as he watched his father's face slowly record the shot, the eyes narrowing and the color fleeing, the boy felt his chest surge with victory.

Then, in fear, he fled from the kitchen.

* * *

It was only much later, crouching in the thick woods of Lincoln Terrace Park with his school satchel filled with *Sport* magazines, after he had decided to skip school and play hookey for the first time in his life, that he felt like an outlaw, a criminal. And there, on Dead Man's Hill, nearly sick from the turmoil swirling his stomach and filling his head, it slowly dawned on the boy that he now understood something of what his father must feel, maybe even what it meant to be a real Commie. And maybe, too, what it was like to have an "infantile disorder," words that he had looked up in the dictionary and didn't really apply to himself, until now, when he remembered the second definition: "Lacking maturity, sophistication, or reasonableness." Yes, the disorder hitting him now was like that, he figured, as the big trees rustled from the wind and his heart beat rapidly from the chaos.

L-A-V-A, L-A-V-A

T he William Waltke Company, of St. Louis, Missouri, began to manufacture Lava, the Hand Soap, around the turn of the century. Then, it was a gray-colored bar, containing a pleasant enough scent, but gritty and "pumice-powered," used especially for tough, grimy jobs. Though most homes carried the bar as an auxiliary soap—along with Ivory, say—Lava was a great success. In 1927, Procter & Gamble of Cincinnati, Ohio, purchased the company from Waltke, and has manufactured the soap ever since. In 1956 the color of the bar was changed to white, and, later, to pink. Along the way, the aroma became a floral spiced scent, a slight concession. But it remained a soap for heavy-duty use, not one for your everyday bath or shower.

If you called the Cincinnati number, you'd get Customer Service at Procter & Gamble, and the lady with a slight twang in her Midwestern accent tried her best to help you out about Lava. However, she knew little about the history of the soap, and nothing at all about the old *FBI in Peace and War*, Lava's claim to legend. This was the radio program that formed part of the native folklore for the boy of eight, beginning in the late forties. Indeed for the whole generation that grew up after the Second World War, and listened attentively to the radio for their news of the world, their sports, their entertainment, L.A.V.A. was immediately associated with *The FBI*, just as, say, Ralston Cereal was part of *Tom Mix*, Pillsbury at one with *Grand Central Station*, Ovaltine with *Captain Midnight*, Wheaties, Breakfast of Champions with *Jack Armstrong, All-American Boy*, *Sky King* with Peter Pan Peanut Butter. It's a little difficult for television-raised watchers to gather the enduring significance of the old radio heroes, characters like Jack Armstrong, Frank Merriwell, Helen Trent, the Green Hornet, the Shadow, the Thin Man, the Lone Ranger. These were mythic heroes, engrained in the consciousness of young kids for a long time, maybe in their hearts forever, and reinforced by tokens, such as magic rings or badges, and theme songs, like the William Tell Overture. The age of heroes was never more secure than in those high victory years, after our Last Just War.

But this was home ground, remember. So, as with L-A-V-A and *The FBI*, the shows' commercial sponsors, aided by their richly voiced announcers and catchy slogans, were equally memorable. "Is it a bird, is it a plane? No, it's Superman!" Or, from Sergeant Preston of the Yukon: "Mush you Huskies, mush! On, King, on!" And from the sonorous bass voice of the Lone Ranger's announcer, those immortal words, "A fiery horse with the speed of light, a cloud of dust, and a Hearty Hi Yo, Silver, Awaay!" And, to make more gloomy your late Sunday afternoons, that thin voice (and ambiguous laugh) declaring, "What secrets lurk in the hearts of men? Only the Shadow knows!" Voices and words to scare you, elate you, transport you, depending only on your imagination. Have those of us who stayed glued by our Philcos or Stromberg Carlsons ever quite recovered from those days of belief in fair heroes—just cowboys and detectives, brave pilots and Canadian Mounties—or replaced them in our adulthood? We try, with literary figures maybe, and maybe even come close. Probably not. For childhood is its own pure realm, where enchantment of the imagination reigns supreme, and where, in the 1940s and early 1950s, radio was its chief handmaiden, a signal for illusion, a frequency for pleasure.

What confusion then when you had a sharp needle of the real

inserted suddenly into that diaphanous bubble of imagined beauty! Real agents instead of radio voices for Case Number 8216? Hey, what was going on here? This was supposed to be a kid's world, fellas. Hold on, will ya? Give a kid a break. Couldn't the boy simply *imagine* the belted trench coat, the villain's mustache, the grimly intimate questions? Did they all have to come true suddenly? And did real father, family bully and foolish leftie that he was, failed father and failed husband too, really have to enter into the scene, and be suddenly converted into a kind of Public Enemy Number One? With son encouraged to be accomplice? . . .

No, America, you can do better than that.

Maybe not in 1951, though.

Home from school, recovering from a cold, I was reading my *Sport* magazine, a long piece about Gertrude Ederle swimming the English Channel, with a picture of her, oil-slicked, entering the icy water, when there came the ringing of the doorbell. Mom was hanging up the wash on the low roof outside so I went to answer it.

Before opening the door, I asked, "Who is it?"

"Is this the Schlossberg residence? Harry and Rose Schlossberg?"

The word "residence" struck me, and I opened the thick steel door. "Yeah, that's us. What do you want?"

The bulkier, darker-looking fellow answered. "My name's Bradley, Walter Bradley. And this here is Frank Dobbs, Jr." He flicked open his wallet, and said, "We're from the F.B.I., son. Is your mother or father home?"

It took me a few seconds to adjust to the words, and finally I said, "May I see that I.D. again, sir?"

The man showed it to me again. Stepping inside the lighted foyer, I looked at the credential closely. Actually, I had to look two or three times to see the resemblance from the younger man in the photo to the older man before me. Only the crew-cut styles in both pictures seemed the same. But the printed words, Federal Bureau of Investigation, with the name (and signature) of J. Edgar Hoover at the bottom, were clear enough. Whew!

"Come in," I offered, and led them through the long hallway to the kitchen. "My mother's out on the roof with the laundry. Should I get her?"

"Well, sure, but there's no need to rush, if she's coming in right away."

"Yeah, she should be in a few minutes. Uh, sit down, won't you?"

My heart was beating rapidly, just from the sound of those three magical letters: F.B.I. Immediately the announcer's guttural voice of the soap commercial for the radio show echoed in my head, "L-A-V-A, L-A-V-A," and I could hear the rattle of the machine gun.

The pair entered the kitchen, Mr. Bradley removing his coat, but Mr. Dobbs still wearing his. A tan trench coat with a wrap-around belt, just like the movies.

"Sit down, please," I repeated, surprising myself with my sudden manners.

They complied, each taking a straight-backed chair and sitting at the wooden kitchen table covered with the slick oilcloth.

Nervous, I said, "Uhm, can I get you anything. Maybe coffee?"

"No need, thank you, son."

I was glad for that, since I was unsure how to brew the stuff.

"Tell us, you must be . . ." And here Mr. Bradley, who had a slight twang in his voice, consulted a small notebook. "Aaron, the son. Age twelve, correct?"

Surprised, maybe even flattered, I corrected, "Almost twelve, sir."

Mr. Bradley nodded, and leaned back, noticing the magazine. "Baseball fan?"

"You bet," I said, happy for that direction.

"Who's gonna win this year in the National, do you think?" Mr. Bradley said.

"Dodgers. Easy."

He nodded, and played with his brimmed hat, turning it every now and then like a top. "I'm afraid you're right. Even though I'm a die-hard Card fan, from way back."

"Well, St. Louie's pretty good, you know," I acknowledged,

and chatted on. "Musial, Schoendienst, Slaughter—oh, they're a tough club all right."

A pause, and then Mr. Dobbs spoke up, for the first time. "Tell me, Aaron, does your father have friends who've come around and talked politics, maybe speaking in Russian?" His short mustache reminded me of Thomas Dewey's, and for that reason alone I didn't take a shine to him.

"Hey, Frank, shouldn't we wait for—"

Mr. Dobbs held up his hand, on which he wore an insignia ring, from college or high school I figured. "You don't have to answer us, Aaron. Please understand that. But you might be able to help your father out, if you do."

My blood began pumping strongly, spinning my head. "Sure," I said boldly, maybe too boldly. For then I sagged somewhat, and took a seat too. "What's he done?" I asked weakly.

Mr. Bradley intervened, and held his hands wide. "We don't know, son, that he's done anything. Anything wrong that is. That's what we're here trying to find out."

Should I tell them about the regular meetings he used to have here, in the apartment, with the group of his Russian cronies? I didn't know, really. But I wished that Mom would come in soon!

"Well, what do you think he's done? I mean, 'suspect' he's done?" I was proud of my distinction.

Mr. Dobbs answered. "Well, we suspect that he's held cell meetings here, or elsewhere. Communist cell meetings." He held his black lead pencil, a Cross, ready by a small notebook. "You're old enough to understand what we're talking about, aren't you?"

I nodded solemnly, and concentrated on his striped tie. Like prison stripes, I thought. The funny thing was, I never much liked my father's Commie sympathies or those meetings—were the cells like biology cells?—indeed conducted in Russian, and sort of blamed his leftist morality for his rough treatment of me. Long ago I held that against him. So here was my chance to get even with him, in a way, but I was doing nothing about it. Why not, I wondered?

I was about to go get my mother when I suddenly remembered, out of the blue, the Bill of Rights that had always been printed, curiously enough, on the inside cover of my hardback Composition schoolbooks. "There's nothing really wrong with speaking Russian is there? I mean no law against it?"

Mr. Dobbs smiled oddly, I thought, and shook his head. "No, there isn't. You're a clever boy, aren't you, Aaron?"

I shrugged, not feeling so clever.

"Do you understand what patriotism is?" Mr. Bradley wondered. "That's really what we want to find out, sort of, if your father is a patriotic man."

"And patriotic toward *which* country," added Mr. Dobbs.

"I see," I said, and thought. "Maybe I can really help you there. Just a second, sir." And I quickly ran out of the room, to the foyer, where, from the wall, I lifted off the cardboard-framed letter that President Roosevelt had written to my father, for his Air Raid Wardens service during World War II. I brought it into the kitchen, and presented it to the gentlemen, as my Exhibit A. "Look, this is a letter that FDR wrote my father, about his patriotism."

Mr. Dobbs looked at the letter, and, showing a thin smile, passed it over to Mr. Bradley. He read it too, and handed it back to me, saying, "Well that's very nice, Aaron. Yes."

"But it doesn't quite answer the question," Mr. Dobbs persisted, doodling with his lead pencil.

I felt he was playing a game with me, and didn't go for that. "Do you think the President would have written him a letter, Mr. Dobbs, if he didn't think my father had been patriotic toward us —America?"

His small gray eyes opened out just slightly, and he half-smiled. "Did he talk to you much about Russia? About his family there for instance? Or"—he shrugged his thin shoulders—"maybe take you with him, to see Russian exhibits, or movies perhaps?"

Mr. Bradley, my buddy, leaned forward and counseled quietly, "You can wait for your mother, son. Maybe that'll be better."

I could have said nothing, of course, and waited for Mom. But I was getting steamed up by this sneaky wise guy.

"How about *your* father, Mr. Dobbs—didn't he talk to you about his hometown, or where the family lived, when you were younger?"

Emitting a deep sigh, he shook his head and gave me a helpless look, meaning I was the helpless one.

I fiddled with my magazine, and asked Mr. Bradley, "Are you a sports fan or just baseball?"

He smiled. "No, I like all of 'em pretty well."

"Good. I'll ask you a football question then. Who was Mr. Inside and who was Mr. Outside and who'd they play for and—"

"Hey, hold on. One at a time. They played for . . . Army?"

I nodded. "Go on."

"Hmm, I should remember, they were quite a pair. But I don't."

"Glenn Davis was Mr. Outside, and Doc Blanchard was Mr. Inside."

He shook his head. "I shoulda remembered their names. I'm a Notre Dame fan. I'll ask you one: when Notre Dame played Army in their famous—"

"That's easy, sir. Zero-zero was the score, and the year 1946."

His eyes widened, and he laughed. "You *are* a sports fan, son!"

I turned now to Dobbs. "Who coached Army, do you remember?"

He shook his head.

"But you must remember who played quarterback for Notre Dame?"

"I'm afraid I don't follow it, Aaron."

I gave him a fishy look. "*No* sports?"

"I'm afraid not."

"Not even the World Series?"

"Not even that, for the most part."

"Then I guess you don't think too much of this country, do you?"

His mouth puckered, and he crossed his legs.

"Yeah," I said, shifting gear in victory, "he took me with him to see films, up at the Stanley Theater, sure. So what?"

Mr. Dobbs, renewing his interest, wrote that down. Nodding, he said, "Yes, a well-known hangout, for émigrés and fellow travelers too. Did you happen to go off afterwards with a small group on a regular basis?"

And now I just couldn't resist an impulse, so I made up a little tale. "Yeah, come to think of it, we did have a small regular group sort of, and we'd go off to the chess club on 14th Street, you know that one don't you?"

He shook his head, face animated, and pencil moving.

"Well, this club had posters up of guys like Trotsky and Lenin, and of course Stalin, and while they played chess and drank coffee, and vodka too"—I don't remember Father ever having drunk vodka, only schnapps—"they really were busy talking politics. And"—I leaned forward, with a special tidbit—"revolution too. In America."

Mr. Bradley intervened, and said, skeptically, "But if they were speaking Russian, how could you tell all that?"

"Well," I said, picking at my lip and stalling for an answer, "you could figure out things by picking up key words here and there. And you see, I knew some Russian—"

"What are you talking about, you knew Russian?" My mother entered the kitchen, wearing a kerchief to keep her hair from blowing, and her faded housedress and cardigan sweater. Though she, unlike Dad, was born here, she looked curiously immigrantish just then, I felt, and somehow resented the awkward dress. "And who are *you* gentlemen?"

"Excuse us, ma'am," said Mr. Bradley, standing, Dobbs following. He introduced them both, flapping open that wallet again, and apologizing for sitting down that way, without her say-so.

"That's okay." She looked them over, asked them to be seated, and went to the sink, where she filled a coffeepot with water, and measured out coffee. "What can I do for you?"

"Well, we're here to ask you a few questions about your husband's activities, political activities. Now legally," Mr. Dobbs said, delicately, "you don't have to answer us without a lawyer present, Mrs. Schlossberg. But you might be able to help us out. *And* your husband too."

She went to the stove and set the coffeepot on a burner, lighting it. "You'll have some coffee, I presume?"

"Why, thank you, Mrs. Schlossberg."

"What is he charged with?"

"Charged? Oh, he's not charged with anything, yet," replied Mr. Bradley. "We're here to investigate, that's all. And, if the facts are favorable, to try to prevent any charging."

"And what could happen to him if . . ." She allowed the sentence to tail off.

"Well, that's not really up to us to say," answered Dobbs.

"It could be jail, it could be deportation," advised Mr. Bradley forthrightly. "At the worst, that is."

"Deport him?" I repeated. "Are you kidding? For what?"

'Treason, perhaps," inserted Dobbs. "But you can also help him, Mrs. S. Please, may I call you Rose?" he offered in his sly way.

Don't Mom, I thought, for some reason.

"Thank you. I'm Frank, and this is Wally. And really, just a few questions should do fine. For example, Rose, does he take any subscriptions to magazines that are political in any way?"

She brought over her sponge cake, laid out plates, and moved over the tall sugar jar. While the coffee was perking, she lit a cigarette, and sat down.

"Magazine subscriptions?" She shook her head no.

Mr. Bradley flipped a page from his notes. "Doesn't he get the IGLWU newspaper? He's a member of that union, isn't he?"

"Well, I think he is. Maybe he does get their paper, I see it here occasionally. Why, is that an illegal paper? Or that union?"

Mr. Dobbs smiled, a smile trying falsely to be forgiving. "Let's say it's very suspect, that union. You realize, there is, or seems to be, a number of Communists in the garment industry. And fellow travelers. So it wouldn't be surprising if the leaders were very suspect."

" 'Scuse me, sir, but what is a 'fellow traveler' exactly?"

"Sure," said Mr. Bradley easily. "Someone who travels with the Communists, who believes in them, though he may not be a regular card-carrying member."

"Well, are they bad too? I mean, just as bad as the Communists?" I almost said Commies, which I didn't feel like using in front of these guys. "Is that illegal too, being one of those?"

"That's a good question, son," said Dobbs. "Let's say we're interested in both sorts, and in sorting out one from the other. And since we're not the judges, we can't tell you if one is as dangerous or illegal as the other."

"But then how can you be hunting down these fellow travelers if you're not sure how bad or how guilty they are?"

"The boy's gonna be a lawyer, Rose, that much is clear!" joked Dobbs.

She stood up now, and went for the coffee. While she poured out three cupfuls, Mr. Dobbs asked, "Any other literature or magazines?"

She hook her head tentatively. "I don't think so." She sat down again, and cut slices of the spongy yellow cake for the men.

"Why, thank you, Rose. What about his family back in Russia? Have they corresponded much between them, back and forth?"

My mother shrugged her shoulders. "Oh, they've written to each other through the years, sure. But how much, or what they said, I don't know."

"He still has three brothers and two sisters there doesn't he?" queried Dobbs. "Besides his mother."

"The mother's dead. And at least one of the brothers and one sister died during the war, I know."

"Hmm, this is mighty good cake," admired Mr. Bradley. "I might come back for seconds." His laugh was jolly, out of tune with the moment, and his true purpose here, I realized.

At the same time I admired my mother, for her poise in facing them and also for her restraint in speaking of Papa. He was not a friend of hers anymore, hardly a husband, and she could have been answering these queries in a different manner, more dangerous to him. Especially since she had continually warned him against his outspoken "Rooskie" desires and leftie talk.

"Were there any explicit Communist activities that he took part in, Rose?" asked Dobbs.

"Not that I know of."

"What about the groups of Russian friends that he had? You know, the ones that used to come over here, for example?"

Reflectively, she sipped her coffee, holding the cup with two hands close to her mouth. "They were friends of his, from the old country. One was a cousin. They came from the same village, or same region. Mostly they caught each other up on news from family and friends back there. Gossiped. Played pinochle. That sort of thing." She had spoken coolly, calmly.

"No political discussions?"

"Of course they probably had political discussion, it's only natural. But I don't think that was the central reason for their meeting. Not at all, from what I could see. And they didn't come over *that* frequently, after all, once every so often that's all."

Once again, she was restraining herself, for she had spoken out strongly against those house meetings, and restraining the facts she offered too. Good and brave woman, I judged.

"Did he try to get you to join any group with him?"

"No."

"To vote the Commie ticket? Or maybe, for Henry Wallace?"

"Mr. Bradley," she said, putting her cup down, "aren't we free to vote for whoever we wish to? And was it *illegal* to vote for Wallace, tell me?"

His face tightened visibly, I saw.

"Besides," I put in, "isn't the ballot supposed to be secret?"

"Sshh," she counseled me, "though he's right of course."

Dobbs returned to the correct track. "Never took you up with him and Aaron on Sundays?"

"No, that was their private activity."

"So you never knew any of the groups he met with up there?"

Uh oh, I was in trouble!

"What groups are you talking about?"

"Why, the ones Aaron told us about."

She gave me a look. "What?"

I shrugged my shoulders, and wanted to slink away.

"Were you kidding us, son?"

I looked up at Bradley. "Just him," I said, indicating Dobbs.

"You really shouldn't do that, you realize, young man," replied Dobbs. "It can be quite dangerous, for your father as well."

I stared at his clever tie, pale smooth face, and Dewey mustache, and said, "Lou Gehrig. What was his great record?"

Dobbs shook his head, not to the answer but to me, and got ready to start the questioning again.

"He played in more straight games, without missing a single one, than any other player in the history of baseball."

"Well, that's very interesting, Aaron," he began.

"Two thousand one hundred and thirty," I persisted, facing those gray eyes directly and forging on. "From June 1, 1925, to May 2, 1939. Fifteen summers of two thousand games in a row. Hard to believe, sir, isn't it?"

My mother put her hand on my wrist. "Enough, yeah? What's with you? Enough." She turned to them. "Is there anything else?"

"What about that Hebrew school that he sent Aaron to?" Mr. Bradley asked. "As we understand it, it was a Communist school of some sort, wasn't it?"

She shrugged her wide shoulders. "A 'Bund' school, that's all I know. I don't think that meant Communist."

"No, Mom, Sholem Aleichem was a real Red, I think," I nodded, sounding most convincing, even to Mom.

"Could you spell that?" Dobbs asked, writing the name down.

"Aaron, what was it like in school there? Was there any political propagandizing going on?"

Yes, for Yiddish instead of Hebrew, for learning by reading and questioning instead of rote drudgery, like my pals were put through at the regular Talmud Torah cheders. "Not for the Russians, if that's what you mean."

"Wasn't that teacher supposed to be a sympathizer as well? A socialist too?" Dobbsie was now taking on my favorite man, my Hebrew schoolteacher, Mr. Goichberg. Somehow, I'd get him for that.

"Well, his favorites were Mendele, Peretz, the Singer brothers, Sholem Aleichem, the guys who wrote in Yiddish rather than Hebrew."

Dobbs looked over at Bradley, who returned the puzzled look.

"Think carefully, Rose. Are you really saying that your husband shows no signs of Red sympathies or inclinations? Never talked about the significance of the Bolshevik Revolution, or thought about the overthrow of capitalist society, *our* society?" Dobbs smiled his best artificial smile, and tapped his pencil against his pad. "Candidly, I, we, find this hard to believe. We already have—" He lifted up his pad and flipped his pages of supposed evidence. "Are you shielding him for any reason perhaps? In one way or another we'll find out the truth, you know."

"Mr. Dobbs," my mother said, "so far as I know, my husband has done nothing illegal that I'm aware of. He may have political ideas and beliefs that are different from mine, but he has never tried to 'overthrow this country.' And, the truth is, we don't talk politics much. Also, if you don't mind my saying so, to both of you, with all due respect, I don't think what a person thinks privately, or even speaks about with his wife or son or close friends, should be a subject of government suspicion or investigation. Not by our government anyway. That's the way the Russians do things, I thought." Decisively, she took another cigarette out from her pack of Camels, and tapped it three times before lighting it.

The little speech stopped them, and surprised me too.

Mr. Bradley spoke up finally. "Rose, we're interested in preserving our way of life, our laws and our freedoms, for you and for your son as well as for us, and the only way we can do that is by investigating those who would seriously undermine our society. If we discover, in the course of our lawful inquiry, that nothing illegal has been committed, then we are as happy as you are, I can assure you. A good American pleases us as much as it should please you."

My mother now glanced down at her wristwatch, and said, "If there's nothing else, gentlemen, I should get to my errands now."

"Why, sure. And we want to thank you for the time you've given us," said Mr. Bradley, moving his chair back and standing.

"Here, Rose, in case we can be of use," said Dobbs, handing her a small white card, "that phone number is direct. If anything comes up that you think is, uh, relevant, or that you may have forgotten to tell us about, or whatever, give us a call, please."

He stood now too. Turning to me, he nodded. and offered, "You're a clever young man, Aaron. And I'll make a deal with you—I'll bone up on my sports. especially baseball, if you promise to try to be *less* clever sometimes. Okay, a deal?" He put out his hand.

Well, it was tempting right there, to take the hand, and make up—you know, smoke the peace pipe. But I remembered how he had dismissed my Exhibit A, the letter from FDR praising Dad, and then cast his slurs about Mr. Goichberg, and I said, "Sometimes the best deals are the ones you don't make. You know who said that? Branch Rickey himself." And I folded up my arms against my chest, like some old Sioux chief, and stood there.

"Well, he certainly has a mind of his own"—Mr. Bradley smiled, uncomfortably I saw—"and a sports repertoire to match it."

After they had gone, and we were alone, cleaning up in the kitchen, I told Mom how grand I thought she had been, handling them so well and protecting Dad at the same time.

"Don't worry, my heart was beating," she said, rinsing the dishes. She shook her head. "They both stink, believe me. Him with his crazy ideas—in his Bolshy Russia he'd have been put away long time ago, I assure you. And *them*"—she threw her head in the direction of the F.B.I. pair—"rotten too. Imagine, wanting to deport him! Is this what they waste their time on? If he were rich, they never would have dared to come here. Well, he deserves a trip back there, to teach him a thing or two about his beloved Russia! Oy, look at the time—would you be a good *kind* and take down the wash for me later? And for lunch, you'll take the pickled herring and slice up a tomato, yeah? And afterwards, maybe a sliced banana and sour cream? Good. Stay in another day, you'll feel better. And I'll be home by four at the latest."

When she had dressed, she looked trim and youthful in her smart skirt and blouse and heels, and I was sorry that Dobbs and Bradley hadn't seen her that way, a good-looking American woman. But that was okay, I told myself, she had performed fine, really fine, even in housedress and kerchief, and that was what had mattered. Despite her fresh lipstick, I gave her a real kiss and hug goodbye, and she widened her eyes in surprise, and said, "What are you up to, you *bandit*?"

An hour later, I was reading my *Sport* when I suddenly found my head pressing with an idea, and got out my lined stationery sheetpad, Shaeffer pen, and wrote a letter.

701 Ralph Ave.
Brooklyn, 12, NY
March 10, 1951

LAVA Soap
c/o "F.B.I. in Peace and War"
WNBC Radio
New York, New York

Dear Sirs:

In the past I have often asked my parents to purchase bars of Lava soap, even though they didn't particularly want to, because of the radio show on the F.B.I. that you sponsor. I am no longer going to do this, and want you to know why. I have just recently witnessed two agents from the F.B.I. up close, in person, and feel that they are very different from the agents on the radio show. I mean, these guys are not interested in capturing big-time gangsters and criminals, or even in pursuing real justice, but seemed to me to be official bullies and crummy citizens. They are not the kind of individuals who should represent our government, in my opinion, and therefore I won't buy Lava any more. This is too bad, since I really like your soap, sir.

Sincerely yours,
Aaron Schlossberg
(11 years old)

A week later, I got a note from the radio show, saying they were passing along my letter to the Lava people. And maybe a week after that, I got a note from the Lava Customer Relations office, in Cincinnati, Ohio. Mr. Bryan Ramsey said they were very sorry to hear of my complaint, but that Lava was committed to sponsoring the show, though there may be some "rotten apples" in every barrel. Grateful for the personal note, I knew my cause was hopeless.

Imagine my surprise when, ten days later, a huge carton arrived from Procter & Gamble, containing a gross of Lava soap! I mean, 144 packets of Lava's gray bars! A note from Mr. Ramsey said he hoped this would make up for any "annoyance" I had experienced.

If I was surprised, sitting there surrounded by mountains of

Lava—I had taken the packets out to count them—you can imagine what my mother felt, when she saw it. Shaking her head, she laughed raucously and said, "What did you tell them to get all this?"

And when Papa saw it, he grew immediately skeptical, saying we would have to pay for it someday, and suggested we return it. I showed him the "Complimentary" tag three times before he relented. But though we had told him of the visit from the FBI agents, I didn't think there was any point in now explaining the peculiar connection. So instead I made up a little tale about a defective bar of Lava, and this is what they had sent me. Well, that made him relax a little, and he shook his head and smiled. "A *meshugenah* country, eh?"

A crazy country is what I thought too, opening my first bar a little later, and figuring I only had 143 to go. And since our regular soaps were Ivory and Lifebuoy, I was going to need a lot of grime to use this gritty L-A-V-A, L-A-V-A.

The Public Schooling

The high schools were famous for their Heinz 57 varieties of education, both in and out of the classroom, and hardly anyone was sent to private schools. (Well, there were religious types, and other zealots from the Old World, who trusted only Catholic or Jesuit schools or Yeshivas, but the suffering kids mostly recovered.) The schools and the sites were well known: New Utrecht and Fort Hamilton over in Bay Ridge; James Madison, Erasmus Hall, and Midwood in Flatbush; Tilden in East Flatbush and Jefferson in Brownsville; Boys High and Girls High in Bedford Stuyvesant; Eastern District, Bushwick, and Manual Training in Williamsburg; Lincoln in Brighton Beach and Lafayette in Bath Beach (both in Bensonhurst); Franklin K. Lane in East New York and Brooklyn Tech in downtown (the all-city engineering school that required an entrance exam and grafted onto your flesh a slide rule as an extra limb for identification). Certain coaches, players, and alumni were legendary. For example, Jamie Moscowitz at Madison, Mickey Fisher at Boys, Mac Hodesblatt at Jefferson formed a Holy Trinity of Hoop Gods. And among other demigods were Lena Horne from Girls High, Red Auerbach and Henry Miller (the "real" dirty-book writer, as opposed to an *Amboy Dukes* teaser) from Eastern District, Daniel Kominsky (Danny Kaye) and the old newspaper editor, Shelley Winters, from Jefferson; Marty Glickman, the fastest-talking sports announcer, from Madison, Sid Gordon, the Giants' slugger, and Sam Levinson, the TV comic, from Tilden; World War II Gabriel Heatter from Boys, and sultry Ruby Stevens (Barbara Stanwyck) from Erasmus. But ordinary eggheads, like physicists or chemists, writers, singers or artists, characters who won Nobel Prizes or sang arias or wrote serious stuff, well, they didn't really count too much. Sihugo Green, Boys' splendid leaper, or Jackie Gleason from Greenpoint, meant much more than the likes of Dr. Jonas Salk or Dr. Isador Rabi.

(Of course we didn't know then that a skinny first baseman from Lafayette would one day strike out Mickey Mantle three times in a World Series and become baseball's premier pitcher; that a funny runt with eyeglasses from Midwood would become the nation's best movie comedian; and we couldn't have cared less that a kid from Erasmus was winning chess match after chess match, and already had been crowned as America's youngest grand master ever.)

The teachers were old pros, mostly boring but sometimes inspiring. The classes were large but disciplined, the sports rivalries between schools combative, the corridors and cafeterias sites of hot gossip and boisterous intrigue. Like the block in the neighborhood, the high school was a special turf, a community center, a stamping ground. The education was many-sided.

While Truman fired MacArthur and McCarthy hunted under beds for Commies, while Oppenheimer was relieved of his duties and the Rosenbergs relieved of their lives, the Cold War heated up and our high school age of innocence sailed on.

Good girls wore white middy blouses and pleated skirts and crinolines, or cashmere sweater sets and club jackets, and studied for college. Others wore tight fuzzy sweaters and hugging skirts, and often took secretarial courses. To show intimacy or going steady, they wore boyfriends' athletic jackets and letter sweaters. Gold-plated ankle chains and silver bracelets were engraved with boyfriends' names, and crucial dates. The hairstyles were (eye-level) bangs, pageboys, ponytails, some permanents, and the virtue level reached French kissing and limited petting. To go beyond that meant having really loose morals, and the status of tramphood. Some good girls achieved that status, especially in long-term relationships, keeping it a secret until the right moment.

The boys too, mostly first- or second-generation children of immigrants (merchants, textile jobbers, garment district workers), were also students of great innocence. They did not have loose change or fancy clothes, knew nothing of dope and little about boredom, and earned their keep by working part-time jobs. Occasionally they drove their fathers' cars, shark-like Buicks or chromy Chevys or black Packards with running boards, but mainly they traveled by subways and busses, and even the toy-like electric trolleys. Athletic and social clubs flourished, like "The Panthers," "The Arrows" or "The Comanchees," groups of fifteen or so, frolicking cubs with club rooms, club jackets, club sports, boasting of reversible jackets, clutch doubles or creamy hand jobs. Softball was their sport, the Dodgers their religion, girls their vocation.

Gangs too roamed, young hoods lurking in selected schoolyards, playgrounds, parks, streets. These tattooed pirates swaggered about with studded garrison belts, D.A. hairstyles, pegged pants with zippered bottoms, push-button knives. Yet these would-be mobsters, known by such quaint names as Black Hats or Syndicate Juniors or Midgets (age twelve), patrolled in known, pirate waters, and hardly ever strayed across boundaries to commit acts of random violence. (If a good girl strayed, hooking up with a "hard guy," it was a hot item.) Though periodically gangs fought each other, and guarded territory, they mostly existed as background staging, shadowy actors in the wings.

(A generation earlier, in areas like East New York, Ocean Hill, Brownsville, the legends of our real gangsters lived on. For there, Murder Inc. was founded, and flourished, with figures like Louis "Lepke" Buchalter, Happy Maione, "the Dasher" (Abbandola), Dutch Schultz, Kid Twist (Abe Reles), Benny "Bugsy" Siegel. These merry pranksters had built themselves quite a little gambling —prohibition—extortion empire, and national reputation, by their unsubtle methods: gunning down new foes and old pals, slipping ice picks in clients' backs, tossing human canaries out of hotel windows. First-generation sons of Jewish and Italian immigrants, these fellows had left their bullet-hole marks in the borough's streets and stores, and their history on its memory. Every red-blooded local boy knew their names and feats like British lads reciting the deeds of their kings and knights.)

The hangouts beyond the school borders served to extend and enrich the public schooling. Just as schoolyards were for basketball, softball, and handball, so asphalt streets and vacant lots were used for pink Spaldeen punchball and stickball with a broomstick and tennis ball ("How many sewers can you hit?" a key question). Pool halls like the Cactus Pool Room on Fulton, Barney's on East 98th Street—and corner candy stores were central command posts, where you hung out waiting for the action, cue stick or Spaldeen in one hand, egg cream in another. Beyond that, pivotal restaurants of the area became, at night, gathering grounds for teenage braves. Dubrow's on King's Highway (or Dubrow's on Utica Avenue) and Famous Cafeteria on 86th Street were always lined by milling circles of heated youth, packs of (post) pubescent warriors on the hunt and clusters of girls, prowling too. (Some parents marked these as dens of iniquity, off-limits to their virginal squaws.) On these sidewalks—or in all-borough hangouts like Coney Island or Prospect Park—young chiefs shadowboxed, kidded, gossiped, preened, dreamed, wagered (on teams or girls), jumped into a car and cruised for an hour, returning for a late-night powwow, look-see, and ice cream or coffee. No adolescent warrior of valor was ever in bed before 3 or 4 A.M.

Coney Island was special. With its old Luna Park on one end, and Steeplechase on the other, it attracted regular carloads from all parts of town. Mrs. Stahls for knishes, Nathan's for hot dogs, the Oasis Bar (on 12th) for the biggest glasses of beer, the Rollercoaster and the Parachute for the sharpest thrills, these were the landmarks. It was here that ethnic groups meandered and mingled, flirted and fantasized, picked up and crossbred. On daring rides that tested your courage, on a wooden boardwalk that ran for miles and stretched your imagination, on neon streets that beckoned with pungent smells and passing girls, the god of Neptune (Avenue) played and sirened to one and all. Out there at the southern tip of the borough, by the continuous breaking sea, Brooklyn was singing.

The Public Schooling

*   *   *

The crucial lesson maybe in all this public schooling was how to scout the territory, read the turf without a road map, know the characters. Where were the boundaries of safety, the zones of danger? Invisibly marked, they were nonetheless there and real. And whatever turf you found yourself on—a Bay Ridge schoolyard, a downtown movie theater (the Paramount or the Fox), a Bedford-Stuyvesant street, a Brownsville pool hall or Gravesend Bay park —there were rules for prudence (if not survival), codes of conduct (and clothing). Brooklyn, and its high schools, was one big, swirling beehive, a honeycomb of different neighborhoods, astir with wily Wops and tough Micks, dangerous Spades and dirty Spics and cunning Kikes, and if you could make your way safely through the zones, why you could get along anywhere, up in Little Italy, Chinatown, even in Harlem, or beyond. (Though what exactly was *beyond* Brooklyn, outside Manhattan, say—or upstate New York in summer—always seemed a little farfetched, unreal, made-up. Well, maybe Texas was real, because it was so vast, but the rest? The borough of Kings or City of Churches was its own galaxy, self-sufficient, wondrous, and endless, and you could spend your life wandering and exploring just it.)

And as you learned to scout the turf quickly, you were trained to read the characters up on stage too, the teachers and the monitors, the principals and the adult strangers. The great teacher was experience, and the real wisdom came from the school of hard knocks. The formal schooling was secondary, simpler. You goofed up here, messed around there, and paid for it, physically, emotionally, mentally. Like having your stomach drop out and heart rate speed going up on the Parachute, and waiting. Whooosh! Now, how about trying it again, out there in life, without a chute? Got the guts, the daring, the gonads, for that sort of adventure? You know, head into some corridor, some alley or room, some unfamiliar situation, where the signs are strange, and the actors are new and different? Well, why not? Wasn't that the lesson too, or the challenge, maybe the major one?

Yeah, sure, at least for this native son.

173

So, switching fields, face the hurdles early on, train yourself in going up against them, alone, on your own, and it didn't matter too much whether you hit them or leaped over; the main thing was meeting the reality, naming it for what it was, and, if need be, facing the consequences. (No backing off or going around those hurdles, though.) The public schooling was that sort of reality-track, a steady testing of one's stamina, street smarts, guts, resilience. Courage and folly too, right along.

Coming of Age

I had just finished a run-through at the synagogue for the up-coming event, my bar mitzvah, you know, all the godawful obligations of that adolescent ordeal. First, meeting the local scraggly-bearded rabbi, who questions me in his thick immigrant accent while stogie-smoking: "Who was your rabbi, Mister?" "My father." He lets fall an ash. "Did you attend cheder, where?" "I went to the Sholem Aleichem school on Topscott Street, for five years." He squints, and looks down at me snottily from above his bifocals. "A Jew you want to be, or a socialist?" I stare at the small man, with the balding dome covered by his yarmulke. Well, nei-ther, Mister, I want to say, but only smile limply instead. In his nasal voice, he croaks, "So what's your Hebrew name, Avraham?" "No," I correct him, "it's Ahren." "Can't be." He shakes his head, and takes a bite of his smelly fish, wrapped in newspaper, straight from the barrel. God! Are we really of the same tribe, this primitive Polish rabbi and myself, a Brooklyn boy and Dodger, not Torah, fan?

Only after about ten minutes of tussling do I convince him I know my own Hebrew name. Finally he shrugs his shoulders, suggesting I'm a hopeless heathen, and curls his finger for me to follow him. Up on the seedy stage, he shows me where to stand, when and how to take up the Torah, when to begin singing my haftorah reading. All the time he's dropping ashes everywhere, on his vest, on the stage, and treating me as though I'm an unwanted intruder. "Sholem Aleichem school, eh?" He fixes my gaze and bites off a bit more of his half-cigar, and spits it out. "So what was wrong with the Talmud Torah cheder?" Not much, I think, except just about everything, especially fellows like you. "I enjoyed my Hebrew school," I explain in defense. "*Hebrew* school? You kiddin' who, Mister? Hebrew you never learn and God or Torah never visit there. Some cheder. Did you bring a check for the shul, or will your father pay me?" So much for the spiritual life, I figure, and tell him I know nothing about it. He nods, drops another ash, and turns away.

Outside, I feel free, released, unbound. Back in Brooklyn, instead of in Lodz or Vilna, wherever that joker comes from. The sun is low in the sky, and the air is autumny brisk. I like my September, though this one brings the ordeal. Even old Straus Street, with its low brick tenements and cheap shops, looks sort of quaint after the seedy shul, and ghetto soul. Well, one thing my stern father did do right was to have me avoid characters like that one. What a contrast to my Sholem Aleichem teacher, Mr. Goichberg, a tall firm man of forty-five, who didn't care about beanies on your head or fringed doilies at your waist, but whether you learned some Jewish history and read real literature. Christ, what a racket those rabbis ran, I always thought, watching them bully my forsaken pals, stuffing Torah down their gullets and charging them nearly a hundred bucks for the pleasure.

I pass the local barbershop where, about a generation ago, one of our local boys, Bugsy Siegel, used to cut his victims' throats while they had a shave or a haircut. Nice landmark, huh? And what a neighborhood altogether, this rich Brownsville. A few blocks away on Hopkinson Avenue you could hear lectures on anarchism and socialism at the Hebrew Education Society, up a few blocks you went to see Yiddish plays at the old Rolland Theater, and in between, meaning everywhere, you had to watch your step. Teenagers and assorted other hoods from gangs like the Black Hats and the Syndicate roamed these streets, on the lookout for some new kid or raw greenhorn to play around with. Thank god I didn't look like a religious toady or wise-ass punk. In my old dungarees and worn sneakers and club jacket, I looked pretty innocuous. Or inconspicuous. That was the key, *not to be there* when you walked around these charming streets. Well, maybe the jacket was a little too new, two weeks old—but that was understandable, right? You get a jacket like we had, a reversible wool and satin jacket with "Charantes, Social and Athletic Club," inscribed on it, saved up out of club dues for three whole years, well, it would be difficult not to sport that around when you got it, huh?

As I was saying, it was a dilly of a neighborhood, and I didn't hang around there much, even though it was only ten blocks away or so from Ralph and Sutter, my homeground. Why didn't I get bar mitzvahed over at Temple Emmanuel, on East New York Avenue, near my house? Too expensive, that fancy place. Here, in the small dingy down-and-out synagogue, becoming a man was much cheaper. Ten or twelve blocks away, but it was a different world. Anyway, I'd soon be up at Pitkin Avenue, the large, spacious shopping boulevard always alive with customers and cruisers, the great escape street of Brownsville. Soon, I'd have a swell time walking home, maybe even picking up a fine girl, and forgetting Rabbi Levinsky and his gracious manners. Of course I might have invited my girlfriend Helen Levine to the shindig after the shul, but in our tiny apartment how were you going to get fifty people in there at one time? And besides, what the hell was I going to get out of having Helen there for that occasion, except a lot of embarrassed smiles and polite words. And that wasn't exactly why I was crazy about her.

Anyway, I'm almost to the top of the street, maybe six buildings short of Pitkin, when I spot these two characters sashaying on down, toward me. Out of the corner of my eye I spot them, and smell trouble. They're wearing their thug uniforms: black motorcycle jackets over white T-shirts, canary yellow and electric-blue pegged pants, white saddle-stitched at the sides, black pointy "spic" shoes. Long hair slicked back in D.A. style, and wavy, greasy pompadours. The shorter fellow is sporting a large crucifix, the second hood comes with huge, angled sideburns. I have a moment to make my decision: cross over the street, out of their way completely, taking a chance that they don't realize why I've crossed, or hug the gutter and pray on by. Which is it? And why now, when I'm almost safe at Pitkin?

My heart begins to pound, against reason, as I stay put on the sidewalk, slowly edging over to the street, and pretending I'm looking at the row of parked cars, keeping the teenage hoods in the corner of my vision.

Easy does it, I say to myself, almost through the danger zone.

"Hey, man, whatcha carryin' there?" Sideburns calls out casually.

I don't answer, but keep on walking.

"I said, baby, whatcha carryin' in your little case?"

Of course I'm carrying nothing, except my Torah and haftorah booklet and the tallis, or prayer shawl, I'm supposed to wear on that Saturday, tucked in the small blue velvet pouch. And they're right, it is a stupid thing to carry around.

I walk, gingerly, scraping my teeth against my lip, trying to think, plan.

The shorter fellow has now run up just in front of me, and stands there by a fire hydrant blocking my way. Built thickly, he gazes at me sideways, trying to figure out what exactly he's caught, by pure chance. A crooked smile breaks across his square block of a face, and I watch him pull out a long, rusty chain, and dangle it slowly around, like a key chain.

Christ.

"What's in the sack, man?"

"Nothing. Nothing much."

The second thug stands close by me, sideburned, wiry, and nasty, and he crosses his arms, crackling his leather. "That's a funny star on your bag. How come?"

Furious but helpless, I feel like a pinned creature, and want to give them the damn tallis bag and fly!

"Hey, come on, I haven't got anything worthwhile."

I see and feel them looking me over, deciding the sentence. The sun is way down now, a dying disc of red, and people are starting to return home from work, but no one seems to notice us. Down here maybe such scenes are everyday stuff. Above, across the lofty, purplish sky, creep a few oblong clouds in the shape of white turtles.

The shorter fellow, fixing me with his steel-blue eyes, handles the satiny lapel of my jacket, and I realize I should have worn it on the duller, woolen side.

"Sure you have things worthwhile, 'Aaron,' " he says, fingering my name written out on the jacket. "Yah got this fancy new jacket for example."

"Plus you got the velvet bag with the funny star on it."

"Yeah, you see. Now let's see what you got in the purse first." Winking at me, he takes the pouch from my hand, and begins to unzip it. My chest is constricting, my head swimming.

They see the booklets in Hebrew, and then hold up the tefillin boxes and straps and tallis. "A kike," he names the fish he's hooked with feigned surprise. "Whaddyah know."

The tall bastard says, "Take off the jacket, jew boy, let's see if it fits me."

I won't go that far, however, and don't budge. Not my *Charantes* jacket!

"Hey, come on now," Blue Eyes says, holding me by the two lapels as though straightening the jacket, "don't make us *take* it off yah, that could hurt."

For some reason I can't budge, as much trapped by fear and fury as by the two hoods. I know I won't give them the jacket on my own, and yet that will mean getting my head bashed or teeth broken.

In turmoil, I sense the barbershop pole has stopped spinning, and imagine that Bugsy, or some other Jewish gangster, will materialize.

"All right, little Hebe—"

Suddenly a nasal voice intrudes, calling out, "Hey, you, Schlossberg, these are your friends?" The overcoated rabbi is calling over to me, and, misreading the situation, mocking me.

I shake my head, in mute confusion. Why hadn't I acted nicer to him, even if he was a schmuck?

He stands a half-minute, watching us, and then throws his hand up in apparent disgust and walks off. My last chance.

"Pal a yours, huh?"

"Hey, look at the old lady's shawl," and the short fellow dangles the white tallis.

"Leave it alone," I say.

"Whoa, the boy's got a temper. Sure." He proceeds to roll the prayer shawl into a ball, nods, and Sideburns grabs me from behind. Then, with precise force, the shawl is stuffed into my mouth, gagging me.

A few pedestrians pass, but don't seem to look over. Tears come to my eyes, and the sky swims in translucent colors.

"Now let's see how the jacket fits. Hold him, Tony." Hard, he tugs open the silver snaps on the jacket, and begins to take it off.

As I struggle, he starts to pull and tear at it, and I go blind with rage, and kick out at him, catching his shin, a mistake I'll pay for, I realize immediately.

Wincing, he holds his shins for a few seconds, and then comes at me, as Sideburns grasps my throat tightly. "Let's see how your prayers do now, you fuckin' Yid!"

A strange guttural shriek from nearby, like a cry from a wounded animal, pulls Blue Eyes up short, his fist cocked in midair, and the small man with the scraggly beard runs toward us, yelling crazily, and holding what looks like a broomstick. In a blur of a moment we all recognize what's happening: the rabbi has returned, clutching a billiard cue. My God!

The action runs swiftly now. The feisty rabbi points at the thugs, and takes a roundhouse swing at the legs of Sideburns. My captor jumps out of the way, simultaneously releasing me. The two circle him, he shrieks at them, "You butchers! No pogroms here!" and he takes another swing, missing again. Only now the short bully leaps upon him, stunning him, and is immediately joined by Tony. To my surprise, the rabbi takes them both on, wrestling and cursing. In the wild motion of the battle, the cue has been dropped, and, along with me, forgotten.

"Schlossberg, help!"

My shouted name urges me to action, and, amazed and baffled,

I retrieve the cue stick, holding it by the thin end. But I don't quite know what to do with it.

The hard guys help me. When Sideburns finally manages to get a half-Nelson hold on the rabbi, his pal finds his old iron chain, and gets ready to use it, doubling it over.

With the fat end of the cue, I butt his ribs, hard enough to twist him about. "Leave him go," I say.

Pleasure flies right through me, parallel with fear, as I see his eyes widen in wonder.

"You?" He gestures with his chain. "You lift that again and I'll whip your ass."

"Take off, kid," warns Sideburns. "This is between us and the mockie now. So scat!"

The noun makes me only more deliberate. "Leave him go," I repeat, facing them. Oh I know now who it's between all right, but I'm praying they'll leave him go, for my sake as well.

"Forget the squirt. Now old Moses," threatens the blue-eyed bully, nodding to Sideburns, who tightens his pressure, "we'll teach you a thing or two about this country." And once again he gets ready to do his work, methodically wrapping his chain around the knuckles.

Clearly, I emit, "Don't."

He turns on me, and points his finger, warning me. "Shut up, and beat it."

Then he turns back, and raises up his chain-wrapped fist, maybe a foot from the straining, gripped figure.

Responsibility mingling with enchantment, I take a short, compact swing, like hitting the ball up the middle, and slam the cue stick into his arm, driving him to cry out in pain.

Stunned, he drops his hold on the rabbi, and lunges at me. I step back and swing again, catching him just below the knees. He drops down onto the ground and wheels about on his back, groaning.

I take a step closer, and say to Tony, in a low sure voice that surprises even me, "Leave him go."

I face him, at a distance, my throat dry, my grip tight.

Sideburns slowly releases the old man, who stands up and

brushes himself off. He finds his felt hat, brushes it off, and puts it on. Then he gathers the religious articles for me, and zips them into my pouch. During the minute or two I stand guard, holding the cue steady in a blur of emotion, ready to defend him, us.

The tall tough is attending to his buddy, still reeling.

"Koom," the rabbi finally says to me in his thick, painful accent, taking my arm, "koom."

Hasn't he ever learned to say "come?"

We hustle back toward the synagogue, where he locks the door, returns the cue stick to the closet in his tiny office, and makes a phone call. Police. Then, another, in Yiddish, to a friend.

He washes his hands and face, and turns to me, shaking his head. "In the old country, they're Nazis. Here, just cheap *trayfe*, bullies, vandals, thanks God."

For a minute, I see him more clearly, I mean like looking through him, through the misshapen suit, the rancid fish smells and the greenhorn accent, through the narrow ghetto perspective and arrogant Orthodox ways, and I see the younger version, dressed better maybe and speaking Polish, walking to his fine Warsaw synagogue, only to be stopped on the way, roughed up. Seeing this, through this sudden transparency, I feel awful, rotten, guilty.

He mutters, "Your haftorah portion, you zing it *shayne*, *mitt zisskeit. Du hust dos liebe, yeh?*" You love it, yes?

I lie easily, "I do."

He nods understanding, and makes a gesture for me to sit down by his desk.

"Tay?" he offers, getting out tea bags and sugar lumps, while we wait for friends to show up soon, or police, to escort us out. "A glass tea?"

And I, who understand and do not understand, neither this stranger nor our connection, our mysterious connection, take a seat.

As I roll my neck and relax my muscles for the first time, I realize that my father, who has been a stern taskmaster, would be surprised indeed to hear that his lessons have worked well, and that I'm coming of age with some style, some merit.

The B-O-Y-S Wars

It's the beginning of the fourth quarter, and we're putting it to 'em. Something you don't usually do at the Boys' bandbox of a gym. So far, it's been a typical Jeff-Boys battle, with bodies banged and bruised on the boards, defenses downright dogged, mistakes turned into wounds. The Korean War, finally finished last summer, was mild stuff compared to this combat. The gymnasium is jammed, maybe two thousand kids all screaming for Boys, except for we lonely twelve from Jefferson. And that great Boys' cheering squad, the eight boys in white sweaters trimmed in red piping, performing their fantastic leaps and agile gymnastics, leading to the famous hand-clapping chant, B-O-Y-S, B-O-Y-S, B-O-Y-S! The fever it produces makes Peggy Lee's pale.

Near the end of the third quarter, we're up by three, when we hit a two-minute run of higher level basketball. You know, where the passes are thrown with blind perfection, the defense deflects balls and creates sudden offense, the shooters swish free and easy from all angles, and the fast break is Pure Flow. Where five individual players suddenly become a Team, five frogs transformed into a prince. (Not that I'll write it that way when I report on the game for *The Liberty Bell*.) It flows like this. First, Harvey misses a jumper from the corner, but follows for his own rebound, and

banks it in. Next, Clarence tips a pass headed for the center, and
Stucky tosses the ball upcourt to the streaking Nurlan for another
deuce. A missed shot and a rebound by Tiebout, my buddy, who
takes it the length of the floor and, without once glancing in Salz's
direction, pushes a bounce pass to him for the easy two. And finally,
Nurlan, pretending casual defense, steals their guard's dribble, and
heads for the basket, slyly allowing the furious guard to catch up
with him, so he can take the sucker in on his hip for the foul and
three-pointer. Oh, it's ravishing, these timeless few minutes of five-
man symmetry, a bright clairvoyance of purpose on the golden
hardwood, something like the Keats ode we've been reading in
English, beginning "Thou still unravish'd bride of quietness." Go
explain that to dainty Violi, poetry counselor.

Bingo! this last steal by Nurlan really sets off the *bad* Boys'
fans, who are not used to their team losing games, let alone being
embarrassed, in their cozy, sleazy backyard. So, they go a little
ape as Nurlan sets up at the foul line. First, they start off with
their rat-tat-tat, B-O-Y-S, B-O-Y-S, B-O-Y-S. Then they proceed
to obscenities (not sparing Nurlan's mother), while tossing out paper
cups and program-dive-bombers onto the floor. Finally, they rave
and rant behind the basket, pointing at Nurlan. You know, part
of the ritual Boys' war dance. If we don't get you here, on the
court, man, we'll get you later. Nurlan gives off a wide sweet smile,
full of pearly revenge for past years of defeat. The noise grows so
loud and so savage that we dozen fans from Thomas Jefferson,
mostly white kids, don't dare turn our heads or glance sideways.
"Avoid the eyes," the motto. At last, the ref blows his whistle,
holds up his hands, stopping the game, and motions to the coach
of Boys.

Well, if you've never seen this act, you've never seen theater.
I mean the real thing, not the stagey stuff.

Almost wearily, the small, sandy-haired man walks to the center
of the old wooden floor, and the deafening unruly crowd suddenly
grows quieter, apprehensive. I mean, you can feel the little white
god's power, down here in the hot Bedford Stuyvesant jungle. It's
kind of eerie, seeing this slender middle-aged man, in sport jacket

and open-necked sport shirt, commanding sudden, focused attention from the packed crowd of mostly black, mostly tough, teenagers. The late afternoon feels like the middle of the night.

Pausing for the attention of all, like some Bed-Sty Olivier, Mr. Fisher calls out, "If you gentlemen don't cut out this nonsense, and I mean cut it out, I'm forfeiting the game." Some mild hisses. "And, friends, there'll not be a body allowed into this gymnasium for the remainder of the season." Slowly he turns all about, and, hands cupped at his mouth like Mr. Goldwyn proclaiming the law to his extras, repeats the same message to all regions of the gym. His gym, you knew.

"Do you believe this?" my pal Art whispers. "MacArthur has nothing on this guy."

I dare not answer.

When the Little God is finished, and all is still, truly still, he begins his trek back to the bench. Only just then a couple of wise guys crack a joke, in a remote region, causing a segment of the crowd on the far side to laugh, and breaking up the somber minute. I mean it's no big deal, right? Just a transition line, you might say.

But the Little God takes it differently—as gods must, I suppose. With a piroutte of surprising ability, the tired coach wheels about, and races across the floor toward the Tommy Jeffs' basket, where the wiseacre had shot from. For just a second Mr. Fisher stops, at courtside, looks about, and then flies straight up the narrow aisle into the stands, maybe twelve rows up. There, he moves in about three seats, and grabs hold of one kid, then another. That's right, two. I mean, how the hell did he know it was *that* pair? And holding two at once?

Not breaking stride, he lifts the two boys up, out of their bench seats, and, on display for their rapt, alarmed classmates, delivers two resounding slaps across their faces, just like the movies. Oh yeah, it is John Wayne make-believe. He then reaches up, swipes away their bopping caps, and calls to two marshals to get the pair out of there. Looking around, he calls out, "Anyone else want to be banned from the gym for the rest of the year? And suspended from this school? Just let me hear you, fellas. Just let out a peep."

And he stands there, hands on hips, looking around that sea of defeated, black faces, the toughest dudes in the city suddenly meek, devoted student lambs.

There being no takers, the coach shakes his head and retraces his steps, out of the stands, weary of his responsibility, his colonial burden.

On the floor he nods to the zebra-shirt. "It'll be okay now, Pat."

It was as though the gymnasium itself sighed, and relented, along with the chastened crowd, who buzzed in awe and appreciation. The God had appeared, spoken, punished, and forgiven.

To our coach, Mr. Fisher said, in his hoarse voice, "Sorry, Hodey."

Hodey gave him a little wave of the hand.

Thus order was restored, and Nurlan got to shoot the foul shot, salting the wound with a good-natured laugh.

The game continued, but anticlimactically, and soon it became nearly a rout. This was highly unusual, since when Jeff and Boys played, the games were so ferociously tight and hard-fought that it hardly produced winners and losers as much as exhausted warriors, backboard battle scars, grim gym wars. This one was just as punishing, but the victor and victim were already clear.

Wisely, our crew of six cheerleaders decided to cool it, and not go out there to perform their preening locomotives or falling pyramids. But Hodey, near the end, couldn't resist throwing up his towel in glee, or accepting a bear hug from old McShain, his assistant coach. We twelve fans, a lonely intimidated jury, also couldn't help standing to cheer our first team as they came off the court, greeted by the subs. After all, we hadn't defeated Boys in their place in maybe a dozen years. In fact, nobody did. Remember, this wasn't merely another gym, you see, but a special place, like a Tintagel Castle or a Crusader fortress. Down deep, we all believed, I bet, that fellas like Napoleon or Rommel might have a difficult time conquering in there.

The crowd caused no more trouble. Like the beaten Boys' players, they accepted the outcome, and feared reprisal.

But for us, beating Boys by seven, 63–56, was like winning the Battle of the Bulge or something. For now we knew, the team knew, we could take the city crown. And to win the New York City public school championship was no small matter in 1953, when a half dozen of our high school clubs were talented enough to have beaten a good many of the college teams. You see, many of our players never got to go to college, and were lucky enough if they managed to graduate from high school. Winning the city also meant going to the Garden, our Taj Mahal. For when you played in Madison Square Garden, it was in front of eight or ten thousand folks, including some very sharp fans, and some big-time coaches. When you won in the Garden, you were hot stuff, and could strut with your school windbreaker, reversible satin and wool in bright orange and blue, all over the city.

Still, the Garden was Goldilocks stuff compared to this place, where the din was deafening, the refs were cowed, the crowd was up close, close and mean.

And where, afterwards, you still had to get out of the building, the schoolyard, and the neighborhood, safely. From one battle to another, see? (And they thought that Heartbreak Ridge was a tough-go.)

After the game we lounged in the hallway, not straying far from the dressing room, still floating on our game high. Was there anything like a high school win over your toughest opponent on their turf? Did Arthur and his Knights of the Round Table feel this good after routing some Saxons for example? You hardly noticed the peeling wooden corridors, the foul bathroom smells, the menacing characters passing. Our small group buzzed and sawed, replaying give-and-goes and tough picks and catching up on every clutch shot and nuance. All the time waiting for the players to emerge, so we could all escape there together.

Analyzing the rough rebounding, Artie and I walked a dozen steps to the corner water cooler, peering narrowly ahead. I awaited my turn behind two others, and was just tasting the jet of cold water when suddenly my arms were seized, and I was shoved up against the wall, in a darkened alcove. A switchblade knife was clicked open in front of me, and held a few inches from my chest.

"You four-eyed fucka, whatcha got on ya?"

In shock, my chest constricted. I couldn't speak, and I shook my head, trying to recover oxygen and sense in this new zone.

My assailant, a brown baby-faced fifteen or sixteen, was wearing a slanted blue beret, a ragged sweatshirt, and dark glasses. He dangled the blade in front of me, dazzling me.

"Give me your money, sucka," he demanded softly, "and move wrong once or holla out, and you're cut."

A noisy silence while the words sunk in. Very slowly I put my hand to my dungaree pocket, and took out the three or four dollars I had. And held them out for him.

He took it, and, seeing the amount, spit in disgust. "Sheet. You betta do better'n that. Or Plug here is gonna get a little upset."

Only then did I perceive the wide mound of a fellow, like a fire hydrant in black T-shirt and trousers, standing behind him.

A school bell was ringing, students passed and friends were talking, but it was all far, far away. Where was Artie? My basketball high? And what could I do?

"Look, I got some change, that's it."

"You white sucka—if you're lyin' to me, you is cut. Search him, Plug."

The hydrant searched me, swiftly and roughly, and shook his head, taking the quarters and dimes from my change pocket. Then the Switchblade said, "Hey, looka here, the boy has a watch, imagine that. Comin' all the way over heah to tell the time." He eyed me warily. "Take it off, mah man."

Weakly, I resisted, saying, "Hey, come on, my mother gave me—"

He stunned my face with the back of his hand.

"Fuck your mother, and don't give me lip. This is mah turf, and you're steppin' on it. Hand it ovah, nice an' easy."

Bewildered, hurt, I unloosed the strap, hands high in front of me. Glancing about, I noticed another presence entering the field of vision.

The boy noticed too, and spoke up. "You need something, man? We doin some bus-i-ness here."

And for a moment, a long five seconds say, I had my chance: to kick him hard in the balls or shins, knock the knife away, and escape down the hall! Fear and anticipation charged me, just as the glee and power of the game had lifted me.

But I couldn't move, only adjusted my glasses. And the stranger, like the last train out, slipped on by.

Now the baby-faced thief turned his attention back to me, pulling the wristwatch from my hand. Eyeing it, he said, with pleasure curling his thick lips, "Ben-rus, tell your mother she has taste." For a few seconds I found myself sliding suddenly into his battered bedroom, shared maybe with two other brothers, seeing his one pair of torn sneakers and change of hand-me-downs, and I figured that this watch might be a real Christmas present.

"Now fuck off, go on! Turn your white ass and move it, 'fore I lose my sym-pathy." And he shoved me on my way.

My head a blur, my heart revving, I reeled down the corridor.

"Hey, you all right?" Art said, "They grabbed you just like that, while a lookout grabbed me off—you look white as a sheet."

I restrained my exploding heart, and head, saying, "Yeah, I'm okay I guess."

He asked what had happened, and I began to stutter an answer when the players emerged, holding gym bags and strutting with pride.

"C'mon, let's move outta here," assistant coach McShain advised, "this is a war zone," and we all moved off together. Our small caravan was escorted outside by several Boys' marshals, identified by armbands, and taken to the waiting bus, on Putnam Avenue. Boys High loomed like a medieval fortress.

Inside, I sat alongside my friend Tiebout, and, trying to disguise my shaking, I asked him about the game.

On the court Tiebout was an aggressive, firm six-foot-four-inch forward who could mix it up with anyone, and who would probably make All-City. Off the court he was soft-spoken and reflective, as skillful with the sketching pen as with a basketball.

"Yeah, we played tough, didn't we? We didn't lose our cool when they caught us at halftime. Except for Hodey—he always gets a little unwound during the game." He smiled, and offered me half his orange.

I took it and ate listlessly.

A handsome, light-skinned Negro, he had had a long romance

with a blond girl at the school, and we had spent many an evening over "Earth Angel" and "I Need Your Love" on the radio, sweating the difficulties of the situation. At the same time I had wound up dating an old flame of his, a beautiful ninth-grade mulatto, with the tender, mottled skin of a doe. For our preferences, considered off-limits, we both had caught some hard flak from schoolmates. Late at night I would scribble notes for a novel about those exotic intimacies, and ensuing attacks.

"Hey, what's wrong? We won, you know. I thought you'd be a little happier—what's goin on?"

"Well, I was . . . until—" In fits and starts, I explained what had happened.

He shook his head in dismay. "They've got some animals over there. Why didn't you say something?"

"When? And to who?"

Considering the matter, he said, "I have a cousin over there who knows his way around. I'll ask him about the watch. Damn, that's tough luck." He nibbled at his orange. "They should close that place down anyway. It's run-down, and overcrowded, and becoming a little Sing-Sing. Sorry, pal."

I nodded. And determinedly switched tracks. "It was a great game, though. You guys really came through."

The bus took off, leaving Putnam Avenue and that witch's castle of turrets and spires, silhouetted in the dusk. As we headed down Fulton, and through the dilapidated streets of Bedford-Stuyvesant, I tried to recover my high, the explosive, punishing pleasure of the game. Crossing my arms, I unwittingly felt the absence on my wrist, and sensed anew my loss.

Had I been chicken, unmanly, not to take that moment's opportunity and kick the bastard in the balls and run off with my wristwatch intact? I told Tee about that opportune moment, and asked his opinion.

He shot me a look. "You crazy? The man had a knife, right? You would have been cuckoo to try anything smart with him." He emitted a little laugh. "Save your 'manliness' for other things, like Shirley and the chickadees. Don't mess with the animals, and never on their ground. Feel good you did just what you did—nothing."

To hear that verdict pleased me, though I wondered how much friendship influenced judgment. Slowly I returned to basketball, savoring the fast breaks, the give-and-goes, the aggressive rebounding, those special two minutes. Remembering my own nervousness during the game, I asked him if he had felt any.

"Sure. Till I got movin, and till I got hit pretty well the first time I went inside." He shook his head. "Still, you gotta stay cool, especially in their place, and when the pressure is on. Otherwise you don't have a chance." He paused. "Whew. I don't know how we did it, you know. *Beating Boys at Boys*," he sort of sang the line. "That just ain't supposed to happen."

I considered his private code. "And rarely does."

"There's a first for everything, isn't there?"

For real fear and folly too? I wondered. And by the time we were back down by East New York, our territory, I had somewhat given up my naive ideas of courage and cowardice, and rather considered the incident as one lost skirmish. Alongside the larger victory. Was that the right way to view it?

"That was a helluva left-hand lay-up you made in the last quarter," I said, "driving in from the right side."

A half-smile. "The cat guarding me was mouthing off to me just then, so I guess I had to get my revenge."

And while darkness invaded the bus as it headed for its first stop, we replayed some of the better moments, lacquering the game with the varnish of spoken memory.

"Well, you'll have something to write about, won't you?" he mused, a fan of my sports writing.

"Yeah. But I'll have to leave out the Benrus, which is part of the story. You just don't win straight and clear over there, do you?"

"Well we did clinch the division," he corrected. "Save the lousy accident for another story."

I nodded. "Are they just a bunch of thugs and criminals," I wondered, "or is it also that they resent white boys visiting?"

He wound his watch and emitted a sigh. "Both. Racists walk both sides of the street, ya know. Black dudes can hate just as well as whites 'cause of color. Remember Betsy Head a few weeks ago, and that little pickup game?"

I started to recall that nasty incident, when I saw that his stop was next. "Hey, Rockaway Ave, you better get going."

He got his gym bag and raised his long form from the cramped seat. Pals called out, "Sharp game, Tee," and reminded him of the small party later on.

To me he said, "Here, take this—" and he deposited his wristwatch in my lap. "I had my real present out there this afternoon, go 'head. I'll catch ya tonight." And he was down and out the folding door.

The bus pulled away sharply, leaving me sitting dumbfounded, holding his narrow golden Longines with the brown leather strap. Superior to my Benrus. The sonofagun was serious too, I knew; generous and spontaneous was his way. *Things* never meant much to him, the few that he had. Friendship did, and a basketball.

What could I do? Well, return it at the right moment.

The bus now turned down the tree-lined boulevard of Eastern Parkway. Here and there trailed bits of dirty snow from the early March snowstorm. I focused back on the game, and in a minute was making notes for my opening paragraph, about the intensity and concentration of veterans on the other guy's court. Especially when that court happened to be a legendary lion's den strewn with Lord Jeff bodies for decades.

Setting aside the stupid theft and strapping on my surprise gift—or loaner—watch, I tunneled back inside the game itself. An experience that had gripped me as much as anything in my youth. Why? Maybe it was like being in real combat, I figured, remembering suddenly Burt's descriptions of flying combat missions—where life was lived more on the edge, with extra intensity, and where honor was frequently at stake. Riding that angle, I scribbled away, my steno pad bumping. Of course I'd have to keep in mind that little blue line of separation: winning a game was not the same as winning a hill (or losing a watch the same as losing a limb).

Yet intensity was intensity, wasn't it? Or was that just me, projecting a value (and a future?), and reckoning romantically?

"Got it all down?" Artie asked, leaning over. "This one should be fun."

"Sure," I answered, figuring, "this one's turned out easy."

"A Savage Place!" or, "Kubla Khan" in Brownsville

It was going to be a great evening, like a World Series game, and I couldn't wait for it to begin. Throughout the day of high school classes and Hebrew School, I thought about my second appearance, and lesson, in that forbidden palace. At dinner, as I wolfed down my steak and french fries and my mother charged, "Where's the fire?" I naturally made up a story about a 7 P.M. punchball game. What was I going to say, that Joey was taking me up to the poolroom for a game of straight pool? Yeah, that's all I needed. To my parents, I might as well have said, "Oh, Joey's going to show me how to hold up Woolworth's." To them, the poolroom was a den of evil, a breeding ground for young thugs and gangsters. To me, the poolroom was like that "stately pleasure dome" of Kubla Khan, our big exam poem in Violi's English class, of which we had to memorize the first sixteen lines by heart. (I really loved those last few lines of romantic horror: "A savage place! as holy and enchanted/As e'er beneath a waning moon was haunted/By woman wailing for her demon-lover!" Great stuff.)

In the pink twilight, even the streets of Brownsville looked promising in the warm spring air, with many shops on Sutter Ave still open and after-dinner pedestrians strolling. Of course my appointed rendezvous gave everything an extra edge, from dull sidewalks to ordinary buses. I crossed the old bumpy trolley tracks on Ralph Avenue, turned up at Sutter and headed toward the theater, where a pack of my pals were hanging around the corner mailbox. Mel called out, "Hey, Schlossy, where you heading? We're choosing up sides for punchball in a minute." I made up an errand to run, and said I'd catch them later. Better to keep my destination a private matter, until afterwards, for bragging purposes. The last thing I needed was for Papa to find out my whereabouts.

I crossed under the El at East 98th Street, a street of shrouded darkness because of the overhead steel girders and tracks (blocking out all daylight), and arrived at Dave's Blue Room, next to the poolroom. By Dave's, Joey, who was smoking, broke away from two fellows to greet me.

"Right on time," he said, putting his arm on my shoulder. Joey was a slender fellow of nineteen, with pallid skin and a hint of despair in his manner. He looked more like a religious scholar than baseball slugger or pool shooter.

I tried to hide my excitement. "Well, you said seven sharp—"

We walked the dozen steps until the entranceway of Abie's Pool Hall, and turned in. We began climbing the long dingy stairway, lit by a naked bulb, a proper ascent to the holy land.

"Now remember, if Barney's there tonight and he asks you your age, you're just sixteen, right? Or I'm facing trouble."

"Absolutely," I said. A lie of one year was not a big deal.

Though I had been inside the pool hall just a week before, it was still like walking onto a strange stage for the first time. My head swirled and my breaths came in gulps. This was the real thing, the legendary hangout for the older tough guys. You'd never catch Stuart Sherman, pre-med at City, in there. Not on your life!

The long cavernous room housed about a dozen pool tables and two billiard tables. Two thirds of the tables were occupied. Green felt tops were lit by flaring cones of yellow light. Clouds of smoke billowed here and there, floating right up past one of the No Smoking signs. Yellow posters of boxing matches from Eastern Parkway Arena or Ridgeway or St. Nick's decorated the walls. Periodically an outgoing train rumbled by, shaking the hall. Behind a wooden counter, the man I took to be Barney clanged change at a cash register, and eyed us from beneath drooping lids.

I followed Joey to a distant table, near a dead, dusty area filled with a few unused tables, chairs, stand-up radio, jukebox.

As we passed through, a buddy goosed him, asking, "Check your gas?"

Joey shoved him. "Don't pay attention to these cruds."

"You gonna make him a straight shooter?" another said.

"Nah, I'm here to put a hustle on the kid."

He pulled the chain on the overhead light, a signal to play, and proceeded with me to the cue rack. From one of the bins he selected a long one for himself, and, for me, two shorter sticks. One felt comfortable when I tried it, and he tested its balance by rolling it on the green felt.

"Looks good, let's play."

Back at our table, Barney was already there, holding a cue ball.

A portly man with large cheek jowls, and those drooping lids, he looked a little like Charles Laughton in *Les Misérables*, chasing down poor Jean Valjean. He asked, "How old's the kid?"

Joey turned to me, and repeated, innocently, "How old are you?"

"Just sixteen."

Barney glanced at me sidelong. "You sure?"

"Sure." My heart beat fast.

He released the white ball onto the table and turned away.

Joey winked, told me to rack up the balls, and began moving the round wooden markers, which were looped on an overhead wire, with his cue stick.

After I had racked up the fifteen solid-colored and striped balls with the triangular wooden rack and lifted it off delicately, Joey said, "Okay, you break. Now let's see how much you remember."

Restraining my emotion, I held the stick on the back rail in a V for the break, with the ball eight inches away, and tried to mix power with control and aim, to make sure I hit the organized huddle. Whack! The rack of balls exploded apart, and one ball rolled into a corner pocket.

"Hey, champ, you're on." Joey nodded.

Pleased, I chalked up lightly after the break, just as he had instructed me. Carefully then, I made the bridge with my left hand, three fingers and half-palm on the felt, and a loop for the cue with my thumb and forefinger. I slipped the cue inside it, aiming for a corner angle shot.

"Hold it," he said. "Take a few practice runs with your cue, nice and easy. Feel the slide. T-h-a-t-s it."

I took the shot, but didn't cut the ball finely enough, and it stayed just by the hole, a setup.

Joey chalked automatically, surveying the table, and quizzed me, "Now where do I want to be, *after* this shot?"

I directed him to a bank position.

"Good."

He hit the cue ball, using follow-through, so that after he made the easy shot, he was in perfect position for the bank. Smoothly he went on and ran a half-dozen balls, hitting firmly but easily, and questioning me about position, and the right shot.

When he missed, he left me with a pretty easy shot, advising, "Okay, I want you to run two or three now, not just one, okay?"

"I'll try." I eyed the table, like looking at a chess board the way my father had taught me, and leaned down, taking aim, planting my feet well. I made the shot, jerking back my cue to get a good draw, which pulled my cue ball back across toward my rail.

"Nicely done."

I chalked up, and tried the rail shot, making sure to kiss the rail and ball at the same time, as he had shown me. Sure enough, the striped ball rolled as it was told into the corner.

Joey nodded, and I felt high.

I now had a shot lined up for the side pocket, but also wanted to get position for a cross-table corner shot. I took my aim, planning to follow through with my cue ball. I shot, but the white ball clacked off my green 6 straight into the side pocket for a scratch. "Damn," I muttered.

"Happens to the best of us. Look, you need some English on that." He gathered the two balls from the side pocket, and set them back into the same position. "Stand over here, by me, and watch where I'm hitting the ball." He had planted his cue on the upper-right-hand corner of the cue ball, "See?" and when he shot it, firmly, the white ball clicked the green ball into the side pocket and kicked rightward, moseying down the far rail, heading directly toward the far corner and ball sitting up there.

"Well, I won't do that too easily," I admired.

"You will, one day."

As Joey chalked up, a friend from the next table elbowed him, gesturing toward a pair of newcomers who had just entered. Joey nodded, took out change, and said to me, "How 'bout a few Cokes? Up front."

I took the two quarters he handed me, and weaved my way through the players and tables to the front counter. Abie, the second owner, was sitting on a chair on a small platform, his short feet not touching the floor, his ear cocked to the radio.

Seeing me, he said, "What is it, son?"

"Two Cokes." I tried to sound nonchalant.

"One second." He was listening intently to a low, fast-paced announcement of the racing results. To me he looked a little like Humpty Dumpty up there, with his egg-shaped face and fragile position. He made a quick phone call after the results, then got down off his high throne, removed two Cokes from the vending machine, and opened the bottles for me. He gave me twenty cents change, taking an extra nickel on each bottle, and said, "You're with Joey, right?"

I nodded.

"Well, you'll learn to shoot well all right, but keep your nose clean, you hear?"

"Sure," I said casually, not understanding his reference.

Returning with my bottles, I passed the pair of newcomers, trim Puerto Ricans sporting sharply pegged pants with white saddle stitching, round-brimmed black hats, long sideburns. I even got a whiff of something sweet, like perfume—holy shit.

At my table now, Joey was conferring with Mugsy, a large strongly muscled bull of a fellow, wearing T-shirt and dungarees, and Stansy, wavy-haired, gentle-souled, and the best pool player.

There was a vague new current in the air, I thought, handing Joey his Coke. He took it absentmindedly.

"Yeah, they were in here a week ago," said Mugsy "and hustled some high school kid for his month's allowance."

"Well, if they want some action," Joey responded, "we'll give them some, whadyyasay?" He poked Stansy.

"I'm game, if it comes to it." An army veteran, he wore his regular army fatigues, with the patch pockets.

"Hey, wanna see my protégé pocket a few, gents?" Joey smiled and laid his hand on my shoulder. "This kid's gonna be a straight shooter in a very short while."

We returned to our game, the guys looking on as I botched a few easy ones, before finally making a decent long-angle shot.

"Hey, not bad, kid." Mugsy said, tapping his cue on the floor. "Stick with it and we'll be calling on you soon to play partners." He murmured something to Joey and Stan and moved off.

We played again. The precise clicking of the balls, the practice of positioning and the different shots, the use of English and draw and follow-through, the endless chalking and racking and scoring —all this became an hypnotic repetition, an intense lesson in cunning angles and degrees of deceit. The "pleasure-dome" was all that I had imagined it to be, and maybe more. No Korean War here, no General MacArthur controversy, no term papers or geometry formulas; just this enchanted, smoky world of green felt and clicking balls and wooden cues.

Pretty soon I noticed, along with Joey, that the two Puerto Rican dandies had been engaged in a game by Mugsy and Sammy Beller, a few tables away. Mugsy and Sammy were just so-so players, I knew, so what was up?

As we played on, I thought how I'd have to try to remember all the details of the hall, to relate to my pals later on. And I felt comfortable enough by now to glance around and observe the swaggering figures with dangling cigarettes and studded belts, as well as the funny pair of owners, little Abie and droopy Barney. Though the reputation of the place was, as I said, that of a tough guy's hangout, it seemed to me to be more of a kind of zoo for odd characters.

Joey was showing me a new way to make a bridge with thumb

and forefinger (and no loop), to raise the cue stick higher for certain odd angle shots.

"Keep that thumb firm," he said, pressing it, "and spread the three fingers farther apart. Y-e-s. Now try."

As I tried it, awkwardly, I saw that Mugsy was back, and murmuring something into Joey's ear. Joey nodded.

"Look"—he came over to me—"how would it be if we cut it short tonight and "—here he probably saw my face drop, and shifted directions—"I got a better idea. Let's suspend our game while I play a little over there, with Stansy, and then we'll pick it up again. How's that?"

"Sure," I said reluctantly.

"You can practice shots meanwhile."

"Can't I watch you guys?" I was half-crushed.

Joey considered that. "Yeah, I guess that'll be all right. But you can't bother us, or the game. No kibitzing at all."

"'Course not."

"And if I say to move away, in case of any trouble—"

"What do you mean, trouble?"

He shook his head. "Forget it. Just listen to me exactly if I tell you to do something, okay?"

"Okay."

He punched me lightly. "And you're doing well, real well."

Two tables away, they were waiting for Joey, who was going to play with Stansy as partners, and replace Mugsy and Sammy.

The exotic strangers were in the act of removing sections of their cues from zippered cloth holders, and screwing one section into another, something I hadn't seen before.

Mugsy gave Joey and Stansy a high-sign nod. "New to me. They were using the regular sticks just a few minutes ago."

"So what should we start out with, sports?" put in Joey, chalking up.

"Quarter a point," said the darker fellow, who wore a tight sky-blue shirt and dark suspenders to go along with a sullen, sleepy look, slicked-back hair, and thin elegant mustache.

Joey looked over at Stan, who nodded easily.

"You're on. Games of fifty, partners rack the points. Call for break." He tossed a quarter in the air, and the second fellow, wearing a red reversible vest over a black shirt, called heads. "Heads it is," Joey announced. "Your break."

Mustache began, shooting with his hat on, and just kissed the pack and a rail on the break, leaving nothing. Stan took a chance, missed the shot, and left an opening. The Vest quickly ran about eight balls before missing. Joey took over, hit two shots but missed a slice he should have made, and then Mustache got into it. He ran the rack, and opened the next by running another eight. They were players all right. And when they continued to do well, I really got worried. Yet, after a while, I couldn't quite put my finger on it, but couldn't quite understand what was wrong with Stansy and Joey; they would make a few short runs, then miss. Not an easy shot, you understand, but for them, one that seemed makeable.

That first game was over in maybe fifteen or twenty minutes, and my heroes got beaten badly, 50–26. As Joey threw the six bucks down, he praised them aloud to Mugsy and Stansy, "These boys can shoot. What do you think, should we try again?"

"Well . . . why not?" answered Stansy.

The Mustache said, "Want to get even fast? Double up on the point?"

Joey made a face as he looked into his wallet. "Mugs, you got some green for me?"

"Sure, I'll cover you. And if you boys don't mind, I'll bet along with them."

The Vest nodded, his sleepy eyes looking up briefly.

I could feel my neck sweat a bit. Did they know what they were doing?

They played again, with a few stragglers coming by to watch. The Spanish boys stayed hot, not speaking to our boys but only now and then murmuring a direction in Spanish, and shooting up a storm after every difficult miss by Joey and Stansy.

"Nice-looking cues," Joey said at one point. "Where are they from?"

"Philippine mahogany, man."

Joey nodded, admiring.

"Stop talking and start shooting," protested Mugsy to his pals. "You and me are getting our ashes hauled here."

The winning score was 50–32 this time. Nine dollars Joey laid down on the green felt, and Mugsy laid down another nine. Wow. I couldn't believe it.

Thank god Joey looked like he was hanging it up, shaking his head. Stansy too.

Just then Mustache spoke up softly. "We give you a chance to win back your money. Dollar a point."

Sammy whistled and Mugsy sighed at the high stakes.

"I dunno," said Joey, loosening his shirt.

Stansy emptied his pocket of bills. "Why not, all the way?"

The tension was as fine and taut as any baseball game in the late innings. My chest felt heavy, and, crossing my fingers behind my legs—I was sitting up on a nearby table—I found myself filling up with tension and passion, a confusing passion.

The tension continued, though taking a different arc as the next game found its shape after a rack or so. This time the luck tipped the other way, a missed shot by one of the Puerto Ricans turning into a long run by Joey or Stansy. In fact, the strangers missed only three shots all game, I think, but that was enough. For in this game all the difficult angles and slices, which our team had just missed earlier, were now made, every bank shot was converted, even an extremely delicate rail roller was pocketed. The win was good for twenty-two dollars! Doubled of course by the outside bet by Mugsy.

The two strangers conferred briefly in a low Spanish. The Mustache said, "We play one more," and, putting a toothpick in his mouth, said, "for two dollars a point."

"That's awful high," said Stansy.

"You have our money now. A small amount. Two dollars a point."

Was that a plea, or a threat? I couldn't quite tell.

Joey shrugged, helpless. "If the man says so. . . . Loser racks."

The Vest racked up, the small crowd increased, and Stansy broke. The striped 14 ball just managed to trickle into the far corner. He chalked up, looked over the table, lit up a cigarette. Then he proceeded to hit, smoothly, firmly, accurately. When he was hot, as he was now, he was something to watch. As smooth with the cue as Cox with the glove, as on target as Carl with his pegs, as daring as Jackie running the bases. He ran nearly two racks, twenty-eight straight points, before he missed a shot. This was my Stan! Pride swept and excited me.

During the course of the run, I glanced over at the Puerto Ricans. Every now and then they eyed each other, and, for the first time, their faces changed expressions, tightening around the mouths and eyes.

After the Vest had a nice run of eight, and scratched on a difficult kiss, Joey took over and ran ten balls, making two shots he had missed earlier. Then the second Spanish fellow came up, knocked in a cool dozen before missing on a long-distance fine slice, and Stansy was up again. Could he really, possibly keep up his torrid pace, I wondered? Studying the table, he chalked up, and began to run: an angled slice, a kissed corner, a side-pocket bank, a pretty draw and stylish table-length bumper bank . . . and suddenly, in the midst of my rooting, I realized the obvious: Stansy wasn't hot, he was playing his normal game. He and Joey had simply *hustled* the Puerto Ricans. Well, after my surprise, I was delighted, doubly so. For it was clear at the outset, when the strangers had changed cues to their fancy private ones, that they were out to hustle our guys. And secondly, hadn't these strangers taken in that high school kid just a week ago? And finally, Stansy, and especially Joey, were my pals, my mentors, my heroes.

Yet, somehow, I felt funny about it, about the approaching victory, though I couldn't figure out why, and didn't have time to. All I sensed was that my full pleasure was being undercut somehow.

No surprises anymore as Stansy, cool as a cucumber, ran out the remaining twelve balls, having to go to another rack of balls to do it, and lighting a cigarette in between. Oh, it was a show, a real show, and there was a light round of applause at the end.

"Let's see now," Joey figured, looking up at the overhead wire for the points, "fifty to twenty, the tally reads to me. That's a thirty-point difference, friends, for a total of—" And here he wet the tip of a pencil point—for drama?—and wrote the figure down on a slip of paper, and handed it over to the Mustache. "That sixty bucks is for us, of course. Mugsy's bill is separate."

There was silence around the table as the two Puerto Ricans conferred for a moment. The silence was filled in with the balls being hit at other tables—though most games had stopped to watch the big action—and it grew in length and unease when no money was produced.

"I use the bathroom first," said the Vest.

Mugsy stood up, and said, "Sure. You don't mind an escort, though."

The bathroom was at the far end of the hall, in a corner, and Mugsy accompanied him down, looking like a huge prison guard walking alongside his slim, condemned prisoner.

The second man, the stylish Mustache dandy, stood solemnly, smoking his brown cigarello, staring out the high window. But all you could see out there, I knew, was the black underside of the elevator tracks of the IRT. Not much of a view.

Now, in the tense quiet by the table, the room rumbled as a train thundered in.

And though I had hated the sly shark earlier on, I had an urge now to go and say something to him. Anything. Why? Simply because he was standing there alone, in a real pickle, surrounded by enemies.

But I didn't—or couldn't—move.

As though on cue, Joey put his hand on my shoulder. "You back off now. Back up to the next table at least. Come on." And he half-jerked me back, a table distance away.

Evidently to pass the time, the Puerto Rican raised his pointy-toed black shoe to the top of the old radiator, and proceeded to give himself a spit shine, using his handkerchief.

Oh, I couldn't help admire that simple act in the midst of his dilemma! The fellow was cool and collected, wasn't he?

Finally, the missing guy was returning with his guard and we'd have our outcome. I still could barely figure out what the hell was going on. I mean, they had to pay, somehow or other, right?

"So, gents," put Joey, "where's our dough?"

Mustache said, "We pay you in one week."

Mugsy laughed, not good-humoredly.

Stansy spoke in a measured voice, "You know the rules, you play for cash, not IOU's. Unless you've okayed it beforehand."

Mustache put his leg back up on the radiator, and tucked his right arm under the other one, fussing with his cigarello. You could hardly see his eyes now under his severe black hat. "We call our friends, and they bring the debt."

"C-o-m-e o-n, we weren't born yesterday," said Joey, taking a step forward, "you call, and we have a nice little gang war on our hands. Spanish Harlem against Brownsville?" He shook his head.

"Hey, you guys, what the hell's going on?"

"Forget it, Abie, no trouble here," Mugsy intercepted the approaching owner, "the boys are just getting their dollars together. No problem."

"I don't want any trouble in my store, Mugs, remember. I can't afford to get closed down again." .

Mugsy eased the small man away, repeating, "No trouble, Abe. Honest."

After he had been shooed off, Joey said to the pair, "Well, gentlemen, would you like to pay the bill now, so we don't disappoint Abie?"

The sharpie with the Vest now edged closer to the wall, and began, slowly, to put away his cue stick, screwing it apart.

It dawned on me, suddenly, that he had reversed the Vest, probably in the bathroom. Why? And his dark eyes seemed well . . . wider, and shinier. How strange. What the hell was going on?"

"If you won't pay your bill, gents," said Mugsy, stamping his cue lightly on the floor, "we'll just have to help you pay it. Right off your body."

"You cheated us, man," Mustache threw out.

"What?" said Stansy.

"You hustled us, man."

"F-u-c-k-i-n-g Spics," said Joey, shaking his head, gripping his cue tighter. "You come across town to hustle a kid last week, and try it on us tonight. In *our* room. You boys have some balls, let me tell you."

"Empty your pockets," Mugsy urged, "or we'll empty them for you."

"All right, man," conceded the Vest, "all right." Reaching into his pocket, and saying, "No hard feelings," he removed a money clip of bills and tossed it down on the felt.

"Go ahead, count them, if you wish," added Mustache with some disdain.

I breathed easier, at last.

What happened next happened fast. As Joey set aside his cue and began to pry open the wad, Vest took an easy step over, apparently to help, and set a switchblade knife down into Joey's hand, pinning it to the table. Joey screamed, and red blood spurted onto the green felt. With his free hand he gripped the fellow around his neck, and held on. Amazed, I couldn't move.

Mustache meanwhile had stepped forward and apparently had kicked Mugsy in the shin, ripping through his dungaree leg and causing blood to ooze forth. (A penknife type-blade was glinting from the pointy toe of the black shoe, I saw.) He then tried to drive his stick into Stansy's head, only Stan had ducked. But when Stansy came up close, and grabbed hold of the man, suddenly Stansy was moving away in shock, saying, "Fuck, fuck!" and I saw his face streaked with blood, running down three grooves neatly.

By this time—maybe ten seconds?—Mugsy had recouped his balance, and whacked Mustache across the knees with the cue stick, crumpling him to the floor. He then held the falling head and brought his knee up to meet it, hard. Sammy Beller meanwhile had gotten a headlock on the Vest, bending his neck back with a struggle while trying to avoid his switchblade. Mugsy grabbed a yellow ball from the table and pushed it onto the fellow's face, causing him to moan aloud, and then forced the ball into his mouth, smashing his teeth, some dropping or flying out, and causing the mouth to bulge unnaturally with blood and ball.

I held on to my table with two hands, transfixed and queasy, the wetness in my eyes fogging over and ballooning the crazy scene. I felt rubbery in the knees, congested in the chest.

There was screaming and shouting, "shits" and "fucks" and

"Spics" every other word, contradictory orders given, people scrambling. They were emptying the fellows' pockets, holding both Puerto Ricans up against the wall. Mugsy wrapped his fist with his garrison belt, the buckle flush with the knuckles, and said to Mustache, "Here, pretty boy, some payment plus interest for using your safety razor, something to fix *your* face up for a year or two!"

Unable to watch anymore, I spun away and saw Joey in a chair, his hand being wrapped in a white handkerchief. Stansy was laid back on a table, his face a site of streaming blood, wiped with toilet paper and wet rags. I was stunned and shocked, as though I too had been hit and mangled and emptied, and I managed to reel away, to the dusty unused area. And there, I threw up, on the floor and on my nearly new Levi's. At one of the rickety tables, I sat facing the wall, tormented, confused, shaking. I couldn't seem to stop shaking, like in some nightmare where you've seen a horrible creature.

Finally Joey came over to me, with another friend, and tried to calm me down. "It's okay now, and I'm gonna be, too, really. Sorry about the mess, pal. Just a couple of Spic creeps, nothing to worry about." He shook me, saying, "Stop now, you hear? Aaron, stop!" and he slapped me twice with his good hand.

"Are you okay? Come on, kid, say something, talk to me!"

Feeling numbed and torn, I shook my head, and then found myself mumbling, "In Xanadu did Kubla Khan/A stately pleasure dome decree:/Where Alph, the sacred river, ran . . ."

Later, I just couldn't go home immediately, I felt too awful, too confused. So, telling Joey outside that I was okay—he and Stansy were headed over to Beth-El Hospital, and the Puerto Ricans?—I went off on my own, up grim 98th Street, and proceeded toward Lincoln Terrace Park, a few blocks away. The spring night air cooled and refreshed me somewhat, and I found my way to a familiar spot amidst the thick trees on Dead Man's Hill. Sitting on the ground, the trees rustling, I tried to figure things out, in my feelings. Why didn't I go to the solitary fellow standing by the window, *when I wanted to*, even if he was a cheap hustler? Why did I feel sympathy for him in the first place, a sympathy I didn't want or need? . . . When Joey got hurt, why didn't I run to his aid immediately? Fear, cowardice? . . . Was it just or decent for our guys to hustle the hustlers with a vengeance, and run up the ante so high? And did they have to beat the strangers up so badly, even though they fought dirty themselves and maybe deserved it? Were "Spics" any worse than "Kikes" (like us)?

The questions were like so many fists, and I couldn't block them or duck them or answer them away. I felt cowardly, stupid, ashamed. And my heroes didn't seem like heroes after all. Did that mean that I was different, freakish somehow, and was fated to remain that way? . . .

And would Papa who hung around Dave's Blue Room, hear about the trouble and find out that his son had been there too?

I tried to rest or hide my head between my legs, but the putrid smell from my jeans drove it back up.

When I thought of returning to the poolroom the next week, as Joey had suggested before leaving in the taxi, I decided I wasn't that eager anymore. Not now. It just didn't seem like a grand place anymore.

And then, suddenly, I was shaking and sobbing all over again, uncontrollably. Couldn't stop either. Nearly choking from my terrible paroxysm, all I could think to do was to start in again on my repetition of the sixteen lines, murmuring aloud in the darkness slowly and deliberately, and thinking how well "Kubla Khan" was serving me:

In Xanadu did Kubla Khan
A stately pleasure dome decree:
Where Alph, the sacred river, ran
Through caverns measureless to man . . .

The Epoch of Incredulity

I was in my senior year when I began using the library regularly in order to compose my sports pieces. I'd go there on Thursday afternoons, after Engelberg's deadly English Novel class at 2:15, and hibernate over in my corner-lair for two and a half hours, scribbling away. Two legal-sized yellow-pad pages made up my first draft, and, later on at night or early the next morning, I'd type the finished draft—*if* I could read the stuff. You see, I had terrible handwriting; though it started out legible enough, once I got going headlong into the story, the penmanship went downhill fast, *r*'s, *w*'s, *m*'s, and *n*'s looked interchangeable, *y* tails looped down and mingled with *b* and *t* tops, penciled-in revisions cohabited the same lines as the original text and ran wildly beyond the boundaries of the margins. It looked more like a child's road map of a fantasy island than a coherent article. But what could I do?

To my surprise—since I was a boy of the schoolyards and the streets—I came to be fond of the library, to experience it as a kind of second home, a hothouse for creative bloom. The rectangular oak tables and captain's chairs, the slanting afternoon light streaming down from the high windows, the museum-like emptiness of the place broken only by the clang of the steam radiators or the sharpening of the pencils by the librarians, all that slipped into my affec-

209

tions. Even the fuddy-duddy librarians, "Doctor" Arthur Goodman and Miss Gwendolyn Brownell, whom I privately dubbed King Arthur and Lady Gwendolyn because they acted like the place was their private kingdom, became objects of some affection. Some, I say, because they remained sentries on watch, always reminding me to keep my feet down and off the chairs, checking to make sure I returned the sports reference books I borrowed during the day, chiding me if I laughed too loud or talked to an occasional pal who might wander in, despite the fact that I was practically their only regular customer. And regular butt of their wit, or attempts at; when I'd leave, something like, "Well, Grantland, what's it going to be this week, the Kentucky Derby?" (Of course I had heard of Grantland Rice, but had never actually read him.)

Why was the place so deserted, except for exam time? Simple. Our school was not famous for its rigorous studiousness. I mean, we had some bright kids, sure, but if you were bright, and you liked to study, well you generally kept that to yourself. You didn't flaunt it by showing up at the library, and earning for yourself a reputation as a common bookworm or college-track grind. No, at Jeff in those days, Thomas Jefferson High in the early 1950s, you were better off as a shrewd-hipped halfback or jump-shooting guard. And if you couldn't be those, well, a class cutup/comedian or an aspiring singer/musician would do all right. Remember, we were a school that had launched Danny Kaye, Shelley Winters, and recently Steve Lawrence, so popular stardom was part of our heritage. Along with great basketball players, like Max Zaslofsky, little Hy Gotkin or big Harry Boykoff. Now sportswriting was okay too; and it was fair enough for me, if I were observed by "the boys"—the elite who counted—to visit the library for that activity. And having it empty most of the time, a museum of sagging shelves and old books, with only an occasional foggy student floating in by mistake, suited me just fine.

How good was I as a sportswriter? Well, that's a good question, which I actually thought about on and off. Among the current sportswriters, fellows like Arthur Daley, Red Smith, Dan Parker, my favorite was Jimmy Cannon of the *New York Post*. I read his column regularly, savoring the second-person projections into the player ("You're Roy Campanella, and you've caught . . ."), the flamboyant style, the hard-boiled unsmiling photo accompanying his columns. Though I sensed a certain purple prose there, I nevertheless tried to copy that style at times in my columns, and found it a kind of useful exercise. (For this I was both encouraged and cautioned by my journalism teacher, Mr. Drachler, who said it was fine to try someone else's style on, but then find one of my own.) I knew I was just feeling my way. Yet I understood that when you wrote about a game, just giving the facts was not enough; indeed, the facts were the dullest part. Something else was at stake, something more passionate, more spiritual at heart, and you had to catch that, if you could. It wasn't easy. But at least that's what I tried to aim for, in a sentence here or phrase there, during those long Thursday afternoons. The cozy familiarity of the dull library was just what I needed to help me concentrate, almost idly, and search for that extra spirit, or passion.

So imagine my surprise, and disappointment, when I came in one day and discovered that our bun-haired Lady Gwendolyn was missing, and in her place was some dyed-haired biddy who wasted no time in informing me that I could only take out one reference book at a time. What? When I complained to Mr. Goodman, he shrugged his shoulders and said Reference was Mrs. McQuillen's province. Well, where was Miss Brownell? "She's having an operation, son, and it may take a while before she comes back, *if* she comes back." He shrugged, forlorn. "One of those things." He was clearly upset, so I didn't push him about the new Reference martinet—my new word for the week—except to say, "Well, if she doesn't drive you crazy, Mr. G., I'll eat my hat." Barely looking up, he retorted, "But you don't own one, do you?" Halfheartedly, he added, "And she's very experienced."

Well, he was right and he was wrong. I didn't own a hat, but she did drive him crazy. Her experience was eaten up by her rigidity, and her tidiness, unlike Miss Brownell's, was somber, so much so that Arthur G. grew more and more morose and grumpy. Almost immediately she began a program to rearrange the entire library organization. The King, being pushed around in his own castle, was walking slower, looking older.

And when she gave me a hard time the following week about walking around in only my socks, even though there was no one around, Mr. G. could only shrug his shoulders in defeat. I decided to come back only every other week, for a look-see, but to try to work in the newspaper office instead, at odd hours.

It wasn't but a month later, with the first March winds gradually blowing in, bearing whiffs of Vero Beach spring training into the Brooklyn air, when I entered the library and saw immediately that Mr. G. was suddenly in his old mood, cheeks reddened and gait absurdly alert, flourishing like King Arthur again. "What's up?" I asked.

He smiled. "Does it show? Well, Mrs. McQuillen has been reassigned, and—"

"Lady Gwendolyn is returning?"

He gave me a look. "Not quite. But we are getting someone new." He shuffled papers, and couldn't resist adding, "And she couldn't possibly be as difficult."

So he too depended on the clockwork order of things around here. Good. With deep satisfaction I renewed my regular place, semi-hidden away from the front desk by a partition of bookcases, sneaked my stockinged feet up on a chair, and doodled on my pad. Warming up. Then I browsed in my three sports books, picking up a hoop fact here, a Clair Bee quote there. And finally I settled into writing, a piece about our best player who had returned to the squad in mid-season, and changed the club from good to special with his all-around court play. Since Tiebout was a subtle fellow as well as swell player, and probably also my best pal, I tried my best to catch the talents of the man along with the player, picking up my head periodically to watch the light dance and slide along the striations (new word) of oak, and count my blessings.

"Have you met her yet?" inquired Mr. Goodman two Thursdays later, with a twinkle in his eye. "You weren't here last week, as I recall?"

"No, the dentist drilled. So I haven't met her. But she can't be worse, to quote you, than that last battle-ax. Is she?"

He smiled, a smile of ambiguity, I thought, sunny ambiguity.

"Well, you'll judge for yourself, my boy, won't you? Here she comes. Mrs. Greenwood, uh, may I introduce you to one of our finest journalists, Aaron Schlossberg."

She came over, put out her hand, and said, "Very pleased. Violette Greenwood."

I shook her hand in an unusual gesture, and sort of nodded my hello. "Welcome. I hope you like it here."

"I hope so too, Aaron, if I may call you that. And please call me Vy."

"Sure. Well, I better get to work. Do you mind if I borrow several works of reference at once? They're sports books, and I'll be sitting right over there, if you should need them."

"Of course not. I don't imagine anyone will be needing such information urgently, except you. Please." Her smile lit up her dark face, and her voice inflection seemed to me lilting, lyrical, exotic. The accent was slightly clipped British.

Well, I took the books, settled into my post with my pad, and tried for my usual balance of idleness and concentration. Instead my thoughts were jarred, my imagination focused elsewhere. It didn't take long to realize that she was the wrong sort for a library: a knockout. Maybe in her late twenties, a trim figure in a springtime yellow suit and low heels, her skin a deep walnut brown (pink-rouged at the cheeks), Mrs. Greenwood (or Vy) looked more like a spectacular wild creature or Hollywood star than a librarian. Though she was dressed conservatively enough, she couldn't hide her attractiveness, at least to me, inured—my word this week—to librarians with bun hair, black shoes, and spinsterish ways.

After a half hour or so of drifting, I set to work, and didn't look up until I could smell her fragrant presence.

"Sorry, it's time to close up."

"Oh, already?"

"You really do concentrate, don't you?"

I shrugged.

"Hmmm . . . are you reading these?" She held up my two novels for Engelberg's course, *A Tale of Two Cities* and *Return of the Native*.

"Yeah, I am," I said, putting on my shoes and standing. "Well, we're just finishing the Dickens, and about to start the Hardy. Why, do you know them?"

Pausing, she responded, " 'It was the best of times, it was the worst of times, it was the age of wisdom, it was the age of foolishness.' "

I suddenly realized what she was quoting. "Hey," I uttered, surprised.

She continued, " 'It was the epoch of belief, it was the epoch of incredulity, it was the season of Light, it was the season of Darkness.' " She smiled.

"More?"

" 'It was the spring of hope, it was the winter of despair, we had everything before us, we had nothing before us . . .' Enough, I *hope*," and she laughed like a kid.

I was flabbergasted. "Where'd you . . . memorize all that?"

"In my high school we had a very strict English teacher. A British scholar who claimed that you had to know by heart some of the greats, like Dickens, Wordsworth, Keats, Shakespeare, or you were illiterate. He'd make us stand up in front of the room, and speak the lines aloud. And they remained."

I shook my head, slightly awed. "Where was that?"

"In the West Indies. On my island, Barbados."

"Well," coughed Mr. Goodman, approaching, "are we closing or are we filing for overtime, ladies and gentlemen?"

For the next Thursday, I memorized that same opening of *A Tale of Two Cities*. Just after we greeted each other, and making sure we were alone, I was in the midst of collecting my reference books, when I sprang my lines upon her. " 'It was the best of times, it was the worst of times, it was the age of wisdom, it was the age of foolishness,' " and continued on to the end.

She listened attentively, not breaking a smile, and when I had finished, she inquired, "By the way, what do you think that 'epoch of incredulity' means?"

Delighted and proud that I had looked up the word, I declared, "A time of disbelief. Maybe an age of skepticism."

She nodded, casually adding, "It's pronounced 'In-kra-dyoolity,' I believe."

I must have blushed, for she laughed and said, "Don't worry, I enjoyed your piece in the newspaper very much. That athlete sounds like an interesting person, not just a basketball player."

During the next six weeks the library took on another flavor, another meaning. Like spring coming on and changing the air, the sports, the habits, so Vy began changing me, in ways I could see and feel, and in other ways I couldn't. My old sense of the library as a cave of afternoon hibernation was vanishing. I found myself going there now on two or three afternoons, not just Thursdays, and dropping by at other moments, on one excuse—to myself as well—or another. And just as I was impressed, and in over my head, with her on that first day, so I continued to be dazzled and heady afterwards. It pleased me to see that Mr. Goodman admired her a lot too, and that they got along really well. Lady Gwendolyn was being replaced by Lady Violette, I thought. Why not? She was smart, kindly, efficient, and brought a special bracing air to the dusty place.

Smart she was—as smart as she was smashing looking. Having majored in drama and literature in college, she was forever giving me plays to read, Arthur Miller and Tennessee Williams, Strindberg and Ibsen. And then discussing them with me. Or beckoning me over to a stack, where she was stocking a shelf. "Here. Have you never read A. J. Leibling? He's a marvelous sportswriter. Do you like boxing as well?"

"Well, yes I do."

"Then you'll especially appreciate him. He writes for *The New Yorker*. Do you read it?"

I shook my head.

"Shame on you. Which magazines *do* you read?"

"Just sports stuff."

Now she shook her head. "We've got to do something about you. Where've you been all your life, huh?" She smiled, and tousled my wild hair as though I were six. But I was sixteen, and felt it, achingly. How had she meant that gesture? I wondered later.

She took a growing interest in my writing as she knew me better. Ordinary sports reporting didn't interest her very much, but if I did a column of interest, she'd comment on it: "You know, you use too many adjectives and adverbs sometimes. Let the nouns and verbs speak for themselves." When I went through the piece, I saw her point. And: "You don't always have to take the coach's or player's view, you realize. And see things only from *their* perspective." I hardly knew I was. "Have you thought of writing fiction —stories or plays? You could use sports figures if you wished. You'd have more freedom with made-up characters than in dealing with the real ones." The idea of more freedom intrigued and baffled me, and I began to consider the notion.

She laughed, flecks of green light entering her brown irises, and said, "If you ever wrote about me, you could be free to make me up. Think how much fun that could be!"

But she was good enough as she was, though I didn't say that.

At times, while this education of sorts went on, people took notice, a student here, a teacher there. Fortunately, Mr. Goodman thought the budding friendship wonderful for me. "So, how's the class proceeding? What does she have you reading this week, Plato's Dialogues yet?" And he slapped my arm, in support. "Watch out, son, she'll get you into college if you keep this up!" Strange how old King Arthur was reading, and misreading, the whole matter. Less happy readings were occasionally made by students who wandered into the library, and, lingering there, would take notice of our five- or ten-minute chats. Both Negro and white kids, but maybe especially the Negro teenagers who were attracted themselves, started giving me hard, almost intimidating, looks. But what could I do, except to look as innocent as possible and to try, at the same time, to be as discreet as possible?

When I consulted with my pal Tee, who, remember, had had his own interracial romance problems at the school, he shrugged and said, "You know I'm not the right one to ask what to do.

Everything *I* do doesn't seem to work out too well. You said she was married, right? Just go cool, so the hubby doesn't get involved." He gave a little laugh, and kidded, "Well, you only live once, kid. But boy, she may be worth it. Did you catch her the other day in that white skirt? Whew!"

Yes, I had caught her actually, and "whew" was just about right. I had never before been so taken, so transported, with a woman's behind. I couldn't take my eyes off of that sight for more than a few seconds at a time. My eye traced, my imagination roamed, the whole curving contour. What a state! Was this wisdom, or was this foolishness? I yearned to ask Mr. Dickens.

We were downstairs, in the acquisitions and cataloguing room, known to us as the "A and C Cave," working and discussing my class novel, *The Return of the Native*. Mr. Goodman had gotten me the convenient part-time job of helping Vy organize the current cataloguing, and on slow Tuesday afternoons, two thus far, we spent a few hours there. In that musky windowless room, crammed with an old desk, ragged daybed covered with brocade, bulging four-drawer files and shelves of books, and decorated with yellowing reproductions of Remington's frontier life, she typed file cards for the updating, and tested me, affectionately. "Why does Hardy give such prominence to Egdon Heath? I'll bet you don't even know what a heath is," she stated. I gave her the dictionary definition, but acknowledged, "Yeah, I guess I don't." She shook her head, "Well, maybe you better go see it sometime. Experience it for yourself."

I nodded, taking the finished card and setting it into a narrow filing drawer.

She pecked with two fingers on the old Underwood standard. "And what do you think of Eustacia Vye—a realistic portrait?"

"Yeah. A great romantic, though."

"Too romantic?"

"For who?"

"For her own good?"

"Probably."

This Vy handed me another card, and teased, "Maybe that type should change her nature. For everyone's sake, but especially her own."

"Maybe."

"You can do better than that."

"Well, it wouldn't be much of a story without her being the way she is."

"Which is?"

"Willful. Passionate. Wrongheaded." ("Willful" my new word.)

She paused, slid her chair away from the desk, stretched like a cat. "God, this is tedious." I couldn't help noticing the smooth, slender neck, and the soft bulge of her breasts as her light jacket edged away from her blouse. "Libraries, god. Why'd I ever choose them?"

I had to refocus my attention.

"Why did you?"

"Silly," she said, standing, "because I love them." She came closer to where I was sitting. "Don't you?"

"Well . . . I'm getting kind of used to them."

She stood there, close above me, and I had to stand up, it seemed. I did. She didn't move, near me, cradling schoolgirlishly two books in her arm, and half-smiling, radiating. I smelled her aroma, a mix of her and musk oil, and stared at her: the large brown eyes with the flecks of luminous green, the exposed forehead due to the brushed-back jet-black hair, the brown-red pigment of the dappled skin, a face of mysterious difference and subtle beauty. Deeply drawn, I was too nervous, self-conscious to move.

She did. Setting down the books, she took the half-step forward, smiled a broader smile, and kissed me on the cheek.

Footsteps approached above, and, as we waited, they moved on.

I kissed her now, on the lips, which were firm and thickly sensual. She kissed back, capturing one of my lips between hers.

As I embraced her, she set her hands on my shoulders, face close, enchantment deep.

" 'The raw material of a divinity,' " she whispered, and I shook my head dumbly. "That's going a bit far, even for Eustacia— incredible, don't you think?"

"Huh?"

"Hardy, in the first chapter." She released herself, just slightly, standing back a bit. "Will you come and visit me?"

What? Not fully understanding, I uttered an "Okay."

"I want you to meet my husband. James."

It took a minute for the words to go through me and register. But what did they mean?

"Really?"

"Yes. That would be . . . appropriate, I think, somehow."

Overheating, held irresistibly, I nodded, trying to concentrate on one of the frontier pictures, "Through the Smoke Sprang the Daring Young Soldier."

"Maybe Friday night?"

I gestured helplessly with my head and hands.

She moved two steps to the desk, wrote down her address and phone number on the back of a file card, and put it into my shirt pocket. "Have you been to Jamaica before?" When I shook my head, she said, "I'll get a subway map and we'll figure out how to get you there. All right?"

"All right."

"And don't look so worried," she scolded, squeezing my hand, "it's all right for friends to be fond of each other."

Friday night seemed like three months later, not three days. The journey to Jamaica, the one in the borough of Queens, seemed like a journey to the other Jamaica, down in the Caribbean. On the hour-long subway trip, I kept wondering what I was doing, what I was heading for; but I couldn't come up with an answer for either. (Tee thought I was somewhat nuts to go; on the other hand, he agreed with me, she'd have to be awfully mean to set me up this way.) Dressed in my innocuous (and only) sports jacket and open-necked shirt, I nevertheless felt more and more conspicuous as the elevated train headed into the Jamaica section, where the faces were increasingly brown and black. I kept my face in my Hardy, except to check on the stations—I had to change once—and periodically peeked out at the vivid passengers in my car.

Descending at St. Albans station, 179th Street, I followed my written directions, happy it was still light out. A busy marketing avenue was filled with shoppers, and I was glad for the activity and the walk. The sounds of Caribbean music mingled with pungent smells of cooking wafting from the houses. I turned down the third street, Oak, and walked down a residential street of shabby apartment buildings and two-family houses, the stucco flaking. At the end of the street, kids my age were playing stickball in the street, using a familiar tennis ball and broomstick. I had an urge to join them, and skip my upcoming ordeal! It was 6:20.

James Olean Greenwood was a large, mustached man of maybe forty who welcomed me with a jolly smile and big handshake. He sat with me in the small living room, asked if I wanted a drink, and made a face when I said ginger ale. "Vy tells me you're the library's only regular. Between you and me"—he leaned forward to whisper the secret—"I don't blame the students. Libraries are the dreariest places in the world. No signs of life anywhere, man. I'll betcha if they put beds in them for naps, or other activities"— he winked and slapped his knee—"they'd do some business all right!" He spoke in a West Indian accent, using a long *a* in man. "She"—and he nodded toward his wife in the kitchen—"don't know any better. Parents. They ruined her with fancy ideas. Sent her to the private British schools and all." He shook his head. "Hey," he called to her, "get a move on, or I'll miss the opening frame!"

Over dinner, a delicious spicy chicken dish with rice and collard greens (new for me), I discovered four things. First, James was going bowling after dinner, and that we could, or could not, accompany him. Second, that James, who worked in a brokerage office, had lots of schemes for making big money. Third, that Vy was not the same person here, in her own apartment. She was less talkative, less cheerful, less literary, less playful. James made up for part of this, by jabbering almost nonstop, and by exuding enough cheer for all three of us. Last, that this jolly St. Bernard in a soft cardigan sweater drank an awful lot and possessed a swift temper. At one point, Vy, speaking quietly, asked if he hadn't had enough beer. James blew up. "Don't you ever tell me, woman, not to have a good time, especially on Friday nights! What you got against me, that I try to enjoy life a little!" His look was murderous. Yet, in a minute, he was back to his former, cordial, laughing self.

I decided it would be a good idea for us to join him for bowling.

We did. For two hours I, we, looked on, and while I was as nervous as heck, my attention was riveted. I may have been the only white kid in the whole place, and attracted some hard, bemused stares. The bowlers, men and women, seemed to be mostly West Indians, decked out in canary yellows, cobalt blues, startling vermilions, like some fantastic flock of tropical birds. (Not Vy, dressed down in simple blouse and sweater.) They seemed to know each other from the neighborhood and the sport. The music was reggae-rich, the ladies (some) were real lookers, and the patrons (many) frequently hugged and held on to friends, moving to the music. The place was alive, like a jam session or carnival. And James, who knew everyone and tried to buy beers for all of them, was cordial, almost protective of me, introducing me whenever the opportunity arose and making sure friends and strangers saw that I was his guest.

Vy had a different view of it all, commenting to me, "Godawful circus, isn't it? Imagine, calling this *fun*. Well, it's good for you to see it."

But why?

And all the way home, I tried to figure out *why*. To the whole evening. What was I doing there, why was I brought there? To watch him get drunk by the evening's end, to watch her pained and resentful silence? Maybe to see the ordinariness of her life and therefore lose my allure for her? To expose him, humiliate her, educate me (further)? Or to see her unhappiness, and make me feel more for her? Riding that bumpy train, practically getting goosed from the loose cane splinters of the seat, I was totally confused. And yet, in my gut, I felt I had done the right thing, especially from Vy's point of view. She had invited me, I had accepted. What was more elementary than that?

* * *

In the library, the next week, she made no mention of the evening, and neither did I. Nor did it come up in conversation between us. It had happened, and was past, as simple as that.

Just as she—and we, together—were as complicated as ever. During the next few weeks, we grew if anything closer. It was as if my showing up at her place and viewing her life closeup proved something to her. Or allowed her to let me into her life more. . . . Something like that. Anyway, in the cave, while filing cards, organizing folders, discussing Eustacia, Wildeve, Clym Yeobright, we deepened our intimacy. Beneath the gaze of Remington's "Cow Puncher" and "Sioux Chief," I learned subtle ways of kissing, intricacies of touching. Her dark skin, her kinky hair, her doe's eyes, her smell, her breasts, her fanny, all drove me wild. She urged me, initiating acts, yet always was careful to define the boundaries, restrain us. All it took was a shake of the head and my pursuit of passion was nipped. And in a minute or two, we'd return to our high conversation—the literary function of Diggory Venn and Thomasin Yeobright—making me frustrated. But I didn't protest, and accepted her way of proceeding.

Naturally, we paid special attention to our conduct upon reentering the library. Sometimes I proceeded to Mr. G. with a listing of missing books, sometimes Vy called him downstairs to check on a catalogue problem. We involved him in our duties, often. It didn't hurt that King Arthur admired us both. I had become her protégé, been turned in a short time from a kind of primitive boy into a reader, a real student, by this idealistic woman. ("Your sports pieces have never been better, lad!" he'd say to me, winking. "And your instructor is the most energetic librarian we've ever had around here.") We were quite a team.

Others had different views.

By mid-April, the situation had become a touch more dicey with certain students, who were now taking more of an interest in her, and in the team. One day, as I left the library and was heading out the large front entrance, I was stopped and taken aside by a group of four Negroes. Forcefully, they held me against a wall, in the darkness.

One said, "Cut the shit out, man. Don't be messin' with no colored chicks."

A second said, "Stay on your own turf, or you'll find yourself under it."

The third flicked out a push-button blade. "This is jes' the warnin', man. The next time comes the sentencin'."

A teacher approached, and they scattered quickly, releasing me into shadows, and fears.

Instead of worrying about the two of us, I was now also worrying about me. My rite of spring had changed, I reflected, so different from previous Aprils, where my attention was focused on the Dodgers opening the new season. How would Campy, Jackie, and the Duke hit, how well would Erskine and Podres and Loes pitch—those were my usual April questions. Now, they were replaced with others. What was going to happen between us? What might happen to me? Would she consider running off with me? Yes, I was feverish, but the sport now was Violette. Remembering Dickens again, I felt smack center in my own age of foolishness.

Except for telling Tee of the threat, who cautioned me to watch myself, I kept the news to myself. And watched myself. Meaning, I stayed away from Vy upstairs except when no one was around. And also, curiously enough, I took a long hard look in the mirror. I saw a wild-haired slender boy of sixteen, with longish nose and alert eyes, a future of adventure in his head. Well, I informed him, if he wanted to hold on to that future, and meanwhile to stay in one piece . . .

The next Tuesday afternoon, we were downstairs as usual, she typing and me filing, and I could see she was troubled.

"You're awfully quiet," I told her.

"Am I?"

"Yeah. Something wrong?"

She stared at me with those big shining eyes. "Is our friendship hurting you—around here, I mean?"

"No," I lied. "What gave you that idea?"

"Oh, a couple of notes I've received lately. Unpleasant ones."

"From whom?"

"Oh, anonymous."

"Did they threaten you?"

"Oh, I wouldn't say they went that far."

"But they . . . hurt you?"

"Well, I suppose so. They're so small and petty."

I waited.

"Would you prefer if I didn't see you again? You know, talk to you and stuff."

She laughed. "No, but I was going to ask you the same thing."

My heart pumped sharply. "Well, I guess we're stuck with each other's company."

We both returned to working. On my side, I felt closer to her than ever, and more resolved to seeing it through, through these nasty threats. But what was that "it"?

It became clearer just that afternoon, strangely enough, when we held each other, kissed, touched, and she didn't shake her head, not at any point. And as petting slipped into full passion—right there on the old ragged daybed—I realized that I had never really been there before, though I had called it that. I was nervous, awkward, unsure; patiently, Vy manipulated me into firm manhood. The turning delicacy of her face (as I observed her during the act), the spreading sensual fragrance, the pleasure of her pliant body overwhelmed me. And pleasing her, this whirled me too, with a new and unforeseen power. I felt like a top, spinning and spinning.

Just as, later on, that night and the next few days, I was excited, on a spinning high that wouldn't recede wherever I went, whatever I did. In class I saw that face; on the subway I smelled that aroma; at home reading, I quivered over that body. Suddenly, all the familiar routines and objects of my daily surroundings were seen and felt anew, as though coated by some new texture, some sensual membrane. The sensation was subtle, and different.

The experience happened again, two days later on Thursday. *It* was expanding, and changing, like a caterpillar evolving into a butterfly, though our full definition remained to be seen.

Dazed and heated by the intoxication, I tried my best to stay cool, and deliberate practically. I had four days before seeing Vy again, so, to plan, I went up to a favorite haunt, the Botanic Gardens. Strolling through the burst of bright yellow on Daffodil Hill, I figured out a proposal. When I graduated, in a few months, maybe we could go away together, to a faraway place. And start over. Maybe somewhere like Hawaii, or Denmark, where the interracial thing wasn't supposed to mean too much. And where we would be perfect strangers. I'd try to land a newspaper job, and she could find a beloved library. I paused at the tropical orchids, leaning very close to observe their irregular intricacy and variety, the subtleties of shape and delicacies of color.

"Easy does it," cautioned a friendly guard. "They're privileged creatures."

Still preoccupied the next day, I again took the IRT uptown to Franklin Avenue, and this time headed for Ebbets Field. There, sitting in the bleachers and watching Warren Spahn toying with the Bums, I made an alternate plan. Why not stay put, in the city somewhere, and live right here? Maybe the Village? That way maybe I could go to college at night, say, and Vy wouldn't be a total stranger. (She had graduated from NYU.) Why not? Less exotic than Copenhagen maybe, but maybe also more practical, doable? Sure. We could see certain old friends that way too. Yeah, I liked that. Well, anyway, two plans were better than one, I figured. Gobbling Cracker Jacks and a frank, and concerned with my own strategy, I hardly cared that Spahn shut out my team that day, 3–0. Who'd ever dream that baseball could be second best to a girl, I thought later. A woman, I realized.

Though I wanted to see her on Monday, to present my plans, I waited till Tuesday, our regular afternoon.

But she wasn't in, to my surprise.

"Called in ill yesterday," Mr. G. said. "Looks like we're both on our own."

"Anything serious?" I inquired.

"I certainly hope not," he replied. "I couldn't afford to lose her too, you know." He glanced at me sideways. "Neither could you, I bet."

I tried to smile. *Lose her?*

"Come on, give me a hand with those two carts over there, you might as well earn your keep up here today." And he slapped me on my shoulder, to cheer us both up. "She'll be in later this week, I imagine."

Should I call her, I wondered, putting away the books? I decided to wait, give it another day or two.

Forty-eight hours seemed like forty-eight weeks, slow and punishing. When my heart stabbed too much, I turned to another sports page. But when she still didn't come in by Thursday, I did call, in the afternoon. I got no answer. And I didn't want to take a chance of calling at night, just in case . . . James answered.

When on Saturday I tried once more and again got no one, I knew something was up. But what? Was she really ill, maybe in the hospital? Had something happened to James? Or maybe a fight between them? Sure. That was it, I concluded.

Later, I tried to concentrate on the Shadow pursuing a lunatic who longed to be a vampire and who had abducted Margo, but my attention kept wandering. The scary voice and gory fright paled alongside my own fears, and despair. When the commercial came on, urging a ton of Blue Coal, I turned it off, in confusion.

On Monday, when I came into the library after class at two o'clock, Mr. G. looked at me, and shook his head, in dismay.

"No luck, I'm afraid, son. No word. I don't quite know—"

He was so down that I found myself consoling him, not myself. "She'll explain herself, sir, I know she will. I mean, there'll be a reasonable explanation, I'm sure. And why don't I just stick around today, and help you out, huh?"

He forced out a little smile of gratitude.

The explanation came on Wednesday, in the form of a note. Shaking his head in bewilderment, Mr. Goodman showed it to me. It read, simply:

> For personal reasons, I must take abrupt leave of you and the Library, without finishing the term, or the catalogue project. Please forgive me. You were a wonderful librarian to work with, and I hate to leave this way. But the matter is somewhat urgent, and

therefore I must. Naturally I will not expect to seek any recommendation from you, now or in the future.

When I looked up, he asked, "Divorce? . . . Death? . . . Grave illness? Take your pick, son."

I shook my head, not wishing to, particularly.

"Well"—he crumpled up the note—"I've lost a colleague, you've lost a counselor, and we've both lost a friend. It's a sad day."

Lost spun round and round in my head. When I tried to telephone, later in the evening, the operator clicked in to inform me that number had been disconnected.

And I too, like that number, felt disconnected. But my heart didn't understand that, during the slow hard fog of the next days, and periodically kept wanting, wanting, wanting.

My explanation, my letter, arrived a week later, at my place. The letter was attached to a book, *Caribbean: Sea of the New World*, by one German Arciniegas. The cover was romantic, adventurous, her letter less so.

Dearest Aaron,

You will enjoy this book. It's a good and real history of where I come from, and where, I imagine, I shall return. You're dear to me, and will remain so. But the mistake, the full responsibility, lies with me. I allowed attraction, and impulsiveness, to get the best of me, and of us, of reason and reasonableness, of professional responsibilities. The result is a loss of confidence and credibility in myself as a librarian, and as your friend. Please remember me. You were a ray of happiness in my otherwise dreary, gloomy existence.

Vy

It was not the easiest of letters for me to read, sitting there in my kitchen at night. Emotion ripping me, I focused on the cover of *Caribbean*. It depicted an aerial view of the blue sea and the chains of green islands. Superimposed on that topography were historical figures, a formally attired Spanish conquistador alongside a subdued, bare-topped native woman standing atop Central America; arising from a large island, a black Caribbean army leader reaching for his sword; in the sea, a pirate schooner and a European frigate; on the jungle tip of the Venezuelan coast, two oil wells rose; and, from the Florida coast, a golden-haired head was blowing down a gust of northern wind. I stared at the illustration, searching for a clue, a hint, of where she might travel. No such luck.

I got out my atlas, and turned to a map of the region, and followed Cuba to Haiti and the Dominican Republic, Puerto Rico to the Lesser Antilles. With precise determination, and a magnifying glass, I traced down that softly curving slope, like a woman's buttock, of tiny yellow islands with black spots for chief cities, the Virgin Islands, Antigua and Guadeloupe, Dominica and Martinique, St. Lucia and St. Vincent, and finally, eastward, Barbados. Her destination? Committing the islands to memory, I closed the atlas, and picked up the history. I read a few sentences, but found my heart wasn't in it. It was elsewhere, floating suspended.

For the next few days, and weeks, I too drifted about, directionless. Nothing meant too much anymore, it seemed. Not baseball, not books, not friends. From the high wire of Vy-intensity, I had dropped into a pit of numbness. In class too I was a washout, even where my experience might have been of use. "What do you mean," Engelberg chided me one day, "that you have 'no opinion' of Eustacia Vye's ending? Come on, Aaron, get with it, or you'll have a tough time of getting out of here come June and graduation."

Even the safe library, my last refuge, had turned into a kind of hall of mirrors. You know, where you get inside and all you see is yourself distorted, misshapen, mocked cruelly.

Old Arthur nodded when he saw me. "Still moping, huh? I understand, my boy. She was special. Well, at least I've heard some good news. Miss Brownell is recovering very nicely, and indeed will be back next fall." He lowered his bifocals, which he wore on occasion. "And you, next fall, any ideas?"

I wanted to say the Caribbean, but simply shook my head.

Slowly, almost involuntarily, I started to disbelieve recent events, trying to erase them from my brain. Saying to myself how it had all been a kind of mirage, made up, created by my overheated imagination. Hurting, I took a kind of sullen pleasure in sharpening my skepticism about who she was, what she had meant to me, and what we had had together. In place of a Dorothy Dandridge look-alike in *Carmen Jones*, she was becoming just another woman, another temporary librarian. And I tried my best to dislodge the strong emotion that was still, every now and then, ravishing me.

I think it would have worked too, had not Engelberg ruined things by giving us a June exam, to prepare for the Regents. There, in the quotation section, he asked us to cite the text and author, and offer an interpretation, of the lines: "It was the best of times, It was the worst of times, It was the age of wisdom, It was the age of foolishness, it was the epoch of belief, it was the epoch of incredulity. . . ."

Suddenly Vy was right there, shimmering like a genie in her springtime yellow dress, reciting the lines aloud, in that singsong cadence and clipped accent.

And I knew that she was not going to leave me for a while yet, a long while—not she or her island spirit—even if her physical self had taken leave. Belief had become incredulity, and incredulity belief again, but a different sort.

Convinced of the meagerness of facts, I started writing, in my newly improved penmanship, about Dickens, *A Tale of Two Cities*, Sydney Carton, the French Revolution. In a few minutes, however, *she* was murmuring to me, about maybe trying to write stories one day, and maybe then being free to reinvent her, make her up anew. Doe's eyes shining, she was laughing, and playfully provoking me. But the thought was intriguing: how maybe, one day, heeding her challenge, I would get a chance to see her dark beauty again, smell her musky fragrance, hear her musical voice.

"Aaron, you okay?" Engelberg was saying, leaning over my shoulder. "You look like you're seeing Sydney or Eustacia in person, right here. How about a drink of water?"

Nodding, and standing, I followed his suggestion, but the slow walk and cold drink did little to end the bewitchment or cut short the bereavement.

A condition which lasted through the spring and the summer (and even beyond), when I found myself paying unusual attention to the world news, not just the sports pages. I noticed for example that the Supreme Court, in Brown vs. the Topeka Board of Education, ruled that segregation by color in the public schools was a violation of the Fourteenth Amendment to the Constitution. And that Senator Joe McCarthy was at it again, this time setting up hearings to prove that Communists had infiltrated the Army. Also, curiously enough, I followed with surprising interest a desert locust plague in Morocco, which was destroying some fourteen million dollars of citrus crops in six weeks. (For a few days I longed to be part of a swarm myself, crawling in the hot desert, hunting for vegetation.) All this factual stuff filled my head, giving my heart a chance to relax, a kind of furlough from its real front.

The Bridge

onstruction was started in 1870, and the Bridge was officially opened thirteen years later, May 24, 1883. Crossing the East River from City Hall in Manhattan to Sands and Washington streets in Brooklyn, the Bridge's river span is 1,595 feet; its width is 85 feet, its height at center, 135 feet. The total length of its "wagonway," about 6000 feet. (Two cables and trolley-car tracks, a wagonway, and a footpath.) Roebling's design marked a new era in bridge construction. At the opening ceremonies it was stated that almost every science known to man had contributed to its accomplishment. After the Brooklyn came the next pair of big bridges, farther up the river, the Manhattan and the Williamsburg. Reasonable copies of the original.

The boy first walked across it at night when he was fourteen or fifteen, and it was the closest thing to that Open Sesame of his reading childhood he had ever experienced. The walk took some two and a half hours, with periodic stops for viewing the scenery. No trolleys or wagons then, of course, just cars and trucks rattling on by, which, after a while, he forgot about. Walking across the Bridge was like ambling through a vast Lionel erector set, with metal pieces maybe fourteen and sixteen inches high hooked together by meticulous labor with tiny nuts and screws, bolts and washers, so you were rather amazed by the whole when it was fully assembled. Like the kind that he and Burt built together when he was seven or eight. And above, the slope of steel cables arching way above him looked like a jumping rope for giants. The wind blew more sharply up here, yet below, way down deep in the East River, he could see the flags of the occasional passing ships stirring. God, it was scary and fascinating looking straight down there.

Crossing to Manhattan by foot on the Bridge was surely the proper way to approach that narrow, legendary island, he thought soberly. The giant skyscrapers with the little yellow lights blinking on and off like a telephone switchboard. The crowded, jagged skyline of horizon, with each thrusting structure fighting to outdo the next. The dark sky, with its silvery stars already blinking, was practically touched by those rising points of steel, making even that sky seem man-made, a part of Manhattan's geography. What a foreign, fantastic island inhabited by those looming steel monsters!

Crossing to Manhattan also meant taking leave from the home ground, of course. But leaving Brooklyn was not all that easy, actually. First there was the stunning walk up high, a high wire of sorts, a bridge of maturity let's say. When he got on the other side, he felt somehow immediately at a loss, a piece missing—what was it? Childhood. Boyhood. Youth. All that was back there, in the old stomping ground. Really, after all, it was such a unique, cozy place, a cocoon of Brooklynites warming and protecting each other, especially living next door to this worldwide celebrity cousin-colossus, that yes indeed, the Bridge was the way, maybe the only proper way, to leave it. Here, on the shores of Manhattan, you felt immediately pressed to be grown up, sober, set and ready for adulthood.

Later he came to see that Brooklyn was made to be departed from, that Manhattan was just right to be there to remind you to get out and try the big world, and that Brooklyn wouldn't go away when you did, but stayed around, hovering in the memory, somewhere in the heart, in the lingo, and in the perception—ways of seeing and experiencing the world. In fact, it was a kind of second skin, or even a coat of arms that grew and wrapped around you as you grew, without your quite knowing it, or naming it. And walking the Bridge maybe sealed your fate, inscribed that heraldry, invisibly, the way all serious pedigrees are etched. In the interior, that is, where your soul was stamped by parts of the borough, and maybe even marked by the ancestral memory of the first six villages, Breuckelen, Midwout, Gravesend, Nieuw Utrecht, Bushwick, Nieuw Amersfoort (Flatlands). Curiously, and circuitously, the Bridge led back to the past as much as it brought you forward, once you walked its stately steel path in your fifteenth year. As much a bridge of dreams then, a spur to suspension of disbelief, as a great suspension bridge.

Adventures of a
Fiction Boy

L et's start down there, underground, in the basement. Where else should a true Brooklyn boy, you know, a boy from the 1950s, hungry, raw, maybe primitive too, begin his full education? In the basement. But uptown, in a Manhattan basement, and surrounded by books. Immersed in books the way a farm boy is dipped in nature, each with his chores as well as love. In my case, thousands of books set on rickety shelves and in wavering piles, and thousands more awaiting sorting out in unopened cartons. And all of them, secondhand and fiction. Thousands of fiction titles, awaiting sorting, cleaning, classifying, shelving. Detective fiction. Science fiction. Fiction for juveniles. (Children's books, along with gothic romances, go upstairs, while Westerns pass on to the Americana room.) But mainly, adult fiction. Everything from D'Annunzio to Dostoyevski, Maurice Hewlett to Hardy, Fast to Feuchtwanger, Conan Doyle to Zane Grey. And thousands of others that neither you nor I had ever heard of. A junkyard for battered, obscure novels. A poor man's graveyard or reservoir of lost souls, discovered delights. Underground, in a used-book store.

And yours truly, Aaron Schlossberg, was the guardian, the gatekeeper, the official fiction boy. At sixteen, he was given the awesome responsibility of bringing order and clarity to the spilling incoherence, of keeping up-to-date on all the ancient fiction down there, some forty thousand titles musty with time and disuse. A vast army of writers to alphabetize, classify, sort out, discover, and remember, above all, remember where I've placed them. Otherwise they're doomed to oblivion. That was my challenge.

"Yeah, don't worry, it sounds like a lot at first," advised portly George with the unpronounceable Polish name. "You'll get the hang of it, and after a while you'll remember the titles easily enough. They just sort of stay with you." Now in his early fifties, George had come to Schulte's as a boy of fifteen, to help out his sister in bookkeeping, and he had stayed on forty years. A pink-faced bachelor who reddened at any offbeat remark about the opposite sex, George was one of the most human fixtures of the store, a kind of innocent Falstaff. There was also Roland the bookkeeper and religious-books man, up on the second tier; Mosey, or Moses the packager, who wrapped books for postal delivery in his corner of the basement; Bernie the cynical assistant manager and night college student; and Lewis ("not Lew," I was told) the manager and owner, and son of the original founder of Schulte's. All of them, and their eccentric predispositions, were indeed fixtures of the place as much as any of the dusty old volumes themselves.

Schulte's, when I came to work for it in 1954, was a three-story house of books situated in an old Fourth Avenue brick office building. Dating back to the 1920s, it was one of the two oldest used-book stores on famous Used Book Row just east of the Village. It had little glamor or spruce, no bright colors or artsy decorations, no sales gimmicks or come-ons for the returning, regular customers. Just used books; hardcover mostly, some not handled in years. Dark, dusty, cranky with age and stubborn with prestige, Schulte's resembled a regal mausoleum as much as a bookstore. It was dimly lit by a series of Prohibition-age light fixtures, where bare unshaded light bulbs went off and on by long chains. And it was manned by men who didn't care much one way or the other if you browsed, bought, or went away empty-handed. Except for Bernie, the help was not particularly diplomatic or concerned, though they were courteous. They were there to serve the books, in a way, which were laid out, or spilled over, everywhere, in rows on wooden tables, or outside, on rolling carts; or on all three floors, on shelves wooden and metal. A mausoleum, as I said.

I came to work there when I was a senior in high school, taking the IRT subway uptown after school in the depths of Brooklyn, and arriving about an hour later at 14th Street in Manhattan. Climbing upstairs, I'd pass the bustling world of dresses and coats "On Sale" always at Klein's Department Store, and then, walking a half-dozen blocks, descend to the seedy planet of used fiction. I arrived about 1:30 or so, and stayed till closing time, at 6:00. I knew little about books, you understand. I was a reality boy, much more interested in the adventures of the streets, the schoolyards, the club rooms, than in those of the printed page. So to enter the domain of the dusty, the vast underground of used books, was something new and strange to me. All I knew was that it was private down there, and all mine; well, almost all mine.

There were the clients of course, who periodically trickled down the wooden stairs and wandered in the dank, airless basement. (The two distant windows were hardly ever opened, for some reason.) Then, in one far corner, Mosey, the light-skinned Negro with the pomaded hair and pencil mustache, wrapped and weighed the books on his wooden table before taking them to the post office at the end of each day. He and I struck it up okay, right off, and I'd visit with him maybe once a day and shoot the breeze. Also, once a week, there occurred the friendly card game, with Mosey, Roland, and Bernie playing, during some very quiet hours. Usually George and I looked on, as observers, and I also played chickee, or lookout, for Lewis, just in case he should saunter on down, or need anything. Though he rarely ever wandered down into our nether region.

After a few months, in November or so, I began to settle in, getting the hang of the place, the feel for the different rooms and slower, grubbier way of life down below. Of the rooms, there was the Special Collections: leather-bound sets housed in a small rag-gedy place, an odd hole for Thackeray, Dickens, Trollope in soft Moroccan leather hues. The Americana room was more noble, a long rectangular area with larger shelving, to accommodate geography, photography, history, regionalism books, with an entrance consisting of two narrow swinging wood-and-glass doors like an old Western saloon. (This was Bernie's domain, and he attended to it once or twice weekly.) Next, a Detective fiction room, whose aficionados, respectably dressed, seemed to resemble their favorite shadowy characters, giving me furtive glances if I tried to help them, and bearing away their books in mysterious paper bags. Of course the main room, complemented by many divergent aisles and alcoves, was devoted to adult fiction; this area was a very large square room so crammed with endless green metal shelves that the space seemed smaller, more suffocating. Chiefly, I became familiar with the thousands of books there: the rows and rows of semibattered spines and dusty covers that faced me wherever I turned, and threatened to eat up all the space. Gradually, however, I felt those books not merely as inanimate objects, but as comrades of sorts, all of us hunkered down below in that boiler room of the Strange Ship Schulte's. In fact, I grew so cozy below, with my pals and me, that I came to resent going up on deck to help out, if Lewis or George signaled for me.

Mostly, however, I didn't need to. For on the whole I was left by myself, below, to bring some order to *L*'s and *H*'s say, to continue to unpack the year- or two-year-old unopened cartons, and to increase my knowledge of which books we had in stock. Periodically, during the day, I'd be interrupted by Lewis buzzing me from upstairs and who, when I went to the bottom of the special, unused stairway, would call down to me, "Aaron, do we happen to have a copy of *The Winthrop Women* by Seton?" or "*Double Double* by Feuchtwanger?" or "*Children of Abraham* by Asch?" or "*The Late George Apley* by Marquand?" And do you know what? It got so, even in the space of those three months, that I'd know immediately, in many cases, whether we had the novel or not, and where, in fact, I could lay my hands on it. If we had it, I'd dust it off, and run it upstairs to the waiting Lewis, standing with his customer.

You can imagine my high when, after one such rescue mission—uncovering *Sorrel and Son* by Warwick Deeping, a name I adored—George said to me, in his froggy bass voice, "You're becoming a real fiction boy!" That commendation was like receiving my wings from flight school, you understand; and I descended below, pride on my shoulder, to carry on the battle. (A losing battle of course; I'd never catch up to the years of stockpiling books, with new cartons coming in weekly.)

As much as the books, I was getting hooked by the place too, not merely the antiquarian mahogany walls, the exposed pipes and ancient fixtures, but by the employees. I had never before been in a position or situation where everyone so bent his will, or succumbed, to the clockwork regularity of the task at hand, without ever crossing the boundary into lament, protest, or passion. Each of the men did no more, no less, than his required labor, as though to do more, or even *feel* more, would throw the whole bookish clockwork order out of whack sharply. Thus, no extra smiles for the customers, no flashy shirt or tie or attractive costuming, no fights or raised voices among workers or with customers, ever. Each man manned his station, his particular area, with chaste, autonomous routine and dull blessed order. They were like monks of different orders, perhaps, quietly pursuing their separate assignments, occasionally passing by each other, and murmuring something polite, even cordial. A monastery of books and monks, then, more than a mausoleum.

At more length, then, consider these book-monks. Roland (or Rollie) worked the religious books, located on the railed balcony ringing the main floor, and he also kept the books in his tiny office. A taciturn man of medium build and rimless spectacles, in old middle age, he wore striped shirts and striped ties, held by a horrible golden tie clasp. Once he had owned his own religious bookshop, but it had failed, and he came over here, some fifteen years ago. Rollie was married, but unhappily so, according to Bernie, and he probably had a mistress somewhere in Manhattan. The only hint I ever saw was that on occasion he'd be using the electric razor to shave off his five o'clock shadow before leaving at night. His religious books, maybe fifteen or twenty thousand titles, he knew cold, never saying, "I don't know that one," but rather, "Renan's *Jesus* is very hard to keep in, sorry." Or, about some papal encyclopedia, "Oh, that set has become *rare* by now, it'll cost you a pretty penny." With me he was quiet and cordial, and after a while I could breathe his unhappiness like some special body odor. This made me respect him, and his silence, all the more.

George was the all-purpose bookman, uncomfortable with the customers, cozy among the books; he knew, it seemed, every one of the eighty thousand or so secular titles. Hard to believe, but true. He also knew where each was placed, on what table, in what pile, under what collection, and at what price. Moon-faced, big-bellied, and bald-domed, George was a saintly soul, painfully shy, a sure virgin at fifty in the year 1955. A practicing Catholic who attended Mass with his aging mother every Sunday, George never bothered anyone with his religion; and though he blushed at risqué jokes and daring women, he never turned away his eyes or off his ears. He was like the fifteen-year-old boy he had once been, still trying to come out from under the weight of his mother and piety, but only peeking through. Routinely he padded around the store like a giant balding turtle, straightening out a pile of books here, checking his dog-eared index cards at his battered schoolmaster's desk. He loved being left in charge, if Lewis had to leave, making sure all was in order. (But how could it ever go out of order, I wondered?) Once, when my high school English teacher couldn't remember the name of an out-of-print title by Howard Fast, I telephoned George during class on the excuse of going to the bath-room, and gave him the problem, and a clue about content. George said, "Oh yeah, that was *The Last Frontier*—we get it in now and then." Mr. Lefferts, my teacher, couldn't quite believe how I man-aged to find that out just like that, and was deeply impressed.

Lewis, the son of the founder of the store, was as regular as John Cameron Swayzee, and as lively as a rod of iron. Sallow-hued, bespectacled, and narrow, about forty-two or three, Lewis was a stiff personality, not much for joking or getting humor, not much for change of any sort. Every day, every season, he dressed the same way: gray slacks, black shoes, an obscure tie, and a bat-tleship-gray windbreaker, which he wore faithfully around the shop. From home he brought his brown-paper-bag lunch, and a thermos of coffee. With Lewis, vitality and vividness were simply out of bounds, off-limits. He wandered about the store like a gray corpse, lending a cadaverous feel wherever he paused or stopped. Not even money, or profit motive, could pump his blood, and he remained a poor businessman. The employees mocked him behind his back, but not too hard, maybe because they knew he was a hopeless case, or maybe out of respect for the dead.

Bernie on the other hand was somewhat dangerous. I mean, he liked to live, and preferred horses, gambling, ladies to books. No doubt he was the odd man out there. In his early twenties, he went to Brooklyn College at night, though his true interest was in making money, maybe opening up his own bookshop one day. Naturally, every time he tried to devise a scheme for providing more profit for the store, by raising all prices say fifty cents, or by acquiring more review books—which we bought for a quarter of list, and sold immediately for double that—he was shot down right off by Lewis, for one vague reason or another. Signs of life like that were simply excessive, a violation of the cadaver's code. Bernie even occasionally spruced himself up a bit—you know, a bright tie here, a catchy pair of argyle socks, maybe a laundered white-on-white shirt. These sorts of items were like whiffs of perfume in the monastery, little sins attracting undue attention through the day. Though we got along fine, Bernie was suspicious, I could tell, that I might wind up bookish on him. Not to say he disliked or distrusted books; his own Americana room he handled with a bookman's care and fastidious overseeing, judging by his steady visits there, and his own lock and key for the place.

As I said, I was settling in during those months, and beginning to like its strange, even exotic attractions.

I made about twenty or twenty-five dollars normally, and often another five for extra hours; this enabled me to save quite a lot. For, after giving my mother one-third for the house, spending another third on train fare and food, I saved nearly ten bucks a week. This added up, you know. And one day, heading down Broadway toward Tenth Street, I passed an office machines and furniture shop having a sale, and my eye was caught by a portable Royal typewriter in one corner, priced specially at $69.95. My gut reacted, and I knew suddenly what I was going to save for: my first typewriter! Inside the store, the salesman said I shouldn't worry, he wouldn't run out of those. When I told him that I worked on Fourth Avenue, over at Schulte's, he smiled warmly, said he knew Mosey, and using a small pencil on a pad, said he'd let me have the machine for $62.50. On the spot I gave him a $5.00 deposit to hold it, thanked him, and walked off, almost flying from my high, not the November wind. Just the sight and thought of the sleek gray machine excited me the way cars had revved up my friends' hearts. I had always written out in longhand my pieces for the high school newspaper, and then had to type them over in school; this way I could type it straight on the machine. Especially since typing had been the best class I had had at junior high. A typewriter. No one in my family had ever owned one, you see, and here I was, going to earn one for myself.

Certainly I was not going to ask my father for it, he who had been kicked out of the house by Mom and me a year or so ago, and who I barely spoke with. Or my mother, who had her own financial worries just getting along. Or Sam, the old family friend, who was now my mother's lover part of the week, and who was generous enough with her. No, I would have to get an item like this, a special prize, on my own. And having my own appointed task like that seemed to give the job at Schulte's an added purpose, I felt, as I entered the shop after fixing an unwieldy mess of books on an outside cart. Excited and determined, I didn't even mind Lewis's request that I stay upstairs awhile and straighten out the new batch of large American Heritage books that had just arrived. Naturally I made sure to sort out anything that looked ripe for Americana, like Lewis and Clark journals or Parkman's *Oregon Trail*. For some reason, I always felt Bernie was pretty sensitive about his Americana, and decided to let Bernie put the books away himself, even though Lewis offered me the key.

And afterwards, downstairs, I told Mosey how his friend at Broadway Office Machines had just given me an extra reduction; he asked how much, and I said $7.00, he said, "Sheet, he can do better than that! I'll speak with the man, he owes me one."

Good old Mosey; a buddy, I felt.

Like the fixtures, the employees, and the used books, there were also the clients who regularly haunted my fiction shelves in those early months. They, too, looked used, worn, sometimes broken, always devoted. Some were New Yorkers, some out-of-towners who never failed to make a book stop if they came to the city, and buy up a batch of fiction for the next several months' reading. The tall lady with the feathered hats and darting glances was always on the lookout for a new Hervey Allen or Vicki Baum. The charming couple from the Village, a short stout silent man and his talkative thin wife, who hunted down the detectives with grim looks and bulldog waggles, filling their brown shopping bags. A fancy East Sider—until Schulte's, I didn't know of the sharp differences between the two sides, East and West—wore the first ascot I had ever seen inside his tweed jacket, and always seemed to ask for books I never had, then, nodding with superiority, found two or three others to take as compensation. Interestingly enough, only after two or three months of seeing me there regularly did these odd souls begin to admit me into their presence, acknowledging tacitly my right to tenant their basement.

One gentleman in particular began to stand out, in part because our earliest meeting turned into a minor confrontation, in which he muttered something like, "Why the hell don't they get a boy who knows real books for a change!" after he asked me for a copy of *The Possessed* and I asked him who wrote it.

It took him a few visits before he saw that I was actually a quick learner, and eager to do my job well. A bulky man who wore a gray fedora and sports jacket, sometimes a tie, he spoke in a brusque voice, but was slightly taken aback when I told him on his next visit I had learned the Dostoyevski titles.

"Hmm," he uttered when I rattled them all off, "have you read any?"

I shook my head.

"What do you read?"

I didn't want to mention the Classic Comics, or the aviator hero books, and said, "Oh, adventure stuff, I guess."

"Aren't you in high school? What do you read there?"

When I explained that in Jefferson High, I read things like *Arrowsmith*, *Adam Bede*, *R.U.R.*, he shook his head. "Dismal. No wonder you kids grow up illiterate. With little interest in reading. What do you want to be, do you have any idea?"

I didn't dare mention writing at that point, so I cited my other chief pursuit. "An explorer."

He narrowed his gray eyes, revealing his high pallid forehead and giving me a kind of inquisitor's look. He reflected, and took out a small notebook. "Here, see if you can get hold of a life of Rimbaud. It might interest you. And I'm also writing down a novel for you, if you feel like reading it." He nodded with authority, and left.

After he departed, George approached me, and asked if I knew who the fellow was.

"What do you mean?"

He laughed. "He's a famous literary critic. Barrett is his name. He must like you, he hardly ever talks to anyone here. Just picks up his books and leaves."

I explained how he was just chastising me for my ignorance. "Barrett, huh? What's he written?"

George recited a few of his titles, and I managed to find one in stock: *Kipling's Legacy*. It looked simple enough to read, but I had no knowledge of the books he was talking about inside. Charles Edmund Barrett. I liked that name, so formal, so long. Anyway, I began to hunt around for one of the Rimbaud titles he had recommended. Instead I found first the novel he had suggested, *Look Homeward, Angel* by Thomas Wolfe. And immediately, that afternoon, sitting on my cushioned bench in a remote corner, away from the stairway or door, I began reading that weighty tome, beneath the bare 75-watt light bulb.

To my surprise, I was immediately taken by the character Eugene Gant, and captivated by the whipping, headlong prose of the author. I read almost forty pages in that first sitting, interrupted three times by buzzer calls, and managed to take the book home with me, sticking with it on the subway. Jostled this way and that on my torn cane seat, I couldn't stop reading it, despite the tightly packed pages and poor light. And for the next week or so, I was hooked that way, poring through the book everywhere, at work, on the subway, at home. Even at school, in English class, while they discussed *Ivanhoe*, I followed Gant.

And when I finished it, I felt heady with excitement, and searched in earnest for that life of Rimbaud, as well as being on the lookout for another novel by Wolfe.

Just around that time, while my informal reading education had begun, something else occurred of interest, also down below.

I was in the midst of emptying yet another carton of long-dead books when Bernie appeared, cigarette in the corner of his mouth, and said he wanted to show me something "special" in Americana. Sure, I said, wiping my hands of the endless dust and happy for the invitation to his private inner sanctum, my first.

"You're about to see the *real* powers of Americana," he advised as we made our way through the swinging saloon doors. Immediately he put his finger to his lips, silencing me, and then pointed me to a ladder leaning up against a high shelf. What the hell was he talking about?

At his prompting, I climbed up four or five rungs, and there, on the shelf marked Southwest, I found a space cleared between the books. A faint buzzing sound arose, alongside *Arizona: Land of Plenty*. Looking closer, I saw a round peephole facing me, maybe the size of a large knothole in the wood; at his gesturing, I leaned closer and peered through. At first my eyes couldn't fathom what was going on, except for a flickering darkness; but presently I realized that I was seeing a home movie of sorts, maybe an eight-millimeter showing on the wall. And there, the picture expanding with my familiarity, I perceived a busty woman entering the apartment of two well-dressed men, smiling and sitting down, allowing her skirt to hike high above her knees. Soon she was having her drink, laughing with white teeth protruding, and leaning far over for a cigarette, her full breasts almost spilling out of her blouse. My throat grew dry, my chest expanded with my breathing, and I threw Bernie a quick glance just to show him I was in full control. He stared at me with a cheap grin. Returning to the peephole, I now also realized something else; inside the room on the other side of the wall a man was whispering to a woman, they were drinking, and there was a brushing movement. Cheesus! I almost fell over. Meanwhile on the screen the woman was already loosening her skirt and blouse, with the two men following suit, undressing.

Bernie was tugging at me. "Hey, better get going—old Lewis is buzzing for you, and I already gave him the bathroom excuse a few minutes ago."

"Huh?"

"Don't worry, I'll let you know what happens," and he winked. "Get going."

Shielding myself, I descended the ladder, my head whirring, and I fled the room, almost hitting the steel shelves straight on.

In a moment I was standing at the foot of the long stairway, and Lewis, cadaver-smiling, said, "Everything under control down there?"

"Oh yeah, Lewis, sure. I just got busy on a shelf."

"Never mind." He nodded. "Can we help out Dr. Almond here? Either of these Silone titles in—*Seed Before the Snow* or *A Handful of Blackberries?*"

I adjusted my thoughts, registered the query. "Sorry, Lewis. A copy of *Fontemarre*, that's it."

Lewis turned to the doctor, who shook his head.

"Thanks, Aaron." And they walked off.

Later on, in the next few weeks and months, I began to learn a little more about the entire basement, and what went on in the far side of Americana. It seemed that Jackson, the large black man who operated the elevator for the rest of the building, ran a kind of after-hours gambling and whorehouse in his rooms downstairs. The gambling took place chiefly on Friday, payday, about six o'clock, when there was a regular card game, liquor, and several women hanging out. From outside, you could enter into Jackson's side of the basement via his freight elevator, which would descend to the basement and slide open its huge doors on both sides, like a cattle car on a train. The floor of the elevator served as a bridge between places, Jackson's Hole, as Mosey termed it, and Schulte's fiction basement.

Jackson himself was a congenial fellow, with a big warm smile and Victorian handlebar mustache. After Bernie had introduced us one day, Jackson invited me to come over any time I wished. "Just remember you're *eighteen*"—he grinned broadly—"in case anyone ever should inquire."

It was Mosey who immediately warned me against going over there. "Sheet," he said, shaking his dusky head over a coffee when I told him of Jackson's invitation, "that man'd hustle his mother for a silver dollar. You stay away from that joint, if you know what's good for you. He's jes lucky I don't blow the whistle on him and his doings."

I listened to Mosey, and trusted him, but the thought of that den of sin just a few steps away from my house of fiction seemed to put the right finishing touch on life in the basement. I mean, I was learning all about the full powers and peculiar charms of life uptown, even though a brothel alongside a bookstore was a little more than my imagination had allowed for. No wonder I felt that real life was to be found downstairs, while simple, shallow commerce was above, and I resented being called upstairs to help out. My place was in the basement, my niche amidst the used novels, and if the lure of illicitness sirened my way on occasion, via that secret peephole, I felt in a way that I was only extending my education.

Immersed in fiction, lured by pornography, semitutored in literature, I felt excited and raw, a kind of rookie in Americana. Back in Jefferson High, I was involved in the basketball season and adventures with pals, but all that seemed high schoolish stuff next to the challenges uptown. I'd sense this as I bumped and rattled my way up to Manhattan on the New Lots Avenue El, which went underground at Utica Avenue, while I journeyed with Eugene Gant or the new fellow I had discovered in the basement, a Chicago kid named Augie March. (I still had not gotten hold of Rimbaud, not in our high school library or in the store.) Once a week or so, I walked from 14th Street via Broadway in order to get a peek at my royal Royal, just checking to make sure it was still there, waiting. All was in order. And as soon as I entered Schulte's, and went downstairs, and changed into my drab uniform of worn flannel shirt and old dungarees, and settled in amidst the used tomes, motes of dust and broken spines, I felt at home, secure. Private again. Firmly ensconced as fiction boy.

Maybe part of the reason too why I felt so secure and firm down there was the confusion taking place in my real home, our Brooklyn apartment. Things had grown somewhat hectic there, with Sam, the new man and lover, trying his best to be kindly and decent to me, but rubbing me the wrong way invariably and inevitably. Small disputes blew up into large battles. If he wanted to watch some inconsequential television show, when I perhaps wanted to tune in to some other silly program, I took it badly and fought him over it. If he mentioned, with good humor, how much he was helping out the household with food and money, I'd leap up and tell him what he could do with it! (Of course the fact that the house needed his help only hurt worse.) The unusual arrangement, whereby Sam stayed over at our place for four nights and at his own for three, with his estranged wife and beloved daughter, was probably also affecting me in school, where my usual mischief-making was becoming something larger. Until, that is, Schulte's entered the picture, and somehow calmed me down in school.

It was not surprising that I spent many hours downstairs idling away the time, daydreaming, projecting, and rearranging reality. After all, I had much time on my hands, and I had been doing that sort of inventing since I was six and my older sister had given up baby-sitting for me, and my parents asked me to stay on my own. I did, and after a few weeks I got very used to those several evenings a week on my own, with my sports magazines, adventure books, radio shows, and my imagination. Every night, late, the lights out and the radio on low, just before sleep, I always told myself a little story—about my pals in the first or second grade, about an adventure involving movie-style cowboys and Indians, about the two girls Pesha and Golda in my Hebrew school. So, daydreaming at Schulte's for part of each day was a practiced habit. I pictured myself traveling up the Congo River, for example, on a freighter heading toward Matadi, say, and then to points inland, to territory previously unchartered by white men. And I daydreamed too of visiting Russia—starting out at Minsk, and seeing the village where my grandfather had been knocked off by some wild cossack; and then, from Moscow, traveling east on the Siberian train, heading toward the Steppes and that wild area where tribes like the Maygars and Tartars had first started out. Naturally, I projected writing a book one day, maybe something like the adventures of Eugene Gant or Augie March, those two boys of the wild, though that would come later, after much travel and adventure. My experience in writing up till then had consisted of a fourteen-page hockey book, with my illustrations, when I was about eleven, a few odd short pieces of character portraits; and sports stories for the high school newspaper. I loved sitting alone with a foolscap pad of yellow paper in my parents' bedroom, sitting on that aluminum beach chair squeezed between mahogany bed and dresser, and writing on the small night table. Hearing the street sounds of Sutter Avenue, and the farther music of imagined places and peoples, I felt the privacy as a halo, the writing by hand intimate, and the evening experience, repeated regularly, bracing.

Now, in the midst of my Schulte's revery, the buzzer would ring of course, and Lewis would ask if I'd show a Mrs. Jamison the Special Collections room as she was on her way down.

And Mrs. Jamison, a handsome middle-aged woman clearly distressed by our underground zone, wrapped her fur coat in her arm more securely, and followed me. On the way she explained, "You see, we've just painted my son's room a light beige, and I think a set of *dark brown* leather would look just right in there." She looked at me, and waited.

"Yes, that would be nice," I approved, recovering my focus.

Inside the shabby room, which embarrassed me more than it did the lady, I showed her the various sets on the swaying shelves.

"Something about two rows' worth of solid brown, say—"

"Well," I offered, going to another bookcase, "we do have an older Thackeray in this dark maroon."

As I brushed away the dust and brightened up the soft Moroccan leather a bit, her face lit up at the sight. She said, "How perfectly wonderful! Just right, that shade. Oh, I loved Thackeray in college, especially his *Middlemarch*! And that maroon is even better than brown!"

Two weeks later, a cold December Monday, with the wind whipping up pretty good, that man with the gruff voice and Sidney Greenstreet manner returned, and leaned by me. What was I reading?

"Oh, good to see you, sir. A great book actually," and I began to tell him about *Augie March*, and then went on to tell him how much I admired Eugene Gant and *Look Homeward, Angel*.

"Oh, you liked that, eh. Why?"

"Well," I said, stumbling a bit, "it inspired me, I suppose. His longings, his devotion to being a writer, and his descriptions of nature. There was, well, poetry in the book"—I thought—"yeah, poetry."

He smiled, for the first time, and his stern face suddenly softened and changed. "Hmmm. I thought you might like it. Later on one develops different feelings about that prose style. But anyway, here, I brought you something, just in case you haven't been able to find a copy." He handed me a book on Rimbaud. "It's not the best, but it'll give you some idea. Read it, and we can chat about it later on. I should be back in a fortnight or so."

"Thanks a lot," I said, figuring to look up "fortnight." "I tried getting a book on Rimbaud and had no luck. Of course I didn't go up to Grand Army Plaza, though I should have."

He stared sideways at me. "What about the New York Public Library? Haven't you ever been? Well, you go there one day. It's up on 42nd and Fifth. You can read there too." He shook his head in dismay. "Do you happen to have *Liza of Lambeth* by Maugham?"

I felt humbled. "Just *Cakes and Ale*, and maybe . . . *Of Human Bondage*."

"Hmmm. That's another good one for you to get to, and soon."

I felt like a hungry boy being offered a candy counter. "There's a lot, isn't there?"

He nodded, and I noticed his tie. I mean the small knot, so different from the wide Windsor knots I was familiar with.

"What about college? Are you thinking of going?"

"Nah. Not really. I have other things on my mind."

"Like what?"

"Well, like shipping out somewhere. Going to sea. Maybe even, later on of course, some writing."

He narrowed those gray eyes, searching my face.

"I don't need college for those sorts of things, do I?"

He laughed now. "No, I don't suppose you do. Enjoy the book."

As he turned away, he paused to add, "But if you change your mind about school, tell me. Maybe I can help you out."

The book on the French poet enchanted and surprised me. A poet so young, a loner so late, and a mixture so odd of peasant, bohemian, adventurer. Then, the bizarre romance with his mentor-friend Verlaine, and the attempted murder. What a life! Next, the escape from Paris and the literary world, and the long disappearance into Africa for the last ten years of his life—how's that for leaving society? And those exotic destinations, like Aden in Arabia and Harar in Absynnia—looked up in my *Atlas*—struck me as childhood magical as the Baghdad of *Ali Baba and the Forty Thieves*. And as youthfully romantic as his abruptly changing careers, leaving poetry for running guns, engineering, business, all performed in the remotest regions among desert rats and killer thieves. The fellow had guts! Absolute conviction! Immediately I understood the sources of my excitement: envy and admiration. He had done much of what I had dreamed about in my Brooklyn Cave. My own notes of adolescence had included destinations like Tierra del Fuego and Cape Horn, Tashkent and Aleppo. I promised myself to get hold of "A Season in Hell" or "Illuminations." And I couldn't wait until Mr. Barrett returned, to narrate to him my rapture. Between Rimbaud and Augie, my head was stirring with plans, projects, dreams!

To calm down from my new adventures in reading—I finished the New Directions book on Rimbaud on Friday—I attended the local poker game in Mosey's packing room. There, on the rectangular wooden packaging table, Bernie, Mosey, and Roland sat on high stools and played their hands, while George and I looked on, kibitzing gently. They asked if I wanted to join in, I said no, and Bernie smiled. "This kid? He probably still has the first dollar he ever earned. Him gamble, are you kidding?"

Though the mockery was uttered in good humor, it stuck in my craw anyway. Was he right, I wondered? Was it overcautiousness that kept me from playing? I thought of Rimbaud, traveling out alone in the desert to sell guns to that dangerous Arab chief, and Augie, racing down to Mexico on his wild binge, and felt myself burning, shamed.

In less than an hour, Bernie had cleaned out the other two, and I felt odd sensations running up and down me.

Afterwards, the room emptied except for Mosey, who bemoaned his fate, sipping milk. "Sheet, every week I tell myself to steer clear a this game, and here I am again, half my week's pay blown. Sheet. You stay away from this foolish stuff, you heah me, boy?"

I nodded, regretful in many ways. Observing that smooth dusky face furrowed in dismay, and those dark nostrils flaring with emotion, I felt for Moses. He had always sort of looked after me, down here. I knew he lived up in Harlem with his family, had two kids, and a hard time making ends meet. And Lewis had once said something about his inclination to gamble, and then, having lost, to begin drinking in quiet desperation. But what the hell could I do?

"That Broadway Furniture man whatever call you yet? I finally got the sucker in, and got him to drop another five down on your machine."

I stared at him. "What?"

"Yeah, go ahead in and check it out. Hey, doncha hear the man calling? Get goin now," and he shooed me out. "No use two a us fuckin' up today, go on!"

Disoriented, I heeded Lewis's buzzer, found a copy of *Mr. Blandings Builds His Dream House*, and returned to my bench perch. I felt down, drab again. A twinge cowardly even for not joining in. And then maybe helping Mosey not lose, somehow. He hadn't even informed me that he had worked privately to help me on the discount of the Royal.

I tried my best to lose myself in Friday afternoon sorting and classifying, for the Saturday crowd. (We always laid out a special used-fiction sale table upstairs.) A few hours later I was rolling my metal cart down to the front shelves to unload some *A*'s and *B*'s when there came a knock at the elevator door, signaling Jackson, and I slid the large door open.

"Where's the boys?" Jackson asked, standing large in his denim blue work uniform, "Still at their penny-ante game?"

"Nah, they broke it up early."

Jackson laughed. "Who won, Bernie again?"

"Yeah."

"That man is either very good or very lucky *or*"—and here he narrowed his gaze—"or very shrewd somehow. Poor Mosey, huh? Oh well. When you see any of 'em, remind 'em we're *on* for tonight after work, and maybe a little partyin' too." He took hold of my bicep. "How 'bout you, slugger? Ready for the big time yet?" He winked. "We got a couple pretty little things comin' on down tonight too. Wanna try it all?"

My chest constricted. "Yeah, maybe I will."

"Well, you're invited—just remember, if you do come on ovah, you're *eighteen* years old. That's, one eight." He went back inside the elevator, and said, "I'll catch ya later then maybe huh," and walked on over to his side of the basement, a hulking, large-shouldered figure.

Lost in thought, I slowly slid shut the door, not bolting it yet, like when I would close up later. Filing away and clearing my cart, I thought about the afternoon and realized that if I were to get lucky, real lucky, maybe I could win back Mosey's half-salary for him. Probably nearly thirty bucks or so. (And maybe even shoot for my typewriter money ahead of time?) The big thing, I knew, was to stay cool when I was winning—*if* I'd get to win, of course—and leave while I was ahead. (Arnold Zweig's *De Vriendt Goes Home* suddenly emerged, and I priced it at $2.50; an occasional called-for writer. What was it doing in the *A* and *B* cart?) I knew poker pretty well, having accompanied my mother to her nightly poker games when I was a boy in the Catskills, and also, playing with my pals occasionally on the block. I was not exactly a card shark, you understand, but if I got the right cards, I could hold my own, and maybe some. I debated with myself, checked my brown pay envelope, and decided to give it a shot for fifteen or maybe twenty dollars' worth. No more. That would give me ten for the week, just in case. Five for tokens and lunches, and five bucks only for Mom, in the worst-case situation.

Later, when I told Bernie rather casually of my evening plan, he was open-mouthed with amazement. "You playing there? You gotta be kidding!"

"No, I'm not."

"Can you play poker?" he asked, lighting up a cigarette, and assessing me anew.

"If I get the cards, sure."

"Look," he said, dropping his mocking grin, and turning big brotherly, "I won't be going over tonight, so here's some advice. When you get in there, they'll be free and easy with the whiskey. You take it easy on that, or you won't have a subway token left. Okay?"

The news that he wasn't going sank my heart, and I almost blurted out a plea for him to change his plans. "Okay." I nodded, restraining myself.

"Good luck. And you're easy about closing up?"

"Sure." I had done it a half dozen times already.

"Don't forget the keys tomorrow, remember."

I nodded, and managed to ask, "Is it uh . . . dangerous over there?"

He laughed, like a small-time Al Capone, and bulged out his Windsor knot for his evening date. "They're not going to roll you, if that's what you mean. But they'll go after your bucks as best as they can. Oh yeah, one other item—make sure Jackson changes the deck every half hour or so. Keeps 'em thinking, if nothing else. And keep your eyes off the broads and on the cards—you know that much, don't you?"

"Sure, I know that," I answered boldly, without knowing a thing.

"You could wait a week, and I'll go with you then," he put to me.

"Nah, I'm okay," I proclaimed.

"See you on Monday then, I'm off tomorrow." He punched my arm affectionately, and slipped into his smart black and white checkered sports jacket. "Who knows, maybe you'll have beginner's luck, and wipe them out. If you do get lucky in there, hold on to the dough, and split. They'll bitch, but nothing more. Remember. See you round, ole buddy boy. Who knows, maybe we'll both score!" He winked. "This Diana is a knockout, even if she is one of the tribe." He departed.

I had an urge to grab on to his sleeve, and say, "Come on with me, Bernie. Just for an hour or so. And then you can leave. Just so I . . . feel I have a friend in there!" Instead I waved him out, and retorted to myself: you're on your own, pal. Fight your fear and play it like a man. You're not going to a duel, but a card game. Just remember: change the decks, keep eyes on the cards, avoid the whiskey. Like a litany I repeated the warnings, and, except for the thumping beginning in my chest, I felt like maybe I could pull it off, with some luck. Why not?

The far side of Americana was a darker, stranger world from ours; luridly lit (including a string of neon lights blinking), cozy and tawdry (old stuffed couch and chairs), a brothel, not a bookstore. One large square room, off which a corridor led to several other smaller rooms. A round wooden table with straight-backed chairs occupied the center, and, on the walls peering down at you, colorful calendars of brown and white females, nude or nearly nude. The music came from a pair of large wooden speakers, soft rock and roll like the Penguins and Smokey Robinson. Smoke ringed the room too, like dirty clouds circling and hovering, looking for a way out. Only there was no exit, it seemed.

"Hey, come on in and meet the folks," Jackson exclaimed, guiding the dazed me.

Four people were lounging about and sitting, including Jackson. A male friend, and two females. The older one, maybe thirty, was a shiny ebony lady enclosed in a tight yellow dress, which barely held in her plump curves; she wore black pumps and big golden hoop earrings. The other was a younger white woman, maybe eighteen or twenty, dressed simply in pale blue sweater and flare skirt, and flat shoes. Slender, strawberry in complexion and hair, she seemed out of place there, like me. They made a very unlikely pair, I thought, and wondered if all this was somewhat fictional too?

The male dude asked, "What's your choice, sport?" Not unfriendly, but, well, chintzy, his smile forced. He was dressed to kill, I noticed; Panama hat, satiny vest, and black and white spats. The first real pair I had ever seen.

"Uh"—I looked over at his makeshift bar—"the 7-Up will be fine."

"Mixed with Seagram's, right?"

"No, by itself actually. Thanks."

"The boy don't drink?" said the man, mocking lightly.

"Give him what he wants, Cecil."

My hands fidgeted in my pockets, and I replied, "Sometimes I do." Foolish lie, which made me even more nervous.

"Here," Jackson said, handing me my soft fizzing drink, "take it easy awhile 'fore we get things going. This heah is Gennifer, with a *G*." He smiled, indicating the younger woman, who smiled shyly from the couch. "And the tiger is called Callie. You watch out for her now, she'll be putting hair on your chest fore you realize it!"

I wasn't sure entirely of his meaning, though I knew the spirit of that phrase.

Callie waved her hand at Jackson and his humor, and reached out for my hand.

Limply, I accepted her grasp.

"Don't you pay no attention to the man's jive. Nice to meet you. What's your name, son?"

"Aaron."

She broke into a smile. "Like Aaron, with that golden calf, huh? Come on over heah and join us, why doncha?" And she led me to the brocade-covered couch, drink in hand. "That way we don't have to listen to the bull that man throws." A good friendly smile, too, filled with flashy gold fillings.

Tucking my wallet deeper into the back pocket of my dungarees, I took the half-dozen steps, and joined the two women on the worn, comfortable sofa. I sunk in, and down, deeply. Chuck Berry was now singing about the faithlessness of his Maybelline.

Callie moved a bowl of pretzels and nuts closer on the coffee table, and I took a few. I tried to refocus on my duty and purpose here as she drawled in a Southern accent, "Ain't seen you heah before. First time?"

I nodded, and breathed in the heavy perfume.

"Oh it ain't too bad. Even Jackson's all right, once you get past his hooey! Right, Gen?"

"Yeah," the girl on my left agreed, gazing at me with quick green-gray eyes. Patches of freckles on both cheeks added to her adolescent, poignant look.

"Where are you from?" I asked.

"Buffalo. Do you know it?"

"No."

That shy smile. "Not much to know." She lifted a drink, which looked like Coca-cola with ice cubes, and I wondered if she was old enough. I noticed now the crucifix around her neck.

Jackson, looming nearby, offered, "How 'bout a little movie, folks, until our two other hands arrive?"

Callie, sipping her amber-colored drink, smiled warmly at me.

I shrugged, not fully understanding the meaning. (*He, Aaron, was beginning to understand, though, that the ground rules here were hotly different from those in Schulte's, or from those he had lived by, like labor, merit, purposefulness, reward.*)

The room darkened even more, my throat went dry and my stomach tingled some. As I found myself drinking all the 7-Up, I wondered if a real drink would settle me down somewhat.

The wall became the same flickering screen I had viewed from the knotty peephole. The reel began, flashing the countdown numbers in reverse, while Callie, casually it seemed, laid her hand on my leg.

In another minute, as the first figures appeared on the screen, Jackson came by offering "fill-ups" to everyone. To his surprise, and mine, I asked now for a touch of Seagram's in my 7-Up.

"Watch him, ladies," he cautioned, handing me the drink, "he may be getting *bad* now."

"How old are you?" murmured Gennifer.

"Eighteen," I pronounced emphatically.

The pornographic film progressed, a man visiting a female doctor and her nurse assistant, and I sipped my drink, trying to keep my temperature down, my thinking steady, my lines of reality clear. At least that's how I reasoned to myself, as the dark mysterious hand roamed my leg, gently squeezing here and there. The eight-millimeter wheezed on, the nurse and doctor began to undress and examine the male patient, and I found it hard to believe that I was but six feet away from Americana, six feet away from my regular station of duty and respectability. For here it was worlds away, like being in a different latitude. I was thoroughly dazed by the strong aromas of smoke and perfume, teased by Callie's hand murmurings. Did you have to go to Aden in Africa or Harar in Absynnia to feel zones apart, strange, on your own, in foreign territory?

For comfort I think, I glanced at Gen, who gave me that same half-smile of shy appeal, and so I patted her knee, for her comfort. (*You see, he was beginning to act like someone else, a fictional shadow self?*) To my surprise, she clasped down on my hand with firmness, edging my thumb up her thigh. Oh, I was getting hooked good and deep now, doubly hooked, and it was confusing, teeming, scary-pleasing.

The movie reeled on, the screen actor and actresses played their porno parts, and soon the real boy and two women played theirs. *First the boy noted that his drink was half empty, and that the room itself had taken on a gauzy impression, like strips of sticky paper laid over everything. Oh he sensed what was happening all right, sensed for example that he was slipping into another element totally, more liquid than solid, as he heard the tinkle of glasses and warm laughter and rolling film. Dusty Schulte's seemed a long way off. And resisting not at all, he fully accepted being led down the narrow, dark corridor by the pair of mermaids, one bulging yellow in front, the other slender, brushing his backside. In the new room sat a potted fern, a blowup color photo of a South Sea island, a dim lamplight by a seedy double bed. Augie, Eugene, Rimbaud, Aaron? The low voices of cajoling and easy seducing, the slow unraveling of clothing and sudden revelation of bodies—all this hit him like being underwater and seeing everything through the medium of translucent blue (here, red). And he was swiftly transformed into a fish of a boy, pulled this way and expanded that way in exercises of the flesh. Callie and Buffalo (her name vanishing) played in tandem, baiting him with honeyed limbs and hooking him with surprise openings, and at sixteen Aaron was dropped down sweet chutes of pleasure that shocked him, scooping his breath away. Though he had been with girls before, this scene was greedier, lustier, fuller pleasure. If you'd have asked him, and he were alert enough to answer, he couldn't have sworn that what was happening was real, and not part of the reel he had been viewing, so much was his imagination filled to the brim, and beyond, with body play.*

Soon, I was welcomed back into the card room with good-natured laughter and joking congratulations, by the old and new (pair of) card players.

"I can see the new hair already!" shrieked Jackson.

"Why pick on a mere boy that way!" noted a white, paunchy newcomer, puffing on a cigar.

I was alert enough to ask for a cup of coffee, before sitting down to play. I drank it straight too, hating the bitterness, trying to collect my clarity. The two gamblers joined us at the table, the black fellow adjusting a green visor on his forehead, and the white fellow revealing a fat roll of dollars.

"Dealer's choice, gentlemen?" Jackson asked, shuffling the deck, and dealing five hands.

Sure enough, beginner's luck. With the women flanking me, for good fortune (I supposed), I did pretty well. We alternated between five-card poker and seven-card stud, for quarters and halves, with a final card ceiling of three dollars. Pretty stiff tariff, I knew. Almost immediately, I caught a run of cards, a good long run for a whole hour or so—you know, a third three to beat two high pairs; a fifth diamond for a flush; a king-high full house in stud to beat a smaller house. Even drew an eight for an inside straight in five-card. The works. Change the deck? Why in the world would I want to do that? I was raking in the dollars so easy that I even handed each of my female good-luck charms an extra fiver, on top of the earlier "tip" I had given them, like a regular gambler. At one point I counted something like eighty-six bucks —enough not only to help out Mosey, and give my mother, but also enough with my savings to buy the Royal typewriter right off. Why not shoot for the whole thing, I thought, while running so hot? Laughing at the jokes, going so well, I even drank a bit more, and played on, and on.

Well, you know the rest. How I blew the winnings, blew Mosey's paycheck, blew my mother's share, blew my initial twenty bucks as well. The cards simply turned against me and nothing I could do was good enough. While the Spinners sang, I lost my charmed life. If I played it conservative, I lost; when I played aggressive, I lost; when I tried to bluff, I was called and defeated; when I didn't call a bluff, I played the sucker. As it slipped away, and my spirit sank, the women stayed right with me, though, Callie whispering I'd come back and Buffalo patting my knee. Inside I was sweating it out, however, knowing I was falling and unable to stop it, looking up at the wall calendars and seeing them smiling, and burning from the rich abundance of a half hour ago, now gone.

Until Jackson shocked me by saying, "Wanna borrow a ten or twenty, Aaron? Looks like you need some now to ante up right here, buddy."

Well, when I realized he was right, my bundle's gone and my big bills gone too from my pockets, I had to restrain my anguish, and tried my best for a manly sort of look. "Nah," I answered him, "I should have just quit when I was ahead, I guess."

Callie tried to console me by offering me "to forget things for a while" in the back room with her, but I declined. There was to be no consolation.

Saying, "I guess I better get going after all," I stood up, and probably wobbled a bit, for Jackson was at my side, steadying me. He inquired, "You okay now? Why doncha rest awhile before taking off, huh?"

"Nah, I'm okay." But when I checked my pockets for my keys, I discovered that I had no real money left, not even lunch money for the next week! My eyes grew bleary, and I cursed myself privately: You stupid prick, you schmuck with earlaps.

Aside to Jackson, I asked if he could loan me five until next week.

"Hey, man, I wouldn't let you leave stone-broke. Here's ten, man, how's that?"

I thanked him, said goodbye to the women, who pecked me on the cheek (Callie calling, "See you next Friday, huh, Aaron?"), and made the return journey through the elevator to the other, more familiar side of the basement. My stomach churned, my head swirled, and a spiral of desolation swept up through me.

I think the next few hours (and next few days) were the low points of my youth. How could I have been so stupid? So totally stupid? As I went about closing up the place, securing the down-stairs doors and windows, and turning off the lights, I felt down and out, depressingly out, having let everyone down. Not only Mosey, but Bernie and Mom too; most of all, myself. Another strange thing: I felt a curious sensation of having betrayed my special friends down there, my books. For I suddenly realized that all those silent dusty novels had become my chums in these months, and now they were like so many witnesses to my cruddy behavior! It was the creepiest of feelings, as though I were on trial, and here were my jurors—Hergesheimer and Hewlett, Archibazoff and Zweig, Hilton and Hobson, all of them, high and low! (And what about Mr. Barrett?) Oh, it stung me, humiliated me!

For five or ten minutes I reeled among my used fiction, not quite in control of myself, stopping at Balax, Belloc, Bellow, Burton, and asking for what?

And when I went upstairs to that huge high-ceilinged hall of nonfiction, it struck me as a prison, a dark and vaulted chamber to hold me forever. Should I take off there and then and say goodbye quickly? Leave a brief note of simple resignation? Haunted by full houses and red flushes, pursued by Southern drawls and flare skirts, taunted by Spats and the porno film, I moved from light chain to light chain, padlock to padlock, door to door: I vowed never again to set foot in Jackson's den, where I had lost my money, my honor, and my special feeling of comradeship in the basement.

Finally I managed to shut the front door, lock up the outside, and pull down the black iron shutter, and turn away, off, to the streets. In the darkened evening, strangers passed (scornful, sarcastic looks?), the wind tossed, and the curving lampposts resembled city gallows. Dumbly I prowled about in the emptying streets, seeking . . . refuge, penance, understanding? From myself, for myself. Shaking with self-torment, I wondered if I were any longer real, or maybe a figment of my own excessive reading? I mean, I was burning with a new intensity of some sort. After an hour or more of meandering aimlessly in streets that I normally would not have entered at night, having been accosted by a man selling a packet here, a woman there, I made my way back, and down into the subway, and soon was being hurtled underground from Manhattan to Brooklyn, memories of dark pleasure flickering alongside afflictions of dereliction.

To my surprise, maybe dismay, no one seemed to know a thing or sense anything different about me the next day, or the next week at Schulte's. (In fact, it was only I who noticed that I had left Americana unlocked the night before.) While I went about my routine with new determination, stricter discipline, feeling a guilty traitor, everyone behaved the same more or less. Apparently Jackson had let on to no one what had occurred, only winking at me when we passed each other once by the elevator, a wink of conspiracy. About my debt to him, he said nothing. To Bernie, of course, I had to say something, so I acknowledged that I had lost, though I omitted the amount. I added that they had treated me okay over there.

"You seem pretty matter-of-fact about the whole thing," he remarked, chomping on a corned-beef sandwich on Monday.

"Yeah, I guess it was kind of . . . disappointing. Not as exciting as I had imagined."

Hitting my arm, he noted, "I knew you weren't exactly any Legs Diamond."

I said nothing, and returned to my sorting and cataloguing.

On Thursday, my despair still filling me, the literary man with the gruff voice and gray fedora came around, and asked how I was getting on.

"Fine, Mr. Barrett, just fine."

"Did you get to that Rimbaud?" He faced me sternly.

"Yes, I did actually."

"And—the verdict?"

I nodded. "He was all right, really all right. Had a mind of his own. Wrote his own way. Moved around a bit too. And"—I tried to think of the right words, but what came out surprised me—"he did a good job of fucking up, didn't he? If you'll excuse the language."

A hearty laugh was his response, and he proceeded to sit on the bench alongside me, removing his hat. "Who doesn't who's anybody?"

I stared at him, in disbelief. "Really?"

"Really. I've done some of that myself."

He had a high forehead, I saw now, and a kind of oval pallid face, and if he had worn a high collar, he would have been a dead ringer for a priest. Was he putting me on now, trying to make me feel better?

"Maybe only those who do mess up, or fuck up as you say, will be able to tell us something new—about feelings, morals, conduct." His small gray eyes fixed me, as though to ask, "What do you think?"

"Well, I'll tell you something then, sir—I'm not sure you have to go so far away, as far as Rimbaud did, to make a real mess of things, see? I mean you can do it right here, right under your nose."

He smiled, folded his arms, said, "Yes, go on."

"Well, maybe that's about it. I mean, I enjoyed, no that's not really the right word—did you really fuck up a lot in your life, a man like you?" Was I getting too bold, my curiosity reaching too far?

The smile changed on his face, and he paused, in mid-expression I thought, to reflect. Then he began, "Look, I once loved a woman, and never married her, for the wrong reason. I even gave her up for another woman whom I didn't feel passionate about, but who had the right social standing. Is that good enough?" He half-grinned, derisively, at himself.

I took that in, tried to register it, observing his tweedy jacket sleeve next to my cruddy red-black flannel shirt. "How about messing up in a cheap, vulgar way?" I put, trying to edge through the protective fence he was constructing for my benefit. "Where you fail yourself in a, a—"

"All the time, son," he said easily. "I'm a writer, remember. That's what you do as a writer, in one way or another."

A writer? "I thought you just wrote literary criticism stuff?"

He laughed, happily now. "That, too." Then he seemed to sigh, remembering something, and stood up wearily.

I stood with him, feeling how Greenstreet large he was.

"Well, are you ready for another book?"

"Sure, though I've still got another hundred pages or so of *Augie March*, and then there's the poetry of Rimbaud for me to get to. But that's not too much."

"Here, come with me." He proceeded to circle around the aisles until he came to the *M*'s, and there, two bookcases in, found a book, and handed it to me.

"Pretty thick again," I observed, handling the battered book, and read aloud the title. "*Of Human Bondage*. Gosh, how'd he think of *that*?"

"Spinoza thought of it for him," Mr. Barrett explained. "The title of one of his books of ethics. Look at the pictures if you get bored with the text." He smiled.

"I'll try to do both, actually"—peeking at the shaded pen and ink illustrations.

"Good. And we'll talk further. You should think more carefully why you like or dislike this book. Maybe make a small list of things? And you should think about college, too, you know."

"Really? Well, maybe, after sailing around a bit."

He nodded, and walked on ahead, with me following.

At the stairway he stopped. "She was Jewish, that woman. Like you, I expect."

"Huh? Yeah, I am."

"And I was somewhat *ashamed* of that." He faced me squarely. "I was a prig, a Waspish prig. Your father, Polish or Russian? And an immigrant?"

"Yes, a Russian immigrant." Not the right moment to ask him the meaning of that odd phrase.

"Hers was Polish, I believe." He draped his arm around my shoulder, appearing to be on the verge of delivering some other words, some deeper confession. . . .

But then he wavered, paused, and gave me a quick goodbye wave as he ascended the rickety steps and moved out.

If it were true, what he had said, then he knew more about "messing up" and regretting it than I did, *by far*. The whole conversation, his spoken words and his deliberate retreat from words, stayed with me.

From Bernie I found out about "Waspish prig," and from Maugham I found out about being gripped immediately by a story. Along with beginning the new novel, I also began developing a new determination, and even a plan of sorts. One which surprised me.

On Tuesday night, when Bernie stayed late to close up, I asked him to "teach me how to drink."

Ceasing his filing, he stared at me. "Have you gone nuts?"

"I want to learn how to hold the stuff."

Shrugging his sloping shoulders, in hopelessness, he mumbled, "After we close up at eight, we'll give it a shot. Boy, you do come up with some, doncha?"

The lesson began in Lewis's small office, where Professor Bernie Gross of Bensonhurst instructed me in Alcohol 1.1. Ground rules: "You take your first drink with crackers or cheese, not on an empty stomach. You don't 'imbibe' cheap stuff, especially cheapo wine— otherwise it's Big Hangover Time next morning. You don't mix drinks, meaning if you start with bourbon you stay with bourbon and don't also accept wine or scotch. What else? Cut a drink with water or soda, and you can nurse it longer. Capeesh? Okay. One last thing—if you want to protect your stomach a little, drink your liquor with milk in it, especially scotch." When I stared in disbelief, he responded. "Yeah, it sounds goofy, but it works. Old Mosey taught me that one. Any questions before we begin the lab?"

"Yes. How do I get beyond the taste?"

"You're serious, aren't you? You schmuck! You get to *like* the taste, that's how. But gradually."

I nodded. "And what do I start with, scotch?"

"No, no. That'll take years. You could try, uh, rum and Coke. Or seven and seven, that's Seagram's and—"

"Seven-Up," I said. "Jackson gave me a bit of that. Yeah, that taste was all right."

"You mean you couldn't taste the whiskey, right?"

"Right."

He shook his head, in futility. "C'mon, we'll start in—I'll buy us a pint of something, wait right here. Cheesus, if Lewis ever saw us he'd hemorrhage."

While he took off, I read about Philip Carey beginning his lonely life, after the early death of his mother. The accompanying illustrations were detailed—lovely, the first captioned by, "You naughty boy, Miss Watkins will be cross with you."

Presently, in the dim cramped office, we were sipping Seagram's from two porcelain teacups, amidst Velveeta chunks and Ritz crackers, sitting by the rolltop desk like two British officers in some remote outpost.

"How is it?" Bernie asked, picking up my book.

"Excellent. Though I've just really begun it."

"The drink, dodo, the drink. Yeah, I've heard of this, but never got around to it. I'll wait till they make a good modern flick out of it. So . . . ?"

"Tastes good." I waited for the full blurry effect to take hold, but all that was happening was that I was coming to like the dark mahogany wainscoting, and the thin, jagged roads of oak in the desk.

"How many fingers do I have up?" he asked.

"Eleven," I answered.

He nodded. "Okay, wise guy, but just hold on willya? Nurse the thing more. Sip a little at a time, otherwise, you'll be on your second. Lay the taste on your tongue"—and he held out his, to show me the way—"and sort of run it around your palate, slowly. Go ahead, just a touch. There you go. And tell me, what the hell is behind all this?"

I now took full notice, letters of book inquiry from Baghdad, Barbados, and Cyprus, and bills going out to Malta, Budapest, Chandigarh, distant places!

"Well?"

"Americana," I answered. "I wanted to turn native."

"Sure," he snickered, "sure. More like you want to impress those whores over at Jackson's, huh?"

Did I? I explained how I had indeed gotten drunk over at Jackson's that night, and didn't want to repeat the act.

"You want another tip, about visiting there again?"

"Sure."

"Stay away from the ladies. They ain't there just for decoration, or diddling, you realize."

"What do you mean?"

"Bozo. First they'll soften you up a little. And then, they might just be hanging around you when you're actually playing." He looked sideways at me, saw I wasn't quite getting it, and came to sit on the arm of my chair, almost tipping us over. "They might just be signaling the house, meaning the dealer, about your hand. Just now and then, when the pot's big enough, honey"—and he ran his finger down my neck in imitation, before I pushed him off.

Christ, I thought, Christ! "I see." I nodded, not letting on about the full impact. Oh was I innocent, stupid! For payment, I forced a drink down too fast, and immediately began coughing like crazy.

"Take it easy, fella, or you'll burn yourself up before the next lesson."

Well for the next few weeks I worked hard, taking more drinking lessons, and getting familiar with the stuff. At the same time I was reading more about Philip's descent into peculiar slavery to the vulgar, anemic waitress, Mildred. What illness!

Two Fridays later, in late February, I was ready for Jackson's Hole again. Of course I had already paid him back his ten bucks, plus a buck interest, the past week. But having written me off as a player when I had skipped a week, he was surprised to see me reappear.

"Hey, folks, look who's back," he announced to the gang.

Callie welcomed me warmly, and with her was a new woman. When I asked about Gen, Callie said, "Oh she might turn up, yuh can nevah tell with that chick. A little high, a lot depressed, most of the time. She sorta liked you though. Hey, come on and tell us what's been happenin', this heah's Jacie."

I said hello to the slim pretty woman, nodded to the two other men, including ole pal Spats or Cecil, and sat down. This time Bernie came on in too, which made me feel easier. Now the sounds of rock and roll and the blinking of neon lights and the sinful appeal of perfumy smoke didn't confuse or startle me. On the contrary, I felt prepared, ready, a kind of student of sin. And when the same routine prevailed, with Jackson asking about a movie while we waited for more hands, I said sure, and watched the flick come on. Ten minutes into it, however, and carefully nursing my one drink, I said I had forgotten something and made my way back out, and over to our side of the basement. There, I opened the Americana room, and entered, and quietly climbed the ladder back to my peephole post, viewing the situation. Seeing the movie on the wall, and hearing the same whirring and voices, here on the outside, made me feel curiously on top of things, apart. Now, I prayed, if I could only get the cards. . . .

But I didn't.

I waited and waited, I played and set the women aside, I stayed clear-headed and goody-goody, and still couldn't get the cards. Steadily, surely, I lost the twelve dollars that I had put away for the game, and dipped into my weekly savings, accepting the punishment as my due. At one point I went to urinate, and stopped to look in on the small dark room of my dingy orgy just a few weeks back. On the wall the blowup photo of that faraway island with white beach, palm trees, and sea-green water was still there, still beckoning. And through the next hour and a half of my steady losing, the color photo hatched itself into a project, or rather, hastened my earlier plan. And even when, at the end, I picked myself up to go, a loser of nearly twenty-two dollars, I felt something else stirring, something larger than the night's poker game. I said good night to Bernie, who, a small winner, tried to offer consolation. "Nah"—I rejected it—"it's okay, just not my night, I guess."

Rumbling home on the subway, I lost myself in Philip's terrible descent into disaster, thinking how maybe the timing was just right to read that book. Above and across the aisle, Uncle Sam, wearing his high top hat of stars and stripes, was pointing and inviting me to join the armed forces and see the world. Good end, wrong means.

A man had fallen asleep over his crumpled *Post*, and the woman next to him, yawning with the long day's fatigue, now and then propped the man up on her shoulder delicately. For a fleeting moment I replaced Sam and his top hat with the gray fedora and oval face of Mr. Barrett, who was peering down at me with a different, sterner message. What was it, I wondered, leaning forward? And what was that deeper confession he was about to make that day, but never did—aloud, anyway? The IRT swerved suddenly and almost tossed me from my prickly seat, jolting my reverie away, and I sat back, with new thoughts and my book. I read: "Philip had few friends. His habit of reading isolated him: it became such a need that after being in company for some time he grew tired and restless. . . ." Was reading really so dangerous? I asked myself. Literature more slippery than reality?

On Friday next, after a week more of planning and reading, I returned to Jackson's. An hour into the game, I was mired in the same pattern, losing ground and my money quietly. I shooed the ladies away, Callie making a face at me, and sipped my whiskey. Down to my last few dollars, I took a shot with my three eights and raised the two high pair showing of Spats; sure enough, he had just the two pair. Beginning with that hand and sizable pot, I turned my luck around. For an hour I got the cards, I had my run. Three aces beating out Jackson's three kings (oh, that stung!). A full house spoiling another player's flush. Pulling a seven for an inside straight in five-card. You know, the works. Oh it was running all right, and I was riding right with it, not bothering with Callie's presence or Bern's absence, not distracted by pornography or Jim Beam, bad jokes or bad looks. Holding my concentration fixed on the cards, remembering as best as I could all the cards showing from that hand and from the deck's previous hands, I galloped on that streaking horse. And before I knew it, I was hearing the moans of the players, seeing the expressions turn hostile, and feeling the piles of dough climb and climb. One for singles, the other for fives, tens, and one twenty. And the second was getting higher than the first. I was rich, friends, rich!

Now, I told myself, get out, Schlossy boy, out. Move up and out. But how? I waited for a simple, quiet loss, checked my watch and pulled up my stakes and waved myself out of the next deal. "Sorry, that's it for tonight. I have an appointment."

The four players, taken by surprise, and maybe by appointment, seemed startled.

I began packing in the piles.

"Yuh just can't quit on us, yuh know—not with *our* loot in your pocket!" declared a round fellow with a cigar in his cheeks.

Tingling, I gathered my nerves as best as possible. "Sure I can, if I want to. A few weeks ago, man"—I inserted the little noun for some reason—"you guys took my money, and now it's my turn."

A short wiry black fellow, the kind that scared me the most ever since, as a kid, I had seen one slash a fellow's face with a concealed razor in his matches, stood up, and came toward me. I stood my ground, and he moved to a few inches of my face, twirling his toothpick in his mouth as though it might go off at any moment. "Yuh-all looking for some trouble, quittin' on us suddenly, jes like that?"

From the speakers, Sam Cook was singing about sweet sixteen, and I held my tongue, counting to six, feeling terror climb my back. Looking at his shining brown eyes, I said, low, "I'm not looking for any trouble. But for tonight, I happen to have an appointment."

An imaginary Mosey winked at me.

If the fellow had snapped at me, or done worse, I don't know what I would have done. His foul breath spilled over me, and I accepted that, and also the menace of his nearness, which seemed to last and last.

Jackson stepped in between us, and eased him back, away. "Hey Jonesy, the boy's got a right to quit, win or lose." And turning to me he said, "But you shoulda let us know aforehand that you had an appointment, sport. Come on now, I'll walk you out."

Without looking back, but feeling the heat on me, I proceeded toward the elevator, and escape. Jackson whispered, "Yuh got some nice little pussy waitin' for you, huh, Aaron?"

I nodded.

"Sho, I dig. Just come back soon and give the boys a chance to get even now. So Jonesy don't stay angry." He patted my back, which was still stiff with tension.

I nodded, said sure, and recrossed the elevator floor, back onto home ground. Fiction boy again. This time I closed up shop with a different feeling, and I was sorry that Bernie wasn't around to celebrate with. But my novels were, and so I shared it with them, preening and promenading through the aisles like a racehorse after a big win.

Outside the store, I felt firm, free and easy, and didn't mind looking strangers straight in the eye. But no wandering for me that night, just a beeline for the subway, my money stuffed down into my front dungaree pocket. The only stop I made was to check out my typewriter in Broadway Office Supplies; there it was, still Royal, still sharp. I could feel the keys on the tips of my fingers.

Later, at home, alone with my chicken dinner waiting in a pot and a note from my mother about how to heat it—she and Sam had gone off to Connecticut for the weekend—I counted my take. One hundred thirty-five dollars, and sixty cents. I whistled at the sum. For one night's work, a few hours really, I had hit the jackpot. Without committing any crime! I sat in our old kitchen, happy with oilcloth, old stove, pale yellow paint peeling, and ate the meal very slowly. I was tasting a victory whose flavors were new to me, and not entirely distinguishable.

For the rest of the evening, my heart fluttered with excitement over my outlandish booty. (In my thesaurus, I had looked up "prize," and found "booty," a word I decided to use for myself.) Even the Friday night fight, with Don Dumphy speeding through each round of Willie Pep's feinting, ducking, and jabbing, couldn't cool me down. Through three or four hours I daydreamed of high adventure, while simultaneously trying to follow Philip Carey's low one. I was being hit by all sorts of impulses, and prowled our three-room apartment looking for definition and resolution. Yes, my plan had to be firmed up, put into motion, and soon, I realized. First, I had to find out about some local particulars.

Before work the next morning I laid out an envelope for Mom with twenty-five bucks, making up for the week I had lost, plus some.

Up at Schulte's, I handed Mosey an envelope too, saying, "Here's some dough, pay me back sometime." He was having to work the extra day nowadays, to make up for his poker loss.

"Huh? You crazy, boy? What the hell you pullin'?"

"Nothing. What you lost a few weeks ago in poker here"—I shrugged—"I made up over at Jackson's last night. That's all. So go ahead and pocket it. When you get hot, you can return the dough."

"Jackson's, you?" He shot me a fishy look, opened the envelope, and handled the two tens and a five and shook his head. "You sho is a fruitcake, ain't you? From Jackson, that crooked fucker, huh? Well then I don't mind takin' out a loan. Thanks, Aaron, thanks. First lucky day I get, you get this back, you heah?"

"Sure, Mosey, sure," I answered, knowing that he hadn't had one of those days in years, and wasn't likely to. Luck was not simply a matter of luck, I was discovering.

"Is he crooked?" I asked.

"Like a three-dollar bill, that's all. If the ladies don't get yah, the cards will. He marks 'em, you know, once he's got the sucker hooked."

I smiled, patted his shoulder, wondering if Bernie was such a sucker.

Throughout the morning I labored industriously to clean up some of the longest lingering piles and bulging cartons, and made some decent headway. (Despite taking a small break when I came upon a Heritage Press *Moby Dick*, and couldn't resist peering at the marvelous drawings.) What would all my dusty novels do without me? In the afternoon, Bernie came around, asked how I had done, and I said "won." Lighting a cigarette, he continued, "Oh yeah, how much?" I announced the sum. He kept the flame burning and looked at me. "You putting me on?" When I assured him I wasn't, he took hold of my arm, and said, "So I'm the one who should be taking lessons, huh?" Suddenly speaking with new respect, he said, "You know, I had you pegged for a deadbeat, an egghead in the making, but you're turning out okay, really okay." A broad smile appeared. "Oh, I wish I had been there to see their mugs when you bid them 'adieu.' I never got that lucky. Hey, what're you gonna do with that kind of loot? Wanna try to go for broke with the ponies on Tuesday night?"

"Thanks, Bern, I have some other plans for it." I'd pass along Mosey's warning next week sometime.

Meanwhile, the next week, in March, I began to take care of those plans. On Monday, on the way to work, I stopped to pick up my new typewriter. A battleship-gray color, clean as a whistle with a new ribbon too, with a speckled gray carrying case, it was a sight and feel to behold, and I took to it like a farm boy getting a new mare. Naturally I tried it out right off, right there on Mosey's table; the keys were high and separate, and the print elite, my favorite. Mosey shook my hand, and said, "If Jackson helped to buy that for you, it should type *extra* sweet, man." Later, the other boys came around, and admired it too.

On the subway home that evening, I guarded it carefully, my hands or legs feeling it at every moment. At the entrance to my apartment building, Steven Werter noticed it immediately, and said, "Looks new, a present for your birthday?"

I smiled sort of. "A present, from myself to myself."

His eyes widened, and he half-nodded. "Didn't know you earned that kind of dough at a *bookstore*."

My mother was astonished, and skeptical too. Did I really need it? Though she conceded, "It's your money, though. Did you get a guarantee?"

Sam, of course, when he saw it at dinner, asked if I had purchased it "hot" uptown somewhere. "How'd you save that kind of money?"

"Overtime," I assured him, "plus a good poker game."

He laughed at that. "Yeah, you poker. It probably would be the best thing for you actually."

On Tuesday I took a longer sidetrack, before work. In downtown Brooklyn I got off the train, and walked along Atlantic Avenue to an anonymous-looking brick building on a narrow street. There, in a large ballroom-sized room, thirty or forty fellows lounged about, many scraggly-looking, dirty blond, youngish. A stubble-bearded fellow pointed out the tiny office in one corner, where a small sign said, "Scandinavian Seaman's Institute." At the counter I waited, and asked the gentleman how I could get a boat out.

"Ships, they're called," he corrected me. "You have your American passport?"

"Not yet," I murmured, reddening at my mistake.

"Get that first," he said in singsong English, "then you can have a look at the board over here. Ships and jobs are listed on the cards." And he turned away.

On a hung cork bulletin board alongside the office, three-by-five cards were posted, listing not merely the ships and jobs, but also, dreams. They were called: Dakar and Lagos, Yokohama and Rotterdam, Oslo and Hamburg. Right there in the heart of Brooklyn! When my brain and heart stopped Ferris-wheeling, in a few minutes, I noted the positions and returned to the busy, brusque man.

"Excuse me again," I interrupted him, "but which of these am I qualified for?"

"With a passport, you can be deck boy, kitchen helper, engine room assistant."

"Is *dekksgutt* the deck boy? What's he do?"

He nodded at the first query, and advised me to ask one of the seamen about the tasks involved, and turned back brusquely to his business.

I found a blond fellow of thirty, an "AB" (or "able-bodied seaman," as he explained), who told me about the *dekksgutt* chores: helping out on deck everywhere, chipping paint, cleaning latrines, handling ropes, "Maybe taking a watch," whatever the "bozz'n" wanted. I gulped it all in, too excited to ask all the details. As I was leaving, he stopped me, and said very solemnly, "Sign on for one trip, maybe three or four months, but not longer. Then you come ashore before you sign on again. You understand?"

"Yes. But why?"

"Because otherwise you get too used to sea, and to ships, and you can't never stay on land for too long. It's not a good life. So"—he smiled gap-toothed—"one trip, and then, if you wish, maybe a year later, another one." He nodded, with regret. "Otherwise, you get . . . I don't know the word in English," and he motioned with his hand.

Later that day, Lewis said, "You seem quite chipper today. And yesterday."

"A good weekend, I guess."

"Oh yes," he said, stopping me for a moment, about to strike my heart with his revelation, "you've been doing a fine job, so I've raised you twenty cents an hour beginning next month. Congratulations."

Surprised, even shocked, I stumbled out "Thank you," not daring to tell him of my plan.

Sallow-faced in his gray windbreaker, he continued, "Everyone agrees you've been the best fiction boy we've had down there in years. Keep up the good work!" and he flashed his best nicotine smile at me before moving on, a cadaver-in-good-cheer.

That week, after making application for my passport, I wrote a letter to the literary gentlemen, in case I missed him. I wrote the letter on my Royal, of course, my first real workout on it.

Thanks, Mr. Barrett, for your course in Reading, sorry it was so brief. (I'm enjoying *Of Human Bondage* very much, though I think Mr. Maugham is quite a pessimist! Is this a "fault" in the book, sir?) On my journey, which is approaching, I'm certainly going to continue the reading. I'm off, you see, in a month or six weeks, as soon as I can get my passport, for some distant destination—though I don't know yet where, or for how long. As for college, well, if I'm going to write someday, I don't really need college, we both agree. I mean, I have to get educated in the school of hard knocks first, right? I've also got a start there, as you may remember, and it really does make an *impression*, for sure. Thanks a lot for your counsel that day, about your own experience; it proved helpful, more than you may know. I bounced back after being rather down.

If I may, I'll look you up when I get back, maybe through George?—if I get back before ten years, as I believe I will. And I'll certainly let you know about my adventures, which may be . . .

* * *

I couldn't think of what to put in there, so I just left in the three dots, like they did in the books. I signed it, "Aaron Schlossberg from Brooklyn not Charleville." The typing gave me as much pleasure as the contents.

Nearly a month went by, spring began in earnest with the Dodgers opening in Ebbets Field, while I waited for my magical object, like my old Captain Midnight badge, to arrive: my passport. (I also checked in at the nurse's office in school, and, from fishy-eyed Mrs. Wallace, got the proper forms for a medical leave of absence.) One Friday evening I returned to Jackson's game, not really to gamble but to show up. I lost a few bucks, but it was my presence that meant something to the players. Privately, Callie handed me a phone number, from Gennifer, and I didn't know what to make of it. And in the fiction department, I was making serious headway in the backlog of books, including a card catalogue for the unshelved stuff. Meanwhile, I kept up with Philip Carey's tumble into hell with the grim Mildred. Could anyone that smart be that dumb, that driven? Was that Philip's case in particular, or the way it worked out frequently?

Mr. Barrett grimaced when I put that to him, in his mid-April appearance in the basement. "Oh, it happens more often than 'smart men' will acknowledge, I'm afraid."

I found my letter and handed it over to him, saying, "Just in case I didn't see you."

He opened and read it and caressed his tie.

"Does the pessimism hurt the book? Well, if it interferes with the characters. If it doesn't seem to come from *within* the characters and their story. Does it, in your opinion?"

Reflecting, I answered, "Well, yes and no, sir. Some of the time, yes, but some other times, not. Sometimes . . . Mr. Maugham just sort of sticks in sentences of gloom from nowhere really, except from himself I guess. Yeah."

He nodded. "Right there, it gets weak, I would think. Sometimes an author can't resist competing with his characters, and it creates a bit of a problem." He paused, gazed at me quizzically. "What about this journey of yours?"

Well, there wasn't much to tell yet. I explained how I was waiting for the passport, about the Scandinavian Seaman's Institute and its "ships," and the far-off destinations awaiting me maybe. "But please," I whispered, "all this is kind of a secret, or private between us. No one here knows anything just yet."

An approving nod. "Mum's the word, I promise. You have . . . courage."

"More like curiosity," I answered. "A lot of curiosity."

"And determination." He stared at me from beneath those curtaining eyebrows.

From somewhere in me a recent line popped out, "Man makes his own fate, huh? That's what Augie March says."

Taking that in, he patted my shoulder. Then, making space on a shelf, he scribbled something down on a loose-leaf notepad, and tore out the page. "Here, my home address, and private phone number. Don't lose it, it's unlisted. When you return, call or write me, and we'll get together. I want to hear about *your* fate."

Unlisted phone? Why? "I don't *really* know what Augie means by that," I admitted. "But I'm working on it. Boy, you live all the way over in *Jersey*. How come?"

"It's not exactly France, you realize," he offered. "A little less than an hour, and I'm here. How long does it take you, from Brooklyn?"

"Maybe a little longer." I nodded.

"Have you been on the other side of the Hudson?"

Like the other side of Americana? I wondered. "Never in Jersey, no."

"You're invited then. By the way, I think I have the perfect book for you to take on your voyage. Let's see if it's in."

He curled around the aisles, turning into the *D*'s. "Look, we got lucky." He handed it over to me. "A going-away present from me. I'll buy it upstairs."

I read, "*Two Years Before the Mast*, Richard Henry Dana. We never get calls for that."

He shook his head. "An American *boy's* classic, in my time. I don't know if it's read much anymore. Too bad. You try it, and tell me what you think."

"Thank you. I will."

And later, after he had given me the book, and shaken my hand goodbye, I noticed he had signed it, with an inscription. The small legible script said, "To Aaron, a fine fiction boy on his way to great adventures, cordially, Charles Edmund Barrett. Schulte's, April 1955." Well, that excited me sort of, and I decided to include it along with my other valuable signatures, like those of Robinson, Reese, Campanella. Oh, I would hate to miss the baseball season, with the Bums so terrific, but it had to be. Carefully I set aside Mr. Barrett's home phone and address, and placed *Two Years* into my knapsack, along with two pads and a pen and pencil case for the trip.

When the passport arrived the second week in May, I think I grew six inches from excitement, for it seemed, in its official manila envelope with the United States of America printed in the corner and a warning to "Return to Sender" if Aaron Schlossberg wasn't there to accept it himself, that my journey, my "great adventures," was actually beginning.

On my way to work on that Thursday afternoon, I stopped again at the SSI, and amidst a blur of seamen's advice and gossip, white index cards with exotic destinations, Norwegian and Swedish accents, and my own leaping blood, I signed on to leave the next morning at 9:30 A.M. for the Ivory Coast of Africa, with stops at Dakar, Lagos, Monrovia, Lobito, Loando, Matadi, among others.

I didn't have too much time, did I?

The news was received with surprising equanimity by almost everyone. Lewis gave it his best nondescript expression, and tepidly wished me luck; he even managed to get a pay envelope ready for me while I said goodbye to the others. Informing saintly George about it, I felt lousy, selfish. He just laughed, however, scratched his head, said he suspected something was up. Bernie exclaimed, "Holy moley, Africa? You're off your rocker? Aah, forget it kiddo, you're a lost cause." Mosey shook my hand with his two hands, and uttered, "Sheet, I wish I could just fly the coop, and blow this city, I'd be gone in a jiffy!"

Roland handed me the pay envelope, standing with the others in a semicircle, a little like when I was bar mitzvahed. An odd bunch, this crew, like chess pieces that could only move in one prescribed direction, but a part of my life. I stumbled out an apology for my sudden leave-taking, but explained how I had cleaned up most of the old cartons and piles, and got a good start on a catalogue. With a smirk, George said, "Yeah, I knew something was up when I saw how clear the corner aisle was the other day," almost making everyone laugh. "Who knows, maybe they'll be full up again by the time you return!" They semi-cheered.

Boy, that made me feel good! And made walking out of the door even harder.

At home my mother took it coolly too, respecting my decision, and knowing my difficult years in adjusting to Sam in the house. She shrugged her shoulders, said dryly, *"Bist du meshuggah,"* and added, "Maybe it'll be the best thing for you. Get the restlessness out of you. But why don't you wait till school's out? What about your exams?"

"Well," I said, keeping my fingers crossed, "if you sign this Mom, and get Dr. Wiener to sign it too, I can take the makeup exams when I return, in September, before school starts." I added, only a small fib, "It'll be no sweat."

"What is this?"

"Just some procedural form saying that because of medical circumstances, it's best for me to take a temporary leave of absence."

"Medical circumstances? Why can't you wait another month or so, what's the great hurry?"

"Because then I'll never get a ship. The college kids'll grab up all the jobs!"

Shaking her head, but showing her usual deep trust in me, she signed the sheet, and I explained what office to take it to. She wondered, "What's supposed to be wrong with you, by the way?"

"A little depressed, that's all. Dr. Wiener will sign it, won't he?"

"Who knows? When do you leave?"

"Eight-thirty, tomorrow morning. We'll go to Baltimore first to load the ship, and then on to Africa."

Sighing in dismay, she asked more particulars, and immediately worried about a suitcase.

Beaming, I showed her the new blue duffel I had just purchased at the local army and navy surplus store, and right off we set to packing it.

My typewriter I carefully stored away for hibernation, tucking it deep into the hall foyer closet, and protecting it with an old blanket.

Over dinner, when Sam began to jibe at me, Mom cut him off swiftly.

I had a hard time sleeping that night, trying to imagine what was coming my way. I called a few friends, said I was "skipping out" for a while and allowed myself about three beats of pleasure before saying I had better get going, cautioning them to stay quiet about me at the school.

And at eight fifteen the next morning Mom and I embraced warmly, she telling me to take good care of myself, and "Don't go picking up any fancy diseases, *farshtay?*"

I knew what she meant, and reassured her. "I'll be okay, Mom."

She nodded, half-believing me.

Outside, a hazy gray day, I passed the corner candy store at East 98th and Sutter, just by the stairway to the El station. I waved to Jack, my old boss, and a reader too.

"Where you heading?" He smiled.

"Small trip," I replied, not wishing to talk in front of his Camel-and-*Daily News* clients.

And by nine-twenty that morning I was at Pier 46 of New York Harbor, showing my papers and walking the plank aboard the *SS Ferngutt*, an 8,500-ton freighter. I was awash with the salty air and the dreamy reality of the fantastic ship suddenly there and alive with little safety rowboats hoisted high, teamsters filling in the holds, Scandinavian seamen moving to and fro with supplies, while our passengers, a dozen missionaries from Florida, looked on from the upper deck. I was taken to the bridge to meet the First Mate. A tall blond fellow in starched, clean khakis, he welcomed me and two Norwegians aboard with hearty handshakes. In good English he explained to me how I was to take orders from the bozz'n, on the main deck, once I got settled into my room, and that the Captain would want to meet me later on, after we had put out to sea. In Norwegian he then spoke to the two others, veterans, and I was freed. Once downstairs, after finding my cabin, I helped out carrying stores to the kitchen.

We pulled out about four-thirty, escorted by two tugboats, and I perceived the island of Manhattan from a whole new perspective, the way I was going to see my life soon enough, I felt. The steel-gray skyscrapers formed a thrusting horizon crossed by bands of late sun, and began gradually to resemble an erector-set construction from my childhood. Was this what it was like? I was transfixed by that jagged skyline and the trailing wake of the ship, and felt as though I were saying goodbye to my youth. Goodbye Schulte's, goodbye used books, goodbye Americana (both sides). Seeing the city more and more as a mirage, I began to feel myself more and more uncertain, made-up, semifictional. What an odd feeling!

Just then, my arm was tugged by a short powerful suntanned man, who asked if I was "the American boy." I answered yes. He smiled shyly, put out his hand, and introduced himself as the "bozz'n," and asked if I would help him gather in the lines and help with the winch.

Taken aback by his modesty and eager for my first sea task, I said sure, and followed him dutifully.

By the thick wet hemp ropes he paused to ask if I had brought gloves, and when I said no, he handed me his old pair. Then, smiling and revealing a row of bad teeth marked by gold fillings reminiscent of Callie, he asked in a lilting English, "So, you've come for some adventure, for some fun? Good. Just remember"— he smiled good-naturedly—"work comes first, and this ship is our home. So there are rules to learn about caring for it, yes? Then, later, all the fun and adventure you want, good?"

After this brief sermon, which seemed to embarrass him, he said somethink like "Comen," and showed me how to handle the thick, unwieldy ropes. No room for daydreaming just then, I knew, as I pulled and tugged, using muscles in my arms and legs that had lain unused for years, and learning a few simple knots too. Soon I began to feel the rocking motion of the great ocean as something natural, something splendid. And as I felt myself losing track of land, of dull solid ground beneath me, I sensed my old self slipping away too, that boy in high school and in the three-room apartment, in the neighborhood and in Schulte's basement, in Ebbets Field, and in Jackson's den. That boy was growing fainter, fainter, maybe already a speck from the past. Bending, tugging, sweating and breathing hard, I figured that maybe that fellow was like one of my used novels, say, a used-character or used-self. Armed with that notion, or weird sensation, I wondered only one thing: what would the new one be like?

"Not like that," the bozz'n said, taking my elbow, "you're using the motion wrong—too much energy, not enough, how you say, touch? Don't worry, you'll get the feel of it. Here, take hold again and tug, comen!"

Rookie Watch

E arly in my journey, the ship and sea fed my hunger for drama and danger, through two incidents. The first occurred on the second day aboard when, on shore still, one of the Mates asked me to climb the mast and change the flags for sea. A real task, I figured eagerly, until I asked someone which mast was in question, and he took me to midships. When I looked straight up at the mainmast, I couldn't see the top.

The able-bodied seaman eyed me. "You're the new boy, yes? Should I get the Mate to ask someone else?"

Embarrassed at appearing or acting cowardly, I shook my head.

Adjusting his blue cap, and smiling curiously, the tall fellow advised, "Hold on with two hands, don't look down, and you'll do fine. When you get to the top, untie the flag and simply drop it down, I'll wait for it. Good luck!"

Quickly I began climbing, and realized in a dozen steps how very narrow the ladder was, maybe half the width of a regular one.

From below, the tall A.B. called out through cupped hands, "That's it, keep going, and remember, don't look down!"

I kept climbing, gripping the ladder sides, and planted each step firmly. Up and up and up, the air windier, the views broader, the blood coursing. About two-thirds of the way, I couldn't resist, took a peek down, sighted the few figures now gathered below, and immediately felt myself swaying and feeling light-headed. I squeezed the iron rungs, took a deep breath, and resumed climbing, moving beyond the flying bridge, the upper decks, the smokestacks. I bit my lower lip, and climbed, repeating the seaman's formula for two hands again and again and following it in act, and making sure to climb one rung at a time, one rung at a time, and not cheat, not look down.

Finally, after what seemed like a long hard hour that was probably no more than five or six tense minutes, I reached the small round platform at top, perspiring from labor and fear. I breathed deeply, tried to relax my leg and hand muscles, flexed my sore fingers. I now had to decide whether to hoist myself over the low railing, or to stay put at the top rung and work from there. At first I thought to hoist myself, but when I realized I'd have to leave my rung footing and leap up into space, I gave up that way. Two sea gulls dived and screamed nearby. Looping the rail with one arm, I used the free one to untie the flag, and then dropped it over the side, having to peer down to make sure it dropped freely, and hardly believing how high I was, seeing no persons below, far below, only tiny creatures.

Holding the railing, I rested a full two or three minutes, pressing my hot forehead against the cold steel of the pole, breathing deeply, and focusing on scudding white clouds and the diving shrieking gulls.

I began my descent, slowly, deliberately, one rung at a time, tongue between lips, heart racing, eyeing the royal blue smokestack for my descending horizon.

When I reached bottom, and jumped the last few steps onto the deck, a small circle of gathered seamen hailed and clapped for me, and the A.B. slapped my back in celebration.

"You see," he said, laughing, "nothing to it, nothing!"

The second incident occurred after we had pulled out of port, heading for the Atlantic, and the Second Mate asked me to go below and take in the anchor chain. He gave me a casual direction about helping to guide the links down. Sounded easy enough. At the fo'c'sle I found the hatch for the chain locker, and practically shinnied down a narrow winding stairway, into a dank, dark windowless oval area. The floor of the room was mostly a cavernous hole, I saw, and heard immediately a twisted creaking. I stared in awe as this huge piece of rusted iron, covered with brine and seaweed like a hideous primeval icon, began its descent into the room, and hole, through the spill pipe. The giant piece swayed this way and that, and finally clanked down awkwardly, with a little push from me. But when it was followed by the rest of the rusty steel chain, huge link after huge link, I knew I should have asked for help, and that it was too late now. It wasn't but a few minutes before I found myself having to push hard here, run halfway around the edge of the hole, and tug there, to make sure the anchor chain was folding straight down, and not piling up unevenly on one side. As the minutes passed, and the links continued to twist and creak down and pile up unevenly, the task grew harder. I was fearful of two things. One was that I'd slip or slide on the oil-slick perimeter and fall into the hole, along with the monster chain. The second was that in seeking to right the weight, the weight would get me instead, pinning me to a side wall, or hooking me down. Either way, my grim fate was to be crushed by the ponderous chain in that dark cave, with no one able to hear my cries.

For nearly thirty minutes I struggled with the unwieldy chain of huge iron links descending relentlessly—losing footing, losing strength, losing oxygen, losing reason; fighting panic, and fighting for my survival more than for the order of the anchor.

When it was over, I wandered dazed into the galley. The crowd looked up, in slow amazement, and asked where had I been, overboard?

When I explained where, and doing what, the bozz'n said, "Why didn't you take someone with you, man? That's a two-man job, for godsakes! Come on, have a beer!"

But the journey fed other appetites too.

We had been out to sea about a week when the First Mate asked if I'd like to take a watch.

"Are you kidding!" I exclaimed.

"It's the gravedigger's, though, from midnight to eight."

I nodded, my heart surging with pride. "That's okay," I said, awed by the prospect. My first sea watch, after just becoming a seaman! (Well, actually, a deck boy.) What more could a boy from the streets of Brooklyn want, right?

And so it occurred, my first real responsibility on the ship. The watch went this way. You worked in teams of three, a Mate in charge and two youngsters paired up. I was teamed with Henrik, a red-haired, freckled-faced fellow of nineteen who spoke a fair English and seemed always in a jovial mood. For one hour, he stayed above, in the wheelhouse (or on the bridge), holding the course, while I was down below on deck, at the prow of the ship. Then we rotated positions, and roles. The task at the prow was to keep a steady lookout for ships in the distance, by means of their lights; if you sighted one, on starboard side, you immediately turned and struck a loud bell once; if on the port side, twice; straight ahead, three times. And a few minutes later, you repeated this signal again. Once the wheel heard the signal, he then steered the ship starboard or port, depending. (You always passed port to port.) There was one other responsibility: at 1 A.M. the fellow below stopped off at the kitchen galley on his way upstairs and made open-faced sandwiches and coffee for the First Mate, Mr. Johannson, who was also on the watch above.

Though the watch was known for its long hours of lonely monotony, of nothing happening, I found it a boy's dream. At least mine. At the wheel, I felt like the Most Important Person alive, the ship's fate—including the forty-odd Norwegian seamen and the half-dozen American missionaries heading for Africa—in my hands. (A mighty illusion, of course.) That curving wheelhouse room became my private world of night wonders; the gyrocompass and whistle lever, light panel and rudder angle indicator, the engine order telegraph and voice tubes, the wooden and brass steering wheel, the wall of windows. Every so often the Mate, a tall blond fellow in his forties who wore a light khaki shirt and shorts, would

come inside from his private map-and-nap room behind and chat
with me while checking the course and the sea. But mostly he
stayed back there, dozing off frequently, once he saw that I was
reliable.

"When will you cut that *shegga* off?" he'd kid me and my youthful
beard regularly, while offering me a sandwich.

Down below, on the deck, I was equally happy. What was a
hopeless stretch of boredom to another was, to me, a rich furrow
of time. Repeating my childhood, I had uninterrupted hours to
think, to fantasize, to daydream, to imagine, to remember, to construct. And I had the most dramatic surroundings to do it in: the
open sea on summer nights. Is there anything more starkly dramatic
and sensuous than the enveloping black sky above, alive and blinking with richly imagined lines of constellations, and the pale lemony
moon? While below, the blue-black ocean swelled and subsided as
our ship cut through it, a shifting sea of lunar reflections and cease-
less roar. What a dazzling field, what a stage setting! With me as
one of the players! The world was clear and purposeful right there,
I thought, the laws of ship and sea more apparent than those on
land. The ambiguities of my youth, the loss of Vy, the pressures
of Papa—all seemed washed cool here, cleansing me. And standing at the very edge of the ship, I felt closer to that sea than was
perhaps natural—I developed deep yearnings to jump in and join
it. That's how intoxicating and hypnotic its billowing romantic
powers could be.

What was there in my past that had prepared me so well for
this first watch? I wondered. Was it my intimacy with the ocean,
or the continuous body of water—ocean, river, bays—surrounding
my Brooklyn, and my periodic walks across the great Bridge? Was
it my early desire for distant explorations, and my detailed lists of
destinations scribbled in my improvised study, squeezed in my
parents' bedroom? Or was it my recent romance with exotic places
hatched in Schulte's basement, inspired by Mr. Barrett's Rimbaud?
Whatever. I cherished my new post almost like a new toy, and
couldn't wait to be jostled awake by a strong hand at about eleven-
thirty P.M., getting me ready. And when my fellow seamen kidded
me, at early breakfast, about all the exciting events that had hap-

pened during the night, I smiled and nodded. Was I ready to jump overboard in boredom yet? Not quite, I replied, keeping my real feelings within.

Indeed I became quite convinced, in those opening weeks at sea, that at sixteen and a half I had found my future home. Who in his right mind would trade in this adventurous life for mundane college? Not I. (And I felt my new nightly watch to be the ideal complement to the sheer romanticism of the whole journey.) For reading, I had just devoured *Two Years Before the Mast* by Richard Henry Dana, a swell book, and had lined up Melville and Conrad. For companions, my Norwegian mates, plus the few Danes and Swedes, suited me just fine. They were friendly (in a quiet way), straightforward, hardworking, helpful. Clearly they proved that Scandinavian seamen were not the dregs of society, as Americans often were supposed to be in the peacetime U.S. merchant marine, but upstanding citizens from a society where "shipping out" was an honorable way of life. Furthermore, on Sundays I even had chess matches; the Second Mate, hearing that I played, would come by to thrash me regularly (with a reckless offensive attack). So, all told, except for the baseball season in full swing, I hardly gave Brooklyn a second thought. The *SS Ferngutt* was my Ebbets Field, you might say, a complete field of action with its own daily team, routine, and play—except that I was more than a fan here, I was a real rookie, exhilarated to be in the league.

One evening, a few days before we hit the west coast of Africa, our destination, I had just finished my first watch at the prow, and made my routine stop at the kitchen galley. I put up the coffee to boil, and made the open-faced cheese and sardine sandwiches that even I had become addicted to. To my surprise, there were two fellows in the room, drinking coffee and shooting the breeze, one of them the ship's carpenter and the other the dark, cynical Dane I liked so much. I couldn't resist joining them for a bit. Switching to English, they moved the discussion to the subject of America, offering their criticisms and praise, based mostly on ten-day stays in New York or Baltimore. Realizing how distorted, or just different, outsiders viewed the country, I guess I got to talking awhile, awhile longer than I realized.

And to my surprise, I found myself defending, in the way of explaining, the country. "No, you guys have to get around more, not just the big cities. And even there, in a city like New York, you have to see different parts of it—like the Cloisters uptown, the Fulton Fish Market or Bronx Zoo, Coney Island. And you *must* go to a ball game, the Yankees or Dodgers or Giants. Then you'd really meet *our* natives!"

I was standing with one leg up on a bench, my prepared tray still waiting patiently, my lecture about to continue.

"Aaron, where you been, man?" Henrik, my partner, was inside the door, looking sober and anxious.

I shook my head, slightly confused.

"You better get upstairs soon—I mean *now*. Where you been? You see the time?"

I checked my watch, and was amazed to see it was already one thirty-five, at least twenty minutes later than usual.

My heart thumping rapidly, I mounted the three narrow flights of steps, balancing the tray. Was the Mate especially hungry for his snack? I wondered. Or . . . ?

Mr. Johannson, the First Mate, was at the wheel, a bad sign.

I set the tray in his room, as was my custom, but when I turned to assume my wheel post, my way was blocked by the Mate.

His blue eyes were icy and unfriendly. "You have failed in your duty, son. A tanker approached us, and we heard nothing from you. It came closer yet, and still we heard nothing from you. Where have you been? And why weren't you at your position?"

The force of his words jolted me. I shook my head dumbly, taking in the meaning first, then the questions. Feebly I explained that I had gone to the galley . . . "And, well, I stayed there, talking."

"I see. And did you go to the galley *before* one o'clock?"

Of course he was right, I had taken off maybe five or ten minutes early. My god! "Yes, before one, by maybe ten minutes."

Towering above me, he said sternly, "You cannot act that way on a ship. You must fulfill your duty, whatever it is. All of us *depend* on this. Each man is as important as the next. And the watch is as important a job as any job, do you realize? An hour on the fore watch must be an hour on the fore watch. You can spend ten minutes, no more, for making the snack. These are the rules. You knew them, didn't you?"

I nodded, my head swirling and my breathing coming hard.

"By the time Henrik spotted the tanker's lights, it is already a few minutes late. If it were a different sort of evening, cloudier or with fog, it could have been a dangerous situation. You would have endangered the ship, and all our lives."

I felt the up-and-down motion of the ship, and listened to the sea crashing, but both felt different now. Not comforting.

"If it happens again," he said, fixing me with those lake-blue eyes, "I must report you to the Captain."

I nodded to that possible punishment, maybe even wanting it.

"Go take the wheel off automatic now."

I left the room, my head and heart swirling, and released the automatic pilot. That next hour I felt in shock, as though I had been scalded by acid. My burning eyes were watery as I considered his damning words, the possible consequences of my folly. I could barely think or understand anything, except that I had been a fool, a dangerous kid, for the ship and for myself. I gripped the wheel as though it were the last secure thing in my life, and when Henrik came up at the end of the hour to replace me, I left without exchanging any word or pleasantry.

For some forty-eight hours I was haunted by my imprudent act, my fall from grace. It was as much a fall from self-grace as a sense of betraying the ship and crew. All my previous dealings with responsibility now seemed like child's play; indeed I felt as though I had never before really broken through the surface of that word, to its real meaning. You know, like being the second-base man in the middle of a double play, and relied upon to catch the peg easily and then make the throw to first, only to drop the peg! I had seen one side of the watch, the glamorous and sensuous one; but its deeper significance I had not really taken seriously. How stupid! I sneaked around the ship, avoiding mates, staying to myself, feeling my stain as a patch of dishonor worn on my sleeve.

Only when the First Mate again was offering me an open herring sandwich a few nights later did I come around, find my normal self again. Though inside, I could feel something hard, like a small weight of lead deposited by my heart.

We hit the coast of Africa at night, and anchored a short distance off from the docks of Monrovia. Though I could barely make out the landscape, so veiled in fog and clouds was it, I nevertheless felt the excitement of the exotic destination. Africa! Why were we anchoring, I wondered, instead of docking? To pick up some workers, I was told, who would help us on the journey down the Gold Coast.

We had our dinner, somewhat later than usual, and waited around, and waited. Finally I went to bed, reading in my upper bunk and figuring that in the morning we'd get our passengers and resume our passage. Somewhere deep in my sleep, however, I heard movement, strange movement, and immediately got out of bed and, seeing Johann missing from the bottom bunk, went to the deck. There I witnessed a strange, indelible sight.

In the soft night air, thin dark shapes, silhouettes of men, were filing aboard the ship. They moved noiselessly, some wearing shirts and trousers, others merely bottoms, and most carrying little laundry sacks in their hands or over their shoulders, like scarecrows bearing their bundles. There was hardly a breeze, and the moon was nowhere to be found, as though the evening was joining us in a mysterious conspiracy.

"Who are they?" I asked

Michael, the Dane, answered, "Our 'helpers.' The Africans. Coming to live with us." He wore his perennial, ambiguous smile.

Bewildered and astonished by the scene, I wondered again, "But where will they live? I mean, aren't all the cabins taken?"

Now his laugh was raucous. "Cabins? That's for this color," and he pointed at the skin on his cheek. "They'll live on deck. 'Camp out.' You'll see. It's something. Really something." And he punched me lightly on the arm. "Something for you to remember, maybe all your life, back on shore. . . ."

And it was something, something indeed.

They proceeded to set up their bivouac on the foredeck, and, in the next few days, to shape their routines aboard. To me, it was like watching the most exotic movie—something like *King Solomon's Mines* or *Four Feathers*—up close, in full color, without understanding what it was about. Odd, eerie. I observed the mundane details, the everyday acts and unadorned appearances, and even understood their singsong English (alongside the tribal lingo), but couldn't make proper sense out of it all.

The fifty or so boys and men lived in a long tent set up on deck, on the forward hold. Scrunched together like black sardines, they slept on thin makeshift bedding; their main meal consisted of a kind of thick gruel dished out from large metal tureens. For a day or two they did odd jobs around the ship. But their real labor was revealed when we docked for a day at a Liberian port and the aft hold was opened up, so that giant sacks of wheat and flour, along with several new automobiles, could be unloaded. In the warm June heat, it was the Africans who did the hard work, lifting, loading, carrying, pushing, pulling, struggling with heavy awkward objects; for eight grueling hours the small, thin-boned Africans did the dirty work. I watched them for a short while—"Ah, they're used to it," I was told—but then, in a wave of guilty despair, moved away.

At sea for several days, they began to relax, at night especially, and have their fun. After dinner, dressed in pajamas or sarongs, they joked each other and held each other (linking waists or arms), laughed, sang, and even began to dance. They made their music with thumb-pianos of different sizes, wooden boards on which were mounted a series of varied-length metal prongs which vibrated when pressed. Simple, ingenious, rhythmical. So vivid and infectious were the Africans in those hours that we found ourselves a captive audience, all of us, from ordinary seamen on the lower deck to the uniformed officers and missionaries on the upper decks. The atmosphere was festive and convivial, and yet, for me anyway, most strange. Where was I? Several weeks ago I was among familiar citizens and recognizable habits and now I was in the midst of a theater performance of the ordinary—*their* ordinary—that was stunningly different from what theater, or life, had been like.

Poorer than church mice, they looked to earn extra money—more than the fifty cents a day they were earning from the Norwegian ship—by washing our clothes and ironing them, or offering to do small errands for us. Always smiling, always gracious, always apparently happy. And when they discovered that I was American, the only one serving as a seaman, I was approached as though I were a prince, a role I didn't particularly wish. For it meant that they believed that I was inherently richer, more powerful, maybe even more just, than the Scandinavians. I worked hard to convince them that I was a mere *dekksgutt*, with no special privileges or dispensing powers. Did they believe me? Well, maybe as much as I believed them—namely that they were really as good-natured and trusting as they appeared. Were inner selves, human intentions and motives matched up so evenly with outward gestures and acts? Hard for me, a native son, to believe such equations.

One night, maybe a week out at sea, I walked out toward my watch on the bow. Though it was after midnight, the Africans were still up in their tent, I realized, hearing their giggling and talking. I continued briskly out to my post. The night was sultry, a new moon was up, and the Southern Cross was visible in the dark sky. The sea had a little extra surge to it too, lifting us up and plunging us down just a bit more. Oh, it was grand, I can tell you, as grand a place as, well, the ballpark at night for a big game. I rolled around on my tongue the names of our approaching destinations, Takoradi, Dakar, Lagos, Matadi, and found the prospects as rapturous as heading for Ebbets Field or Yankee Stadium. I'd have to drop Mr. Barrett a card from one of those towns, and maybe even show him my journal.

As the sea lifted me, I felt at one with the whole scene, and didn't ever want to be anywhere else. And as it dropped me, I felt the renewed pleasure of duty too, duty and responsibility. Not just a tourist tour, this freighter journey. It all seemed so right, so secure . . . save maybe for the bizarre campsite and strange creatures just behind me there. Hard to believe they were real, or really what they seemed. Especially since I had heard a grim story of a Norwegian seaman on a recent journey who had been robbed and killed in an African port for his wristwatch and shoes. Sprayed by the ocean, I figured that it wouldn't take much for a pair of our Africans to sneak up behind me, grab me, and remove my shoes or wristwatch, and dump me overboard nice and easy, then return to bed. Who could ever prove anything or even know what had happened to the boy from Brooklyn?

Shutting down my fantasy, I turned about to look up at the wheelhouse high above. Standing just before me, however, like dark apparitions, were two ebony souls, maybe ten feet away, silent and grinning. The moment and their shocking presence stunned me. They seemed unreal. My breath came in sudden gulps. I faced them, and nodded, and maybe half-smiled too, wondering if they weren't phantoms of my imagination after all? The wheelhouse, my Norwegian mates, the civilized world of the ship, seemed far, far away.

And we seemed to stand that way, suspended in time, they, bare-chested and barefoot and smiling—blocking any escape—and I, numbed and tense and backed to the edge of the bow. I was an easy mark, an easy drop to oblivion. I wanted desperately a sign of familiarity, a way of sizing up the situation. All my Brooklyn street smarts seemed of little use here. This was not Marcy Ave. or a dangerous corridor in Boys High, where some thug was angling over, signaling trouble. Here, with these smiling Africans, I couldn't figure anything, had no buoys or internal compass. But suddenly it struck me, in one of those unforeseen moments of reeling memory, that my paralyzing fear was akin to the boy of eleven feeling the dark stare of Robinson in that parking lot, before he autographed his scorecard. A signal of Otherness that scraped the nerves like chalk on a blackboard, but that remained puzzling in its meanings.

The long staggering minute hung in the sultry air, with the two young men grinning, and the sea roaring, and I not knowing whether to talk, run, swing out.

The taller fellow said, "It is most beautiful up front here, no doubt."

The second fellow, wearing a crucifix on a chain around his neck, added, "We hope you won't mind. Us, here."

Dimly recognizing this short squat fellow, I found my voice. "No, it's all right."

"I am Peter Obongaloo," the first one announced, and put out his large hand.

Weakly I clasped it, surprised by his soft grasp.

"And I am Azinne. We have met before. You remember?"

They sang their English in high-pitched voices, and continued to grin broadly, their teeth filled with gaps and shiny fake gold. While Azinne recounted our brief meeting, I felt my breath returning to normal, the night's order re-emerge quietly.

"You are the American, yes?" Peter wore absurdly long and threadbare Madras shorts, and sported thick sideburns.

"Yes."

"From New York?"

"A part of New York, yes."

"We know many things about America," stated Azinne. "You will help us get there perhaps?"

I almost smiled. "Well, I don't think I'm able to do that, actually."

Peter understood. "Naturally, you do not know us yet. But we work hard, and you will see us for yourself. On this journey."

Azinne spoke. "Is it true that we can buy a car easily in your country? I myself would like a Chrysler New Yorker."

I mumbled some sort of equivocal answer.

"I see many American movies," stated Peter. "They are my favorites. They have the best action!"

Azinne shook his head, unsure. "But too much *pich, pich, pich!*" He had set his thumb and forefinger into the L shape of a gun, and pulled the trigger three times, grinning at his mocking act.

"Is it true too that they murder every day in New York? Or is Philadelphia worse?"

How to take these clichés? "Well, maybe, but . . . you don't feel it. The private citizen I mean."

Presently, as they proceeded to ply me with more questions while chattering like crazy, I began to sense the unrealistic fahrenheit of my fears, the folly of my imagination. These strangers were in fact a pair of amiable visitors, innocent company. My judgment was off, way off. (For a second I saw the icy blue eyes of the First Mate, and heard his hard words.)

"So, it is agreed then—we may work for you during our stay?"

I was taken aback, and backed off. "Whoa, hold on. Look, if I have any work, I'll look for you two, okay? I promise."

"That is excellent," declared Azinne, taking my hand.

"We will be available. You will ask only for Peter and Azinne, yes?"

"Yes."

Beaming still, they bid me "Good night" and moved off. Gone.

My hour up front was nearly over, my wristwatch read. I turned back to the roving moonlit sea. Its rhythms and orders were intact, even though my own were shaken still. I peered out into the vast sensuous darkness, aflutter with movement and surprising shifting lights. It was all beauty and mystery, wasn't it? Out there, maybe down here. To reason my way through the maze, I saw, meant to see through my own clouds of biases and prejudices. A long journey that, maybe a lifetime's. Meanwhile, the *SS Ferngutt* was not a bad college. Finding the four bright stars that formed the unique Latin cross, I began sighting something else, a flashing luminosity high overhead, all around, an exploding radiance of myriad colorings and magnitudes. Dazzled and enchanted, I couldn't help staying on for ten extra minutes, soaking up that unfamiliar sky and unknown hemisphere as though I understood its brilliant signaling.

In the next two weeks as we glided down the Gold Coast I observed the Africans at length, especially my new pair of pals. Whenever possible, I found them the odd small task, though there wasn't much of it. I also looked on, and then away, as they bent their brown bodies to the hard jobs in the hold, loading and unloading in the murderous sun. (Rough stuff, glad we Americans weren't the bosses.) At their departure, I gave them my name and address, a pair each of shirts and trousers, and some dollars. (I made forty-two a month.) They donned the shirts, laughing at the misfit, shook my hands, smiled graciously, and promised to write me. Promising back, I was moved.

Of course I had been mistaken. I mean, about the Jackie Robinson memory serving as a kind of model for the Africans. No, not at all, I thought. He was an angry man, a defiant man, a unique man, and player. Azinne and Peter were not any of those things, not by a long shot. My daring base runner hero, like his truest fan, was a native son, shaped volcanic and heroic by home-ground forces, while these fellows were true foreigners, the same color maybe but different souls and different cultures. Theirs was a whole different ball game, I knew.

I steadied myself and became a respectable rookie at sea. I learned lots of things in a very short while. My Norwegian pals, for example, were not so fine once they had some beer in their bellies. Many turned berserk and violent, banging each other around at night and, bloodied and bandaged, turning peaceable and gentle the next day again. I discovered what ardent fanatics were our blond Christian missionaries, who made a last-ditch attempt to convert me before heading for their real prey in the jungles. I got to see the detailed madness of our Captain, who, one day, dressed in his formal immaculate whites (including brimmed hat and shorts), paraded me across midships, while everyone looked on, and got down on his knees in the latrine to show me how to wash the shower area properly. And I also learned how to defend myself better in chess, against those relentless all-out attacks by the Second Mate; if I built a secure castling area, and held on, trading pieces, I could actually turn the tables on him. He grew red-faced and furious at his first loss aboard the ship.

Still, I didn't expect the reward I was given, or permitted. I mean, when the *SS Ferngutt* headed up the Congo River toward Matadi, I was trusted with the wheel on my regular watch. Oh, I was not alone in the wheelhouse; the Mate was there, and we had also picked up an African river guide just as we turned upstream, and he directed me. But when the First Mate told the Captain that "Yes, *shegga* can handle it," my blood pumped and spirit surged.

The ship moved swiftly, maybe twelve knots an hour, and land was so near on both sides you could hear the squeals of the hyenas and behold the silvery prancing zebras and loping ochre giraffes. A boy's dreams mingled with dense green realities. Yet, as I held the wheel, turning it just slightly this or that way, I thought curiously enough of my Brooklyn, and figured that, after all, home ground had prepared me well. Not yet seventeen, I was at the helm of a freighter in a tricky, legendary river, ready and able to take it on in, and once there, plunge deeper into adventure. My fate seemed at hand now, fixed by that notion. All this, on my rookie journey. Not bad, I thought, as the thick jungle came wildly alive with calls and screeches, something like the fans rooting in a crucial late inning. Not bad at all. .